THE SUPPOSED SISTER

PAMELA BELLE

Pamela Belle Books

The characters and events portrayed in this book are fictitious. Any similarity to real persons, living or dead, is coincidental and not intended by the author.

ISBN-13: 978-1-0686784-3-1
ISBN-10: 1-0686784-3-1

Cover design by: Pamela Belle

For my own sister Vicki. I hope this makes up for the spider I put in your hair on your seventh birthday.

CONTENTS

CHAPTER ONE

In Coffee-houses you began …

Covent Garden at night was not a quiet area. Whores, drunks, brawls, street vendors, hackneys, carts, all contributed to the cacophony that surged along every street, court and alley. Even so, the noise emanating from the coffee-house in King Street drowned everything else. Stamping, cheering, shouting, it echoed between the tall houses, bounced off the cobbles and rendered thought impossible. A little group of urchins, ragged and filthy, huddled together in an unobtrusive doorway nearby and nudged each other, waiting eagerly for what they knew would be next.

The short, plump man in a plain brown wig threaded his way patiently through the throng. His clothing marked him out as a provincial, a country bumpkin ripe for the plucking by pickpocket or whore, but something in the confidence with which he carried himself deterred anyone lurking with malicious intent. Just as he arrived at the door of the coffee-house, a few yards from the famous tavern at the sign of the Essex Serpent, silence fell so abruptly that it seemed some paralysing spell must have robbed those within of all ability to make a sound. Behind him, a subdued shuffling noise indicated that the boys were moving closer.

A woman spoke sweetly into the hush. Even with the windows open on the summer night, he could not catch the words, but he knew the voice as well as he did his daughter's. There was a murmur of anticipation within, and he seized the moment and nodded to the big man who kept the door against troublemakers and other undesirable elements.

"Good to see you, Mr. Jessop," the man said, his accent betraying his Welsh origins. "Madam is about to sing, but if you can find a space at the back for now ..."

Sam Jessop, successful Oxford draper and loving but often exasperated father, slipped the doorman a coin and edged past his bulk into the hallway. The door to the main room was open, but all he could see were backs and bewigged heads, all shrouded in the inevitable tobacco smoke. There was no hope of progressing through the packed crowd without serious disruption, so he leaned against a section of wall that was less crowded with advertising bills, and waited with the others.

"I'm pleased to see so many of you here this evening," the unseen woman said, her voice clear and young, with just a trace of a West Country burr. "I shall give you three songs for your delectation and delight, and then no more, for it is growing late."

A muttering of discontent rumbled around Sam, and the small man standing next to him shook his head in disappointment. The woman continued. "The first two I shall choose, but the last you may suggest - *suggest*, I say, though I may not take any of you up on your suggestions. Now, Isaac, are you ready?"

The answer came as a thin pure sound, played on a fiddle or viol. There was an intake of breath, and then she sang.

Sam had been expecting this glorious torrent of words and music, but even so, the hairs raised themselves on the back of his neck. He knew the song, of course, everyone did, but not like this.

"'*Go from my window my love my dove*
Go from my window my dear
For the wind is in the west, and the cuckoo's in his nest,
And you can't have a lodging here.'"

A movement to his right caught his eye. A gap had appeared in the rapt, devoted listeners as they shifted to gain a better view of the singer, and through it he could see a man sitting at the end of the long table next to the wall. He was dressed in a shabby black coat and a dark tie wig in the military fashion, and he was using a stick of plumbago to draw something on a scrap of paper. Sam smiled to himself. All was right in this little world.

"'Go from my window my love my dove
Go from my window my dear
The wind is blowing high and the ship is lying by
And you can't have a harbouring here.'"

The song finished on a last plaintive note, echoed by the melancholy violin. There was a reverent pause, and then an explosion of cheering. The gap closed, and Sam could no longer see the man in black. No matter: he would meet with him later. It was enough to know that he was here.

"I thank you, sirs, for your kind appreciation. And now, pray silence. Isaac?"

Once more, the fiddle began: a jaunty tune this time, in contrast to the previous lament.

"'An old man came courting me, hey dorum darrity
An old man came courting me, me being young
An old man came courting me, all for his wife to be,
Maids when you're young, never wed an old man.

When we went to bed, hey dorum darrity,
When we went to bed, me being young,
When we went to bed, he neither done nor said
Maids when you're young, never wed an old man.'"

Being a sober and respectable person, he did not know the words, but most of the other men did, for they joined in heartily with the last verse.

"'And when he was asleep, hey dorum darrity,
And when he was asleep, me being young,

And when he was asleep, out of bed I did creep,
And into the arms of my handsome young man.'"

When the applause and laughter had eventually dwindled into something approximating silence, the singer spoke again. "Well, kind sirs, what is your wish for my last song tonight?"

Someone shouted a coarse suggestion, and was instantly hushed. Another man shouted, "*The Fair Maid of Islington*," and sparked a chorus of alternatives. Sam craned his neck, but could catch no glimpse of the young woman he had come so far to see. He was right at the back, of course, and she was made small and slight, but it was very strange to hear her so close, and yet be invisible to her.

He sensed a movement at his side, and glanced round. The man in black had moved to stand next to him. He was considerably taller and leaner than Sam, with a keen, rather grim face. Then he smiled, and it was completely transformed. "Well met, Samuel Jessop. How do you do?"

"I do very well, thank you, Dark." Sam indicated the crowd pressing about them. "And I see the Paradise is likewise doing very well."

"Indeed it is. I would have thought that by now it would no longer be a novelty, and the Town would have grown bored. But it seems not."

"*The Cuckoo*!" a man just in front of Sam bawled, and his cry was taken up by others, while feet began to stamp rhythmically and the floor shook. The noise ceased as abruptly as it had begun, and Sam could imagine the imperious gesture with which the singer had silenced them. The fiddle gave its note again, and she spoke. "Thank you all, kind sirs, and *The Cuckoo* it shall be - an excellent choice, for it is one of my own favourites. And then I will bid you a good night, and may God bless you all.

"'Oh, the cuckoo she's a pretty bird, and she sings as she flies,
She bringeth no tidings and she telleth no lies
She sucketh white flowers for to keep her voice clear,
And when she singeth 'cuckoo', summer draweth near.

As I was a-walking and talking one day
I met my own true love as he came that way,
The meeting was a pleasure, though the parting was a woe
For I've found him false hearted, he'd kiss me, and then he'd go.'"

When the last note had died away, echoed by a gentle sigh from the fiddle, there was a reverent hush. Sam noted that more than one of the audience was wiping tears away. Acutely aware of the sardonic nature of the man beside him, he refrained from doing the same. Fortunately, the wild applause which then exploded around them diverted Dark's attention, and he was able to brush a hand surreptitiously across his own eyes.

It took some time for some semblance of calm to return to the Paradise Coffee House. Many of the audience, accepting that there would be no more music tonight, left in search of tavern or home, but an obstinate group persisted around the bar, stamping their feet and calling for another song, until the doorman Evans firmly and implacably persuaded them at last to go. And only as they were shuffling reluctantly out into King Street, did he set eyes on the proprietor of the Paradise Coffee House, the young woman whose voice had captivated them all.

He had been lurking at the back, waiting for everyone else to leave, so the room was almost empty before she realised he was there. Then she came rushing out from behind the bar with a cry of delight, and embraced him warmly, with a fragrant kiss on each cheek. "Sam! What a surprise! I am so glad to see you! How are you?"

"I am very well, thank you, Polly my dear," he said, smiling down at her: he was not a tall man, but Polly Paradice stood barely five feet in her stockings.

"And ..." She glanced round at the almost empty room, and then continued. "I hardly dare to ask it, but what of your daughter Mary?"

His frantic search for his wayward only child had been the reason for his friendship with Polly, and her return home with him, full of tears and contrition, had come after many scrapes and misadventures which had put them all in danger, and had nearly put an end to Dark. At least now he could give her good news. "She is well, and happy, and married these five months."

"Thank God for that," said Polly, with feeling. "And who is her husband? Is it the young man you found for her before she ran away again?"

"It is - fortunately, he was willing to continue with the arrangement despite what she had done."

Polly raised her eyebrows in surprise. Since what Mary had done had been to run away with her Scottish Jacobite lover, not once but twice, and in addition to assist his escape from Newgate prison, this indicated that the young man in question was either exceedingly tolerant, exceedingly besotted or exceedingly stupid – or a combination of all three. Sam opted for the kindest interpretation. "He is very much in love."

"I should think he needs to be," was Polly's comment. "And Mary did not object?"

"Not in the least. I know she has learned from her experiences. After all she endured at the hands of Sinclair, the prospect of a cosy and uneventful marriage with a man who genuinely adores her proved irresistible. They are very happy, and she told me last week that she is expecting their first child."

"So you will be a grandfather! Sam, I am so pleased for you. Dark, did you hear that? Miss Mary is married, and in the family way."

The tall man in black was helping himself to the last of the coffee in the pot next the hearth. "Indeed, Sam? My congratulations. I trust that this is a *recent* development?"

"Dark!" Polly cried. "You should not insinuate such things!"

"Should I not? My apologies, my dear Paradice." He bowed, but Sam saw the secret look that passed between them. So the passion had not yet been slaked.

"I have spent the past six months attempting to make him fit for polite society," Polly said, turning to Sam, her hands spread in exasperation. "And as you can see, it has been to no avail."

"I was unaware that you desired to enter polite society," Dark said, a glint in his eye.

"Well, even if I did, I would not be able to, if I had you in my train."

"Mr Jessop!" A young maidservant had entered, bearing a stack of used coffee dishes. Her shining brown hair was neatly pinned up beneath her cap, and she wore a spotless striped gown that hinted, no more, at the trim figure beneath. It took Sam a moment to recognise her, so great was the change from the child he had last seen back in January, outspoken, untidy, still awkward in her true but unaccustomed guise as a girl. "Nobody told me you was in town!"

"That's because no-one knew, until I came here," Sam said. "Gin, how you've grown!"

"My name ain't Gin no more, as you well know, Mr Jessop, I'm Jane now. Jane Maggs."

"Maggs? I did not think you had any other name. Pardon me, Gin – that is to say, Jane."

"Everyone called my ma Mag, so Madam thought I may as well be Maggs." The girl grinned. "It's as good a name as any other."

"Well, Jane Maggs, you look uncommonly fine on it, and I'll swear you've grown several inches."

"Four to be exact, sir," she said, with some pride.

"Hardly surprising, since she's eating us all out of house and home." Polly nodded to her maid. "Put those dishes down before you drop them, Jane, and make your curtsey to Mr. Jessop."

The girl did as she was told, and then stood decorously, hands folded in front of her, awaiting further orders. The room was now empty of customers, and the big Welshman came back in, a bunch of keys in his hand. "All gone, madam, and the door locked. Shall I close the windows and shutters?"

"Yes, please, Will, and then you may go." Polly gave him her brilliant smile, that had enchanted half of London. As Evans turned away to the nearest window, Sam said, "There is one face I do not see - where is Hannah?"

"Here, sir." A tall, sturdy black woman bearing a tray laden with silver coffee pots and more stacks of dishes, had followed Gin - he would never be able to think of her as Jane - into the room. She put it on the bar counter and beamed at Sam. "Welcome back, Mr Jessop."

"And you too, Hannah." Now this little family of waifs and strays - Gin saved from the streets, Hannah from slavery, Evans from penury and Dark from black despair - was together, and Sam surveyed them with a pleased and approving eye. He too had been rescued, along with his errant daughter, and they all owed Polly Paradice a great deal.

"Is there any of the Arrack left, Hannah?" she was asking, and as the maid answered in the affirmative, she set out some Delftware punch cups alongside the plain silver bowl that held the potent mixture of lemon juice, rum, sugar and spices, made to Hannah's special recipe from Barbados, and ladled the liquid into them. "We must celebrate Sam's arrival in style. Jane, if you wish you may have a small amount, when you have handed round the other cups. Carefully, now, without spilling. Welcome back, Sam Jessop, and your very good health!"

With the windows shuttered and the fire still burning, the room had grown very warm. Outside, the life of the night-time street, busy, raucous, full of danger, could be heard as a sullen blur of sound, with the occasional shout or shriek rising above it. Sam drank his punch, finding it as delicious, and as perilous, as he remembered.

"So, Jessop, are you in London on business? Or have you another daughter to find?" That was Dark, who knew very well that Sam had only the one daughter.

"Partly business brings me here, yes, but I also have a letter for you, Polly." In the warmth of his welcome, he had almost forgotten it. He put his cup down on the nearest table and felt for his waistcoat pocket. After some fumbling, he drew out a rather battered sheet of paper, folded and sealed, with the direction on it in an erratic hand. *Mrs Mary Paradice, at the Paradise Coffee House in King Street in Covent Garden.*

"A letter? For me?" Polly stared at it as if she had never seen anything like it before. "Do you know who it is from, Sam?"

"Of course. Last week I had business in Bath, and took the opportunity to call on your old friend at the Bear - "

"Oh, is it from Kitty?" Polly's face, already flushed with delight and the effects of warmth and the punch, lit up with joy. "My dear Kitty, who was as good as a mother to me when I was young! How is she, Sam? Is all well there?"

"All is well, and your old friend Ephraim sends his affectionate regards to his little Farthing."

"Was he that wizened old cove?" Gin asked. "He looked as if a puff of wind would blow him away."

"Ephraim is a deal stronger than you might think," Polly said. "But I do not recall asking you for your opinion, Jane."

"Sorry, Madam," said the child, though she did not look it, and added immediately, "Ain't you going to take the letter?"

Polly, stepping forward with her hand outstretched ready, gave her recalcitrant maid a withering glare. But she accepted the paper from Sam with a conspiratorial wink, slid her thumbnail under the blob of wax, and opened it.

He was closest of them to her, and so he was the first to see all the colour ebb away from her face, and her eyes grow wide and dark. As she read, her free hand crept, shaking, to her mouth. "Oh, my God," she whispered.

"Polly?" Sam moved forward, suddenly fearful. "Polly, what is it? Is it bad news?" Perhaps Kitty was mortally ill - though she had appeared in robust good health when he had met with her only yesterday. He could think of nothing else that might be contained in that letter that could affect Polly in so drastic a fashion.

"No, it can't be!" Her voice was a feeble, trembling shadow of its normal clear and confident tones. "It can't be! It can't! She's dead!"

"Dead? Who's dead?" Sam demanded in bewilderment. "Not Kitty - she was hale and hearty when she wrote the letter."

"No - Mattie!" And her face as white as the paper in her hand, Polly dropped to the floor.

Sam moved swiftly, but Dark was quicker. He caught her just before her head hit the boards, and pulled her into his arms. All Sam could see of her was her lace cap, and the shining brown curls beneath it, and a few folds of her rose flowered gown. But the expression on Dark's face was so plainly, painfully exposed, that after a few heartbeats he had to look away. It was not only passion, then.

Hannah brought more punch, with an extra dash of rum. By then, Polly had recovered a little: she sat on the floor, leaning against Dark, her hair disordered and a touch of colour back in her face. Sam, looking down with compassion, thought, as he had so often thought before, how lovely she was, how well she knew it, and yet how warm and generous was her nature. He bent and picked up the letter, which lay near his feet, and resisted the temptation to glance at it. "Polly? Do you want this?"

She looked up at him, and gave him a smile that had something of her usual spirit. "Thank you, Sam, I will take it in a moment. Will you help me rise?"

Between them, he and Dark assisted her to a chair which Evans had brought from the inner room. Hannah, her face full of anxiety, proffered the cup of punch, and Polly shook her head. "No, I thank you, dear Hannah - pray make me up a dish of tea, as strong as you can, sugar it well, and that will restore me."

"If you say so, madam." Hannah retreated to the hearth, where one of the kettles was still steaming gently. Gin went to help her, fetching the tea caddy down from a shelf behind the bar, and scraping some crystals off the sugar loaf. Together they made the tea, and Hannah brought it over and put it gently into her mistress's hand. Dark was there to steady her, but Polly had mastered herself now, and the trembling had ceased. She sipped the steaming liquid, while her friends gathered round her, watching anxiously. At last she gave the empty cup to Gin, and looked up at Sam. "May I have the letter?"

"Of course," he said, and handed it to her. She took a deep, rather shaky breath and unfolded it. Her lips moved soundlessly as she read it over carefully, and then she laid it down in her lap. There were tears on her cheeks. She said quietly, "I am so sorry for giving you all such a fright. I believe I must owe you an explanation. Sam, will you read the letter aloud? I do not feel equal to the task just at this moment."

He did not feel equal to it either, but he would do the best he could. Kitty's hand was haphazard, her grammar untutored, her spelling worse, and punctuation completely lacking. In consequence, the sense was very difficult to interpret. At length he began, slowly and hesitantly, to read.

"'*My dearest Poll I hope this finds you as well as it leaves me forgive my Haste but I have some News for you a Week or two ago a young Woman came to the Bear asking for you and would not leave until she had some Tidings of you which I could give her but not your Direction as I did not know of it then by God's Blessing Mr Jessop came to this Town and so I was able to write this to you and hope this News will be welcome to you though what Use you may make of it I do not know as I made Enquiries afterwards for her but could not find her though I heard that she had left Bath some Days previous with a Band of strolling Players bound I know not where she told me she was your Sister and I did not at first believe her as you had told me previous with Tears and much Sadness that all your Family were dead but she insisted it and said her Name was Martha Paradice and indeed she did have a Look of you she is taller than you are and more slender her hair though brown has a touch of red but her Eyes are a lighter Colour than yours more grey than blue she told me a little else about your Father and Mother and Brother that I knew to be true and so at last I came to believe her and asked her what had she been doing these past dozen Years and more at which she grew Melancholy and said she did not care to speak of it but that her one Wish was to find you again so I told her you were living in London and had a Coffee House but I could not remember where having lost your last Letter I do think Nance must have used it to light the Fire it is a wicked Habit I have often scolded her for but no Matter for Mr Jessop came by so I could send you Word by him I hope I have done right if you wish to find her she is with a Company of Players as I said their Manager is one Amos Crowley I do not know where they were going but as you have Friends in that Business perhaps you will discover where they are or she may find you I hope this News is welcome for I remember how you have long thought you were all alone with no Family and now it seems your Sister lives so it is a time for Joy and I give you all best Wishes for a happy Reunion with affectionate Regards your dear Friend K.'"*

There was a little silence after Sam had finished. Polly wiped away more tears and said, "I thought she was dead. I truly thought she was dead."

Dark's voice was very gentle. "Why were you so sure of it?"

"Martha - we all called her Mattie - she was a Parish Apprentice as I was, but she did not have a good mistress as Kitty was. She was much younger than me, only six years old when I saw her last. The magistrates bound her to a tavern-keeper in Bath, and he and his wife worked her hard and treated her very unkindly. Then after a year or two, they all moved to Bristol, and I had no more word of her until much later, by chance, I heard some tale that she had been accused of thieving, and had been so severely beaten for it that afterwards she had run away. I could have no more news of her, and I ... I assumed she must have died." Her voice broke. "I never imagined that she could survive such treatment, let alone living on the streets. And now ... and now it seems she did. And

I must find her. I *must*, or I will never have peace, for I failed her before, and I feel the guilt of it still."

There was a small, intense silence. Gin, characteristically, was the one to break it. "You can't go gadling off all over the countryside *again*," she said. "What's to become of us and the Paradise if you leave us?"

"I am sure that Hannah and Will and the rest of you will be equal to the task," Polly told her. "In any case, I should be gone for no more than a few days. Strolling players usually have a regular route, so it should be easy to discover where they have gone and where they will be next. I can ask Jenny Garnet, or at the playhouses, someone is sure to know."

"Forgive me, madam." That was Hannah, frowning. "But who's to say this - this female really is your sister? She could have heard you was doing well for yourself and thought to share in your good fortune."

"But how could she know, if she is not truly my sister?" Polly asked. "You heard what Kitty said in the letter - she knew things about my family that a stranger would not know. And if I see and speak with her myself, I will know for sure that she is Mattie." She looked round at them all, her expression fierce and determined. "You may think what you choose, but I *will* do this. I trust you to ensure that the Paradise will be safe while I am gone. And I will not be gone long. I promise you I will not. Now, Will, are you done? Then you may go home."

"I must go back to my inn," Sam said, realising belatedly that it was almost midnight, and that it would be unwise to leave his return to the Black Swan any later. "Forgive me, Polly, for causing such upset, I had no idea - "

"Oh, Sam, there is nothing to forgive!" She jumped up to embrace him. "You have given me such news as I never thought to have all my life long, and I shall be forever grateful. And you must not go alone. It is your usual one? The Black

Swan? Then Will shall walk with you, he lives in Holborn now."

"Thank you, Polly," Sam said gratefully. "I will come back tomorrow morning, if you wish."

"Of course I wish it! You are one of my dearest friends. Now, be off with you, and keep yourself safe."

He took his leave of her, and of Dark and Hannah and Gin, and set off through the dark, perilous streets to Holborn, with the stalwart bulk of Will Evans comfortingly by his side. He had exchanged no more than a few words with Dark, and it was, Sam thought, a safe bet that he had very little desire to go off gadling, as Gin had put it, given the dance that Polly had led them both last year, in pursuit of Sam's errant daughter. He would have given much to know what the artist thought of this entirely unexpected news, and of Polly's impetuous plans.

*

"I have never told you of what happened to my family," Polly said. "It is a subject very painful to me, and for many years I tried to forget, and look to the future rather than regret the past."

"That is something I also try to do," said Dark. "And as you reminded me once, on a very memorable occasion, if there are five things you have not told me, there must be five hundred I have not told you."

"As few as five hundred? I had thought it was many more than that." Polly surveyed him with a wry smile on her face. She was sitting in her favourite chair on one side of the empty hearth in her parlour upstairs. A lock of her dark hair had come loose and curled over her shoulder: with a sudden, impatient movement she gathered it into one hand, twisted it and pinned it back on top of her head.

The man seated opposite her smiled in return. "You

may reduce the number to four, if you wish, dear Paradice. But if you decide it is a tale too sad for the telling, I will not press you."

"It *is* sad – in fact, some would call it a tragedy, though an old tragedy. And I thought I had left it in the past, until Kitty's letter brought everything back to the present. It was such a shock - I have never fainted before, in my whole life. I have been alone for so long - "

"You are not alone." His voice was suddenly rough, betraying his emotion. "Poll, I am with you now, and for always. You know that."

"Do I?" She studied him, her dark blue eyes once more full of tears. "We have been lovers for a mere six months. If you tell me the same in two years, or five, I might begin to believe it. No," she added, as he made an indignant movement, "I know you are not lying. I know that you mean what you say. But experience has taught me that promises of future happiness have a way of coming undone, even when made with the best of intentions."

"Then I hope to be the exception," Dark said.

"I hope so too." Polly closed her eyes for a moment. "And now, I must begin my tale, or I will lose all courage."

"Then begin, and I promise not to interrupt again."

"My family were not always poor. My father's father was a prosperous farmer, and my mother's father called himself a gentleman, though I suspect he was no such thing, but aspired to be. He was angry that my mother had married beneath her, as he supposed, and cut her off. Not long after they were wed, my other grandfather died, and my father took over the tenancy of his farm. It lay just outside Bradford in Wiltshire, with a fine neat farmhouse, orchards and paddocks and good fertile ground, and for years all was well. I was born, and then my brother Tom - there was another boy who died when he was a baby, and lastly my sister Mattie, who was six years younger than me. Her birth was very difficult, and both she and my mother were given over by the doctor, but they survived, though my mother was never in good health again, and Mattie was always slender and fragile-looking. But she was such a sweet, pretty child, we all made a pet of her, and my father doted on her, he called her 'Cutty', which is the Wiltshire word for a wren." She swallowed, and added, "If - *if* I were to find her, I would ask her what our father's pet name for her was. Only she and I are left to remember it."

"And you are set on finding her?"

"You promised not to interrupt."

"My apologies, dear Paradice. Pray continue, and I will be silent."

Polly sent him a doubtful look, eyebrows raised, but he said nothing, and she went on. "Then there was a harsh winter, followed by a wet cold summer. The harvest failed, and a murrain killed most of the cattle. My father had spent much money making the house beautiful, and he had very little left in savings. I remember the farm workers coming to the door for their wages, and shouting abuse when he turned them away with empty promises. The new furniture was sold, even the hangings on the beds, and my mother's riding horse, and the pony I shared with my brother and sister." She smiled sadly. "I wept all night when Acorn went. I was only eleven years old, and I did not understand. But still there was not enough money, and my father took the fancy that the farm was cursed. He said that he had had nothing but bad luck there, and so we must move on. He gave up the tenancy and we moved to another farm, many miles distant, near Gloucester, which was owned by a kinsman who was growing old and needed help. But we had not been there above a year when my father was kicked by a horse, and his leg was shattered." For the first time, her voice faltered, and then grew strong again.

"The bone could not be set, and the wound turned bad. A few days later, he died. And although we were kin to the farmer, he said we could not stay now, and turned us out of the cottage. It was January. My mother was too ill to work, I was twelve and my brother Tom was ten, Mattie was only six. The parish would not assist us when we applied for poor relief, but said we must return to Bradford. I begged the magistrates to let us stay, I said my mother was not strong enough for such a journey over many miles in a wagon, but they would not listen. And so we were forced to leave. We were nearly a week on the road, and at the end of it my mother died, mostly I think of grief and shame. So I and my brother and sister were cast upon the mercy of the good men of Bradford, and bound as Parish Apprentices. I was fortunate, I was sent to the Bear. Tom was 'prenticed to a tailor, who was not an unkind master, but he lived in a part of the town where fever was rife, and before a year had gone by, he was dead too." She smiled, though her eyes were full of tears. "Kitty heard of it, and allowed me to go to his funeral. There was no-one else to mourn him, and he was laid in a pauper's grave. So, Dark, that is the sad and sorry tale of my childhood, and perhaps now you will understand why I must find Mattie, if it is indeed Mattie, for she is the last of my family and I cannot rest easy until I can see her face and know that she is my sister." She looked up at him, sitting quiet and self-contained on the other side of the hearth. "And now that you have heard it, do I dare ask how your thoughts run?"

For answer, he rose, and knelt beside her, taking her hands in his. "Darling Poll, I did not know - what can I say?"

"You need say nothing. It is not an uncommon tale, after all. Farms fail, families fail, children are orphaned every day, there are Parish Apprentices in every town and village in the land, some treated well and some treated ill. I am not claiming any special tragedy, and besides I realise now that, much though we all loved him, my father was a superstitious fool. If he had not taken it into his head that our farm near Bradford was cursed, he would be there still, God willing." She smiled down at him. "And I would not be sitting here now, and I would never have known you, or Hannah, or Gin, or Sam, I would be long married to some fat red-faced farmer, I'd be fat and red-faced too with a brood of brats, and my proudest boast would be of my uncommon skill with the butter churn."

"Do not blame me, my dear, if I say that of those two incarnations of Poll Paradice, I prefer the one that sits before me now."

"So do I, Dark. I only wish that my family had not died to achieve it."

There was a long pause. At last, she bent her head and kissed him lightly on the cheek. "Then will you allow me to go in search of her?"

He let out a bark of laughter at that. "I? *Allow* you? I have long ago abandoned all attempts at trying to control you, Paradice, you know that only too well. You are a law unto yourself, and I like you the better for it. You are not some milk-and-water miss too timid to exchange words with a goose. But can I ask one thing of you?"

"And what is that, pray?"

"That you do not go on this quest alone."

"You do not wish to come with me, Dark? I cannot imagine why that should be."

"I don't deny I have some ... *interesting* memories of the other time I went gadling, as Gin would say, around the western parts of the country in your fragrant wake. But that is not the reason. I have a portrait to complete, remember? Mr Henderson wants it finished for his wife's birthday."

"And when is that?"

"The Friday after next, to be precise. And while I would

like nothing better than to accompany you, Mr Henderson will not pay me the ten guineas we agreed unless it is delivered on time, and even I cannot live on thin air and promises."

"I know you cannot, Dark, and I am quite happy for you to stay in Half Moon Street and paint your stock-jobber until you have his fat and florid face set on canvas to perfection, so do not worry on that score. I will take Gin."

"*Gin?* But she is a child."

"She is fifteen years old or thereabouts, and you know as well as I do that she has a courage and wisdom far beyond her years. And the Paradise can spare her, whereas it cannot spare Hannah. She and Will and Ned and the pot-boys are perfectly capable of running the coffee shop between them, though Hannah will not like being thrown together with Will." For the first time, a note of levity infused her voice. "He wishes to propose marriage to her, and she is terrified of the prospect. I think she also feels that as a former slave, she does not deserve any man's love. It took me a year to persuade her that she was worthy of my friendship and regard."

"She is certainly more than worthy, but surely she could do better than Evans? He is only a door-keeper who was formerly – "

"One of my hired bully-boys, yes. But he has a position here now for as long as the Paradise will serve coffee, and he may give the *impression* of being slow in his wits, but in fact he is not, he is kind, he loves her truly, and will treat her well. You could not say the same of many better-placed men. And despite what she says, I am pretty sure she returns his affections, but is afraid to take such a bold step." She grinned at him, and added with a return to her usual playfulness, "I have spent much time over the past few weeks trying to convince her that marriage to him is not to be feared, but so far, to no avail. She has pointed out, several times, that I am the worst person in the world to advocate wedded bliss."

"And why should that be, Paradice?"

"I am sure I do not know, sir." Her smile, by design, was enchanting and tempting both. She glanced pointedly at the little clock on the mantelpiece, which showed that it was half an hour past midnight, so late that the street outside had grown almost quiet, and rose to her feet, stretching out a hand. "And now, Dark, shall we go up? Otherwise I shall fall asleep in my chair."

"Willingly, so long as you do not instantly fall asleep in your bed."

"I doubt you will let me," Polly said, and with a sudden mischievous whirl of flowered skirts and white lace, ran from the room and up the flight of stairs which led to her bedchamber on the second floor. When Dark arrived there, having deliberately taken his time, he found her seated at her toilette table, undoing her hair and laying the pins, with their jewelled heads, green and amber, azure and pearl, in a little porcelain dish by the mirror. Their eyes met in the glass, and he came over to stand behind her, his hands resting on her shoulders. She brought one of hers up to touch his fingers, and he bent to kiss her lightly on the top of her head.

"Be careful of pins, Dark, there should be a dozen and I have only found ten."

For answer, he ran one hand lightly through her dark hair and brought out the missing pins, one topped with a garnet, one with a little silver ball. "These ones?"

"Yes, those." She took them from him and put them in the dish, then rose and turned to embrace him. They kissed, leisurely at first, then with increasing passion, until she drew back a little, her face flushed, and said softly, "Will you unwrap me, Dark, for I do not want this gown creased beyond hope?"

Over the past months, their lovemaking had changed

from the urgent slaking of desire, pleasurable though that was, to something deeper, richer and infinitely more satisfying. And tonight, too, there was tenderness, gentleness, and for her part an emotion which Polly knew, though neither she nor Dark had ever said the words out loud, could only be described as love. They had each loved before, and been cruelly betrayed, so it was not surprising that they were both wary of admitting, even to themselves, that they had taken that final leap of the heart.

Later, she lay with her head on his shoulder, his arms warm around her, both wrapped in a delicious afterglow, and said drowsily, "Dark?"

"Hmm?"

"Are you truly happy for me to go in search of my sister? Or do you think it another wild-goose-chase?"

"You wish for my honest opinion?"

"Yes."

"Then I must tell you that I *do* think it another wild-goose-chase, if you want to call it that - but I also know that you will have no peace or rest until you find out, one way or another, whether your sister is still alive, or whether there has been some unfortunate misunderstanding."

"You are right on that score." Polly thought of Mattie as she had last seen her, small, fragile, her dirty face wet and streaked with tears as she was given into the keeping of her new master. He had shouted at her to stop crying, which had made her wail the louder, until his wife boxed her ears and she was dragged away. And as clear as day, she remembered Kitty, standing next to her, holding tight to her arm to prevent her rushing forward to ... to do what? She had wanted to hit that bitter, sour-mouthed woman, scream abuse at her angry husband. But it would only have got her into terrible trouble, perhaps even prison for assault, and it would undoubtedly have made poor Mattie's plight worse. She had railed against Kitty at the time, but she had quickly come to accept that her new mistress had been right to restrain her.

"And so you must go," Dark said softly, his breath warm against her hair. "And I pray that you find this girl, and that she proves to be your sister. But do not hope too much. And promise me that if there is trouble, you send for me."

"Why should there be trouble?"

"Poll Paradice, thou art born to trouble, as the sparks fly upwards. And if your sister - your *supposed* sister - is the same, then the sparks will start a conflagration. Add Gin to the mix, and you have a powder more deadly than any of my fireworks." His arms tightened round her. "But whatever happens, do not put yourself in hazard."

There was a small silence, broken only by distant shouting from the Piazza, where a brawl had obviously broken out. Polly said softly, "If I promise, will you also? Three times, in the first months of our acquaintance, you could have died."

"Three? I make it only two."

"When Sinclair attacked you in the meadow near Bath. When the fireworks set the warehouse ablaze above your head. And if the Jacobite prisoners in Newgate had suspected you were a spy, they would not have hesitated to knife you in some dark corner."

"Well, they did not suspect it, until that old schoolfellow of mine was brought in, and I had to leave forthwith. But I grant you it was a possibility, so I will agree with you - three times it is. Rest assured, Paradice, I have no intention of embarking on another dangerous exploit. In any case, most of the leading Jacobites are in prison, or executed, or fled back overseas, so my services are no longer required, for the moment. I am entirely at your disposal, once Mr. Henderson's portrait is finished."

"And I am very grateful for your assistance, sir," said Polly, rather tartly. She let the silence lie a little, and then added, "When I thought Sinclair had killed you, in that fight in the meadow, I realised that however grim and unfriendly you might pretend to be, I actually enjoyed your company."

"Do you remember later, when we fell out? It was then that I discovered that however provoking and infuriating you might be, life without you was tedious in the extreme."

"Yet, unlike most men, you do not forbid me to go."

"I am not most men."

"I know that, Dark, that is why I am here, and why you are here beside me." She yawned, and snuggled closer to him in the dark. "Let me go, and I will always come back to you. And when you want to go off on some wild-goose-chase of your own, I hope you will always come back to me. Now, shall we sleep? Because I intend to rise early tomorrow, and make enquiries after Amos Crowley."

CHAPTER TWO

Your friendly Visit

"La, Poll, it's been an age!" Jane Garnet, known familiarly as 'Long Jenny', leaned in for her friend's embrace, and then held her at arm's length, studying her. "You look better than I've ever seen you. You obviously haven't grown tired of your phiz-monger yet - he must be doing you a power of good."

"My thanks for your kind words, Jenny. And you? How do you do?"

Jenny Garnet was an actress, recently moved to the company at the Drury Lane theatre. She would never be as admired or as notable as Mrs Oldfield or the incomparable Miss Santlow, but she had a prodigious memory, a flair for comedy, and a tall, boyish physique that had led to many breeches parts, and once, memorably, a eunuch in *'Valentinian'*. She waved a languid hand. "Oh, I do pretty well, Poll, and all the better now I'm no longer with Rich. I've had more good parts in the last two months than I did in two years at Lincoln's Inn Fields."

"I know - Dark and I were in the gallery to see you in *'The Rover'*, back in May. You played Lucetta, a 'jilting wench', as I recall. I'm so glad for you, Jenny, you deserve to do well."

"I believe I performed that role to perfection, so much so that I am shortly to take the part of Betty Frisk in *'The Country Wit'*, another jilting wench, so my fortunes are on the up, especially as I have bid Mr. Perrett farewell. He was growing uncommonly tiresome, with his notion that actresses are three parts the whore. Do you know, he actually asked me to repent of my sinful ways, and take up a sober and godly life. I told him I would not give up the stage were he to offer me marriage and three hundred pounds a year, and kicked him downstairs."

"You did not."

"Oh, I can assure you I did, Poll - though I admit I did not actually *kick* him, that would have been far too much effort. The mere threat of it was enough."

Polly had been introduced to Jenny's erstwhile lover, but had not formed a favourable impression, and she said so now. Her friend smiled. "Oh, he was entertaining enough at first, but he comes from a Dissenting family, and was taught to think all plays and players the spawn of Satan. So good riddance. Now, Poll, can I tempt you with some of this fine claret here?"

It was midway through the afternoon, and Polly would rather have had tea, or chocolate, but she accepted the proffered glass of wine and settled herself on the couch in Jenny's pleasant chamber. The sun flooded warmly in through the open windows, along with the sounds, and smells, of the street below. For a while, the two women sipped their drink and made small talk, exchanging news and gossip about mutual friends and acquaintances, many of them concerned with one or other of the two theatres in London. At a convenient lull in the flow, Polly seized her opportunity. "Jenny, have you ever heard tell of a player called Crowley? Amos Crowley?"

Her friend was both an avid receiver and an even more avid disseminator of news, rumour and gossip, and, being a Londoner born and bred, seemed to know half the town, which was why Polly had decided to ask her first, before making enquiries at the two playhouses. True, once Jenny knew of the reason for her interest, she would poke and pry as she usually did, but it was worth it if she could discover more about Crowley, and where he and his company might be found.

"Lord," Jenny said, her plucked eyebrows arching in surprise. "That's a name I haven't heard in an age! What do you want with that rogue, Poll? You surely can't be thinking to join his company - they're living hand to mouth and sleeping under hedgerows, from all accounts."

Then he did exist, and was not a figment of Kitty's, or the supposed Mattie's, imagination. Polly said carefully, "Of course I don't. I am very comfortably situated at present, in every respect." She ignored her friend's suggestive chuckle, and continued. "But I have heard that an old friend may be with him, and I have a fancy to get in touch with her again."

"Are you planning to rescue her, Poll, so she can join your little band of waifs and strays?"

This was very close to the mark, but Polly refused to rise to the bait. She took another sip of claret - mid-afternoon or no, it was very good, she must remember to ask Jenny where she had obtained it - and said casually, "I doubt she would wish to be rescued, as you put it. But tell me more of this Amos Crowley. What sort of man is he? And do you know where he might be?"

It was Jenny's turn to drink her wine while she considered her answer. "Crowley? He's a charming scoundrel, as long as you don't cross him. But he never charmed me, despite all his efforts. He acted with Betterton in the old company at Lincoln's Inn Fields, and then moved with them to the Queen's Theatre, as it then was, in the Haymarket. So that's, what, ten years ago and more?"

"At the least."

"But then Betterton died, and Cibber took over, and Crowley fell out with him - not very difficult to do, I grant you. He'd fallen out with Rich's father as well, so he took himself off with some other disaffected actors, out into the country. And there he's stayed, from what I hear, travelling with a raggle-taggle band and playing in barns and inn yards and risking being taken up for vagrancy. Or thieving. If you find your friend with him, Poll, tell her she could do better."

"I will," Polly said. "So - do you know where they might be? They played in Bath not long ago, so I've been told."

Jenny finished her claret, frowning, and set the empty glass down on the windowsill behind her chair. "Bath? I thought he kept more to the south, his usual route goes through Hampshire and into Sussex and Kent. But perhaps he has good reason to avoid those places now." She leaned forward, her face unwontedly serious. "And I'll tell you this as your true friend, Poll - you have good reason to avoid him too. He's trouble."

"I thought you said he was charming."

"I did, but his charm don't run deep, and that's the worst kind. He uses it to get what he wants, and if he doesn't, he'll eat your friend up and spit her out and never care if he breaks her heart and crushes her soul. Is she young? Younger than you? And seen less of the world?"

"Yes," Polly said, though in truth she did not know whether her sister retained any of her childhood innocence: it was unlikely, given what she had heard from Kitty. She knew about superficially charming men, however: her late lover, Robbie Sinclair, had been just such a one, delightful when it suited him, ruthless, even murderous when it did not. Suddenly she feared for Mattie, if it was Mattie, in company with a person whom even Jenny mistrusted and disliked. Her friend was famously easy-going and often commented that she was too idle to waste energy and effort on enmity or spite, but Crowley was obviously unpleasant enough to warrant the exertion.

"Then she is certainly in need of rescue, and the sooner the better. Do you plan to go to Bath? Is your phiz-monger going with you?"

"No, he has a portrait that must be finished first."

"Oh, is that the way the wind blows?"

With the memory of last night's delights warming her heart, Polly said, "No, he really does have a portrait to finish. I'm taking Gin – Jane – with me."

Jenny crowed with laughter. "That little imp of mischief? You need a man to escort you. Your muscular door-keeper should suffice."

"Evans will look after the coffee-house, with Hannah and the boys. I don't plan to be absent for more than a few days, a week at most - *if* I can find Crowley and his company quickly. Once I reach Bath, it should not be too difficult to pick up their trail."

"La, Poll, of course, why did I not think of it before - Tony is your answer," said Jenny suddenly. "I heard he was in Bath earlier in the year, and he may be there still. He will know all the travelling players. If you can find him, he will set you on your way, without a doubt."

"Tony? Do you mean Tony Aston? I thought he was in Ireland."

"And so he was, all last year, but he's back now from what I've been told. Apparently he's concocted a hotchpotch of dances and comical songs and short pieces that he calls a Medley. You know Tony, he'll be only too eager to help you."

Polly did. Tony Aston operated on the fringes of the theatrical world, sometimes acting with one of the established companies, but more often travelling, with his wife and young son and a motley and ever-changing crew of associates, all over the land, and stopping wherever there were people willing to pay to see their performances. He was an amusing, witty man with great, and genuine, charm and considerable generosity, and was regarded with much affection by those who were his friends and acquaintances, but money seemed to slide through his fingers like water, and he was perpetually casting about for new ways of making it, some legitimate, some not. She said, "Thank you so much, Jenny. If anyone is able to help me find Crowley's company, I should think it would be Tony."

"I hope you do," said Jenny Garnet. She leaned forward in a confiding way, her eyes eager and bright, her bronze hair, artfully lightened and curled, lit to fire by the sun at her back. "So, Poll, who is this friend you are so eager to trace?"

Polly hesitated. Now it had come to the point, she found that she did not really want to tell her friend the possible identity of the person she sought. But although Jenny famously could not keep a confidence to herself, were she to be offered a winning lottery ticket to do so, she was also kind, and she had been helpful. So she said, "I do not know for sure, but I believe that she may be my sister."

"Your *sister*!" Jenny sat back, eyes round, mouth open, hands to her face. "Lord, Poll, I did not think you *had* a sister! I understood you were alone in the world!"

"Once I had a brother and a sister, and a mother and father too, until they died. I know my brother is dead - I saw him buried - but I never knew for sure what had happened to my sister. I thought she was dead too, I had long given up all hope, and then yesterday I received news that she had been asking after me in Bath. And my - my informant mentioned that she had left the city with a band of players under the leadership of this Amos Crowley. So I feel I must do my best to find her."

"She may *say* she's your sister." Jenny was suddenly thoughtful. "But is she?"

"Why would she say that she was, if she was not? What

could she hope to gain by it? How could she know that her supposed sister has done well for herself? Surely it can only be the natural desire to be reunited with the last member of her family, without any thought of reward." Polly paused, and then added, "And if she is not my sister, how would she know where to ask of me? Very few people know my past history."

"You sound as if you are trying to convince yourself, Poll."

"Curse you, Jen, you know me too well. Yes, I suppose I am. But the only way to discover the truth is to find her, and I mean to do that as soon as possible. I knew you would be able to help me, and so you have, and I thank you from my heart. Now, pray tell me where you obtained this excellent claret?"

Jenny Garnet looked almost coy. "I fear I am not at liberty to say, it may be more than my life is worth."

So it had been come by illicitly. Polly smiled. "No matter, I will not press you."

"Just as well, for I would not tell you if you did. Now, pray forgive me, but I must ask you to leave soon, I am due at Drury Lane later and I do not want to be late. It is not the chiefest part, but I have some telling lines and I mean to impress Cibber with my ingenious acting. Mark my words, Poll, I shall be the toast of the theatre before long!"

So Polly gathered her parasol and her straw summer hat, and bid her friend goodbye, with expressions of her sincere gratitude, and a warm hug. Jenny laughed. "I hope you find her, and that she proves indeed to be your sister. But remember what I told you, concerning Crowley, and be wary of him."

"I will, I promise," Polly assured her. "And I will tell you all about my adventure to Bath, when I see you next - which should be at the most in a week or so."

"A week? I hope your coffee house, and your phiz-monger, can survive so long without you! If you wish it, I shall look in from time to time, to keep them all up to the mark." During lean spells without a part, Jenny had frequently helped out behind the bar, distributing her dubious brand of wit along with the tobacco and punch.

"I thank you for that, but pray do not put yourself to any inconvenience on my account."

"On the contrary, Poll, I shall enjoy it, for you have tutored them very well, and besides, you are such a harsh mistress that they are all terrified of you."

Laughing, Polly took her leave, but her friend's words echoed in her head as she walked back to King Street. It was not true, of course: if anything, she was too soft on her servants, particularly Gin. But they had not, yet, taken advantage of her generosity: rather the reverse, for they had responded to her kindness with fierce and dedicated loyalty. Hannah was her beloved friend, Evans would do anything for her, and the child now called Jane Maggs had done her utmost to bring her and Dark back together, when it had seemed to them both that their brief affair was finished for ever, burned to ashes in a conflagration of betrayal, misunderstanding and rage. Yes, she and Dark owed Gin their present happiness, so she could forgive the plain-speaking bordering on insolence, the sometimes inadequate standards of cleanliness, even the occasional mutiny. And on her quest to find her sister, she felt that she could have no better companion.

*

But when she climbed into the Bath Flyer, very early in the morning three days later, Gin was not her only escort. Sam Jessop had insisted on accompanying her on the first part of her journey: as he had pointed out, it was only a little out of his way, and he could pay a second visit to a prospective customer who had needed more time to think about the deal Sam had proposed when last in Bath. His business was varied - he traded in fine cloth, lace, braids and trimmings - and from a lowly start as a draper's apprentice, he had built it up over thirty years with hard work and a reputation for fairness and probity, and was now a wealthy man, living in comfort and able to provide his wayward daughter with a generous dowry.

Polly could not help but remember that other time, in the autumn of last year, when she, Dark and Sam, with Gin a stowaway, had made this journey in search of the missing Mary Jessop, who had eloped with Polly's former lover, the Jacobite Robbie Sinclair. They had eventually found her, after some adventures, but for all of them, those days had been a transformative experience. Sam and Polly had become firm friends: Polly had discovered Gin's true, female identity: and she and Dark had moved from outright mutual hostility to mutual and later passionate attraction. That jaunt, begun so inauspiciously, had turned out all for the best, and she hoped now that this second trip to Bath would have a similarly happy outcome.

The weather was fine, the roads were in good fettle, and the journey passed with no more incident than their coach having to negotiate a stranded wagon just past Marlborough, in the morning of their second day. Many hours later, they rattled wearily into Bath as the sun was sinking languidly towards the horizon, and drew up in the yard of the White Hart in Stall Street, the other of the two principal inns in the town. Polly had sent a letter ahead, warning Kitty of their coming, and there were a couple of porters ready to carry their bags up to the Bear, a few minutes' walk away, where their hostess was eagerly awaiting them.

It was the better part of a year since they had last met, and there was a flurry of welcome, loving greetings, enquiries as to the journey and the state of the roads. Polly had not forgotten her first fears when Kitty's letter had arrived, and was relieved to see no change in the small, spare, energetic woman who had come to be a second mother to her during her time as a maidservant at the Bear, long ago. Kitty, for her part, greeted Sam warmly and then asked after Dark. She was pleased to be told that he and Polly continued to have, as she rather coyly put it, an 'understanding'. Finally, Gin was brought forward, suddenly and unwontedly awkward, even shy, in her neat gown and cap, to be admired in her proper guise as a girl.

"And I trust Mistress Paradice is keeping you in proper order, and showing you the best way of doing things?" Kitty demanded, looking Gin up and down with an expression that anyone who did not know her would have described as menacing.

"Yes'm," said Gin, eyes on the floor and bobbing a curtsey to be on the safe side.

"And of course," Kitty continued, "her way of doing things was taught to her by me, so they are unquestionably the best. I trust you will follow the path of righteousness and obey her instructions to the letter?"

"Yes'm." Gin risked a glance up at her tormentor, and what she saw there must have reassured her, for she added, "Though sometimes I can't help myself, I say things I shouldn't cos they leave my mouth without my say-so."

"Well, Jane, you must do your utmost to prevent that happening. Now, be off to the kitchen and help Nance to bring us the refreshments I have ordered. You were here last year of course, so you will know where to go."

"Yes'm," said Gin, and scurried out. Polly, who had been watching with a gleam in her eye, waited until the door had shut and the sound of her maid's footsteps had dwindled away, before dissolving into laughter. "Oh, Kitty, I had forgotten how terrifying you can make yourself appear! It's not often Jane is so cowed."

"So you haven't rubbed all the corners off her yet, lamb? For shame!"

"I seem to remember," Polly told her with a smile, "that even you never succeeded in rubbing all the corners off me."

A few moments later, Gin returned with a tray of refreshments - tea, cakes, pastries - and Kitty's guests were able to take the edge off the thirst and hunger that had assailed them during the last stages of their journey. Then Polly, who had hardly been able to contain her impatience, wiped the crumbs from her mouth, swallowed the last drop of tea, and turned to her hostess. "Tell me about the woman who calls herself my sister. Tell me everything you can remember, I beg you, for I am on fire to know more of her than what you set down in your letter."

Sam and Gin leaned forward attentively. Kitty put her cup on the table beside her chair - they were in her private parlour, which was comfortable if a little shabby round the edges - and looked thoughtful. "I'll tell you what I can, Poll, but it won't be a great deal, for she was here for no longer than it took young Jane to fetch that tray. She came to the yard asking for you, and as good fortune would have it, spoke to Ephraim, for he's the only one of the ostlers who remembers you. He said you lived in London now, but that I might be able to give her your direction, so he sent her in to me. Sat in that very chair you're sitting in, but she didn't want to trouble with tea, though I offered it, she just wanted news of you. So I told her that you'd been here last year, and that I knew you had a coffee house in London, but I could not for the life of me remember where it was. She was uncommon disappointed, I could tell that, and she upped and left straight away in a huff, before I could ask her more. When I had the leisure, I asked about, pretty young girl like that would turn heads, and I was told she was a player with a strolling company, but they'd left the morning after she came to me. So I wrote the letter you had, but of course I did not know where to send it, until Mr. Jessop happened to come by a few days later, for which I thank you wholeheartedly, sir."

"Glad to be of service," said Sam, rather indistinctly: he was still working his way through the last of the pastries, and had his mouth full.

"So, how did she look?" Polly demanded, and something of her urgency seemed to spur Kitty into a more concentrated answer.

"How did she look, lamb? Well, a bit shabby to be honest. Her gown had seen better days, the hem was frayed and she'd mended a tear in the sleeve, her linen wasn't too clean either, but she was slender and tall, taller than you, and from the way she carried herself, you'd think she was Queen of England. And as I said, she was a pretty girl. Though not so pretty as you are, lamb."

"What colour were her eyes?" Polly asked, knowing she was blushing. "You said in your letter that they were more pale than mine."

Kitty, pinned down, screwed up her face with the effort of recall. "Aye, they were, I'd say grey rather than blue. Her hair was reddish brown, some would call the colour chestnut I think. And her face pale but her cheeks quite rosy. Does that sound like your sister?"

Polly was silent as she also searched her memory. The image of Mattie, that she had kept in her heart for twelve years, seemed to lose all definition just as she sought to fix the details in her mind, and vanished like smoke in a gale. All she could remember was a little girl, her face streaked with tears and her lank hair snaking down under her dirty cap, sobbing as she was dragged away to a life which had proved intolerable.

"I don't know," she said at last, aware of how feeble that sounded. "She was only six years old. Children change so much as they grow up. And the more I try to remember her, the more she fades away. But you said that she spoke of my parents, and my brother Tom?"

"Yes, she explained very briefly what had happened to them, and that tallied with what you had told me, so I thought she must truly be your sister. And why would she not be?"

"Why indeed, for what could she gain by pretending such a relationship?"

"A dry bed and regular meals rather than going on the tramp," said Sam, joining the conversation for the first time. "Forgive me, Polly, but you are a woman of consequence and standing now, you are comfortably situated, perhaps she thought to presume upon your generosity."

"But how would she know about Madam or her family?" Gin said suddenly from her stool in the corner, where she had consumed cakes silently and as quickly as if she feared she would not eat again for some time. "She wouldn't, unless she really was Madam's sister - or had known her. So either way, if you catch up with her, you'll find out what happened to her." She grinned, revealing uneven teeth smeared with crumbs. "So you'd better track down that Tony Aston fellow what Long Jenny told you about, and see what he has to say!"

"Aston?" Kitty enquired. "Tony Aston? That name seems familiar ..."

"He's an actor," Polly told her. "He has a little company and travels all over the country, but apparently he's playing in Bath at present. They perform songs and dances and brief scenes."

"Of course!" Kitty cried, clapping her hands. "I knew I'd heard that name - he's the Medleys man. Very popular they are, a good crowd every night, apparently - if they weren't," she added bluntly, "they wouldn't have been playing so long. I think they've been in Bath since May. Of course, I ain't seen them, no time to waste with such fripperies, but the gentry seem to like them. If you want a word with Mr Aston, he'll be at the playhouse."

"I did not know that Bath had a playhouse," Sam observed.

"Indeed it does, Mr. Jessop, and has done for more than ten years - though I don't suppose it compares with your fine London theatres, Poll. It's just behind our yard, on the corner of Vicarage Lane and Borough Walls, a few moments' walk. But I should leave it until tomorrow morning - you'll be all the sharper for a good supper and a comfortable night's sleep."

*

"This ain't no playhouse!" Gin exclaimed, staring round at the interior of Bath's only theatre. "It ain't no more'n a common barn!"

Though she would never admit it aloud, Polly knew her maid had a point. They were both accustomed to London's glorious establishments at Lincoln's Inn Fields and Drury Lane, with their elaborate scenery, spectacular decorations and elegant boxes where the politer elements of society could watch the performance in comfort, while ensuring that those in the pit and gallery had an excellent view of their fashionable attire. Although Bath's playhouse had been built only ten years previously at considerable expense, with contributions from many aristocratic patrons, it was not entirely clear how their money had been spent. The seats were tiered, one above the other, rising so high that those wishing to occupy the rearmost row must be forced either to bend double before they sat down, or knock their heads against the ceiling. The stage, for so the space not taken by the seating should presumably be called, was bare and unadorned, without scenery or any furniture or props, and the only decorations to be seen were the armorial bearings painted on the walls, apparently commemorating the generosity of those who had paid for this Spartan accommodation.

"And there ain't no boxes neither," Gin continued, in her penetrating London whine. "Where's the Quality to sit?"

Polly, standing in the central aisle, looked round and pointed. "There's one, see, above the entrance." She lowered her voice, forestalling another derogatory comment. "And I suggest you keep quiet, or you'll have us thrown out."

Gin sent her a mutinous glance, but obeyed. Polly cupped her hands and called. "Hello? Is anyone about?" There must be, for the entrance had been unlocked, and even a place as bare and unpromising as this would not be left unoccupied, at the mercy of every passing thief. She spotted a door at the side of the stage. Did it perhaps lead to a green room or a tiring room?

Just as she began to walk in that direction, it opened, and a man emerged, clad in a rough, homespun suit in a muddy shade of brown, which Polly recognised as the conventional costume for a rustic in a comedy piece. He saw her at once, and frowned. "Can I help 'ee, ma'am?"

It was some time since she had last encountered Tony Aston, but Polly knew him at once: that clever, mobile face was unmistakeable. She did not think he recognised her, for he was peering at her in a short-sighted way, still frowning. "I very much hope that you can, Tony," she said cheerfully, holding out her hand. "Do you not remember me? We have met several times, at the Playhouse. Poll Paradice."

At once his frown cleared, and an expression of delight took its place. "Polly! Such a beautiful songbird! Dare I hope that you are seeking to adorn my humble Medleys? Some fresh blood would be very welcome, very welcome indeed!" He seized her hand and shook it vigorously. "This is an unlooked-for pleasure, yes, my dear, a real pleasure. I cannot promise you more than a small share of the profits, of course, but with you as part of the company, we can look forward to full houses for the rest of the season - "

Polly felt it would be wise to interrupt him before his mistaken assumption became reality. "Tony, I am sorry to disappoint you, but I have not come to join your company. I've come to ask for your help, and information, if you can give it."

Instantly, he deflated like a pricked bladder. "Oh, my dear, are you not? I thought - well, never mind."

"Perhaps in the future, yes, I would be happy to sing for you - if you come to London, seek me out at my coffee house in King Street by the Piazza, and we can discuss it." Polly deliberately kept her tone business-like. "But at present I fear I have a more pressing matter to hand. Long Jenny thought you might be able to tell me about a strolling player and manager called Amos Crowley."

Tony Aston's changeable face altered again, in a way that disturbed her. "Crowley?" he said. "What do you want with that skellum? Take my advice, Poll, and steer well clear of him. He's trouble, that one. Took my best actress, enticed her away with false promises, and I still haven't found anyone to replace her." He looked at Polly hopefully. "Unless ..."

" You are kinder than I deserve, Tony, but I fear I must decline."

"Ah, well." He let out an exaggerated sigh, and she wondered how many of the emotions which played so swiftly across his features were genuine. "It was worth the asking, just in case. Now, will you come and meet my wife and my boy? Walter is only ten but you would not think it if you saw him act, and he has a remarkable voice for one so young - "

Gin coughed pointedly. It was astonishing, Polly

thought, how much meaning such a brief, wordless sound could convey. She smiled at Tony. "Of course I would be delighted to be introduced to Mrs. Aston and Walter, but could you tell me first where this man Crowley might have gone? A friend of mine may be with his company and if what you say about him is true -"

"Oh, it's true as I'm standing here." As if his legs were not truly joined to the rest of his body, they performed a little caper without Tony apparently realising that he was doing it. "He's a bad lot. Has a finger in all kinds of nefarious pies. If you find your friend, I should tell him to leave before trouble finds him too."

Polly decided not to correct him. She said, "I certainly will - *if* I can catch up with them. Where might they have gone? Do they have a regular route? Jenny said she thought they usually travelled through the southern counties - Hampshire, Sussex, Kent –"

"Salisbury," Tony said. "I'd heard they were going to Salisbury. But they left Bath at least ten days ago, so they may have gone on from there by now. After that, Southampton perhaps, or Winchester, who knows?" He smiled hopefully at her. "You might not find them at all, or spend the whole summer chasing after them. Why not stay in Bath and give us the joy of your incomparable voice?"

"*No*, Tony."

He was obviously either obtuse or desperate - Polly inclined to the latter view - for he began again, in a wheedling tone, to try to persuade her to change her mind. Fortunately, the door to the side of the stage opened once more and a boy came charging out, followed by a tall woman in a lavender coloured wrapping gown, edged with rather grubby lace. "Papa, Papa, I have the song off perfectly now!"

This must be young Walter, a well-grown child who had

the same quickness of movement and liveliness of expression as his father. Tony beamed at him fondly. “Well, my boy, we must hear it, but first let me present - my dear, this is Poll Paradice, who has sung at Lincoln's Inn Fields, and whom I have been attempting to entice into our company.”

“Without success, I’m afraid to say,” Polly put in hastily, before there could be any misunderstanding.

“Polly, my dear wife Abigail, and my son Walter.”

“Delighted, I'm sure,” said Mrs. Aston, taking Polly's hand with fingers that felt limp and rather clammy, and giving it a perfunctory squeeze. “Lincoln's Inn, you say? I know it well, though when *I* sang it was at Drury Lane.”

Polly knew the gossip that Tony's wife had actually performed in a booth at Bartholomew Fair before her marriage, but had no intention of mentioning it. She listened politely to Walter singing 'The False Lover' in a piercingly high treble, and when he finished, on a note that was perilously close to a shriek, she complimented his parents on producing such a talented child.

“Thank you,” said Mrs. Aston, attempting graciousness. “And what brings you to Bath, Mrs. Paradice? Since you are not to be of our company,” she added, with no trace of regret.

Polly explained again that she was searching for a friend who had apparently joined Amos Crowley's band of roving players, and for the first time Tony's wife displayed some animation. “Why ever would anyone of sense ally themselves with that dyed-in-the-wool villain?”

“Tony told me that he had enticed away your best actress,” Polly prompted.

“Indeed he did, with who knows what promises and temptations he had no intention of keeping, and she fell for his lies, the stupid girl. You may know her, she goes by the name of Isabella Wright. She does have some talent, though, which presumably the silly minx intends to waste in barns and inn yards."

"I have seen her act, some while ago," Polly said cautiously. In her opinion, the Astons were well rid of Bella Wright, who had the reputation, entirely deserved, of being vain and demanding, as well as being promiscuous to a degree noticeable even amongst the theatre community, who were not usually famed for their chastity. "But surely Crowley already had sufficient actresses in his company?" She glanced across at Tony, who was giving his son advice on his performance.

"Oh, he had some, to be sure, a sorry crew of sluts and trollops. But you said you had a friend who might be amongst their number?" Mrs. Aston looked Polly up and down, and Polly, who had deliberately dressed modestly for this meeting in plain dark blue cotton calico, with a muslin kerchief decorously covering her neckline, gazed blandly back. "My friend is neither, so far as I know. But she may not be with them. Do you know the names of the other women with Crowley? How many were there?"

Abigail Aston waved a dismissive hand. "Four or five. There's Mother Ellis, she's little better than a bawd, plays comedy parts. Rebecca Barrett, a harlot if ever there was one, and Sukey Mason too. And a couple of pert little misses, already in a fair way to following in their steps. What is your friend's name?"

Polly had already thought of the answer she would give. "Martha."

"I do not think there was anyone called Martha, but I may be mistaken. If there was, she was young and insolent. I pray you do not chase after them to no purpose. Now, tell me truly, do you not think my Walter a fine young singer? He could match any cathedral choirboy for his clear tone and perfect notes."

Polly readily agreed. She did not care for Mrs. Aston, but she had been very helpful, so it would be impolite and impolitic not to spend a little time in their company, praising their young prodigy. She glanced at Gin, who had sat down on one of the benches with a look of extreme boredom, and then accepted Tony's invitation to refreshments in the Green Room, which turned out to be little more than a cupboard to the side of the stage area, the space almost entirely taken up with ancient props and musty-smelling costumes, with frowsty wine and a platter of stale cakes and sweetmeats on offer.

"So did you find where they've gone?" her maid demanded a while later, as soon as they had gained the fresh air of Vicarage Lane. "Madam," she added as an afterthought.

The sun was very hot, and Polly paused to unfurl her parasol. "According to Mr. Aston, Amos Crowley's company planned to visit Salisbury."

"Where's that?" Gin was a Londoner, born and bred, and apart from that foray to Bristol and Bath last year, had never been outside the capital in her life.

"To the south-east of here, in Wiltshire. It's perhaps forty miles, easily done in a day if we set out early."

"Is there a coach?"

"I don't know - I'll ask Kitty. If not, we'll hire a horse, and you can ride pillion."

"Ain't Mr. Jessop coming too?"

"No, Jane, he still has business in Bath, and then he's going home to Oxford. We shall do perfectly well on our own."

"What if there's footpads or highwaymen?"

"I thought that being held up by a handsome rogue on a fast horse was every young girl's dream."

Gin's only reply was a contemptuous snort. Polly, chuckling to herself, made her way down Vicarage Lane, which was quicker and easier than trying to negotiate the Bear's yard, at present filled by someone's private coach being readied for an onward journey to Bristol. She did not place much reliance on Abigail Aston's derogatory remarks about the women in Crowley's company - which she suspected were founded on malice and resentment rather than actual fact - and Tony's words of warning, though they appeared to echo what Jenny Garnet had said, also seemed more to do with the defection of Bella Wright to the rival company, rather than any serious villainy.

So, they had gone to Salisbury. She had never been there, but she had heard talk of its fine cathedral, the handsome Close around it, and beyond them a bustling and thriving city. No playhouse had been mentioned, and Polly doubted that Salisbury possessed such a thing. If a place as wealthy and fashionable as Bath could only boast the glorified barn she had just left, then it was very unlikely that a small rural city would have a proper theatre. As Mrs Aston had predicted, Amos Crowley's company would probably be playing in inn courtyards or in outbuildings in the countryside. She had met actors who had experienced the strolling life, and most of them had been very glad to leave it behind for the security, regular wages and appreciative, sophisticated audiences of the London theatres. Surely only desperation could have driven Mattie to join such a band, and she would welcome her sister's arrival as if Polly was her saviour.

A moment's honest reflection was enough to overturn that comforting vision. They had set out to rescue Sam's daughter Mary, last year, only to find that Mary, in love with her abductor, did not want to be rescued. It had taken a brutal revelation of Sinclair's true character – Mary had overheard him and her landlady planning to sell her to a brothel – to persuade her that she was better off at home with her father. Perhaps Mattie, in love with the theatrical life, would not want to leave it. And Polly knew that whatever decision her sister – her *supposed* sister – might make, she must accept it, and be content with the knowledge that Mattie was alive, and well.

Salisbury. It was not so far, and might prove to be the end of her quest.

CHAPTER THREE

That's a Lie, and a loud one

"Players, you say?" The landlord of the Red Lion, one of the city's most well-appointed inns, regarded Polly with deep suspicion. "We don't hold with they folk here. Salisbury be a *respectable* place."

It certainly looked it. A fine broad Market Square, a cathedral whose spire, thrusting gloriously towards heaven, had been visible for several miles along their road like a beacon of hope, and neat, well-kept buildings, some half-timbered in the old-fashioned style, others newly built of brick with stone quoins and sash windows, testified to the fact that Salisbury was indeed very respectable, and also, Polly suspected, rather dull. Certainly, if the innkeeper knew the half of her distinctly chequered history, he would bar her from his salubrious and very expensive establishment forthwith.

But he did not, and she had once more dressed modestly, she had her maidservant in attendance, and Kitty had arranged for her to travel in a private coach, which was returning to Southampton after conveying its owners to Bath for the season. Polly had therefore arrived in Salisbury as decorously and respectably as its inhabitants might desire, and with high hopes despite her weariness: she had been awake since well before dawn, and the roads were so bad that any slumber, or indeed even a brief nap, was completely impossible. She swallowed a yawn and gave the innkeeper a small version of her brilliant smile. "I can see that it is. Such a pleasant place! But you say that the players have not been here for some time?"

"Not since the Year Six," said the innkeeper. "Corporation bade them go and never come back, and good riddance. Corruption of youth, disorderly conduct, vice and debauchery, we don't hold with that sort of behaviour here."

"So there have been no players here for ten years?" Polly said, struggling to keep the disappointment out of her voice. Indeed, the landlord was looking at her so doubtfully now that she feared she might have to find another inn to spend the night.

"Ten year of peace and order we've had without 'em, and long may it continue. I've heard Winchester Corporation did the same, last year, because all the young scholars had gone to see the play, to the neglect of their studies and the corruption of their minds." He fixed her with a suspicious stare. "If you'll forgive me asking, madam, why do you wish to know?"

"I am seeking my unfortunate niece, who has been enticed away by a band of players," Polly told him blithely. "These young people seem to be irresistibly attracted to such an ungodly way of life. I hope to rescue her before it is too late."

Behind her, she heard a little scuffle and a huff of breath, and prayed that Gin would not disgrace them both. But the innkeeper seemed to be mollified by her words, and nodded sympathetically. "I very much regret that I cannot help you, madam. But of course you'll be welcome to stay while you make your enquiries."

A servant who was probably the same age as Gin showed them to a comfortable chamber on the first floor, and informed them that supper, if they wished it, could be brought up to them. Polly thanked her, and as soon as the door had shut behind her, turned to her own maid. "I will unpack, but can you go down to the kitchens? You may order our supper and at the same time enquire about the players. The innkeeper appears not to know where they are, but I'll wager his servants do." She smiled reminiscently. "When I was in their position, I remember we all knew every detail of the entertainments on offer in Bath, and for miles around."

"Indeed, Madam," said Gin. She paused, with a look of hopeful curiosity - Polly had always, by design, been rather reticent about her past as an inn servant at the Bear - but when no further information came, bobbed a curtsey and nodded. "Yes, Madam. But I'm not sure as how I'll be able to understand them, they talk strange in these parts."

"Well, do your best," Polly said. She added, "It would hardly be proper for me to go, and I likely would not receive much in the way of helpful information if I did. Whereas you have a good chance of finding out where the players can be found."

"*If* they're anywhere near," Gin said doubtfully.

When she had made her reluctant departure, Polly turned to the bags which had been carried up by a burly young manservant. She took out the two gowns and the riding habit she had brought with her – all plain and 'respectable' – shook them to get rid of the creases, and laid them on the bed. Keeping busy was the best remedy for apprehension, and she could not deny that she was anxious. Having come so far and invested so much in her search for the girl who claimed to be Mattie, she was now beginning to fear that, as Dark had pointed out in London, she might have embarked on a wild-goose-chase.

Very quickly, she heard clattering feet outside - Gin had never lost the habit of galloping everywhere as if there was a fire at her heels - and the door banged open to admit her, in the company of the girl who had earlier shown them up to this room. "Madam, this here's Betsy. I can't rightly make out what she's saying, but she knows about them players, that's for sure."

Betsy, obviously a rather shy girl, looked distinctly overwhelmed by the attention paid to her. She curtseyed, blushing deeply. Polly said kindly, "Thank you for taking the trouble to answer my maid's enquiries. Apparently you know where Mr. Crowley's company of players can be found?"

Betsy, seemingly struck dumb, nodded in confirmation.

"Tell Madam what you told me," Gin said helpfully. "'Cos she can understand what you say and I can't, or no more'n a word or two."

The girl gathered her resources with an effort, and said, "They be playing up Amesbury way, ma'am, so I've heard tell. At Mr. Kenton's barn."

"Amesbury." Polly had heard the name, long ago, but could recollect little else about the place. "That's north of here, am I right?"

"Aye, so 'ee be, ma'am, 'bout eight nine mile away."

"Excellent, thank you, Betsy. And whereabouts in Amesbury is Mr. Kenton's barn to be found?"

Even Polly, Wiltshire born and bred, struggled to make sense of the girl's answer, for her dialect was very broad, but she thought she had the gist of it. "Coombes Court Farm, just before you reach Amesbury town on the Salisbury road. Is that correct?"

"Aye, ma'am. Be off highway on..." Betsy paused for thought, then flapped her left hand. "*This* side. 'Ee can't miss it. They be there till market day Friday, so they say, or somewhen after."

Polly hoped she was right. She thanked the girl, rewarded her with a sixpence, and told her she could go. When the door had shut behind her, she turned to Gin. "That was very well done. Here's sixpence for you too."

"Thank you, Madam," said Gin, with a delighted dip of a curtsey, and secreted the coin in the pocket of her gown. Polly wondered what she would spend it on. After years in her boy's disguise, her maid seemed to have little interest in personal adornment or feminine frivolities, and still had to be reminded occasionally of the need to keep her nails clean and her hair tidy. It was very unlikely that Gin would want to invest in a bundle of silk ribbons or some scraps of lace, and certainly Polly had seen no evidence that she had done so. Given the rewards and tips she had deservedly received during the eight months she had been in Polly's service, she probably had quite a tidy sum tucked away under the mattress in her attic room at home.

Later, when they had eaten a plain but substantial supper in their chamber, Polly went downstairs to enquire after hiring a horse to take them to Amesbury. In contrast to the suspicious innkeeper, his wife was all smiles and helpfulness, promising a fine mount with a side saddle and pillion pad, and adding that if she wished, there would also be a groom to escort her. "For the downs often be lonely, ma'am, and there be highway robbers about. And what would 'ee do if 'ee came to grief?"

Polly would much rather have gone on her own, with Gin, but she knew that the advice was sensible, and she could amply afford the extra expense. So she thanked her, and arranged for an early breakfast and a start soon afterwards. It would take no more than an hour or so to ride to Amesbury, if the weather was fair, the road reasonable and her horse as good as was promised, but she could not countenance any further delay. Mattie was so tantalisingly close, and if she was indeed still a member of Amos Crowley's company, tomorrow they would meet again, after so many years apart.

The morning dawned bright, and fresh with expectation. Polly had spent a restless night, disturbed not only by her excitement and apprehension over the coming day, but by the snores of her maid, fast asleep in a truckle bed in the corner. She arose heavy-eyed at the knock on her door, dressed in her riding habit, and with Gin bright and refreshed at her heels, went down for a substantial breakfast involving coddled eggs, thick rashers of bacon, bread and cheese and cake, all washed down with copious amounts of coffee which did much to restore her energies. Then they went out into the stable yard, where two horses were waiting, a stout dapple-grey cob which must be hers, to judge from the side-saddle, and a dark bay hack, their reins held by the groom who was to ride with them. He was a sullen-looking young man, but he brightened considerably at the sight of Polly's trim figure in her new dark red riding habit, and proved most helpful in assisting her to mount. Gin, muttering under her breath, clambered up onto the pillion pad behind her and, at Polly's instruction, reluctantly held onto the back of the saddle. The groom, whose name was Jacob, swung easily onto his nag, and they set off for Amesbury.

Of necessity, it was a stately amble rather than a brisk pace. If she had not had Gin, precariously perched behind her, to consider, Polly might have suggested they at least break into a trot, but this was only the second time her maid had ever ridden pillion, and she knew that the jolting rhythm of a faster gait would probably shake her off. So she curbed her impatience, and determined to enjoy the ride. It was a lovely day, and the roadside was bright with June flowers, white hemlocks and purple cranesbill, the yellow of toadflax and everywhere the deep blue cornflowers and the brilliant, searing scarlet of poppies in great drifts amongst the ripening wheat and barley in the fields outside Salisbury, while clouds of butterflies, brown and bronze, dappled and copper and azure, danced around them. Larks sang joyfully overhead, and when she looked up, hoping to see their distant specks in the infinite sky, three buzzards were circling above them, riding the warm summer air with broad, stiff wings. It had been some days since the last rain, so chalky white dust swirled around their horses' hooves, and coated the trailing hem of Polly's habit with a silvery sheen.

For several miles, they rode along an old straight road, heading north-east out of Salisbury, before turning north near one of the many villages called Winterbourne, along the way to Amesbury. This part of the route was uphill at first, and Polly's grey laboured under its double burden, though she and Gin combined must have weighed less than a single sturdy man. On the downs there was much to look at: views in all directions, into the blue distance, flocks of sheep, clumps of trees, and everywhere the flowers and the butterflies and the warm air shimmering above the road and stirring Polly's hair beneath her stylish three-cornered hat.

They had passed a few travellers, and had others overtake them: once they pulled aside to make way for someone's coach, very smart and new with matched chestnuts between the shafts and a coat of arms painted on the doors, and there were a couple of farm carts too, as well as walkers and others on horseback. Polly found herself enjoying this interlude much more than she had thought she would. It was very pleasant to feel the gentle motion of her mount beneath her, and the warmth of the sun on her back. She was reminded sharply that she had been born and bred on a farm, and these rural surroundings evoked many happy memories of her childhood, before her father's foolishness and improvidence had brought ruin and death to almost all his family.

Except for her. And, perhaps, except for Mattie. And if this supposed sister was truly Mattie, how would she know? What would she say? What could she do? And what would she be, the child whom Polly had last seen dragged away sobbing to a cruel household and a life of miserable drudgery?

The distant beat of hooves behind them intruded on her thoughts. At her back, she felt Gin turn cautiously to look. “Gawd, someone's in a hurry,” she observed. “Better get out of the way.”

Polly remembered the innkeeper's warning words, and

steered her mount to the side of the road while Jacob, riding a few yards ahead of them, did the same. She twisted round and peered past Gin's shoulder. In the distance, a cloud of dust was growing rapidly, eating up the empty road between them. This was surely no highwayman, who would choose a lonelier spot for an ambush rather than riding down his prey in a one-man cavalry charge, but she could not help a thrill of apprehension as the horseman approached. The earth seemed to shake, the air quivered, the dust rose up to engulf them, and in a tumult of sweat and leather and flying mane, horse and rider thundered past and away along the road to Amesbury. Polly caught a very brief impression of a young man in a brown coat, crouched low over the animal's neck, urging it on, and an acute spear of envy caught her: she would have loved to be able to ride as fast and as furiously as that, but it simply was not possible on a side saddle, unless she wished to break her neck.

Coughing, they rode on much more sedately in his wake, and in due course the outlying houses of Amesbury appeared ahead of them. Jacob knew of Mr. Kenton and his barn, and led them straight there. It was a substantial building, constructed of tarred wood on a flint and brick base, and set a little apart from the farmyard. Like most barns, it had a large central door and another opposite, to assist in the threshing, and a thatched roof in excellent repair. As Polly rode towards it, she saw a woman sitting on a bench outside, in an attitude of considerable relaxation, and smoking a pipe. For a moment, her heart leapt, then she realised that the woman was far too old to be Mattie: she was in her forties at least, and the hair escaping from under her battered straw hat was turning grey. Was this Mother Ellis, whom Mrs. Aston had described as 'little better than a bawd', and who played comedy parts?

Polly's heart began to thud. She drew the grey cob to a halt, and signalled to Jacob, who dismounted and came to help her. After two hours in the saddle, her legs were stiff, and it was a relief to feel the earth beneath her feet again. Gin was less discreet about her feelings. “Gawd, I'm glad that's over! My arse is as sore as a flogging cully’s!”

At a significant look from her mistress, she subsided with a grimace, and stretched her aching limbs. Jacob, blushing, took the reins of both horses and led them over to a water trough. Polly brushed the worst of the dust off her riding habit, then gathered up its trailing hem in one arm and walked towards the barn. The woman did not get up at her approach, but continued to survey her suspiciously from her sprawled position on the bench, legs apart, puffing vigorously on the long clay pipe clenched between her teeth. Polly felt a prickle of annoyance. The woman was a member of a profession which depended entirely upon the goodwill of the populace for its success. Common courtesy, surely, was an essential qualification.

“If you've come to see the play, you're too early,” said the woman, in accents that were a sneering echo of Gin's London whine. “It don't start till six.”

The actress, if that was what she was, might have been a stranger to charm, but Polly had practised it for most of her life, with, usually, dazzling results. She smiled and held out her hand. “Mrs Ellis?”

“Who's asking?” A pungent aura of stale tobacco hung around the woman, and her teeth were stained a nasty shade of yellowish brown.

“My name is Polly Paradice. I wonder if you can help me.”

“I doubt it.” The woman took out her pipe, hawked and spat. The phlegm landed just shy of Polly's feet, and she knew it had been aimed deliberately. With an effort, she mastered her temper. It would do no good at all to scream and shout, however far she had come for this moment, however desperately she wanted to find Mattie. Still smiling, keeping her voice soft and persuasive, she said, "I wish for a word with one of your company, who I believe is a relative of mine."

"Oh? And who might that be?"

"She is called Martha, or Mattie."

"No-one of that name here."

"But she told a friend that she was with a company of strolling players led by Amos Crowley."

"Did someone mention my name?" A man had emerged from the barn, and stood looking at Polly, a hand shading his eyes. "I see you have greeted our charming guest in your usual inimitable style, Peg. Perform the necessary introductions, I pray you."

Sullenly, the woman rose to her feet, setting down the pipe. "This here says she's Mistress Paradice," she said in quite a different tone, with an unconvincing smile. "She's seeking some mort called Martha."

"Martha? I don't know of any Martha." Amos Crowley was probably in his late thirties, dressed in a coat of dark green velvet that had obviously cost a great deal of money, but some while ago. He was of middling height, and sturdily built, with strongly muscled legs and a thick neck. Polly had seen men like that competing in wrestling matches at fairs, or guarding the doors of dubious inns and taverns. But although he looked like a roarer, his accent was certainly that of a gentleman, and his face, with regular features, smiling mouth and vivid blue eyes, was undeniably handsome.

"I was told, sir, that a relative of mine was a member of your company. The intelligence seemed certain." Polly took a deep breath. He was looking at her speculatively, and also with admiration. She gave him her most charming smile, and added, "Of course, if she does not wish to be found, she may be hiding behind an alias."

"Eh?" said Peg.

"Going under another name," Crowley told her, with an impatient gesture. "Well, why not join us, Mistress Paradice? We are resting before the performance later today, and all our company is present. You may see for yourself whether your relative is part of their number."

She indicated to Jacob that he should take care of the horses, and then, with Gin close at her heels, followed Crowley into the barn. As her eyes adjusted to the dim light, she heard voices, and smelled fresh straw, and also tobacco. Obviously no-one had reminded the company of the dangers of smoking in a building made of tarred wood and burnable thatch. Polly shivered. Only six months ago, she had witnessed the destruction by fire of a warehouse constructed in a very similar manner, and had nightmares about the conflagration still. Dark had so very nearly died in it - indeed, for a terrible half hour, she had thought that he had.

At this time of year, before harvest, it was a high echoing space that would normally be empty. But the floor nearest to her was filled with several haphazard rows of stools and benches, and beyond it, on either side of a clear area that was presumably the stage, faded red curtains, incongruously opulent in this agricultural interior, hung from the rafters. Another large piece of cloth, clumsily adorned with a scene of trees and hills, formed a backdrop. The comparison with the beautiful scenery at the Drury Lane theatre, painted by Dark, was rather sad. Polly thought of the life of a strolling player, constantly harassed by puritanical officials, tramping from village to town to village without any idea of what welcome, if any, they would receive, begging space for their productions, performing in front of a raucous unsophisticated audience for shillings and pence. It was not a life she would choose, but apparently her sister had chosen it.

If her sister was here. Both Peg and Crowley seemed adamant that she was not, but Polly had to see for herself. She remembered Kitty's description. *"Eyes grey rather than blue. Her hair was reddish brown, some would call the colour chestnut I think. And her face pale but her cheeks quite rosy."*

Crowley led her past the rows of seats, across the 'stage', and through the curtain at the side. The barn was very large, and there was as much space behind the backdrop as there was in front. Here the company were taking their ease amongst all the paraphernalia of their profession. Bags, baskets, assorted props - a stand of spears, armour, a rickety table and chair on which were laid out a bundle of papers, ink and quill, a pile of heavy drapery, an ancient musket, the components of a bed – were all heaped chaotically around, and a variety of costumes hung from ropes strung across the barn. Light came from a small doorway at the end of the building, and from a couple of lanterns hanging from nails at each side. Polly paused, her eyes searching the assembled faces, most of which had turned to look at her. There were about half a dozen men, probably the same number of women, and a scattering, surprisingly, of children, including a very small girl perhaps two years old. She recognised Bella Wright, her stays unlaced and a bottle at her elbow, staring back at her with insolent curiosity. Another, younger woman sat next to her, sewing up a tear in a shift, but her hair was too fair to be the girl of Kitty's description. Beyond them, in the shaft of sunlight from the door, two more girls sat on stools together, perusing a battered book, presumably a play script. Either of them could have been Martha, but not the middle-aged woman brushing the dust from a yellow velvet gown, a boy of perhaps seven or eight assisting her with more energy than was helpful.

"This," said Amos Crowley, "is Mistress Paradice, who is seeking a young relative whom she believes is with our company. Are any of you connected with Mistress Paradice?"

Puzzled and curious faces turned towards her. A fat man wearing a full wig said with a snigger, “I ain't, but by God I'd like to be.”

“That'll do, Jack,” said Crowley sharply. “Show some respect to the lady.”

“Poll Paradice ain't no lady,” said Bella Wright, taking a swig from her bottle.

“Enough!” Crowley roared suddenly, and his actors fell silent. The smallest child wailed, and was shushed by the middle-aged woman. He went on, in a quieter tone. “Mrs Paradice has asked for our help, and even if we cannot furnish her with the information she requires, the least we can do is to treat her courteously. I ask again - do you know where this young woman might be found?”

“She is called Martha,” Polly said. “Martha, or Mattie, Paradice, but she may be using another name.”

Blank looks and puzzled shakes of the head followed her words, and she felt suddenly as if she might burst into tears. She had come so far, invested so much, been so certain that today she would meet her sister, that she did not think she could bear this final disappointment. For how would she ever find Mattie if this trail turned out to be false?

“As far as I know, none of our actresses have ever gone under that name,” said Crowley. He pointed them out, one by one. “Isabella Wright. You met Peg Ellis, at the door. The lady brushing the yellow gown is Rebecca Barrett, and Sukey Mason sits next to Bella. The girls studying their lines are Nancy Hobbs and Hester Johnson.”

At their names, the last two looked up. Polly studied them. They were the right age to be Mattie, who would now be twenty. Miss Hobbs, though, was a plump, pasty-faced girl, nothing like Kitty's description, and Miss Johnson's dense black hair was very far from chestnut. Disappointment washed over her. She swallowed, and said to Crowley, "It seems my intelligence was mistaken. I apologise most profusely, sirs, ladies, for troubling you all. I will take my leave."

"But my dear Mistress Paradice," said Crowley, with a frown, "surely you will need to rest before returning to..." He paused, with an enquiring look.

"Salisbury," said Polly. The years had taught her to disguise her feelings when she wished to conceal them, but she suspected that Crowley had sensed her distress. She mustered all her resources with a valiant effort. This might be an opportunity to question them further. There surely could not be more than one company of strolling players in the West Country at this time, and Kitty had mentioned Crowley with certainty. What if Mattie, under an assumed name, had left them just a few days ago? She could, even now, be making her way to London to find her sister: indeed, they might have passed each other on the road. The thought heartened her, and she gave Crowley her most charming smile. "Why, sir, that is most kind of you, and I do own that some rest and refreshment would be most welcome before I ride back."

"Capital, capital," Crowley said, clapping his hands. "Our fare is humble, but satisfying, and there is, I believe, a little wine if you would care for it, or small beer. If you would take a seat?"

A stool was found for her, and a little table, and one of the boys brought bread and cheese on a pewter plate, while Crowley poured wine for her with a flourish. Many of the company came to introduce themselves, and she kept searching the women's faces, looking for any that might conceivably be Mattie: but all too obviously, none of them were. She noted that Bella Wright stayed in her chair, swigging from her bottle, which was unlikely to contain a liquid as mild as wine, and sending her sour looks. Polly suspected that the reason for her hostility was due not only to simple jealousy, but to the fact that she herself knew quite a lot about Mistress Wright, and none of it to the actress's credit. Since she had no intention of peaching on her to Crowley, Polly ignored her, and sipped her wine with genteel appreciation. It was very good, and she said as much to him.

"A fine claret indeed," was his response, "but I pray you, Mrs Paradice, do not ask from whence it came." He gave her a knowing wink.

Because it is smuggled, Polly thought, but did not say so. Instead she contented herself with another sip, thinking. She did not wish to question the company too closely in his presence, and he was certainly - perhaps deliberately - making his presence felt. Was it because he wanted to prevent them giving her information? Or was he - as some of his actors evidently were - just seeking the opportunity to be close to an attractive woman? Certainly the lecherous Jack was, for he had come to stand just behind her, close enough for her to smell his unpleasant odour, but not quite close enough to cause open offence.

Munching the bread and cheese, which was very welcome, she took better note of the male members of the company. Apart from Jack, there was Crowley of course, and a very elderly man who might be lame, for his chair was softened with cushions, and a stick leaned against his knee. Polly recollected Jenny's assumption that her sister was Crowley's lover, but of course there was always the possibility that another, younger actor had caught her eye. There was a man about Crowley's age, but larger and greyer, with the flushed and lumpy face of the hardened toper: she could not imagine Mattie choosing him. The two younger men were much more likely candidates. One was about Polly's age, very handsome and all too obviously very aware of it. The other was hardly more than a boy, and wore his own hair tied back.

His brown coat looked familiar, and suddenly she realised that he was the rider who had passed them so furiously, an hour or so before. He was looking thoughtfully at her, and when she caught his eye, he turned away. Polly hid a smile. Certainly her powers of attraction had not waned, despite her advancing years, and she was vain enough to be pleased. Yes, she had Dark for her lover, and depended on no man for her bread, but it was still good to know that a pretty boy thought her worthy of attention.

"So," she said, when the brief meal was finished, "I have had another thought. Has there been any young female in your company who perhaps has recently left you? In Bath, or before? It is possible that my informant might have been mistaken, and thought she was still with you."

"No, Mrs Paradice," Crowley said at once. "We have been the same number for months now, since last winter in fact. No-one has joined us since then, and no-one has left."

The actors around her nodded in confirmation. At last, Polly was forced to accept defeat with all the good will and grace that she could muster in the face of such a blow. She finished her wine, thanked Crowley as prettily as if he were royalty, bade the others farewell, which took some time, and eventually left the barn. Jacob was still outside with the horses, talking to a glowing, dimpled girl with a bucket, who was probably one of Mr. Kenton's dairymaids. If so, she made good cheese. When he saw Polly, he straightened, said something to the girl that made her giggle, and sent her on her way with a pat on the shoulder. "Aye, ma'am?"

"Time to go," said Polly crisply. "Have you eaten?"

"I've had bread and cheese and cider, ma'am, all good."

"Excellent. Then let us return to Salisbury." She turned round, expecting to see Gin, but there was no sign of her. With an exclamation of annoyance, she gestured to Jacob to remain with the horses, and went back to the barn. Just as she approached the doors, her maid emerged, looking flushed and rather smug. "Sorry, Madam, I dropped something."

"Well, kindly be more careful in the future." Polly's tone was sharper than usual. She was bitterly disappointed at the failure of her expedition, and the urge to take it out on her maid was so strong that she was almost tempted to give way to it. "Now be quick, I have no intention of lingering."

Gin glanced back at the barn. Crowley had appeared at the door, smiling benevolently. When he saw them looking, he raised a hand in farewell and turned back inside. As soon as he had gone, Gin said fiercely, "Didn't you see her, Madam? She was there all right!"

"Help you mount, ma'am?" Jacob had come over to them, but Polly waved him away. "One moment, if you please."

Gin was hopping from one foot to the other in agitation. "Didn't you hear me? She's there!"

"Oh, Jane, you are sadly mistaken. I looked at all the women there most carefully, and there was none who could have been my sister."

"You didn't look at the *men*, though, did you?" said Gin triumphantly.

"What do you mean?"

Gin came up close and hissed, "Lord love us, you're as bad as Dark for not seeing what's under your nose! I knows what a woman dressed as a man looks like, don't I? I spent long enough in breeches myself! That lad in the brown coat what rode past us like the devil himself was after him, he ain't no lad, I'd stake my life on it."

Polly stared at her in astonishment. "Are you sure?"

Gin gave a contemptuous snort. "Course I'm sure. And I'll wager that's your sister. She wants you to find her, don't she, or she wouldn't have gone to the Bear, but for some reason she needs Crowley and the rest to think she has to stay hidden. So I pretended to look for something I'd dropped, and went up to her, and said, 'Do you want to meet her?', and she said she'd be at the George in town by noon." And then, as Polly turned, intending to go back into the barn, her maid caught her arm and said urgently, "No, Madam, don't show you've guessed! We can ride away like we're none the wiser, and then wait for her at the inn."

"But why would she not want to reveal herself to us in front of them? I don't understand."

"Perhaps she's feared of one of them - that Crowley perhaps, I've met his sort, all toadying and kind to your face, but plotting to stab you soon as your back's turned. I don't know, and I don't care," Gin said in exasperation. "Let's just go, before he realises something's up."

"But what if she doesn't come?"

"Then we has a good dinner and goes back to Salisbury," said Gin, always keen to ascertain when her next meal might appear. "Come *on*, Madam."

So it was that, a quarter of an hour before the clock on the parish church struck twelve, Polly, with Gin her faithful shadow, was ushered into a small parlour in the George, Amesbury's principal inn. She ordered a mutton pie and bottled fruit tart, with wine for herself and small beer for Gin, for the rough and ready meal in the barn had failed to slake her hunger, and she knew that her maid would never turn down the offer of food. When it arrived, born by a waiter on a broad wooden tray, she thanked him, and added that they were expecting a visitor, and that whoever enquired after Mistress Paradice should be shown to the parlour straight away. She did not care to specify the gender of the person who would be in search of them, but if Gin was right, and Kitty's description was also accurate, then her sister might present herself as either a young man, or as a woman. It was an intriguing prospect.

As she ate, hardly tasting the rich meat and savour of mint, she cast her mind back to the scene in the barn, and the boy, so she had thought, who had looked at her with curiosity, and then turned away. She blushed now, to recollect how she had assumed, in her vanity, that he was ogling her.

"It ain't the done thing," Gin said, through a mouthful of pie, "to go round dressed like a lad when you ain't. I mean," she added, swallowing, "I know I did, but that was 'cos I *had* to, or end up like my ma. And your sister's an actress, and actresses do play breeches parts, but that's on the stage. They're back to being a woman soon as the play's done - or before." She looked at Polly wistfully. "But them days was good in some ways, I still ain't got used to these." A scornful kick indicated her skirts. "Perhaps she don't like them neither."

"Perhaps," Polly allowed cautiously. She found that despite her earlier hunger, she did not want the rest of her pie, and pushed the platter away. Gin's hopeful gaze followed it, and she smiled. "Have it, Jane. It is too good to go to waste."

The maid needed no second bidding. She devoured the remains of the pie with gusto and washed it down with generous gulps of small beer, while Polly, trying to quell her apprehension, sipped at her wine, which was vastly inferior to that which Amos Crowley had given her, being only just on the right side of vinegary.

It was a warm day, so the window was open, and as Gin mopped up the last of the crumbs with a licked finger, the church clock began to strike noon. The girl's head went up, and she stared at Polly. "She'll be here any moment," she said.

"Indeed I hope so." Polly was doing her best to give an impression of being cool and collected, but she noticed, hoping Gin had not, that the hand which held the wine glass was not quite steady. She set it down carefully, and to calm herself, counted the chimes. And at the eleventh, there was a knock on the door.

This is the moment, Polly thought, her heart beating so wildly she thought it might burst out of her chest. *This is when I meet my sister again - or know that she is not.* She spoke, marvelling at how calm her voice sounded. "Pray come in."

It was one of the inn's maidservants. "Your visitor, ma'am," she said, bobbed a curtsey and withdrew. And in the doorway stood the boy, or girl, in the brown coat.

CHAPTER FOUR

Were I a Man

Polly had imagined this meeting a hundred times, had rehearsed what she would say and do when she came face to face with her long lost sister, but at this moment every prepared utterance fled her mind, to leave her bereft of speech. She said at last, her voice hardly above a whisper, "Mattie?"

The person in the brown coat came forward, shutting the door, and stood a few paces from Polly. The answer came louder, and with more certainty. "Yes, I am Mattie."

All at once, Polly was on her feet, her arms outstretched, and after a moment's hesitation, the other accepted her embrace. For a while they clung to each other, and then Polly, aware of Gin's bright-eyed gaze upon them, drew back a little and stared into the face of someone who, it seemed, was her sister. She could not connect this watchful, composed creature with the sobbing little girl who had been dragged away from her long ago, but fourteen years had intervened, and the child had become an adult. Grey eyes, as Kitty had said, and chestnut hair, tied back with a black ribbon, taller than Polly and with a faint scattering of smallpox scars at the edge of the face, she looked nothing like the Mattie she remembered, or like either of their parents. And surely Mattie had not had the smallpox before their separation. Sudden doubt assailed her. Was this truly her sister?

She found her voice at last. "Will you not sit down? There is a little wine left."

"Thank you."

Gin, obviously remembering her training, got to her feet and indicated the chair. Mattie took it with a nod. Polly noticed that she sat like a man, legs apart, confident and assertive. It was only now, at these close quarters, that she could see what Gin had discerned: the subtle roundness of the hips, the faintest hint of femininity in the contours of the chest, the softness of skin and the complete absence of a beard. She said, "Why do you dress like that?" To her ears it came out too abruptly, almost aggressively, but the person opposite her did not seem to take any offence.

"Because I choose to. Why do *you* dress like that? Because you are a woman, and you assume you have no choice." Mattie's accent was more strongly tinged with the flavour of the West Country than her own, but then Polly had lived in London for nearly ten years.

"Then do you play breeches parts?"

"Of course. It was that which gave me a taste for wearing them off the stage as well as on. How did you know I was not a man?"

"*I* did not – you had me fooled completely. It was my maid Jane who suspicioned it."

Gin assumed an expression of satisfaction at her own cleverness. Mattie glanced at her, and nodded approvingly. "She has unusual perception, then. Very few people ever guess the truth."

"It's on account of how I spent four years dressed as a lad myself," Gin explained, unbidden. "So I knows what's what."

"Indeed?" Mattie looked at her with interest. "Why so?"

"Didn't want to be no man's whore," said Gin baldly.

"I can understand that. So how did you manage with pissing and all?"

"Oh, there's always somewhere private," Gin said. "Anyways, folks see what they wants to see. They see boy's clothes and think it's a boy, even if the other signs are plain as the nose on your face. Madam only saw because I was hurt, and she tended me. Dark never knew till he saw me in a gown, and he calls himself an artist!" Her tone was scornful.

"Dark?"

"A friend," Polly said quickly, feeling it was time to intervene before the conversation escaped from her intentions entirely. "Mattie, please - I am sure it is a long tale, and you do not have to tell it all, but what happened to you after we were parted? Those people who took you - they did not seem kind. And some years later, I was told a story that led me to believe that you were dead."

"They were not kind," said Mattie, and an expression close to loathing briefly twisted her face into ugliness. "Master Swift was a brute, and his wife no better. Once, she beat me so badly, I was knocked senseless, and a neighbour reported them to the magistrates. But they claimed I had been stealing food from the kitchen, and they were let off any punishment. I was given back to them and of course they treated me worse. In the end I thought that even if I were hanged, that would be better than what I was enduring. So I pretended to be so cowed and terrified that they no longer watched me very carefully. And when opportunity offered, I stole some of her jewellery and ran away." For the first time, she smiled, rather chillingly. "They never caught me. I did what I could, to survive."

There must be many, many more stories behind her brief words, but Polly knew she could not ask, not yet, for if she did she would almost certainly receive no answer. She said, her heart aching for what Mattie had suffered, "Do you remember much of – of before? When we were a family?"

"I remember the farm," said Mattie slowly, her brow furrowed. "There were cattle, brown cattle, and a barn full of hay. There was a garden with cabbages and leeks, and a bed of pink and red roses, and the kitchen was big and dark, and if you looked up the chimney when the fire was low, you could see the sky."

The same, of course, could be said of almost every farmhouse in the land. Polly wanted this to be Mattie, so much that her chest hurt and the words burned in her throat, but she knew she must persist, gently, so that there could be no doubt. She asked, "Do you remember me?"

"Of course!" Mattie sounded surprised. "You were always singing, and you taught me so many songs and rhymes. My voice was not so tuneful as yours, though. And I remember a lullaby our mother would sing to me." She hummed the first few bars of a soft air that Polly recognised at once. Yes, she could also recall her mother sitting, rocking Mattie's cradle, and crooning in her gentle voice.

'Golden slumbers kiss your eyes,
Smiles await you when you rise.
Sleep, pretty baby, do not cry,
And I will sing a lullaby.
Cares you know not, therefore sleep,
While over you a watch I'll keep,
Sleep, pretty darling, do not cry,
And I will sing a lullaby.'

But many, many women up and down the land would know that tune, and sing it to their babies as they slept. Polly said, "And do you remember our brother?"

"Tom? Yes, of course I do. I know that he died a year or so after we were all parted."

"Yes. Kitty allowed me to go to his funeral. He had a pauper's grave, but at least I was there to bid him farewell." It had been raining, she remembered, as if heaven itself were weeping for his loss.

"You were fortunate in your mistress," Mattie said, a thread of bitterness in her voice. "Mine told me that Tom's master had got a bad bargain because he'd died so soon, and she hoped I would not prove similarly unreliable." Again that twisted smile. "I vowed then that one day I would run away, and a few years later, I did."

"So - how did you come to be with Crowley's players?"

"A woman called Moll found me, half-starved in a hedge near Gloucester, a couple of months after I'd run. She took me under her wing."

If this kind and selfless deed had occurred in London, she would have assumed that Moll was a bawd trying to entice an innocent young girl into her clutches. She made no comment, though, and Mattie continued. "Moll was a player, not with Crowley, but another company. They were happy to take me on, there's usually a part for a young girl, or a boy – that's how I got the taste for wearing breeches. When their leader fell ill and retired and those players split up a couple of years back, Moll joined Crowley, and I went with her. She met a man she liked last winter, though, and left, but I stayed on."

"And do you enjoy the life of a strolling actress? Surely it must often be hard?"

Mattie gave a contemptuous snort. "Believe me, nothing on this earth could be so hard as being in Master Swift's house. It's not easy sometimes, when the rain falls and folk don't turn out, but then I think back to what I suffered from those two brutes and reckon myself lucky." Her glance at Polly, her good clothes and soft hands and pale, protected skin, was eloquent. "You had it easy, I can see, while I did not. And I'll be no-one's bond-servant again."

"So you plan to continue with Crowley's company, then?"

"Of course," said Mattie, with some impatience. "Why would I not? Did you think I wanted to come and live with you, in London? To wear skirts all day and never ride a horse nor breathe fresh air? I'm not looking for a life of comfort, sister, I'm not accustomed to it as you are. I need a life of interest and freedom. Plant me in London and I'll likely die of it."

Polly found herself flushing, to her shame and annoyance, because that was exactly what she had planned to suggest. She changed tack. "So you have no ambition to play at Drury Lane or Lincoln's Inn one day?"

Mattie made a dismissive gesture. "Proper theatres? They wouldn't touch the likes of me, there's no chance they'd have a travelling player on their fine polished boards."

"Why not? Tony Aston travels from town to town, and has also played at Drury Lane. There are others, I know. Both the theatres are crying out for new blood and fresh faces. If you are good, they will welcome you, especially if you bring something a little different. London audiences love nothing better than novelty."

"Yes, and they'll also soon tire of it," said Mattie. "But our audiences never have the chance to grow jaded. We rarely stay more than a few days in the same place - just long enough for word to be spread around and gather people in. Then we're off somewhere new."

Before the magistrates catch up with you, Polly thought. There were many towns and cities such as Salisbury, where players were not welcomed. At best, it was a precarious, hand-to-mouth existence, but she could see how such a life would seem attractive to a girl who had experienced such miserable servitude. Pauper children such as she, Tom and Mattie had been were cheap commodities - easily obtained, easily abused, easily discarded.

"Then I cannot tempt you to come back to London with me? You will not be persuaded?"

Her pretty mouth a resolute line, Mattie shook her head. "No. I will not."

"Then why did you seek me out?"

"*I*? Seek *you* out?" There was no mistaking the hostility now. "I did no such thing, sister. I enquired after you because I wished to know, out of curiosity, whether you still lived, or whether you had joined the rest of our family in the grave. No, it is *you* who have sought *me* out. Did you wish for a serving girl, perhaps, to scrub the floors in your coffee house? If indeed it *is* a coffee-house, and not a Covent Garden nunnery. Well, you must go back without me, for I'm no woman's cinder-garbler, not even for my sister!"

Polly stared at her in horrified disbelief. She opened her mouth to explain, but Gin, who had been quiet for much longer than was her wont, leapt forward to stand in front of Mattie, her face crimson with fury. "What do you think Madam is, you stupid little tib, she ain't no Abbess and she don't run no leaping house neither, she wanted to find you 'cos she *cares* about you! She thought you was dead and when she had the news you wasn't, she fainted clean away! She's come to find you, she's followed you to Bath and then Salisbury and now here, she wanted to find you 'cos you're her sister and she loves you!"

"Jane –" Polly began, but her maidservant ignored her and swept on. "So tell her you're sorry and kiss and make up, 'cos you've done her wrong."

Mattie had flushed a very deep red. Ignoring Gin, no mean feat, she said coldly to Polly, "How can I trust what you say?"

Polly drew in several long breaths, calming herself, trying to find a way to reach out to her. At last she said, "You cannot, because you do not know me. I have given you no proof even that I am truly your sister - as you have likewise given me no proof, though I can think of no reason that either of us would have, to lie about such a thing. So I will make no demands. I respect your decisions, and I will trouble you no longer. But I will give you this. It was our mother's, and there is no other like it." She unclasped the little round locket on a cheap chain, that she always wore about her neck, and held it out to Mattie. "Take it. There are three plaited strands of hair within, from my head, and Tom's, and yours, that she kept from when we were babies. If you are ever in trouble or have need of me, send me that token and I will know it is from you, and I will help. My coffee house is called the Paradise, in King Street in Covent Garden, and I can always be reached at that address, and you will always be welcome there. And have this too, you may do with it what you wish, pawn it or sell it, it is yours." A quick twist of her fingers removed the sapphire ring from her right hand, and looped the locket chain through it. "This is no bribe nor purchase, Mattie. It is help if you should ever need it."

For a moment, the young woman in front of her stood stiff and still, and Polly wondered if she had miscalculated again, and harmed their brief acquaintance past mending. Then slowly, reluctantly, Mattie's hand came out, and took the chain with its two burdens. She said, as if forcing the words out, "Thank you."

"No, it is I who should thank you, for finding me, otherwise I should have lived all my life thinking that I was the only one left of us." Polly smiled at her. "And now I know that you are also in the world, and I cannot tell you how much that comforts me, that you survived."

"I would say the same." For the first time during this curious reunion, Mattie looked less than confident, even ill at ease. She added, "I am sorry for what I said, just now. I thought - I could not believe that you did not want to use me for your own selfish reasons."

Because everyone else has used you, since our parents died, Polly thought. She was filled with sudden admiration and love for her sister, who had survived - no, triumphed - despite all that she had suffered. She said quickly, "I understand - you have no need to apologise."

As she finished speaking, outside, the church clock struck the half hour. Mattie started, and an expression of alarm came over her face. She said, "I have been here too long, and I will be missed if I do not go back now. Do not fear for me, sister, I am stronger than I look, and I have a place in the world as you do - even if our worlds are very different. Thank you." She sketched an elaborate bow that would not have been out of place at court, and moved to the door. As she opened it, she turned with a smile. "I had not thought that I would have grown taller than you. 'Cutty' no longer!" And with a last, flamboyant flourish of her hat, she was gone.

Polly's knees felt suddenly so weak that she groped behind her for the chair, and sat down. Gin gave her a sharp glance, and then poured more wine into the glass and handed it to her. "Here, Madam, drink this, won't you, it'll put heart back into you. Well," she added, with a disapproving glance at the door, "that one's a high-flyer and no mistake. A proper romping girl with a shrew's tongue in her head."

"May I remind you, Jane, that you are speaking about my sister." Even this sour wine was very welcome: Polly felt it creep through her, fortifying and warming.

"But *is* she truly your sister? She don't look much like you, Madam."

"She may not, but she knew the pet name that our father used to call her when she was a very little girl - 'Cutty', which is a wren."

"Someone could have told her that," said Gin, but she sounded dubious, and then added with a frown, "No, that can't be right, because who else would know apart from you, and her? So she must be your sister! Ain't you glad, madam? You wanted to find her, and you found her, and she may be a right rantipole, but she's alive, ain't she?"

"Yes, she's alive." Polly set down the glass and looked at her maid. A dozen different feelings filled her, so that she hardly knew what to think. Relief, joy, pride, that her sister was well and apparently happy and had made some small success in the world. Dismay, that the joyful reunion she had envisaged had not happened, and disappointment that Mattie had refused to join her in London. And still, despite everything, despite that mischievous last utterance of the word that should prove beyond any doubt that the girl she had just met was indeed her long-lost sister - still she could not put her hand on her heart and declare herself completely certain. For she had no sense, no sense at all that they had ever met before, no matter how long ago, and how young they had both been at their last parting. She could not link that sobbing, terrified child with the self-contained, almost disdainful creature who had stood before her in coat and breeches, defying the limitations of her gender and revelling in her freedom from restriction.

"Did you see her face, when the clock struck?" said Gin, obviously pursuing her own train of thought. "Scared her half to death, it did. Something ain't right there, to my way of thinking. If she's so happy with them players, why'd she need to keep meeting us a secret from them?"

"I noticed that too." Polly felt as if she had been turned upside down and shaken until all her past life, all her previous certainties, had vanished, leaving her bewildered, shocked and bereft.

"So what do we do now? We can't hardly follow her about to see if all's well with her."

"No, we cannot. We shall have to leave her here with them. She has chosen her life, after all, and who am I, to naysay her? I can't *force* her to come back to London with me. No, if she does change her mind and feel the need of my company, or my help, she knows where I can be found, and she knows that my door will never be barred to her. Hard as it is, we must return to Salisbury without her, and take coach back to town."

"Will there be any coaches, madam? Salisbury seems a very *small* sort of place." Gin's disdain for what she perceived as a backward provincial city was obvious.

"The coach to Exeter passes through, so I surmise there will be one returning to London tomorrow or the day after. Or if necessary, we will go back to Bath." Polly took a deep breath, forcing herself to be calm and decisive. "And now, I think, I will pay our bill and we shall be on our way."

The church clock struck one as they rode out of Amesbury along the Salisbury road, with a long, hot afternoon ahead of them. Polly glanced at Mr. Kenton's barn as they passed. There were now quite a few people, mainly children, idling near the doors, obviously hoping to catch a glimpse of the players, but none of them were in sight, though she could see the horse that Mattie had ridden, tied up in the shade of an elm tree beside the building. She longed to dismount, and run inside, and beg her sister to change her mind and come back with her to London, but she must respect her decision. And of course there was still that niggling, uneasy doubt. Was this *really* Mattie?

The journey back to Salisbury was uneventful, and they arrived at the Red Lion hot and dusty. Jacob led their horses away, and a maidservant greeted them at the door. "Mistress Paradice? There's a gentleman waiting for you in the back parlour."

This was the last thing that Polly had expected, for she had no friend or acquaintance that she knew of, either in Salisbury or Wiltshire, apart from Crowley and his players, and no-one had overtaken them on the road back. She commanded refreshments, sent Gin to wash her face and hands and brush the dust from her clothes, and then, alive with curiosity, and not a little apprehension, allowed herself to be escorted through the rambling inn to a small room overlooking the courtyard.

And there, sitting before a mug of beer and a half-eaten fruit tart, was Samuel Jessop. Surprised, Polly stared at him. "Sam! I had not thought to see you here - when we left you in Bath, I thought you would be returning to Oxford."

"So did I," said Sam, rising to his feet. He looked tired, and even more travel-worn than Polly felt. "But last night a letter for you from Dark arrived at the Bear, and I felt I must bring it on to you." He felt in the pocket of his coat, and handed her a small, folded square of paper, with her lover's unmistakeable black scrawl across the front. *'To be given only into the hand of Mistress Paradice at the Bear in Cheap Street in the city of Bath, with all haste'.*

"It seemed important," Sam added, as she turned it over and pushed her thumbnail under the seal. "So I thought it best to come in search of you. I knew you were planning to seek your sister in Salisbury, and so I set out this morning."

"This morning? But Kitty told me that there would be no coach today."

"I know," said Sam, with a wry grimace. "So I took horse instead."

"But you hate riding, Sam! You have always preferred to travel by coach."

"And so I have, but I felt it best not to delay."

"Oh, Sam!" Polly hugged him warmly. "That was very kind of you. But I wonder what could be so important that Dark must write to me in haste? Ten to one he has mislaid his second-best wig, or some such nonsense."

Since Dark, though a daily and often nightly visitor, was

not actually a member of her household, the whereabouts of his wig was no concern of Polly's, and she knew that this, or any other domestic matter, was very unlikely to be the reason for his urgent communication. She released Sam and unfolded the letter with sudden apprehension. Would it be bad news?

Not precisely. She scanned the scant, typically ambiguous lines. Dark was an artist, making a living from painting portraits and embellishing the scenery at the Drury Lane theatre, but he also spied for the government. Despite the defeat of the Jacobite armies the previous year, George of Hanover was still precarious on his newly acquired throne, and she had come to accept her lover's occasional unexplained absences. It was best to ask no questions, because then he would not be forced to tell her lies.

'Dear heart, I urge you to have a care, for the gentleman you mentioned is, I discover, not to be trusted. If you have now found the person you sought, or even if you have not, I pray you return to London without delay, for your business is here, and needs you, and so does your most humble and affectionate servant.' And he had ended with the brief scrawl of his signature, that she would recognise, but would be illegible to unfriendly eyes.

"It's a warning," she said to Sam. "I think it must concern Crowley, who is manager of the playing company my sister joined."

"I am glad it does not bring bad news," Sam said, with a sigh of relief. "But tell me, Polly, did you find her? Did you find your sister?"

Gin arrived with a tray bearing refreshing mugs of cool cider, along with another very good strawberry tart and a big bowl of thick cream. As they all ate and drank, Polly told Sam about her meeting with the players, and with the girl who claimed to be Mattie. She did not mention her doubts about her supposed sister's true identity, but she did confide that she had not liked Amos Crowley, and that Dark's letter only confirmed her feelings.

"Well, I am glad that his warning has proved unnecessary," Sam said, licking cream off his spoon, while Gin eyed the last slice of tart hungrily. "But of course your sister has decided to stay with the company, so she will be at risk from this man. Dark did not specify *why* he was not to be trusted?"

"No, he did not." Polly thought about Crowley, about his watchful, slightly intimidating manner, the way he had commanded the other actors, and Mattie's apparent fear. "It could be anything, any reason. He could be an abuser of young women, or a thief, or even in league with smugglers for all I know - the wine he gave me was surprisingly good."

"It often is," Sam pointed out. "Best not to ask too many questions about that sort of thing. But you have left your sister with this man, have you not? After this warning, will you go back and make another attempt to persuade her to leave him?"

"I would like to," Polly said sadly. "But she was adamant that she had no wish to come to London with me. She professed to like the life of a travelling player, and she certainly relishes the freedom she has, to ride round the country in breeches. At first she thought I was seeking a cheap servant, but now I think she suspects me of trying to put her into a respectable cage - and that is so very far from my intention. I want her only to be happy, and safe. I thought she would be, in Crowley's company, but now I have read Dark's letter, I'm not so sure."

"Well, there ain't nothing to be done about it now," said Gin philosophically. "So, does either of you want the rest of that tart? Acos if you don't ..."

*

After the quiet of Wiltshire, London seemed even more like Hell's cauldron, filled with shrieking, tormented people, demonic smells, and the taste of foul, rotting things on the tongue, but Polly relished her life here, for it held everything she had ever wanted, and all those whom she loved, with two exceptions. One was on his way back to Oxford, where his flourishing business and his son-in-law and pregnant daughter awaited him. The whereabouts of the other, she did not know, and could not envisage - a barn, a house, a hedgerow? Mattie seemed too wild and unconventional a spirit to be at home anywhere, save in the pages of a scandalous tale by some Grub Street hack. Polly prayed that she would be safe, and well, and happy, but somehow she doubted it. The world in general was not kind to women like her sister. Or, indeed, to herself.

She had forged her own path, and made a success of it, but she was keenly aware that her success was transient. Riot, fire, a sudden illness, even a change in fashion, any one of these could see her enterprise doomed, and she and all her friends and servants cast back into poverty. So she always kept a tight hand on the books, and hoarded the profits, along with certain valuable jewels, with an accommodating and very discreet banker in Cheapside. Mr. Fanshawe did not mind dealing with an independent woman of dubious repute: in fact, she suspected that he would not mind dealing with Beelzebub himself, if he thought there was an advantage to him. And when she had enough gold saved, she would purchase a house in some pleasant village to the west of the city - Chelsea, perhaps, or Fulham - for her retirement when she grew disenchanted with London and her coffee house. As Mr. Fanshawe had advised her, there was no investment more sound than in bricks and mortar and land.

The Paradise had only been open for six months, but already she had amassed a very respectable sum. If business continued so brisk, three or four more years should see her achieve her aim. She did not know whether her present staff would accompany her into the country: indeed, if Hannah married Will, she intended to hand the coffee house over to them. And Gin was a Londoner through and through, and obviously found rural idylls boring, if not actually threatening. No, she could not see her maid happily feeding chickens and gathering blackberries. Nor, if she were honest with herself, could she envisage Dark as part of this bucolic existence. He, too, was entirely urban, completely at home in the heart of the city. But she would cross that bridge when she came to it - *if* she came to it. Meanwhile, she would do her utmost to ensure the continued success of the Paradise, and enjoy her present life to the full, for there was no point in wasting time worrying about what might never come to pass.

The Salisbury coach finished its journey at the Angel in the Strand, near the church of St. Clement Danes, and Polly hired a hackney to take them and their bags up to Covent Garden. It was a very warm July evening, still and stifling, and her incipient headache hinted at the prospect of thunder later. Even after so short a time away - it had not been a week - she was anxious about what she would find at the Paradise. She was confident in Hannah's ability to keep the place running smoothly, and yet could not believe that nothing would have gone wrong in her absence. So much of her life had been beyond her control, that now she had her grasp firmly on the reins, she found it very difficult to let go.

"Don't fret, Madam," said Gin, who sometimes seemed to be able to read her thoughts with uncanny accuracy. "It'll all be right and tight, you'll see. Hannah don't stand no nonsense."

Nor had she. To Polly's anxious eyes, her coffee house seemed exactly the same as it had always done since its opening: the witty sign, painted by Dark, that swung above the cheerful red door, the sound of animated voices debating some thorny political or literary question emanating from the open windows of the main bar, and Will Evans, large and reliable, guarding the entrance from troublemakers. She had sent no warning of her arrival, and he looked at the hackney curiously: then, as Gin opened the door and jumped down, his broad face split into a beaming smile, and he came forward to welcome them. "Good to see you back, ma'am! I'll take your bags up."

"Is all well?"

"Of course it is, ma'am, no trouble at all beyond some of the regulars asking after you. They're eager for a song and no mistake." He shouldered one of the bags and picked up the other, then turned back into the house. Polly noted, with approval, that he kicked shut the inner door to the coffee room as he passed, so that she would be able to go upstairs to her quarters without her arrival being noticed. The journey today had been long and hot, she ached all over and she longed to wash away the dust and change into cooler clothes - the calico round gown printed with sprigs of flowers would be perfect. With Gin at her heels, she climbed the familiar stairs, and followed Evans into her bedchamber. He put the bags on the floor, and looked at her expectantly. "Forgive me if I'm forward, ma'am, but did you find what you were looking for?"

"Thank you, Will, and yes, in a manner of speaking I did." Polly smiled at him, not minding the query, for of course he knew the reason for her journey to Bath, he had been there when she opened Kitty's letter. "Hannah is at the bar, I take it?"

"Yes, ma'am, and Mrs. Garnet is helping her today. Dan and Joe have been working hard. It's all run like clockwork, madam, though I say so myself."

"And Dark? Has he called in?"

"I haven't seen him since the day you left, madam, I understand he's busy."

"Then if either of them can be spared, send one of the boys round to Half Moon Street with a note." Polly went through to her parlour and opened her writing desk.

Without pausing to think, she ignored the spluttering quill and scribbled a few lines in a hand rather less careful than was her usual habit.

'Dark,

I am come safely home and have good news. Kindly do me the service this evening of waiting on your most humble and affectionate servant,

Paradice.'

She gave the folded paper to Evans, not bothering to seal it, and the Welshman bowed briefly and left the room. She heard him clattering down the stairs, and went back into her chamber, where Gin was waiting. Usually Hannah helped her with her hair and her clothes, but Polly had been training Gin up for the past few months, and she was now sufficiently competent to be allowed to perform these duties whenever her other maid was busy with the coffee house.

Disrobing, washing, changing her garments and repinning her hair always took time, and it was some while before Polly, looking into her gilt-framed mirror, could be truly satisfied with her appearance. She knew she was vain, but her beauty was the principal reason why she was sitting here, clothed in fine garments with pearls at her neck, and not working for a pittance in some tavern. And, more tellingly, it was one of the reasons why she had attracted Dark, even while, in the earliest days of their acquaintance, he had been infuriated by her duplicity and her guile. She had had good cause, which he had acknowledged when made aware of it, but in a spirit of mischief and intrigue, she had set out to captivate and enchant him, and she had spectacularly succeeded.

He made her so happy. Her blood tingled at the thought of him, of his presence, of his touch on her skin and of what they would do in the night to come.

And as if her longing had conjured him up like some

menacing, black clad devil, he was suddenly at the door of her chamber. Polly saw him in the mirror, and her heart leapt with joy, but also with apprehension, for he wore his habitual grim look and she had cause to be wary of it. But when she turned and rose to greet him, her smile was one of pure delight. "Dark! Thank you for coming. I had no great expectation of it so soon, I thought you might still be busy with Mr. Henderson's picture."

"No, I had already called it a day." He embraced her, and they kissed, before he drew back, setting his hands on her shoulders and looking thoughtfully down into her face. "You said it was good news, Paradice, do I then take it that you found her?"

"Yes, I found her." She became aware of Gin, hovering, and said quickly, "Bring us up a pot of coffee, Jane, and something light to eat – you may send out to the confectioner's if there is not. Unless you want wine, Dark?"

"A pot of coffee will be very welcome, thank you - I have spent all day in a fug of paint fumes, trying to give Mr. Henderson's countenance some semblance of humanity, and I am desperate for a little relief. Every time I close my eyes, his face appears to haunt me." For the first time, he smiled at her, and it made his face seem much younger and less forbidding. "Still, I am optimistic that I shall prevail, eventually."

"Then the portrait is not going well?"

"No, my dear Paradice, it is not. Mr. Henderson has revealed himself to be a man of many and decided opinions, few of them pleasant and many of them unfit even for your ears. It has been all I can do, these past few days, not to lay murderous hands on him and poison him with the same vile green paint I have been using to depict his appalling waistcoat."

"I am sorry your customer is not to your liking. But at

least you will be ten guineas to the good." Polly paused, then added, "Thank you for your note. It arrived after I had left Bath, and Sam brought it on to me. I take it you meant to warn me of Amos Crowley?"

"I did. But tell me first, what happened. Tell me how you found your sister, and what transpired. I assume you have not brought her back with you?"

"No, she would not come, and would not be persuaded, so I dropped the suggestion, or I fear she would have become angry, and I did not want that - I could not bear it, after finding her again when I had thought her dead. But come into the parlour, where we can be comfortable, and I will tell you everything."

Gin, puffing back up the stairs a while later with a laden tray, found them in the twin chairs on either side of the empty hearth, while Polly's tabby cat Sly had taken up her preferred position on her lap, and was vigorously purring her satisfaction at her owner's return. By this time, the tale had almost been told, and Dark looked with approval at the maid, who had once, in a previous and precarious existence, been his link-boy. "So you realised that the supposed boy was in actual fact a girl? From your special knowledge of the subject, I assume."

"Plain as a pikestaff if you knows what's what," said Gin, with a pert look: she had been in Dark's casual employ for nearly four years, and in all that time, he had never guessed her true identity.

"And she really is your sister, Polly?"

"Why would she not be? What would she have to gain? Only a comfortable roof over her head, and she spurned my offer of that in no uncertain terms. And she knew the pet name our father had for her. No, it must be Mattie."

"But?"

Polly spread her hands ruefully. "But ... oh, Dark, I do not sense that I have ever met her before. She *must* be my sister, yet she seems like a stranger."

"But you last saw her, what, fourteen years ago? There is a huge gulf between a young child and a grown woman, and moreover you are much the elder."

"I suppose so," Polly said sadly. "I *know* that she is my sister, but I do not *believe* it, in my deepest heart. Does that make sense?"

"A little. But I think it safe to assume that she is, until we receive proof to the contrary - and that may never arrive. Now, tell me about Crowley. Describe him, as minutely as you can."

Polly put aside her doubts about Mattie, and concentrated. She closed her eyes, and brought his image once more to her mind's eye. She said at last, "I did not like his manner. It was over familiar, ingratiating even, but I felt he was suspicious and hostile underneath. The rest of the company were no better, though he kept them in order sternly enough. They are a sorry band for the most part, little better than vagabonds. I do not know why Mattie was so set upon staying with them."

"Crowley?"

"Of course, apologies, my mind is wandering off the point. Crowley is a man of thirty-five or so, I would guess, some four or five inches shorter than you, but built big and bluff, much in the mould of Will Evans, in fact, but from his speech and manner, it's plain he was bred a gentleman. Very piercing eyes of a light blue, a short brown wig, a rather too ready smile. Is that sufficient? Is that the man you warned me about?"

"I think it is." He glanced at Gin, who was waiting for

instruction, and jerked his head towards the door. "I expect you have business elsewhere."

"Can't say as I do," said Gin brightly.

"You may go to my chamber and do your best to brush and shake the dust from my travelling clothes," Polly told her. "And no listening at doors, Jane. No, don't protest, I know your habits."

"Yes, Madam." The maid bobbed a curtsey and reluctantly left the room. Dark got up and went to the door, checked behind it, and then shut it firmly, before turning back to Polly. He said quietly, "I believe that is the man, yes. He has a long and disreputable history, and I do not think that Amos Crowley is his real name."

So her instincts had been right. Polly stared at him in dismay. "How, disreputable?"

"He has been connected to Jacobites both here and in France. And he has previously called himself Ambrose Rookwood."

"I have heard that name before, I am sure of it."

"You may well have done. Ambrose Rookwood plotted to kill King William. He and his accomplices were executed for treason more than twenty years ago."

"Then how –"

"This is probably his natural son, or some other Rookwood offshoot – Ambrose is a favoured name amongst the family. They are extremely prolific, both in numbers and in treachery, they are fervent Papists, and they are dangerous. I do not know the reason why he has chosen to roam the countryside under an alias, but I can readily guess it. What better disguise, than to be the manager of a company of players? They may mingle with common people and gentry alike, hide arms and equipment amongst their stage effects, and pass on messages from other Jacobites or even from the Pretender. One rebellion has been defeated, but that will not stop them trying to stir up another, or encourage unrest amongst the disaffected. It is a great pity that your sister would not leave them, Paradice, for she has surely been drawn into Rookwood's web, and from what I know of him, he does not scruple to use any means to hand, to further his own ends and those of his master in France."

"But what can I do? She was adamant that she would not leave them. And she seemed afraid of something or someone, she was certainly afraid of being found talking to me, and Crowley - Rookwood - denied that she was in the company, though he must have known the truth."

"You can do nothing, Poll, for if you try to contact her again, or let this go beyond the two of us, it may well put her in serious danger. You can only pray," Dark said, his voice grim, "that she knows nothing of any plots, and has the sense not to pry or to become involved. Because if she does, she risks being taken up for treason."

CHAPTER FIVE

A Song to rouse me

"Mistress Paradice, your humble servant, madam – and what a feast you are for my eyes, as always!"

Polly looked up from yesterday's copy of the *Flying Post* – the current edition was being avidly perused by an elderly gentleman seated near the window – and beheld a familiar and not altogether welcome figure on the other side of the counter. The very young man whom she had secretly dubbed 'Beaky Nose' had been absent from the Paradise recently, and she had not felt the lack. However, he had always spent his money freely, so she ignored the feelings of irritation his arrival engendered, and gave him a warm smile. "Why, thank you, sir. And it is good to see you. Have you been in the country?"

"I have the honour to be a scholar at Oxford, madam."

That was surprising. She had thought him a typical young man about town, wealthy enough to do as he pleased and unencumbered by intelligence. And what was he called? John? Jack? James? It surely began with a J, though she was damned if she knew his surname. And she could hardly ask him, for he probably wished their acquaintance to be on a far more intimate level than she did.

"Indeed, sir? Which college?"

"Corpus Christi."

Sam Jessop lived in Oxford, and he had more than once mentioned that place as a nest of recalcitrant Jacobites. *Interesting*, Polly thought.

Young Dan, who served in the coffee house, appeared from the back room, wiping his hands on his apron. "What is your pleasure, sir? Will it be coffee? Tobacco?"

"A dish of coffee and a pipe." Beaky Nose waited until Dan had gone to check on the pots keeping warm by the hearth, and then turned back to Polly. He leaned forward, coming a little too close, and said in a whisper, "I have a proposition for you, Mistress Paradice."

"Indeed, sir? Will it be to my advantage?" She was glad that Dark was not present: he had given little indication of being a jealous man, but he had been angered by her visit to her Jacobite ex-lover, Robbie Sinclair, in Newgate last year, and for a while they had seriously fallen out over it. In any case, past experience had taught her to be wary. Most of her previous lovers had disliked her giving any man not in his cradle or his dotage a second glance, while being remarkably free with their own favours to all and sundry. But Mr. Henderson's portrait had been finished at last, and Dark had gone into the country, visiting his sister, who had just been brought to bed of twins, and she did not expect him back until next week. Moreover, he was well aware that much of the Paradise's success lay in its owner's ability to indulge in lively and flirtatious conversations with her customers, while making sure not to let them take any liberties.

"It may be." Beaky Nose – why could she not remember his name? – hesitated, and then said, "I have cried your prowess as a singer to my mother and sisters, who are all very fond of music, and Mama has asked that you visit her house to perform for her. Of course," he added, seeing her obvious astonishment, "you would be handsomely rewarded. And our coach will be sent to pick you up – you need do nothing but step out of this door and into the carriage." He looked at her with a hopeful expression. "What say you?"

Polly gathered her thoughts. It was not uncommon for wealthy gentlemen – or ladies – to command private performances of scenes from a play, or dancing or singing, and it could be a useful supplement to an actor's or actress's income. Sometimes the venue and audience were not entirely respectable, but there could surely be no harm in performing for this young man's family, and if they were as rich as it seemed, it might be very much worth her while.

"Indeed, sir," she said at last, "it is more than a little tempting, and I am flattered to be made such a generous offer."

"Then you will say yes?"

His puppyish eagerness was endearing. Polly thought of the comfortable house she wished to build or to buy, in Chelsea or Richmond or Kew, and of the cost, and of how much she must yet save up to make her dream a reality, and smiled at the young man. "I will say yes, sir, and I thank you. When would it be convenient to visit?"

His face lit up with delight, and a certain amount of relief. "I am so glad. Once Mama takes hold of a notion, there can be no stopping her, and my sister Nan is the same. How are you placed for this Wednesday? Perhaps after we dine?"

Hannah, bearing a tray stacked with used coffee dishes and cups for her Barbados punch, came through from the back room. She raised an eyebrow when she saw her employer in a huddle with Beaky Nose, but said nothing, only carried her burden into the little storage closet behind the counter, where there was a large bowl of water for washing and some old cloths for drying. She would probably disapprove of the arrangement: Hannah was very protective of her mistress, and quick to point out any flaws in a plan.

"I see no reason why not," Polly said. "But in case there is something which prevents my coming at the last minute, can you give me your direction, so that I may send word?"

"Of course – it is Lady Oglethorpe's house, in Little Ryder Street, which is just off St. James's."

Oglethorpe. The name seemed vaguely familiar, but it

was an old memory, and she could not recall the context in which she had heard it.

"We usually dine at three o'clock," he added. "So shall I tell Mama to send the coach for you a little earlier? And then you may have something to eat before you sing for us. Also, would you be agreeable to some of our friends attending?"

"Of course," Polly said. If she could gain a reputation for her singing amongst the wealthy who lived in and around St James, it might bring considerable reward. And the timing was perfect, she would be back in the Paradise before evening, the busiest part of their day. Indeed, she suspected that the only difficulty might lie in persuading him, or any other male friends who might be present, that she was not in the market for a lover. Though he must be well aware of her liaison with Dark, since it was common knowledge around Covent Garden.

Three young men, handsomely dressed and wearing powdered wigs in the latest style, came swaggering in. One of them called out. "Jemmy! When you've finished sweet talking your mistress, order coffee for us, there's a fine fellow!"

James Oglethorpe (though she doubted that she would ever think of him as anything other than Beaky Nose, just as, despite all her efforts, her maid remained Gin rather than Jane), flushed a deep and unattractive crimson that reached to his ears. He muttered an apology, handed over a few coins, and bore his own dish over to his friends. Hannah, emerging from the closet with some clean cups and a sniff of disapproval, gave the little group a disparaging glance. "So he's back, madam. I thought we were rid of him. What did he want? You looked mighty close together."

Low voiced, so as not to embarrass the young man further, Polly told her what Master Oglethorpe had proposed. Her maid listened in silence, and then said, "You've said you'll go?"

"Yes, why should I not? I have been promised a handsome payment for my services."

"Are you sure that singing is the only service he'll want of you?"

"I hardly think so, since I am to perform for his mother and sisters."

"So he *says*, but are you sure of that, madam? After all, they'd be respectable people. Polite society don't have nothing to do with the likes of us."

It was true. Polly had spent some time on the town, and Hannah was a freed slave. Neither of them would be admitted into any wealthy household, unless discreetly by the back door. She said, "I have been asked to perform for them, not to engage in conversation. They will listen to me sing, and I hope they will applaud, and then they will send me back to Covent Garden with a well-mannered smile and a fat purse. It has all been arranged, and my lady's carriage will call for me at half an hour past two on Friday."

"Hm," said Hannah dubiously. "Well, let's hope it's all above board, madam, and you're not carried off to his country house for ravishment instead."

"I shall be perfectly safe," Polly assured her, with a smile. "I shall be taking Gin."

Her maid's only answer was a contemptuous snort.

*

"Mistress Paradice? Pray enter my lady's carriage."

The liveried coachman held open the door of a magnificent conveyance, freshly painted, with a coat of arms on the side. The shield was white, with a black chevron and three ferocious black boars' heads. They did not look particularly friendly, and Polly hesitated. She had taken the decision to do this on impulse, and had spent the intervening time wondering if it was wise. Hannah disapproved, and so, she was sure, would Dark. But Dark had already sent word that he was staying with his sister for a few more days – one of the babies was frail, and Bonne feared for him and needed her brother's support – and Polly was guiltily glad of it. If she was chasing a wild goose, she did not want him to know just yet, or at any rate not until she had made an amusing story out of it, to deflect any anger he might feel. And if the Oglethorpes were everything they seemed, and as generous as Beaky Nose implied, then no harm would be done. She did not especially like having secrets from Dark, but she had long ago developed the habit, from choice and also for reasons of self-preservation, of keeping some of her thoughts and her life private and apart from her lovers. And even after so many months, it was too soon to know if Dark was different.

Thinking of what she would wear and what she would sing had provided a very welcome distraction from her fears and wonderings about Mattie. Dark had mentioned treason: so small a word, with so great a burden. During the day, she had usually been able to forget about her sister for hours at a time. But if she woke in the dead of night, she always thought of her, and wondered whether she was well, and safe, and happy. It was like a deep splinter in the finger, that would hurt only when touched.

Nor had she felt able to talk to anyone about her fears. Dark hated all Jacobites with a passion: he had said that she must do nothing, or she might put Mattie in danger. And although Jenny Garnet was sympathetic to the Jacobite cause, she was also a notorious gossip. Confiding in her about Mattie would ensure her sister's situation was known all over town. No, she could not tell Jenny.

Now, after much deliberation, she was wearing her favourite gown, of silvery blue satin. To enhance it, she had recently bought a petticoat of Spitalfields silk, exquisitely embroidered with cornflowers and pinks, entwined with flourishing green leaves. It had cost a considerable amount, even though she had paid less than the going rate because the embroiderer was distantly related to Dark, and Huguenots looked out for each other. But she had decided that it was too showy for such an occasion. The Oglethorpes would not consider her their equal, either in wealth or in birth, and she had no wish to offend them. So instead she wore a plain petticoat in a darker shade of blue, and covered the low square neckline with a lace-edged kerchief which gave, she hoped, just the right indication of modesty and respectability. Lady Oglethorpe probably suspected that the beautiful songstress that James had recommended was in fact angling after her son, and Polly had no intention of confirming her suspicions.

The coachman helped her inside, and she thanked him graciously. Gin, of course, in her less elaborate attire, needed no assistance, but gave the man a pert and searching glance, as if wondering whether she knew him: her years on the streets of London had given her a very wide acquaintance with the more disreputable elements of society. She sank onto the brown leather upholstery opposite Polly, and once the door was shut, let loose a gusty sigh of pleasure. "This ain't no common hackney, that's for sure, Madam."

"It certainly is not," Polly agreed. The interior of the coach smelt of fresh leather and new paint, with a hint of some more fragrant and floral aroma, and was as unlike the usual odour of mould and stale sweat inside a hired conveyance as it could possibly be. She waited until they were moving, with some shouting and cracking of his whip from the coachman to warn the inevitable crowd of curious bystanders to get out of the way, before adding, "Do you know him?"

"Ben Atkins," said Gin promptly. "Used to drive a hackney, his sister keeps the Ivy Tavern off Cheapside. He's come up in the world and no mistake. He didn't know me, though."

Since the coachman would have last seen Gin in her former guise as a ragged link-boy, this was not surprising: nearly a year's worth of plentiful food, kind treatment and appropriate clothes had wrought a vast change in her.

"He's a good sort, though – always treated his prancers right," Gin went on. "Which is more than you can say for some of 'em. So if he's working for these Ogellers they'll be square coves."

"The family's name is Oglethorpe," Polly said. "If they like my singing, they will pay me well, and if you are quiet and obedient and helpful, they may tip you handsomely."

At the thought of this, Gin's expression grew brighter, and she looked down at her attire. "Am I dressed proper, Madam? All well-rigged?"

"Yes, you look neat and tidy and respectable."

Gin smoothed her spotless white apron and assumed a smug smile. "I learn quick, don't I, Madam. You'd never guess I used to be a boy."

"Until you gallop up the stairs like a runaway horse," Polly said. "Yes, you have learned some things very quickly – others, not so fast. But I am very pleased with your progress, Jane, and more to the point, so is Hannah, and she is a much harder task-mistress than I am."

"And don't I know it," Gin muttered darkly.

The coach's progress was slow due to the press of traffic, though in summer London was usually less busy, as many of the wealthier sort abandoned the hot and unhealthy city for their cooler and more comfortable country houses. They turned out onto St. Martin's Lane, negotiated the usual tangle of hackneys, carriages, carts, horses and walkers at

Charing Cross without too many delays and a minimum of abuse, and entered the quieter, broader and more salubrious thoroughfare of Pall Mall. Polly used the time to go over her repertoire in her mind. The songs she planned to sing were a very mixed collection of popular ballads and merry ditties, together with *Dido's Lament*, a difficult aria calculated to appeal to more sophisticated listeners than her usual audience. She knew it well, having learned it long ago in Bristol, and it was often sung in the interval at the theatres. Experience had taught her that singing improved with much practice, and she had certainly had much practice over the past few months, giving her customers a varied selection of songs three or four times a week. But would she still be able to reach that astonishing high note?

Perhaps she would save the Lament for another occasion, although she had tried it out last night, and her audience had seemed to appreciate it.

"So, what yer going to sing?" Gin enquired, as the coach approached St. James's. "*Maids When You're Young?*"

Polly tried to suppress a snort of laughter. "No, of course not – it's hardly suitable for polite company."

"*I* knows that," Gin retorted, but she was grinning too. "But I weren't sure you did."

"You presume too much familiarity," Polly said, trying, and failing, to speak severely. "Now quiet, we must be almost there. Remember your manners, I would not have you disgrace us."

"What do you take me for?" demanded Gin, indignant. "I knows what's what. Don't you fret, Madam, I won't let you down."

Ryder Street was a narrow opening off St. James's, lined with terraces of tall houses perhaps forty or fifty years old, handsomely built of brick with elegant sash windows. The coach made the turn with some difficulty, and filled the width with little room to spare. It drew up outside a house about half-way along. Polly looked at Gin, and saw the child's face sparkling with excitement. Knowing that her own expression must be similar, she smiled, and put her finger to her lips. Then the coachman was opening the door, and helping them out into deep shadow. Above, a narrow ribbon of blue summer sky threaded between the roof tops, and the square cobbles under Polly's thin-soled shoes had obviously been recently swept clean of rubbish.

Gin said not a word, but she looked around her with an expression that spoke eloquently of a mixture of envy, admiration and contempt. It said, '*These fine people might think themselves better than us, but they fart and piss and shit and rut just the same under their silk and lace.*' In her view, frequently expressed, respect should be earned, not demanded, and Polly tended to agree with her.

Another liveried servant opened the door to them. Polly had wondered if they would be escorted to a rear, and therefore inferior, entrance, but that would probably have involved a detour into another street, if indeed such a back door existed. He showed them into a dim hall, very similar to that in her own house in King Street, but much larger. To the right, instead of the broad space and scrubbed wooden tables and counter of her coffee house, there was an informal dining parlour, furnished with comfortable chairs and a gate-legged table, already pulled out and laid in readiness for a simple meal. The street outside was so narrow that even the high window let in little light, but to compensate, the wainscot panelling that lined the walls had been painted a pale creamy colour, and there were candles in sconces on either side of the plain mirror above the fireplace.

"My lady has ordered that refreshments be brought to you as soon as you arrive," the footman said. "She directs me to instruct you to take your ease here, and as soon as the family have finished their dinner, I will summon you." He glanced at Gin, who was standing decorously by the door, her hands neatly folded over her apron and her eyes downcast. "Will your maid remain here?"

"If Lady Oglethorpe will not mind, I would like her to stay with me," Polly said quickly. "I plan to train her up as a singer, and it will be useful for her to watch me as I perform." Since Gin had a voice a corncrake might envy, and a repertoire of songs popular on the street but hardly suitable for a lady's ears, this was a glaring falsehood, but the footman was not to know that.

As soon as he had gone, Gin turned to her, panic on her face. "What do you mean, Madam? I ain't no singer, and not likely to be neither! Don't ask me to sing, I beg you, please don't!"

"Don't fret, of course I won't," Polly said briskly. "But I would like you with me, and that seemed a good enough excuse. You are an excellent observer, Jane, and I plan to ask you for your thoughts upon the gathering later. Now tell me, did you also know that footman?"

"Nah, never seen him before in my life," Gin said, more cheerfully now she knew she was not going to be asked to sing.

"I am glad of it – I was beginning to think that you were acquainted with every living soul in London, good or bad."

At that moment there was a light tap on the door, and two maids, very little older than Gin, bore in a tray apiece, both laden with platters of cold meats, roast chicken legs, bread, cheese, a custard tart and a bottle of wine and glasses. All this was set out on the table, and the maids curtseyed and withdrew.

"I thought it would've been grander than this," said Gin, looking disappointed. "There ain't no fancy French fare, nor sauces!"

"That will be above stairs. We are below. In any case, this is good food, and plenty of it, and I for one do not plan to let very much of it go to waste." Polly sat down, feeling suddenly hungry: she had not eaten since early that morning, before the coffee shop was opened.

"Nor I, Madam," Gin said, and took her place opposite. For a while there was no sound in the room but the scrape of cutlery on china, and the more distant noises from the street outside or in the much busier thoroughfare of St. James. The meal was plain, true, but the meat was succulent and tender, the cheeses full of flavour, the soft white bread obviously from that morning's baking, and the tart was sweet and delicately spiced. It was all served on good china plates, and washed down with an excellent light claret which reminded Polly, suddenly and sharply, of the wine she had been offered in the barn at Amesbury a few weeks previously. Perhaps the Oglethorpes patronised the same merchant? It seemed very unlikely, but if so, that merchant operated under cover of darkness, and paid no taxes. She raised her glass and studied the ruby liquid with an assessing eye.

"Smuggled?" enquired Gin, who seemed increasingly able to read her thoughts with alarming accuracy. "That's what I thought."

"If so, it's best to keep quiet," Polly warned, taking an appreciative sip. "Where smugglers are concerned, everyone looks the other way."

"Because if they do, there's profit, and if they don't, there's danger," said her maid darkly.

There was certainly no mistaking the smooth taste, richly aromatic and fruity. Had Gin also sampled Crowley's offering? She could not now remember. In any case, it had no bearing on the task ahead of her. She put the glass down and took from the pocket of her dress the slip of paper on which she had written the titles of the songs she planned to perform, going over them in her head. Of course, it was best to be flexible, for she had no real idea what style of singing the Oglethorpes might prefer, so there were soulful ballads, lively but decorous ditties, lyrics of love exchanged or love denied, and of course the Lament, which she was still not certain she wanted to attempt.

When they had finished, Polly rose to her feet and walked to the window. It was sparklingly clean, and provided a good view of the street and the houses opposite, all still in deep shade. She performed the breathing exercises which her singing master had taught her, long ago, and then tried a few snatches. Behind her, Gin was polishing off the rest of their meal, though she did not take more than a few sips of the wine. Her mother had died a gin-sodden wreck at an age younger than Polly was now, and Gin, out of principle, rarely drank anything stronger than small beers or cordials.

"They're taking a long time over their dinner," the girl grumbled when she had finished.

"In polite society, it can last several hours." Polly turned from the window and smiled at Gin. "We may be kept here for some time yet. But at least we are now neither thirsty nor hungry."

At that moment, there was a tap on the door, and the footman entered, bowing slightly. "Mistress Paradice, Her Ladyship is ready now to receive you, and bids me ask you whether you have enjoyed your refreshments."

Her heart leapt with a mixture of excitement and apprehension, but Polly kept her face calm and smiling. "Thank you. Indeed we have. A most excellent repast."

He led them back into the hall, and up the elegant staircase, the banister of smooth polished pine, the balustrades carved in a twisting fashion that was now rather old-fashioned, but Polly thought were nonetheless very handsome. At the top, they were conducted into a splendid room, which must occupy much of the space on the first floor. The bright sunlight poured in here, illuminating painted panelling in a soft sage green, an elaborate plaster ceiling, and a marble fireplace. The windows had been left slightly open, and the fresh air was welcoming and surprisingly cool.

"Mistress Paradice, my lady," the footman said, with a deep bow. Polly, rising from a low, graceful curtsey, saw a group of perhaps half a dozen people, and sitting at their centre a tall, angular woman in a hooped gown of iron-grey satin, with a petticoat in a paler shade of the same colour, and a plain black stomacher, trimmed with gold. The effect of rich severity was enhanced by the ring of steely curls which edged her lace cap, looking as though they had been forged by Vulcan. She surveyed Polly with a grim, assessing stare. "So you are the songstress of whom my son speaks so highly?"

"He is too kind, my lady, but yes, I am."

"And I understand you have agreed to sing for us today, Mistress Paradice."

Gin, just behind her, muttered under her breath, "Well, she ain't here to scrub the floors," and Polly had to squash a mad desire to laugh. She said with a smile, 'Yes, my lady, and my humble and heartfelt thanks for your kind invitation."

"Excellent." Lady Oglethorpe peered at her across the prominent nose which she had bestowed on young James. "Do you have a musician with you?"

"I often sing unaccompanied, my lady." Isaac, who had played his violin for her on the night when Sam had brought the note from Mattie, was rehearsing at the Haymarket Opera House, so she had been forced to dispense with his services today.

"Hmm. Interesting. So how do you keep to the tune?"

"I was told by my music teacher that I have perfect pitch."

"Indeed. Remarkable. My daughters, alas, have no such gift, save for Molly here."

The girl sitting beside her, arrayed in a remarkably fine mantua of patterned silk that was almost as elaborate as the petticoat Polly had chosen not to wear, blushed and fluttered her pierced ivory fan. Her mother cast her a quelling glance and turned back to Polly. Before she could speak, a young woman on her other side, also a daughter to judge from her strong resemblance to Lady Oglethorpe, leaned forward and said, "I understand from my brother that you keep a coffee house."

You make it sound as if I keep a brothel, Polly thought, suddenly and sharply annoyed. Why had she agreed to this? No matter how beautifully she sang, she would never be treated by these people with anything other than contempt. Then she caught sight of Beaky Nose – she really must stop thinking of him under that name – standing just behind his mother's chair. He was looking at her with some sympathy, and then smiled encouragingly, as if he knew of her thoughts. She did not respond but squared her shoulders and made herself a little taller, thinking that after all, she was as good a woman as any of them, if not better. "I do," she said. "At the Sign of the Paradise, in King Street in Covent Garden. Mr. Oglethorpe has been a regular visitor."

"So we understand," said his mother, as if she thoroughly disapproved. "However, that is neither here nor there, Anne. Mistress Paradice, pray sing for us now."

Lord, what a Tartar, Polly thought. For an instant, under that glittering glare, she could not remember any of the songs she had planned, although she knew them all off by heart. And then memory came back, and she calmed herself with several measured breaths. "I will, my lady. First, I will give you '*The True Lover's Farewell.*'"

A pause, filled with the faint rustle of silk, the distant noises from the streets outside, and the lazy buzzing of a bee, bumbling against the window. One long breath, and she could begin.

"'O fare you well, I must be gone
And leave you for a while:
But wherever I go, I will return,
If I go ten thousand mile, my dear,
If I go ten thousand mile.

Ten thousand miles it is so far
To leave me here alone,
Whilst I may lie, lament and cry,
And you will not hear my moan, my dear,
And you will not hear my moan.

The crow that is so black, my dear,
Shall change his colour white;
And if ever I prove false to thee,
The day shall turn to night, my dear,
The day shall turn to night.

O don't you see that milk-white dove
A-sitting on yonder tree,
Lamenting for her own true love,
As I lament for thee, my dear,
As I lament for thee.

The river never will run dry,
Nor the rocks melt with the sun;
And I'll never prove false to the man I love
Till all these things be done, my dear,
Till all these things be done.'"

Polly had learned this many years ago from her mother, and had sung it countless times since, which was why she had decided to begin with it. Moreover, it was a lovely tune, and no-one, not even the fiercest stickler for polite behaviour, could take exception to the words. As she sang, she could see some signs of appreciation amongst her small audience. Young Molly was listening with rapt attention, and even her disdainful sister had stopped the small, impatient movements of her fan, while Beaky Nose – James – was gazing at her with unrequited longing in his eyes. When she finished, there was a smattering of genuine applause, and a young man sitting next to James called, "Bravo!" Daringly, she flashed a smile in his direction, and waited until they were quiet. Then she gave them *'Love Will Find Out The Way'*, *'The Nightingale'*, and *'The False Bride'*. It was gratifying to note that their appreciation grew with every song, and at the tragic conclusion of the last, Molly had brought out her handkerchief, and was dabbing at her eyes, while even her mother's forbidding features had noticeably softened.

"Will you favour us with one more tune, Mrs Paradice?" James's friend asked. Polly smiled at him again. "Yes, sirs, ladies, if it please you all, I will sing for you *'Dido's Lament'*."

It would be familiar to anyone even slightly acquainted with the theatre, and there was a muted buzz of interest amongst them. She had not thought to include it, but their response to her performance had encouraged her, and she was now confident that her voice was equal to the task today.

And judging by their reaction, it was. As she sang the last, lingering *'Remember me ... but ah, forget my fate,'* even Lady Oglethorpe was wiping away a tear. Polly stood quite still, silently receiving all the praise and applause as her due, as she had done when performing at Lincoln's Inn Theatre, last year, and trying not to let her own emotion show on her face.

"Mistress Paradice, I must confess that was exceedingly

well done." Her hostess rose graciously from her chair and approached her. "You have a most beautiful voice; I cannot recall when I have heard the like. James? James, thank you for suggesting that she sing for us."

"My pleasure, Mama." They were all crowding round her now, as they did at the coffee house, but there, if she felt suffocated, she could escape. Here, she must tolerate their interest and answer their questions with courtesy but without giving too much away: for surely, if they became aware of all the murky details of her history, they would instantly bar her from the house, lest she contaminate them.

But she had learned the rules of polite behaviour and etiquette long ago, in Bristol from the Colonel, who had loved her singing and had treated her as if she were his own child, so she could smile and receive their compliments with grace and humility, until Lady Oglethorpe said abruptly, "You must be thirsty, Mistress Paradice, from exercising your voice. Will you take tea now, with myself and my daughters?"

Polly had to make an effort to stop herself gaping in surprise. She had come here to sing for a private party in return for a handsome purse, and an invitation to sit down with the Oglethorpes had never featured in her thoughts about the afternoon. But my lady was ushering her into another room, where stood a table covered with a white damask cloth, and set with the paraphernalia required for the elegant service of tea. It was a most impressive display, intended to flaunt its owner's considerable wealth and excellent taste. Polly thought of her blue and white Delft cups, pretty but chipped, and the silver teapot with a dent in its side where Gin had dropped it during polishing, and was glad that she was most unlikely ever to be in a position to return Lady Oglethorpe's unexpected hospitality.

She took the chair indicated, careful to move with the same instinctive, well-bred grace of the other ladies, and glanced around. Of course Gin had not accompanied her into this more intimate, private space – presumably she would be taken down to the kitchens and given something to eat – and she felt oddly unprotected. She noted the pale blue painted panelling, the gilt-framed mirror above the hearth, and the subtle, comforting signs of considerable wealth. The array on the tea table gave a similar impression: the silver kettle on its stand, the fragile porcelain cups, brought all the way from China, the basin for slops, the jug containing milk or cream, the bowl full of sugar lumps and the gleaming silver tongs with which to serve them. With a proprietorial air, Lady Oglethorpe inspected everything, and nodded to the maid who was waiting beside her. "Very good, Peggy. You may leave us."

"And so, Mistress Paradice," said Miss Molly, turning eagerly to her, "you sing exceptionally well. Where did you learn such things?"

"Sadly, my parents died when I was young, and I was adopted by friends of our family. They ensured that I was taught all the necessary accomplishments," said Polly, omitting entirely the fact that she had been a lowly parish apprentice and maid of all work at the Bear, before the Colonel had taken her in.

"Indeed." Lady Oglethorpe surveyed her with beady curiosity. "And now, my son tells me, you are the proprietor of a coffee house."

"Yes, my lady. My benefactor unfortunately died when I was sixteen, and I was sadly forced to make my own way in the world." It had not seemed so sad at the time, despite her affection for the colonel, for opportunity had beckoned her to London, but she had swiftly been brought back to earth.

"You seem to have done very well for yourself, Mistress Paradice. I commend you. Your voice is exquisite."

"And that is high praise indeed from Mama," said Miss

Molly, who possessed an uninhibited liveliness very much at odds with her mother's stiff dignity. "I wish I could sing so well, but James – my brother whom you know of course – James says I sound like a London sparrow, all chirp and no tune."

"If you would but address yourself to your task, you would fare better," said her sister, whose expression rivalled her mother's for severity.

"How can I, when Signor Capelletti is always unwell?" Molly complained. "He has come to the house perhaps twice this year, and last time he was coughing so much he claimed he could not hear me. It's not my fault if the London air has left too much dust in his lungs." She turned to Polly, her round pink face suddenly alive. "Mistress Paradice, would you be so kind as to give me singing lessons? I am sure you would be a much better teacher than ever the Signor could be!"

"Mistress Paradice undoubtedly has many calls on her time. She will not want to make her days more crowded by indulging your whims." Anne Oglethorpe sent her sister such a quelling glance that Polly felt a pang of sympathy for the girl. However, she neither sulked nor dissolved into tears, but continued cheerfully, "I am very sure it is not a whim, for Mama has said that every young lady must learn to sing in tune, and I think that if I had Mistress Paradice as my teacher, I would certainly do so without delay. Mama, do you not agree with me?"

Of course she will not, Polly thought, and at the same moment Lady Oglethorpe said, "It seems an uncommonly excellent notion, my dear. What do you say, Mistress Paradice? You would, of course, be handsomely rewarded."

Once more temptation, in the form of that sweet commodious house in the country, rose to Polly's mind, and once more, after the briefest of struggles, she succumbed. She liked Molly's artless good humour and irrepressible spirits, and if she could succeed with the girl where the unfortunate

Signor Capelletti had failed, the Oglethorpes would perhaps recommend her as a singing teacher to other wealthy families, and her distant dream would become a little more real.

"I would be delighted to teach your daughter, my lady," she said, and Molly clapped her hands in delight.

CHAPTER SIX

But good intentions justify the deed

"Well?" Gin demanded, as soon as they were back in Lady Oglethorpe's coach. "Did they like your singing, Madam? I hope they paid you well for all your trouble!"

"Indeed they did," Polly said, and showed her the guinea in her hand.

Gin sniffed. "He's an ugly old cove," she said dismissively, looking at the King's profile.

"I'm not at all sure that's not treason, but I don't care how ugly he may be, this coin is good honest gold, and that will more than suffice for an hour or two of my time. Did they treat you well, below stairs?"

"Well enough," Gin said. Polly had seen that look of bright-eyed eagerness before, and knew her maid must have information to impart.

"So," she said, "what did you learn about the Oglethorpes?"

"That her ladyship is called Old Fury behind her back, and rules with an iron rod, but can be bent and softened if you know the way. That Miss Anne bids in a fair way to being worse than her Ma, which is why they call her Young Fury, and what's more – " Gin lowered her voice, though the coachman could not possibly have heard her above the rumble of wheels and the noise of the street – "They say she used to be the Earl of Oxford's conveniency!"

"Really?" said Polly, finding it very hard to reconcile the prim and rigid young woman she had just encountered with the general assumption that a mistress should be soft, pliant and accommodating.

"*Really*." Gin seemed delighted at the reception of this choice piece of gossip.

"So what else? I can see you're eager to tell me."

"Miss Molly spends far too much at the mantua-makers and the milliners and the goldsmiths, and she'll be dished up if she don't watch out. It's all kept from her ma, but the servants know, because them what she owes money to come knocking and have to be sent away."

"I see." It fitted in with the girl's extravagant style. "Anything else?"

"Well ..." For the first time, Gin hesitated. Then she said, "From the talk in the kitchens, madam, for sure they're all a nest of Jacks!"

Somehow, it was not a surprise. After all, Beaky Nose – James Oglethorpe – had been a scholar at Corpus Christi, which could also fairly be described as a 'nest of Jacks'. And the fact that his eldest sister had supposedly been the mistress of the Earl of Oxford, who was widely suspected of being a Jacobite and currently languishing in the Tower after being impeached for 'High Crimes And Misdemeanours', added weight to the revelation. Determined not to make too much of it, Polly shrugged. "I cannot see how that will count for anything."

Gin looked at her. "Dark won't be pleased. Is you going to tell him?"

She hesitated, and the maid at once jumped in before she could answer. "You've got to tell him! You knows how he feels about Jacks."

Polly did indeed. Dark came of a Protestant family of silversmiths who had been forced out of France more than thirty years previously, and had found refuge first in Amsterdam, then in London. He had been reared on tales of the atrocities committed against the Huguenots, the rapes, the murders, the forcible conversions and separation of families, and had seen at first hand the horrors of war when fighting in Marlborough's army against the Catholic French. The threat of rebellion and civil strife if the Jacobites tried to set their exiled King James on the English throne was very real to him, and he had become a spy for the Hanoverian government to counter that menace.

"Still," Gin added, "you ain't going back, so maybe it don't matter if you don't."

Polly said slowly, "I have agreed to give Miss Molly singing lessons."

"You done *what?*"

"You heard me."

"Well, you can't," said her maid decisively. "Dark – "

"Will not like it. I know. But Lady Oglethorpe has offered me such a handsome reward, I felt I could not refuse."

Gin stared at her. She said, "And you ain't thinking, now you know, as to *why* they want to cuddle up to you all of a sudden? Perhaps they're hoping you're still one of them."

"I never was 'one of them'. Sinclair was, and while I loved him, his cause was my cause. But I realised in time that his plans would only bring death and misery. If you remember, he was planning to kill the Prince of Wales and blow up the Frost Fair with Dark's fireworks."

"And you stopped him, and he was killed in the fire. Good riddance," said Gin, fervently. "So do these Ogleys know that, do you reckon? Or do they still think you're a Jack?"

"Oglethorpes. No, we did not talk about him at all. I had no idea they were Jacobites until you told me just now." This was, of course, not strictly true, but she had no intention of letting Gin know that.

And, curse it, the girl was right. She must ask herself why they had sent this sudden invitation, this unlikely offer to a woman whom Lady Oglethorpe would surely never usually allow to enter her house, even to clean the scullery, and certainly not on the terms of intimacy with her daughter which giving singing lessons would entail.

"Well, you can't," Gin said decisively. "And Dark'd say the same, I knows he would. And then you'd fall out over it and I ain't going to let that happen again, because you and he love each other and it wouldn't be right!"

There was a small, fraught silence, filled by the coachman shouting insults at a wagon driver apparently blocking his way. Polly took a deep breath, wondering at her own sudden anger, and then said calmly, though with an effort, "It is not usually part of a servant's duties, to give advice." Though Hannah, of course, was the exception.

Gin sniffed. Her rather protuberant brown eyes stared unapologetically at her mistress. She said, "I can't help it. I can't sit by and let you ruin all you've got for the sake of a few guineas! Tell Old Fury you've changed your mind! You ain't broke, you can afford to let a coin or two slip past you."

"Listen, Jane." Polly took a hold of her wayward emotions – love, the child had said love, the one word she and Dark, by some unspoken alchemy, had never mentioned even in their most intimate, private moments – and tried to speak decisively. "I will do what I think best, whatever you might say to try to influence me."

"Tell me you ain't going back!" Gin begged, tears beginning to fill her eyes. "Please don't go back, Madam, *please!* I don't know what they're up to but they must be up to no good, Jacks always are! If they knows you stopped Sinclair killing the Prince of Wales, they might want revenge on you!"

Polly's patience, usually on a long string where Gin was

concerned, was by now decidedly frayed. "I hardly think that is a likely possibility. We are not in a stage play, are we? No, Jane," she added, as her maid opened her mouth to protest, "I know you mean well, but that's enough. I don't want to hear another word from you on the subject, do you understand?"

Gin opened her mouth, closed it, swallowed hard, and said in a meek voice quite unlike her previously strident tones, "Very good, Madam."

The ensuing silence lasted all the way back to King Street, and Polly was at leisure to consider the future, with care and forethought. Gin's fears were ridiculous, of course, there would be no danger from the Oglethorpes, and in any case James, her fervent admirer, would never have suggested anything that might imperil her. True, she did not much care for Lady Oglethorpe, or for her disapproving elder daughter, but Molly, young, lively and garrulous, was a very different proposition, and she thought that teaching her might be a welcome diversion from fretting at Dark's absence, or her worries about Mattie.

As for telling her lover, well, that could wait until he returned from Bonne in Richmond. It was not something that she wished to entrust to a letter, even if she had known his sister's direction. She would love to meet this woman whom he held in such affection, which seemed to be mutual. But she, like the Oglethorpes, was wealthy, respectable, and unlikely to wish for any contact with the likes of Polly. She had not often regretted the fact that she was unacceptable in polite society, but where Bonne was concerned, it was different. And even if Dark's sister desired to meet her, her husband assuredly would not.

On their return to the coffee house – with half of King Street hanging out of windows or cluttering the street to gawp at the Oglethorpe's carriage – she sent Gin to scrub and clean the dirty cups and stained coffee pots, and took her place behind the bar, guiltily aware that she was leaving more and more of the daily running of her establishment to Hannah and Will. Not that either of them ever seemed to mind, though Hannah cast her an enquiring glance as she tied her apron round her waist and enquired of the elderly man who had just entered, what he wished to be served with this afternoon. When he had gone away with his cup and pipe and tobacco, young Dan following at his heels with a fresh pot of coffee, Hannah came up to her and hissed, "I'm glad to see you back safe and sound, ma'am! How was it?"

"Interesting," Polly said softly. "But all entirely above board. His mother is an eminently respectable lady, with two daughters. She wishes me to give singing lessons to the younger one."

Hannah's eyebrows shot up. "And did you agree?"

"I did, after a little consideration."

"I do hope she offered you a fine purse!"

"She did, which is why I accepted. I am thinking of my future, Hannah, and yours." She smiled at the other woman. "You know, I think, what I envisage."

"I do. But I can't help but wonder, madam, whether you'd readily take to a quiet retirement in the country. You're at ease and at home here in Town, same as me."

"If I'm honest, I sometimes wonder the same. But I am not planning on moving to Chelsea or Knightsbridge tomorrow, or even next year, for that matter. Once I have saved enough money – and Miss Oglethorpe's fees will hurry that along nicely – I will buy a house there, and if I am not then tired of life in Town, I can let it out at a high rent until I feel the need. I long to have a garden, Hannah, and perhaps keep chickens, and go for pleasant walks in the fresh air. I was born and bred in the country, and I do hanker after green fields and open skies. And the day will come, I know, when I will have had enough of city life."

"So what will become of this place?" Hannah gestured at their pride and joy, their trim, busy, welcoming coffee house, on which so much time and effort and expense had been lavished over the past eight or nine months. "You cannot think to let it all go to waste."

"And I will not. It will be yours." And as Hannah stared at her in astonishment, Polly added, "No-one could deserve it more. And I know it would be in good hands, with you and Will. You can marry, and change the name if you like – though there is already a Will's Coffee House, of course – and it will flourish." She smiled. "If you want it, that is. But the one thing I would ask, is that you do not tell anyone else this – except for Will, of course, you may confide in him."

Her maid seemed lost for words. At last, she said, gasping, "Thank you, madam. Thank you!"

"There is no need for thanks. You are my true and loyal friend, and you deserve it." Polly gave her a swift hug, and then had to turn back to the counter to serve a group of actors from the Theatre Royal, taking a break from rehearsals. They were regular customers, and greeted her with appreciation and good-natured banter, before turning to reminiscences of a play they had performed a few weeks ago, called *The Ignoramus*, in which Norris had played the title role. Much amusement was derived from their descriptions of the comic actor Will Penkethman reciting the epilogue while riding upon an ass – something which, for reasons Polly had never been able to fathom, he frequently did.

"But it weren't his usual ass, you see, Mrs Paradice," said the diminutive Henry Norris, leaning over to pick his pipe from the selection in the jar on the counter. "His usual ass was taken poorly, so Wilks had to bring in a replacement. And it wouldn't stand still, it was all of a shuffle and a fidget – "

"And shat on the boards," Penkethman interrupted. "Begging your pardon," he added belatedly, as Wilks, the theatre's actor manager, who was famously insistent on politeness in female company, nudged him in the ribs and glared at him. "Mind your manners, Will, in front of the lady."

Polly smiled. "I should think so too, Mr. Penkethman. This is a respectable house. So, apart from the disobliging ass, how did your play go?"

When at last they were settled at the table by the further window, Evans came up to her, his face flushed and his eyes bright with excitement. "Oh, madam, Hannah's just told me! Is it really true?"

"It is, Will, as true as I'm standing here. Have you actually asked her yet? Or are you still thinking about it?"

"I ... I ..." The bashful doorman hung his head. "I haven't quite dared, madam. You know what she's like, if you catch her at the wrong time she can be so prickly, see."

"Well, I should dare, because if you don't you'll never give her the chance to say yes." Polly gave the counter a brisk wipe with a damp cloth, and grinned at him. "I do not think she will turn you down. You are a good, kind man, and such as you are rare as hen's teeth these days. She is afraid of change, that is all – she is so settled here."

"I do know that, madam," said Will Evans. He managed a nervous smile. "Shall I go ask her, then?"

"Why not? There's no time like the present. She's sweeping the inner room, and there are no customers in there, you can be private for a moment or two." And then, as he still hesitated, Polly gave him a little push. "Go on, Will. What's the saying? Faint heart never won fair lady."

At last his face cleared. "Aye, madam, thank you, I will. Oh," he added, suddenly stopping in the middle of turning away. "I clean forgot, in all this excitement – this arrived for you this afternoon while you were out. I'm sorry, madam, I should have given it to you as soon as you came back."

"That doesn't matter, Will, I have it now." Polly took the small, tattered fold of paper, knowing the sender even before she saw the thick black scrawl on the outside. *'Mrs. Paradice, at the Sign of the Paradise Coffee House, King Street in Covent Garden.'* She could make a good guess at the contents, too, and so it proved.

> *"Darling Poll, I am called away on urgent business which I am unable to put off, and cannot tell when I will return. At least, though, my sister does well now, and so do the babes. She wishes to send you her regards, and expresses the hope that one day soon, we might all meet together. That is also the desire of your very humble and devoted servant,*
>
> *A. Dark."*

Of course, she could not imagine that Dark had ever been humble in his life, and the thought of it made her smile briefly, before disappointment inevitably filled her. She missed him, his sardonic, dry wit, his unspoken but very real affection, his presence in her home, by her side, and above all in her bed, at present a wide and lonely place which her cat Sly could not fill.

Treacherously, she felt her eyes prickle with tears, and turned away so that Evans would not see it. But he was already hurrying into the back room, shutting the door firmly behind him, so she had a moment to compose herself, and to wonder, not without a stab of annoyance, what was the 'urgent business' that had prevented her lover from returning to her. Government affairs, no doubt, investigating Jacobite conspiracy, apparently still a danger despite the overwhelming defeat of the Pretender's army last winter. So it was just as well, she thought, pinning a welcoming smile to her face as Wilks returned to the counter to replace the pipe he had just broken by carelessly knocking it against the table, that he was in ignorance of her arrangement with the Jacobite Oglethorpes.

*

Polly had thanked Lady Oglethorpe but told her that there was no need to send her carriage to King Street in future, and her hostess, despite her gracious manner, had managed to convey the impression that she had had no intention of offering it anyway. So on the morning of her first lesson with Molly, she sent Dan out to find a hackney, and when it arrived, a while later, she climbed into it with a reluctant and surly Gin in tow. She had been tempted to leave the girl behind, but it would hardly be proper to arrive alone, and Hannah was once more in charge at the Paradise. So here she was, sitting hunched in the corner of the hackney, looking as she would rather be having a tooth drawn at the barber-surgeon, and mercifully mute. Polly resolved to have her under her eye at all times during their time at Little Ryder Street: she could not risk her maid airing her derogatory opinion of Jacobites in front of the servants in the kitchen.

Over the past few days, she had spent some thought on how she would teach Miss Oglethorpe. She had never given singing lessons before, but she had a clear memory of those she had received, many years ago, from an ancient German opera singer. Breathing exercises, scales, airs to extend and train her voice: she could certainly introduce the girl to these fundamentals, but they would have little effect without concentration, practice, and above all the possession of a voice capable of responding to tuition. Her brother's description of her as 'all chirp and no tune' did not sound particularly promising, and Polly suspected that her lessons would be in vain. However, she was being paid handsomely for them, and she would do her best, however unsuitable the raw material turned out to be.

To her relief, there was no sign either of Lady Oglethorpe, or of her intimidating elder daughter, and she was shown into the same parlour in which she and Gin had eaten a few days previously. Miss Molly was there already, dressed in a stylish gown of rose-coloured silk, which prettily set off her glowing complexion and dark gold hair, and accompanied by an even more stylishly clad maid, who was French, to judge from her mistress's fluent stream of instructions in that language. If the Oglethorpes were fervent Jacobites, they probably had strong connections with Catholic France, where the Pretender was currently residing. *Well,* thought Polly, *at least that will prevent Gin from letting slip something incriminating while I am occupied with teaching young Miss.*

"Mrs Paradice! I am so glad you have come!" The girl beamed as Polly made her curtsey, and Gin scuttled over to a corner as far distant from the French maid as she could get. "I declare I have been looking forward to this for days! I am persuaded you will be a far better teacher than Signor Capelletti, and unlike him, you are punctual, which is a very good start. How shall we begin?"

"I think it is best if you sing a song for me, a tune you like and know well," Polly said, unable to resist smiling at her enthusiasm. "Then I will have some idea of your capabilities and what, if anything, I can teach you."

"I thought you would wish to hear me sing, so I have been practising this." Miss Molly drew herself up with a deep breath and a look of fierce concentration. "You sang it when you came here previously, it is called *The True Lover's Farewell.*"

Polly's heart sank, not because it was a poor choice – it had a good tune that was easy to sing well – but because at the present, with Dark's brief note haunting her mind, the words were rather too close to the bone. But she smiled and listened as the girl sang, finding, somewhat to her surprise, that she did not mangle it as much as she had expected, though she employed many trills and arpeggios which she must have learned from the Signor. "That was very good," she said, as Molly finished, her plump cheeks flushed with effort. "You have been well taught."

"*Really*?" Miss Oglethorpe seemed astonished. "But Jemmy always says – "

"Pray do not pay much attention to what your family might say, because most families are too familiar and inclined to tease," Polly said. "Especially brothers," she added, with a wry smile, remembering the good-natured banter and bickering she had once enjoyed with Tom, before disaster struck their own family.

"And Jemmy is the greatest tease in the world," said the girl, with some feeling. "But at least I feel he *likes* me. Unlike Mama and Nan."

There was a low tsk from where the French maid sat. Molly flushed deeply, and turned away. Polly said gently, "I think you have a good voice, Miss Oglethorpe, and I can certainly train it so that you will be able to sing with confidence for the entertainment of your family and friends. But you will need to do as I say, and practise all the exercises I will give you, at least once a day. Are you prepared to do that? Because if you are not, then there is no point in continuing these lessons."

"Oh, I am, be sure of that!" Miss Molly cried. "I want more than anything to be able to sing without feeling that I – that I – "

"That you are all chirp and no tune?" Polly queried, smiling at her. "I am glad to say that your brother was mistaken there. But, I pray you, do not insert all those extra notes into your singing, that is a florid Italian fashion. If you are to sing for me, you must learn to sing plain, and pure, and true, and pay attention to the sense of the words. Now, let me demonstrate the proper exercises you must perform before you launch into the first song, for if you do not make a habit of doing them, you will hurt your voice."

For the next hour, she instructed Miss Molly in the art of breathing, led her through various scales, and emphasised that the sense of the words she was singing needed to match the way she sang, in the English manner. The girl proved an apt and eager pupil, and when the footman entered to announce that their allotted time was up, he seemed to have come too soon, and Polly was surprised to find that she had thoroughly enjoyed herself. The arrangement was made, for the same hour next week, and she climbed into a hackney in St. James Street, feeling very pleased, and with the guinea which the footman had discreetly passed to her stowed safe in her pocket.

Over the next few days, Polly decided that she should devote as much time as possible to the Paradise, which she felt she had sorely neglected of late. It was less busy in this pleasant weather – winter, when a customer could sit all day in the warm for the price of a few cups, was their most profitable time – but she had come to rely very heavily on Hannah. Hannah these days was a very different person from the frightened, defensive woman she had first engaged as her servant, two years ago, and she was now, first and foremost, a friend, albeit a friend who did not scruple to speak her mind when she thought it necessary. That was the result of the confidence she had gained in Polly's employ, and also because she was now no longer a runaway in fear of her master, but a free woman, with a lawyer's paper to prove it. And Polly was sure that the bright eyes, the infectious laugh increasingly heard, and the joyful manner in which she mixed the Barbados Arrack punch for which the coffee house was rapidly becoming famous, were because she had, at last, accepted Will Evans' offer of marriage.

So, even though they did not need, most afternoons, to open the back room, working in the Paradise was a pleasant, companionable experience, and on the evenings when Polly sang for her customers, the coffee house was so full that curious passers-by were unable to come inside and had to stand on the doorstep to listen. She half expected another offer from Rich, the manager at Lincoln's Inn theatre: she had sung on his stage once or twice last year, with much success. But he sent no word, and she suspected that he had decided that now she was singing to her customers, who could see and hear her at close quarters for the price of a cup of coffee, they would not wish to spend rather more for the same privilege at a distance in the theatre.

Her next lesson with Miss Oglethorpe passed off well, and she was becoming better acquainted with the girl's voice. It would never be exquisite, but she could carry a tune, and although the highest notes were beyond her range, she was proving competent in the lower registers. Once more, there was no sign of Old Fury, or of the elder daughter, and at the end of the lesson, Molly let slip that her mother had gone to their house at Godalming in Surrey, where some domestic crisis had apparently arisen. "And I cannot say that I am sorry, for she rules with a rod of iron and treats me as if I was still a child, and Nan is little better, since Oxford was sent to the Tower she has been well-nigh insufferable – she was reputed to be his mistress, you know, though I do not think that can have been the case, for she is as sour as any lemon and I cannot imagine any man looking desirously on her. Is that a very terrible thing to say about my sister, Mistress Paradice?"

Polly could hardly agree with her opinion, so she smiled, and said something non-committal. Molly prattled on. "I have two other sisters, you know, and another brother too, and I am sure they would be far more kind to me, but Theo is in Italy waiting on the King of Sicily, and Fanny and Nell are in

France, and I do wish I was there with them, for they are such fun even though Nell has been married these eight years and has several children, and you would like Fanny exceedingly I think for she is very lively and such good company."

"I did not know you had other sisters, Miss Oglethorpe."

"Oh, that is no secret, but Mama does not care to mention them very often, I think because it reminds her that they are gone beyond her reach. Still, Nell made an excellent match, to a Marquis, but the French did not like it because although she is very pretty, they did not feel her blood was blue enough, despite the fact that we Oglethorpes are a very old and respected family. And Fanny of course would like to make a match as grand, but she is not so old as Nell, nor as pretty neither, though you do not notice it because she is so good natured and has such spirit. Anyway, I have not seen Nell for many a long year and I daresay she has grown stout and plain, she has so many children I've lost count." Her face grew solemn. "I wish I could go to France, for then I would be free of all my troubles."

"Troubles?" Polly queried, for she could not see how this pampered creature, surrounded by luxury and wealth, could have any troubles, save for those which might attend upon having a domineering mother – or, of course, the debts which Gin had mentioned.

"Oh, no matter," Molly said, with an airy wave of the hand that did not convince. She turned and strolled to the window. The weather was less warm than in the previous week, and it was a dull, cool day with the threat of rain in the air. Polly saw her pause for a moment and glance casually up and down the street outside, perhaps checking something. She moved quickly away, as if she did not wish to be seen, and turned with a rather too cheerful smile. "Mistress Paradice, are you agreeable to coming again next week?"

"Of course," Polly told her. She liked Miss Oglethorpe,

though she thought her spoilt – but not as spoilt as Sam Jessop's daughter Mary had been, for Mary had been cross and peevish, whereas Molly's good nature was obvious. "I shall look forward to it."

As she and Gin left the house, she noticed a shabbily dressed man loitering near the junction with St James Street. He looked at them closely as they went by, but did not speak. If Miss Oglethorpe was indeed heavily in debt, perhaps he was waiting for the chance to accost her and demand what was owed. But it seemed unlikely, for even if the girl was in deep water, surely her mother would bail her out? Even a parent as severe and intimidating as Lady Oglethorpe must surely help her child when in trouble, rather than abandoning her to the mercy of her creditors and the shameful danger of a spell in some squalid sponging house. And she felt that the guinea at present in her pocket would have been put to better use in paying off the debt.

But it was no business of hers, and she would not make it so.

It was not to be her decision, though, for after the lesson the following week, when she was giving Molly the words, copied out in her best hand, for the songs she should learn before their next meeting, the girl turned to her and said diffidently, "Pray excuse me for asking you, Mistress Paradice, but were you once acquainted with a Scotsman called Captain Robert Sinclair?"

Much of Polly's surprise and alarm must have been displayed on her face, for Miss Oglethorpe added hastily, "Oh, pray do not distress yourself, I did not mean to upset you! But I had heard ..." Her voice trailed off unhappily.

Polly took a stern grip on her wayward emotions. There was no point in denying it, for it was the simple truth, and many people must know the name of her previous lover. She said cautiously, "You have heard correctly – I was indeed a – a friend of Captain Sinclair at one time. But I had broken off the connection some months before his death."

"He was a very loyal gentleman," said the girl, her round, guileless eyes fixed earnestly on Polly's face. "And he has been much lamented."

Not loyal to me, Polly thought grimly. She had loved Robbie Sinclair once, deceived by his charm and his generosity, until she had realised that, in fact, the only thing in the world that Robbie Sinclair truly loved was not herself, nor young Mary Jessop whom he had seduced, nor even the Jacobite cause he espoused, but Robbie Sinclair. She gathered herself, trying to think of a reply that would not reveal too much. "So I understand," she said at last.

"But – forgive me – you do not sound very unhappy? Despite your friendship?"

"He had given me ample cause to think that his regard for me was at an end," Polly said, choosing her words with care. She saw that Miss Oglethorpe seemed puzzled, and added more bluntly, "He had decided that he preferred someone other than myself."

"Oh, I am sorry for that – and sorrier still for his death, of course. So sad, and so unnecessary. Such a brave and loyal servant to the King!"

For Miss Molly, of course, the King was not George of Hanover, currently on the throne, but the Pretender, ensconced in Avignon and plotting to regain his birthright with, presumably, the enthusiastic assistance of all the Oglethorpe ladies. Polly decided it was high time to steer the conversation into more innocuous waters. She said, "Indeed he was. Now, are you clear about the songs you are to learn? It would greatly help you if you were to have them by heart before our next meeting."

"Yes, Mistress Paradice." The girl looked as if she would

like to say more, but Polly was already beckoning to Gin, huddled in her corner. "Forgive me, Miss Oglethorpe, but I must leave now – there is a friend from the country expected soon, and I have much to do." She stood as her maid draped her light summer mantle over her shoulders, and then curtsied. "Until next week?"

Miss Oglethorpe seemed disappointed, but it was plain she lacked the tenacity, not to say the confidence, of her formidable mother, and Polly was able to escape before any more awkwardness ensued. The footman ushered her out, slipping the guinea discreetly into her hand, and with Gin beside her, she briskly walked the short distance to St. James's, where it would be easy to find a hackney.

"What friend from the country, Madam?" Gin demanded accusingly, as soon as they were seated inside. "You ain't said nothing about no visitor!"

"The note only came just as we were about to leave." Polly pulled it out of her pocket.

"Is it from Dark?" Gin asked hopefully, but even she, still struggling with her letters under Polly's patient tuition, must be able to see that the neat hand on the paper was quite unlike Dark's ferocious black scrawl.

"No, but it is the next best thing – Mr. Jessop has just arrived in town, and he will call on us tomorrow morning."

"Oh." Gin sat back against the worn leather with a look of angry disappointment. "I wish Dark was back with us, he'd soon tell them Jacks where to go."

Polly could imagine it only too clearly. Not for the first time, she felt a prickle of unease about her agreement with the Oglethorpes. On the surface, there should be no harm in it, but Miss Molly's apparently artless questions had surely not been her own idea, and an indication that the request for singing lessons had not been as innocent as Polly had assumed. They knew who she was, and of her association with Robbie. What did they want?

Dark would not like it. Dark would tell her to cease the lessons forthwith, and be damned to the easiest guineas she had ever earned. And she knew he would be right. As the hackney jolted its erratic way back to King Street, she resolved to send a message to Little Ryder Street telling Molly that she could no longer be her singing tutor. Or would that indicate to Lady Oglethorpe and Miss Anne that she had something to hide?

She would see Sam tomorrow, and she would ask his advice.

CHAPTER SEVEN

Rising Mischief

"Sam! It is so good to see you!" Polly received his affectionate kiss of greeting, and then stood back to inspect him. "You are looking very well, I must say. Did you have a good journey?"

Sam Jessop nodded. "I did, and the weather has been kind too." He looked down at her, frowning slightly. "So – any further news of your sister?"

"None whatsoever, which I have persuaded myself is a good thing. Will you not come upstairs for a dish of tea, Sam? Or coffee, if you would prefer? And we can have a pleasant chat."

They were soon ensconced in Polly's pretty parlour above the coffee shop, and Gin, face set with concentration, brought tea and warm rolls fresh from the bakers down the road, with butter to spread on them, and little curd tarts sprinkled with nutmeg, for Sam had confessed that he had come straight from his customary inn in Holborn, without stopping to have breakfast.

He consumed his share of the food hungrily, and Polly, who had already eaten a couple of the rolls as soon as the boy Dan had walked in through the door with a cloth-covered basket full of them, sipped her tea in its chipped blue and white cup and thought of Lady Oglethorpe's very superior tea table, with its very superior paraphernalia.

"That was most excellent, I thank you, Polly," said Sam, putting down his empty cup at last, and dabbing up the final crumbs of pastry and bread. "So what is Dark up to at present?"

She gave him a wry grimace. "I have absolutely no

notion. He has been gone these four weeks – first to see his sister in Richmond, and then, so his note said, called away 'on business'."

Sam could guess what that meant as well as she did. "That seems a long time for him to be absent with no further word. Do you suppose he might have gone overseas?"

Polly spread her hands. "I have no more idea than you have, I regret to say. I just hope that he is not putting himself in danger."

"That is hardly likely, knowing Dark. Would that old lady with whom he lodges have some knowledge of him, do you think?"

"Madame Rousselle? I doubt it. She is not privy to all of his doings, though she likes to pretend that she is. And I have little wish for another of her interrogations at present. She is too nosy by half."

"So you are not missing him, Polly my dear? Not the smallest scrap?"

"And so are you too nosy, Samuel Jessop! Yes, of course I miss him. But in his absence I have begun a new enterprise which has so far proved gratifyingly lucrative, though I suspect he will not like it." And she gave Sam a brief account of the singing lessons with Miss Oglethorpe, and how the arrangement had come about.

"Forgive me if I am sadly obtuse, Polly, but why would Dark not like you giving singing lessons? He is not the kind of man who thinks he owns you."

"He is not. He will not like it, Sam, because apparently they are all fervent Jacobites."

Sam, who disliked the Jacobites almost as much as Dark, but for different reasons, frowned at this information. "That pleasant young man is a Jack?"

"Beaky Nose? Or James Oglethorpe, as I should now call him? Yes, and all his family too. Or so Gin says. As you can imagine, she has heard all the servants' gossip, and servants' gossip never lies."

"You are right, Dark will not like it. But I cannot see any harm in giving a young girl singing lessons."

"Well, that is what I thought, but Miss Oglethorpe asked me yesterday if I had been acquainted, as she put it, with Robbie Sinclair, and that has changed my mind - so I would very much appreciate your advice, Sam, as to what I should do."

"But how is that significant?"

"It means that they know of my past association with Sinclair, they may know that you and I and Dark foiled his attempted assassination of the Prince of Wales, and that Dark was responsible for his death, and even if they do not, they must surely have some secret reason for engaging me as Miss Molly's singing tutor. Perhaps they mean to recruit me to their cause. And do not look at me like that, Sam, I have no interest in Jacobite conspiracy and I have no intention either of joining them, or of spying on them. I do not care for Lady Oglethorpe, the servants call her Old Fury and she is a haughty creature who keeps her daughters much under her thumb, but I do like Miss Molly, she's a sweet innocent and has surely been ordered to sound me out, she seemed reluctant and unsure of herself and did not press me. My head tells me to cease the lessons forthwith, but I confess that they pay me so well that I am reluctant to abandon such easy money."

"I would not have thought you were in want of funds, Polly. This place must be very profitable."

"Indeed it is, but I am saving as much as I can. I have plans to invest in property, and when Lady Oglethorpe proposed the singing lessons, it seemed a good opportunity to add to my store."

"An opportunity too good to be true," Sam said drily. "As it has proved. Well, you have asked my advice, and I will give it – and I am certain that Dark would say the same, were he here now. Do not go back next week, but invent some reason why you can no longer oblige Lady Oglethorpe or her daughter, and write and tell them so."

"You don't think that will arouse their suspicions? That it will indicate my guilt?"

"What guilt? You are guilty of nothing more than an error of judgement, which you have now remedied. Anyway, they are already suspicious of you, it seems. I should have nothing more to do with them, I cannot say it plainer than that. And what harm can they cause you, without drawing unwelcome attention to themselves? Break off the connection, and forget about them."

He was right, of course. Polly sighed, thinking of the three guineas she had already earned, and the others which had beckoned so temptingly. "Thank you, Sam. Your advice is very sensible, even if it is, I confess, a little unwelcome, and I will do as you suggest. Now, tell me all your news. How is Mary doing? She has some way to go yet, I recall?"

"The child is due in December, so I understand. She is blooming, and grown quite plump and contented. I hope and pray all goes well with her."

Polly could not imagine Sam's spoilt, petulant daughter being contented, but she had heard that pregnancy could sometimes have that effect. She let him continue to describe Mary's devoted husband and comfortable life, and his hopes for her future, before asking, "So what brings you to London, Sam? Business?"

"Of course. I hope to find a supplier of cottons and fine linens, the merchant with whom I have most recently been dealing is elderly and plans to sell off his stock and retire to the country. You do not happen to know of any such? Of course," he added with a smile, "that is not the only reason. It is always a pleasure to come to the Paradise and see you, Polly – and Dark and Gin and Hannah and everyone else."

"And it is a pleasure to see you, Sam, you will always be more than welcome here. How long do you plan to stay?"

"A few days, perhaps a week? It depends on how long it will take me to find a suitable merchant and come to an arrangement that will satisfy us both. I have an appointment in a couple of hours with a man in Cheapside who has been recommended to me, an importer of undyed Indian calicos, but I thought I would pay my respects to you first."

"Thank you! And is there anything we can do to entertain you while you are here? *The Duke of Guise, or The Massacre of Paris,* is playing at Drury Lane tonight. It is a tragedy, but supposed to be acted well, and besides, it is so hot against Catholics that it has not been performed for many years, so you are bound to approve."

"I have no particular animosity towards Catholics, so long as they are loyal subjects of King George," Sam assured her. "But I have not seen a play since last year, and I shall much look forward to it."

*

It had been an interesting evening, Polly thought, as the players left the stage to considerable applause, and even a nosegay of flowers thrown to Mrs Christiana Horton, the leading actress. True, the theatre was not above half empty, but the audience had been appreciative, and the play was full of eloquent drama and high sensibility, notwithstanding the tragic ending. Sam had insisted on paying for a front box, and he and Polly had a splendid view of the action, even if, close to, Mrs. Horton was not quite the dewy young maiden she would appear from the upper gallery.

Even with the reduced audience, it took some while to leave the theatre and gain the fresh summer evening air outside, where they met up with Gin and Dan, who had been in the lower gallery, also paid for by Sam. Gin duly declared her appreciation for his generosity. "I likes a deserved death!" she said, with considerable relish. "Thank you, Mr. Jessop, that was proper kind of you."

"It was my pleasure. An excellent play. It was, I fear, a little far-fetched in parts, but nevertheless it held my interest."

"That demon certainly weren't very likely," Gin continued. "I ain't seen no fiends from hell traipsing about London lately, have you? Still less one that talks in *poetry*." This last word was said with deep contempt.

"It's a play, Jane," Polly reminded her. "It's not intended to resemble real life."

"I knows that, madam, I ain't soft in the head."

"*Jane*!"

"I'd rather have seen a comedy," said Gin, unrepentant. "I likes a comedy what'll make me laugh." She was evidently of the opinion that there was quite enough demonic behaviour already in London, without adding a supernatural element.

"Comedies should make you laugh," Sam pointed out with a smile. "And next time, I promise you it will be a comedy. Now, Dan, did you remember to book a chair for me? And a link-boy?"

"Yes, Mr. Jessop," said the boy, gesturing to where a sedan waited, illuminated by a scrawny child carrying a torch, on the corner where Playhouse Passage gave onto Bridges Street. "Best hurry over, sir, or someone else'll nab it."

Indeed, the throng was considerable in the narrow confines of the Passage, and several voices were bawling

"Chair! Chair!" Sam took Polly's arm and steered her through the press. She kept a sharp eye on the shifting figures around her, for this was an ideal opportunity for thieves, while Gin and Dan hastened on to make sure of the chair. Just as they reached the fringes of the crowd, someone bumped into her, so hard that even with Sam's support she gasped in dismayed surprise and almost lost her balance. She felt a fumbling at her side, near the slit for her pocket, and then Dan shouted something and in a flash he and Gin were off in pursuit.

"Polly!" Sam exclaimed. "Polly, what is it?"

"A cutpurse, I think – Dan's gone after him, and Gin too." As Polly turned to see what was happening, she felt something slither down the folds of her gown. Just in time, she bent and caught it.

"What's that?"

Something small, and quite light. She looked down at it, but could not discern much detail in the flickering dusk. "I don't know," she said. "Whoever bumped into me must have dropped it." She paused for a moment, thinking, and then added aloud, "Or given it to me. Sam, let us move closer to the linkboy, so I can see."

The package proved to be a small bag fastened with a drawstring. Polly opened it and tipped the contents out into her palm. A folded square of paper, and a locket on a cheap chain.

She knew that locket.

"Got him!" Gin and Dan returned in a rush, pushing a small snivelling urchin in front of them. As soon as he saw Polly, he whined, "I didn't do nothing, I swear it!"

"You're a thieving cutpurse and known for it, Dicky Barton," said Dan contemptuously. He had been a linkboy like Gin, and Polly had employed him on her maid's recommendation. Although since then he had behaved impeccably, obviously conscious of the good fortune that had removed him from the streets, she had always suspected that his past life had not been free of crime. The child Dicky's next words confirmed it. "You ain't so lily white yourself, Dan Wicks."

"Quiet," said Polly, before Dan could respond. She addressed herself to Dicky, and held out the bag, the locket and the paper. "Did you give me this?"

Dicky nodded, and wiped his nose with the back of his hand. A bruise was coming up on his face, and the front of his ragged shirt was splattered with filth. "Didn't take nothing off you, Mrs. Paradice, on my honour!"

Gin snorted. Polly gestured sharply at her, and turned back to the child. "I know you didn't. But tell me – who gave you this bag, and told you to pass it to me?"

"Don't know his name, never seen him before. Short gundiguts in a full wig. He was asking who knew you, and I said I did, 'cos I used to light your chair sometimes. So he gave me the bag and sixpence and told me to slip it to you without you knowing."

"Well, you couldn't even manage that, could you?" Dan said scornfully, but Gin nudged him in the ribs. "Hold your noise, he's just a little dandiprat."

"Thank you, Dicky. I'm sorry that Gin and Dan were a little rough with you, but they thought you had stolen from me." She fumbled in her purse, and drew out two sixpences. "You may have these for your trouble."

"*Thank* you, ma'am!" Dicky secreted the coins somewhere within his ragged coat, and made a surprisingly competent bow. "Your humble and obedient servant forever!" And before he could suffer any more abuse from Dan, he turned and ran off down Bridges Street, towards the Strand.

"Sir!" It was one of the chairmen, a big burly man with a strong Irish accent. "Would you be wanting us still?"

"Just a moment, if you please," said Sam, and turned back to Polly. "I don't understand – is this your locket?"

"Yes." Polly opened it with her thumbnail. Inside, each neatly plaited, were three strands of hair, one dark, one chestnut brown, one lighter: herself, Mattie and Tom. She closed it and took a deep breath, feeling herself begin to tremble as the full import of it struck. "This is the locket I gave to Mattie in Amesbury, and I told her that if she was ever in trouble, she should send it to me, and I would help her. Though I don't know why she did not address it to me at the Paradise, I gave her that direction. Perhaps she had forgotten it."

"Is there something written on the paper?"

There was one scrawled word. The three ill-formed letters swam and flickered in the light of the link-boy's torch. Bewildered, Polly said, "Rye?"

Gin was peering round her shoulder. "Rye bread," she said helpfully.

"What would rye bread have to do with Mattie needing my assistance?"

"There is a town called Rye," Sam said. "It's a little port, rather decayed now, down on the south coast, near Hastings."

"Ain't never heard of neither of them," said Gin.

"Nor I." Polly turned the paper over and over, but it offered no further clues. "But if there is a place called Rye, then I am sure that is what this must mean. She is in Rye, and in trouble."

"Sir," said the chairman again, more forcefully this time. "Will you be wanting us, or shall we carry that gentleman over there?"

If Sam did not take this chair, there might be a long wait for another, and as darkness had fallen, Polly did not want him to return to his inn in Holborn alone and on foot. She swallowed her fear and anxiety for her sister, and spoke briskly. "Yes, he will take it now. Sam, come to the Paradise tomorrow morning, and we can talk about this then. And do not protest, I insist on it."

"As you wish," said Sam, plainly unhappy about it. "But will you be all right, Polly? This is very distressing for you –"

"Yes, Sam, please take the chair and the link boy – I shall be perfectly fine, it is a very short distance back to King Street, and I have Gin and Dan with me. I will see you tomorrow – at nine o'clock? Until then, goodbye." She gestured to the two servants and turned away to end the argument.

But as they walked along Russell Street to the Piazza, Dan carrying a lantern to light their way, she could hardly supress her sense of dread. *Oh, Mattie,* she thought, *Mattie, what has happened to you?*

*

"Good morning, Polly," said Sam, coming into her parlour at the appointed hour. "Forgive me for saying so, but you do not look as if you have slept much."

"Oh, Sam, I hardly think I have slept at all! I have told Gin to bring coffee upstairs as soon as she sees you come in – is all in hand?" She came over to give him a kiss of greeting. "And I have to say, I do not think you look particularly spritely yourself. Pray sit down, you are quite pale."

Sam took the chair opposite her, the one in which Dark usually sat. He nodded to the little round table beside her. "Is that the locket? May I see it? The light did not allow me to have a close inspection last night."

Lying in her bed in the wakeful hours with her mind revolving hideous possibilities and dangers, Polly had held it clutched tightly in her hand, as if by doing so she could keep her sister safe. She passed it over to him, and watched as he turned it over. "Does it open?"

"Yes, quite easily. Slip your thumbnail between the two covers."

Sam looked down at the three plaited locks of hair within. "Do these belong – "

"They are mine, and Mattie's, and Tom's. The locket was my mother's. It's – it's ..." For a moment she thought her voice would fail her, and then she found the strength to continue. "She gave it to me as she lay dying, and I hid it because the poor law commissioners would have taken anything of value off me, to pay for our keep. It is the only memento of my family that I possess."

He handed it back to her, and she slipped it over her head. The cheap chain would look tawdry alongside her pearls, but she did not care.

"And the paper?"

"I have looked at it over and over again, I have turned it every possible way, I have held it up against the light and I've held it over a candle, and there is still only one word on it. Here you are, study it for yourself."

After careful perusal, Sam nodded. "You are right, there is no sign that anything else has ever been written on it. So, it must mean that she is in Rye."

"How long would it take, to get there? Are there coaches?"

"I don't know, for I have never been there myself. But it should not be difficult to find out. I take you are planning to go?"

"Of course I must go there to find her, what else can I do? You have not met her, so you will not know her character – she seems quite a prickly and defensive person, proud, unwilling to accept help. If she has sent me this, it is a sign that she is in desperate need. I can't ignore it."

"I understand that, Polly, but have you considered that if your sister is in danger, so you may be putting yourself in harm's way yourself?"

That was one of the fears that had kept her awake for much of the night, but there were plenty of other possibilities. Polly shook her head. "I am not concerned about that. I *must* help her, whatever she has done or has happened. I also gave her a valuable ring, perhaps she has been accused of stealing it – in which case, the sooner I go to Rye, the better."

"And I will come with you."

"Sam! You do not have to do that! I know what Dark would say – "

"And so do I." He smiled at her. "I suspect the words 'gadling', and 'wild-goose-chase', and quite possibly 'fool's errand' would be used. No matter. You cannot go to Rye on your own, without an escort."

"So you really are going to this Rye place, then, Madam?" Gin demanded, coming in at that moment with a laden tray. "Well, never fear, you won't be on your own, because I'll be with you, of course."

Polly and Sam looked at each other, and despite her fears, Polly could not help a snort of laughter. Gin glared at them, offended. "I can look after Madam, better than most people."

"I know that, Jane," Polly said. "But there may be danger."

"So? I learned things when I was a lad that you wouldn't

want to know about, but they'd be more'n useful in a tight corner."

"I will be travelling too," Sam put in hastily. Gin cast him a glance of withering contempt. "I never knew you was handy in a fight, Mr. Jessop!"

Sam ignored her. "Polly, you have not replied – would you permit me to accompany you to Rye to find your sister?"

"Of course, Sam, you would be most welcome!"

"Then when we have finished our breakfast, I will return to the Black Swan and make enquiries about coaches to Rye, they are certain to know, or to know of where I may find the answer. I suspect there may not be a direct service, it is a very small place and much out of the way. It is possible that we will have to make the journey on horseback. Let us hope the weather will be more pleasant than it has been of late."

"That is very kind of you, Sam." Polly poured out the coffee and handed him the dish. "But I have to say, I do wish I knew where Dark is. He seems to have vanished into thin air."

"If anyone knows, it'll be Madame Rousselle," said the irrepressible Gin. "Shall I go round to Half Moon Street and ask her?"

"That will not be necessary," said Polly. "But a good idea, nonetheless. Sam, when we have finished our coffee, can you spare half an hour or so to walk there with me?"

The redoubtable Madame Marie Rousselle was Dark's landlady, and a relic of a bygone and very much less polite age even than this. She had probably been born plain Mary Russell, but had appeared on the London stage at a time when French names were all the fashion. As a reward for, as she bluntly put it, lying on her back, her aristocratic (or perhaps even royal) lover had bestowed on her the freehold of the tall house in Half Moon Street, just off The Strand, and no more than a few minutes' walk from the Paradise. Here she held court, attended by a small staff of bullied but well-paid servants, and drawing news and gossip into her rather unsavoury web. Polly, walking down Bedford Street on Sam's arm (Gin, despite her protests, had been left behind to help Hannah with the morning rush in the coffee house), could not help but feel a little apprehensive about this imminent encounter with a woman she admired for her shrewdness and indomitable spirit, but could not like. Madame Rousselle saw altogether too much too sharply, and had a penchant for pertinent and very unwelcome questions.

The footman John, an old acquaintance of Gin, answered her brisk knock, wearing the carnation and yellow livery which displayed his employer's lamentable lack of taste. He bowed them inside, and bade them wait while Madame was at her morning toilette. Polly and Sam sat bolt upright on old-fashioned, uncomfortable chairs in the lady's saloon, hardly daring to exchange glances, let alone converse, in case they were surprised by their hostess. Dark occupied the top floors of the house, with living quarters, the long attic where he painted, and a large room like this one where he exhibited his finished work for his customers' approval. Polly could picture his lodgings only too clearly, all perhaps now in darkness, the shutters closed, the paints congealed and the bed cold. Since entering the house, her longing for his presence beside her, which she had managed, more or less successfully, to suppress during daylight hours, had grown to a physical ache, as if she had been sorely wounded. Where was he? And was he, like Mattie, perhaps in danger?

"Madame will see you now," the footman announced, with a bow and a look of complete disdain which Polly knew to be hypocritical in the extreme: no-one who had once worked at the notorious Hole in the Wall tavern was entitled to give himself such airs. She and Sam rose to their feet and, with some trepidation, walked into Madame Rousselle's bedchamber.

Although today there was no fire burning, the room seemed to have absorbed and increased all the warmth from the sun streaming in through the east-facing windows. The lady sat stiffly in an upholstered chair, propped up by fat velvet cushions, her stick in her hand. She wore the hideous scarlet wig which Polly remembered from their previous meetings, and a fashionable floral wrapping gown which would have looked much better on a young girl. Her eyes, faded but still sharp and malicious, travelled from Polly to Sam and back again. "Who's this?" she demanded.

"Samuel Jessop, at your service, ma'am." Sam made an elaborate leg. "I believe we have met, some months ago."

"Ah, yes, I remember now. You're Dark's friend. Well, you won't find him here."

"We know that, Madame," said Polly patiently. "But we would very much like to know where he is."

"Why ask me? I'm not his keeper." Madame Rousselle opened a little silver box on the table beside her. She took a pinch of snuff, inhaled, and only then proffered the box to Sam. He politely declined, and she shut it with a snap and put it back on the table. "One of those puritanical Dissenters, are you?"

"No, ma'am, I am not, but I prefer a pipe."

"As you wish. Your loss." The old lady surveyed them. "So you want to know where he's gone, do you? Well, I can't tell you. Unless he's at his sister's in Richmond still."

"I believe he is not," Polly said, stalwartly resisting the urge to shake Madame until her remaining teeth fell out of her head. "He sent me a note saying that he had been called away on business."

"And we all know what kind of business *that* might be, do we not? When was that?"

"About three weeks ago, if I recall it right."

"Hm. He could be anywhere in this world – or the next. Don't look so downcast, girl, you know as well as I do that he's got more lives than a cat." She leaned forward avidly. "Why d'you want him, anyway? Lovesick, are you?" She glanced meaningfully at Sam. "Well, when the cat's away ..."

Polly saw her companion blush, and felt her irritation rising. She fought it down with an effort. "Of course not. But I may have to go into the country on family business, and I wish to let him know where I am."

"Well, you can write a note for him, and I'll see he gets it when – if – he returns." She uttered a malicious cackle at the expression on Polly's face. "You need to grow a thicker skin where Dark's concerned, my girl, or you'll fret yourself into an early grave. John? *John!* Fetch quill and ink and paper for Mrs Paradice, and look sharp about it, you whoreson idler."

"I marvel that you can keep your servants so long," said Polly demurely, feeling that she must discharge at least one shot across Madame Rousselle's withered bows.

"Oh, don't waste your pity on him, I pay him well enough to make him deaf and blind to any insult. *Thank you*, John," she added with heavy emphasis, as the footman reappeared, bearing a brass-bound walnut writing box. "On the table if you please. Now leave us."

"Very good, madame," said John, bowing. The old woman beckoned to Polly. "Come here, girl. There's everything you need in this box, so you may write your note."

"Wait!" Polly said to the servant. "Is there also wax?" She had no desire to leave her message unsealed, for Madame Rousselle would doubtless have no scruples about reading it.

"What d'you want wax for?" the old woman demanded.

"I wish my note to be for Dark's eyes only, Madame."

"Pouf! We've become very prim and proper, haven't we, girl? I can tell you, it don't suit you. Yes, there's wax, and you may seal it, more's the pity. John? A candle for Mistress Princum Prancium, since she's so finicking."

As the harassed footman left, Polly picked up the writing box and retreated to her chair. Under Madame Rousselle's inquisitive gaze, she picked out a pen, uncorked the ink, placed the paper on the sloping board, and began to write, not caring when the ink spluttered in her haste and left a trail of blots across the page.

"Dark,

I do not know where you can be found, but I am forced to go into Sussex to a place called Rye to find my sister, who has asked me most urgently for help, though I do not yet know why she has need of me. Sam will be with me, and Jane too. I do not expect us to be away above a week, but if you should return before we do, I beg you have no fears for

Your most faithful servant,

Paradice."

She wrote the date, sanded it, and Sam passed her the candle which John had just brought in. A blob of hot wax, a press of his signet ring, and the letter was safe from Madame's prying eyes.

"Give it here, and I'll make sure he gets it," said the crone, holding out a skeletal hand. Polly kept hold of the note. "If it's all the same to you, Madame, I will leave it in his chamber. After all, you may be indisposed or asleep when he returns, and I wish him to see it as soon as possible."

Madame Rousselle glared at her. "Don't you trust me, you little chit?"

Polly produced her most enchanting smile. "I regret to say, Madame, that I do not."

The old woman gave a delighted screech of laughter. "And you'd be right! Oh, a girl after my own heart, you're more than a match for him – and me! Well, leave it in his chamber, I'm sure you're perfectly familiar with all its nooks and crannies." She cackled lasciviously. "And when he returns, I'll tell him to hunt for it there. Are you going so soon? You will not stay for a dish of tea?"

"I regret that will not be possible, Madame," said Sam apologetically. "We have much to plan and to arrange today, and time is pressing."

"Well, you can come and tell me all about it when you get back. And mind you do, or I'll know the reason why."

"Of course we will," Polly assured her, edging towards the door with the precious note safely in her hand. "And my heartfelt thanks to you, Madame, for your help."

"Pouf!" The old lady waved her hand dismissively. "It was little enough. You know your way to Dark's chamber, of course," she added, with a suggestive leer. "John will show you out when you're done. Good day to you, Mr. Jessop, and *bon voyage* to you both."

It was the work of a moment to run upstairs to Dark's bedchamber on the first floor. Polly glanced around, then propped the note on the plain marble chimneypiece, where he would certainly see it as soon as he entered. Madame Rousselle could no longer climb stairs, so she would be unable to purloin it herself, but there would be nothing to stop her asking John or her maid Sukey to take it. Polly found a shilling in her purse, and smiled at the footman, waiting for her in the hall, as she came back down. She slipped the coin into his hand and said softly, "If Madame asks you to bring you my note, pray tell her that I have hidden it too well and you cannot find it. Mr. Dark will be most displeased if it transpires that it has gone astray."

"Of course, ma'am," John murmured, palming the

shilling into his pocket with the fluidity of long practice. "Good day to you, Mistress Paradice, Mr. Jessop."

"Phew!" said Sam, as they walked back up to King Street. "She is a remarkable old lady, to be sure, but I marvel that Dark has been able to tolerate living under the same roof for so long. For myself, I would find it extraordinarily difficult."

"I do not think their paths cross very often. He is safe from her above stairs, and ill-mannered enough to ignore her except when it suits him. She does not charge him much in the way of rent, so it is a satisfactory arrangement for them both."

"Well, I confess I would not be so content with such a situation, but that is all by-the-way. Polly, my dear, I will leave you here and make enquiries about our journey to Rye, and I hope to see you back at the Paradise in due course. And with any luck, there may be no need of that note, because we will return well before Dark does."

Polly thought that would be less than likely, but decided to hold her peace.

CHAPTER EIGHT

Heav'n grant your Journey safe

If Polly had been asked, a mere two days previously, where she would be standing to take her first view of the town of Rye, she would not have imagined that she would be looking over the rail of a ship, across lurching, murky water, towards a hump of land on the horizon. But she was here, after one of the most miserable journeys she had ever experienced, wondering why she had been mad enough to agree to this. At least Sam had been on a ship before, having voyaged regularly to Holland during his apprenticeship and after, but until Polly had beheld the thin, ominous grey line between the Thames and the sky, she had never even seen the sea, and the same went for Gin, who had turned green before they passed Wapping.

As he had promised, Sam had made enquiries about coaches to Rye, and as he had feared, there were none. The best that could be hoped for was to take one to Tonbridge, and hire horses there for the onward journey, nearly forty miles, to Rye. It would take at least two full days, and the weekly coach to Tonbridge had left the previous day. However, so the landlord of the Black Swan had informed him, the *Susannah* of Rye was at present loading below London Bridge, and would be sailing on the morning tide tomorrow with a varied cargo and room, if they did not mind the limited space, for three passengers.

The *Susannah* was an elderly hoy, small enough to be berthed alongside at St. Saviour's dock in Southwark, rather than being anchored out in the river downstream. Polly had surveyed her bluff bows and air of sturdy competence and felt reassured, but Gin, unusually pale and quiet, said dubiously, "It's not very big."

"Hoys are built for the coasting trade," Sam informed

her. "So they can enter small harbours and shallow waters. They're not intended for sailing to the New World."

"I don't want to sail to Rye," Gin muttered miserably. "Why couldn't we go on the coach?"

"Because it would take too long," said Polly. "Of course, you may return to the Paradise if you wish, I'm sure Hannah will find plenty for you to do while I am away."

As she had expected, this cured the girl's grumbles, and she climbed carefully on board, her bundle clutched tightly in one hand and the other clinging to the rail. A burly young sailor helped Polly, and Sam, not the most agile of men, followed them. They were welcomed aboard by a tall, pot-bellied man in a worn blue coat, who introduced himself as Captain Oake. A small boy showed them through a hatch and down a ladder to two tiny cabins at the back of the ship – or, as Sam informed her, aft. He would have the smaller, and Polly and Gin would share the other. From the trunk and boxes shoved into one corner, it seemed that they had displaced one of the sailors, perhaps even the captain himself, but Polly had paid handsomely for their passage at such short notice, and could not feel guilty about it. There was a bunk made up with sheets and blankets, and a pallet on the floor for Gin, who looked about her in some alarm. "How long are we going to be on this here boat, Madam? I thought you said it was a short voyage!"

"It depends on the wind, so I understand, but I'm hoping we will spend just one night on board. If we went by land, we could not do the distance in a day. With luck, we should see Rye tomorrow evening."

"I'll believe it when I sees it," Gin muttered.

The ebb tide and a westerly breeze carried them down the Thames. Polly had taken a river boat to Greenwich several times, once with Robbie, then more often with Dark, and walked in the pleasant park there. She stood on deck, watching the banks flow smoothly past, pointing out some of the landmarks to Sam, whose ventures overseas had always begun at Harwich. Gin, groaning and tinged with green, had stayed in the cabin, and Polly had found her a bucket, just in case.

As the buildings of Greenwich disappeared behind them, the river broadened and the banks became low and marshy, the hills more distant. With little of note to see, Polly turned her attention to the *Susannah*, sailing merrily along with the wind filling her sails and the thick brown Thames water rippling along her tarred sides. Now, Sam was able to tell her that this hoy was around a hundred tons burthen, and crewed by half a dozen men and a couple of boys. She had been built in Rye and under Captain Oake, a native of that town, she traded with London, Southampton and other south coast ports, as well as the Low Countries and France.

"And what her cargo might be when she crosses the Channel, who can say?" Sam had glanced quickly round before speaking these words. "It's against the law to export raw wool to France, to protect our weavers, but there's so much profit in it, it's more than worth the risk. In any case, there are very few revenue men to prevent them. And in France, they can load up with wine and brandy and tobacco, all very cheaply, and sell it here for handsome prices."

Polly thought of that surprisingly good wine which she had recently tasted, offered to her by people as diverse as Jenny Garnet, Amos Crowley, and Lady Oglethorpe, and wondered if it had all been smuggled on vessels like the *Susannah*. Very probably it had.

"And what is more interesting still," Sam continued, in the same low voice, "apparently sometimes the ships carry hidden, human cargo. The Jacobites in France still plot against King George, and they send their spies over to England to encourage rebellion."

Suddenly, it all began to make sense. Jenny Garnet was a Jacobite sympathiser, and as a native of London, had family, friends and acquaintances everywhere. The Oglethorpe household was Jacobite, according to Gin, and Dark had said that Crowley was a Jacobite agent. It was a warm day, but Polly shivered. Did Mattie's plea for help have something to do with Jacobite conspiracy? Had she discovered some plot and thereby put herself in danger?

"How do you know all this?" she asked softly.

"The landlord of the Black Swan is beyond garrulous, indeed if you do not take care he will keep you listening all day, and his wife is a native of Kent – from Deal, I think he said. When he heard I wished to go to Rye, he not only told me about the *Susannah,* but was happy to give me more information about the town than ever I had needed - or indeed desired."

Captain Oake was approaching them. He bowed politely, and asked them if their accommodation was adequate, apologising for the cramped and spartan conditions. Polly gave him her most charming smile, while wondering if this pleasant, apparently ordinary man with his weathered face and calloused hands could possibly be a dangerous smuggler. "How long do you think this voyage will take, sir?"

"Ah, that depends on the wind, Mrs. Paradice. It's at our backs now, as we sail down river, but once we reach the sea we'll need to round the North Foreland, and beat south past Ramsgate and into the Downs. If it hasn't changed to a more favourable direction by then, we'll let anchor and wait for it to change, for we can't head straight into it. All being well, we'll reach Rye by tomorrow evening, but alas, I have no power over wind or tide."

"Then I shall pray for a wind that's fair and following," Polly said. She glanced up at the huge mainsail, which was drawing nicely in the breeze. "You have a fine and commodious ship, sir."

Captain Oake beamed with pride. "She is certainly as excellent as I had hoped for, when I bought her not two years ago – as sweet and responsive as a good woman."

"I am glad to hear it," said Polly, as sweetly and responsively as she could manage, though the Captain was looking at her earnestly, with an expression in his eyes that she had frequently seen before. "Tell me, sir, what cargo are you carrying?"

"On this voyage, chiefly goods that have been ordered from merchants in London by various gentlemen and ladies of Rye. Barrels of tobacco and pipestaves, glassware, china, wines from Portugal and Spain, even a dining table and chairs for Mrs Tucker, who was the widow of Samuel Jeake, one of our most prominent citizens, but is now married again."

"No French wines?" Polly asked mischievously.

Captain Oake shook his head. "No, I regret that the tariff on French wines is too high. A pity, for they are usually the best and most popular. Now, if you will excuse me, sir, madam, I must attend to my ship."

"Polly, you are very wicked," Sam said, once the Captain was out of earshot. "You were insinuating that he was a smuggler."

"I was not!" Polly looked at him with mock indignation, and then laughed. "Yes, of course I was. And you noticed, I hope, that he did not like it."

"Smugglers are ruthless men, and do not scruple to threaten or even harm those who might betray them to the Revenue. We should be very careful."

"Indeed we must, for these are murky waters we are about to swim in, I think, murkier even than the Thames above the bridge, and if I am to find and help my sister, I must gather all the information I can."

"I know that, but you must not rouse people's suspicions, or they will be less likely to assist you."

"I know that too, but I hope he took me for a frivolous, empty headed gill-flirt." Polly looked up at the sunlit sky, the gulls crying overhead, the grubby white sails of the *Susannah* urging the little ship downriver, and sighed. "It is a guise that has served me well in the past. Most men do not expect a woman to have any intelligence or cunning, and most are susceptible to the most shameless flattery."

"Your view of us is disappointing, but I suspect it is deserved."

"I do not include you or Dark in my censure, of course. You are both the exceptions that prove the rule. I have only survived and flourished because I have been prepared to employ whatever weapons I have at my disposal, to keep me safe. And if that means that I stand accused of exploiting my looks and my wits in the process, then so be it."

The river slipped past them, growing ever broader, with gleaming grey mud flats and featureless marshes on either side. They passed big merchantmen bound for London and anchored to wait for the wind and tide to turn more favourable, and large numbers of smaller craft, fishers and ferries, nimble and speedy despite the breeze against them. Sam pointed out the sails fore and aft of their masts, like those the *Susannah* carried, and told her that such a rig meant that they were much more manoeuvrable, since they did not rely so greatly on the wind's direction.

Towards noon, Polly went down to check on Gin, and found her looking a little better. She persuaded her to come up on deck, and the girl clung to the rail and watched with a mixture of fascination and terror as the *Susannah,* tide-borne, sailed on towards the sea. Soon, she had so far forgotten her sickness as to sample some of the bread and cheese they were offered by the ship's boy, a barefoot, wiry lad with his hands already calloused by constant handling of the ropes. But as their union with the sea approached, the water growing choppier and the *Susannah* beginning to pitch and roll, Gin uttered a strangled exclamation, her hand over her mouth. Sam knew what to do: he rushed her over to the side furthest from the wind, held her while she vomited copiously into the Thames, and then made her walk down to the bows of the ship, with a leather bucket beside her, and concentrate her gaze on the distant grey line of the sea.

Polly was not so badly affected, but when the *Susannah*'s movements became more exaggerated, she went over to her maid at the bow and left Sam to admire the work of the crew as they bustled around the deck, hauling on ropes and setting the small square tops'l high on the mast. As they approached the open sea, the waves grew stronger and the little ship bucked and plunged like an eager horse, the spray flying onto her deck, and Polly forgot about dignity and decorum for several hours, and joined Gin in misery.

Much later in the afternoon, however, she became aware of different noises and different motions: the deck had left off heaving, and her innards, in sympathy, were likewise settling down. She looked up and saw that the mast was no longer tossing wildly against the sky, and that men were busy furling the sails.

"Polly, my dear?" Sam was bending over her. "Polly, how do you feel?"

She was cold and wet, her limbs were stiff, her throat was sore with so much voiding, and her stomach was scoured empty. But from somewhere, she managed a faint smile. "I do a little better, thank you, Sam, now the wind and waves are not so violent. In fact ..." She paused, wondering at herself, and then continued, "In fact, I feel almost hungry. Are we come to

Rye?"

"Bless you, no, we are in the Downs, off the coast of Deal, and the wind is not in our favour at present, so we have dropped anchor to wait for it to turn." He offered her his hand, and Polly took it gratefully and allowed him to help her to her feet. She looked around with interest. The *Susannah* was indeed at rest now, and everywhere, for as far as Polly could see, many other ships large and small were also lying idle on the gently swelling waters. Gulls swooped and cried around them, and the sun sparkled on the blue sea and lit the distant land. It was a very pleasant sight, and for the first time that afternoon, Polly could appreciate it.

The wind, however, continued to blow inconsiderately from the west, and brought clouds and rain before sunset. They ate supper sitting in a row on Polly's bunk, enjoying bread and cheese, a meat pie and an apple tart, all washed down with more of the surprisingly good red wine. That night, they all slept well, and woke to the motion of the ship, much gentler than it had been on the previous day, as the *Susannah* began the second leg of her voyage. Hurrying up to the wet, gleaming deck, Polly saw that the rain had ceased, the rising sun was shining, and the wind had changed. And an hour or so after noon, they rounded the dangerous shingle point of Dengeness, jutting out into the sea, and crept carefully up through the treacherous shifting sands of Rye Bay, towards the distant town on its hump of rock.

Polly glanced from side to side as the land narrowed to a funnel around them. Where, amongst these shingle banks, the furtive spits of sand, the desolate empty marshes, was Mattie? Was she even still living? Or had Crowley, a man she neither liked nor trusted, done away with her because she knew too much?

She was being ridiculous. The most likely possibility, if her sister were truly in trouble and in need of help, was that she had been suspected of theft because of the sapphire ring which Polly had given her in Amesbury. In which case, she would merely have to explain the truth to the constable or the magistrate, and Mattie would be exonerated and freed. Polly could not imagine her defensive, prickly sister being overcome with gratitude to the extent that she would be persuaded to leave Crowley's troupe and join her in London. But at least she would be safe.

The sun was beginning to sink towards the cliffs and hills of the land stretching away to the west before they reached Rye at last. It had been a cautious creep between mud flats and marsh on a turning tide and an almost imperceptible wind, with a man at the bow calling directions to the steersman, and the town piled up, house above house, on the hill ahead of them, with the church tower and its short steeple crowning all. But after many twists and turns, they came at last to the wharf, with huts and warehouses, a crane, and a variety of other boats already moored alongside. Everything had the rather ramshackle air of a place that had seen better days, and small hope of them returning.

There was, however, much bustle on the quayside, and plenty of men and boys ready to help the *Susannah* as she approached her berth, which had obviously been cleared for her. Polly wondered how they had known of her arrival, and then remembered that the hoy's approaching sails must have been plainly visible from the town, almost as soon as she entered Rye Bay. Within a very short time, the vessel was securely moored, a boarding plank in position, and the Captain was beside them to bid them farewell.

Sam thanked him for his care of them during the voyage, and asked if he knew of a suitable inn where they could stay. Neither he nor Polly had divulged their reason for visiting Rye, and although Oake was obviously curious, he had not asked. Now, he said promptly, "Most strangers to the town go to the Mermaid, the George, or the Red Lion. They're all comfortable, respectable places, but if you mention my name to Will Bird, he'll see you're well looked after. He's a good friend of mine." At Sam's assent, he turned and beckoned to a scrawny young man on the quayside, standing hopefully beside a barrow. "Malachi! See these good people to the Mermaid, will you?"

Polly set her feet on dry land with a sensation of profound relief. Even in their relatively smooth final progress up the river, she had felt unsettled and disturbed by the slight motion of the ship beneath her. Strangely, however, the act of walking on hard ground, after more than thirty hours afloat, was almost as difficult as moving around on the *Susannah* had been, when she was rolling and pitching in the turbulent sea, and she held tight to Sam's arm, while Gin looked as if she would have liked to have kissed the quayside, even though it was wet and filthy with fish guts, and spangled with scales. She said urgently, "Madam, please, as the Lord's my witness, I ain't never going on a ship again as long as I live. I'll walk every step of the way back to London, as long as I don't have to get back on that boat."

Polly forbore to laugh, because she had much the same feelings herself. "You need not fear, Jane, I suspect we will be returning home by horse and coach, since I hope that there will not be the same need for haste."

"Thank the Lord for that!" said her maid fervently.

One of the *Susannah*'s crew had loaded their bags into the barrow, and the little procession set off. The river curved round the base of the hill on which Rye was set, and they must climb up into the town. The way led through a crumbling old stone gate, flanked by two towers, and looking as if it was about to fall down on their heads. Malachi, however, wheeled the barrow underneath it with no anxious glance upwards, and began to ascend the steep cobbled street beyond it. Most of the houses here were built in an older style, with crooked half-timbering and whitewashed plaster, though here and there Polly saw new brick and large, fashionable windows. She noticed one ancient but particularly imposing edifice, tall and wide, capped by three gables, with a shallow step up to a studded oak door. As they passed, it opened and a girl, perhaps a couple of years younger than Gin, emerged. Unlike Gin, however, this child was obviously no servant: although she wore a plain dress of russet cotton, it was topped by a kerchief of fine muslin, and her cap was edged with lace. She looked at them curiously, and then turned back towards the open door, calling for someone. Polly, her attention diverted, stumbled on an uneven cobblestone and would have fallen but for Sam's steadying hand. When she glanced back at the house, the girl was walking briskly down the street towards the harbour, with a woman who was probably a servant hurrying behind her, carrying a basket.

Their destination proved to be a large and handsome building, despite its obvious age, with a spacious courtyard and stables at the rear. They were welcomed by Mr. Bird, the landlord, a big man with the inn-keeper's professional affability. Within a very short time, they had been accommodated in two splendid chambers on the first floor, accessed by their own staircase, and food had been brought up to them by a cheerful young maid who was evidently very curious about their new guests. Indeed, the girl, whose name was Mercy, went so far as to enquire of Polly why she was in Rye. "For our visitors mostly be furrin gentlemen here on business, begging your pardon, ma'am."

Polly had known that this sort of question was bound to come, and had pondered it at intervals all that day. Despite what Sam had said, she had decided to be fairly open about the reason for her coming. If that was risky, then so be it: she was too anxious to find Mattie as quickly as possible, to tiptoe daintily round the subject. So she said, "I have travelled here on a matter of some urgency – I am trying to find my young sister, who I fear may be in trouble."

"Indeed, ma'am?" The maid's eyes were bright with interest. "What sort of trouble?"

"That's the problem – I do not know. She has fallen in with a disreputable band of strolling players, and –"

"Players, ma'am? They were here last week, in the Red Lion's courtyard. I wish they'd have stayed longer, but they only played one night, so many on the Corporation are Dissenters, and they don't like plays and players because they lead the young men into the paths of wickedness. So they made them move on."

Polly thought of that innkeeper in Salisbury, who had expressed very similar views. She said, "Do you know where they have gone now?"

"I heard they were going to Appledore, ma'am, and then on to Romney and then Lydd I do believe. They may be there still."

"Are those towns far away? I'm a stranger here, and I don't know how the land lies."

"No, ma'am, Appledore be an hour's ride away, no more, to Romney a little further, and from there south to Lydd be no more than three miles, and back to Rye two more hours, because there bain't no bridge across the river, and you must take the ferry. But you could ride it all in less than a day, easily."

"And has there been any trouble here in the town? I have wondered if my sister had been perhaps accused of thieving or suffered some other mishap."

Mercy shook her head emphatically. "No, ma'am, there's been nothing of that sort here to my certain knowledge. Of course, she might have been taken up in some other town perhaps, I think they played in Hastings afore, but I've a brother there working on the fishing, and he was here two days ago and had no news of that sort."

Polly thanked her with a sixpence, and the girl curtseyed and withdrew. Gin went next door to summon Sam, and they sat down to a pleasant meal of roast meats, a raised pie, a compote of stewed apples with cream and sugar, and a lemon posset. Once they had assuaged their hunger and thirst with good food and, again, surprisingly good wine, Polly told Sam what the maid had said.

"So your sister is not in Rye." Sam, replete, leaned back in his chair and folded his hands over his generous stomach. "Or so it would appear."

"The girl could have been lying," put in Gin, who in this private space was very much part of the discussion.

"I don't think she was," Polly said thoughtfully. "Not everyone is as devious as you, Jane. There are still some innocents in the world, and she is one of them, I believe."

"Well, if we assume she is telling the truth, there are several possibilities. First." Sam began to tick them off on his fingers. "That your sister is not in trouble at all, but wishes for some reason to bring you here. Second, that she is indeed in trouble with the law, but not here in Rye."

"Then why did she write Rye on the paper?" demanded Gin.

"Well, yes. And there is a third possibility – that she is in trouble, but not with the law. We know that Rye is concerned with the smuggling trade. Perhaps she has knowledge that has put her in danger."

"None of it seems very likely," Polly said, after an unhappy pause. "It is all so far-fetched and fanciful."

"I agree," said Sam. "And I think our first action should be to find these players, and see if they know anything. After all, this may be one of Dark's wild-goose-chases, and the odds are that your sister is still with them and perfectly safe and sound."

"Then we should ride out tomorrow," Polly said decisively. "I am sure there will be horses for hire here. And go to Lydd first, so that hopefully we shall meet them rather than forever be chasing after them."

"I have no idea where Lydd is," Sam pointed out.

"Nor have I, but we can ask. After all, there are only a limited number of directions in which we can go. South or east, you must inevitably come to the sea."

"And I ain't going on no boat for love nor money," Gin muttered resentfully.

It turned out, however, that there would be no alternative. The maid Mercy came back to clear away their plates, and Polly asked her how they would get to Lydd.

"You go through the Landgate and up to Saltcotes," said the girl, pausing in her careful stacking of the crockery on her wooden tray. "And you take the ferry cross the river, and ride eastwards 'long the Marsh till you come to Lydd. Bain't so far. And you can't miss Lydd, ma'am, the church tower sails over all the land like a ship."

"A ferry?" As Polly spoke the word, Gin looked aghast. Polly ignored her. "Is the way clear to see? Are there signposts?"

"I doubt that, madam, for all the roads on the Marsh are changeable, because of the sea and the dykes and the ponds – or fleets, as we call them here. But you can ask at Guldeford, that's the village you come to on the other side of the ferry. Or Mr. Bird will give you directions, his sister lives in Lydd."

"And horses?" Sam enquired. "We will need to hire horses."

"Mr. Bird has excellent horses for hire, sir, at very reasonable rates."

"But how will they get across the river?"

"Oh, they go on the boat," said Mercy cheerfully. "Don't you worry, sir, all the horses be used to it, and there bain't nobody drownded for years and years."

Polly did not dare look at Gin. She said, "You have been very helpful, Mercy, and I thank you. My father will speak to Mr. Bird later." They had thought it best that she pretend to be Sam's daughter, for reasons of propriety. After all, she bore a close resemblance to his real daughter, and did not look so very much older than Mary, though in fact there were almost ten years between them.

The maid had barely shut the door behind her before Gin said vehemently, "I ain't going on no boat, nor ferry neither, and that's my last word on it." She folded her arms and glared first at Polly and then at Sam. "You can send me to walk back to London if you like, you can send me packing for good and all if you want, but I ain't – going – on – that *ferry,* not if you offered me a golden guinea."

"Well, in that case, since you are so resolved, you may stay here and see what information you can gather, about the players and my sister. But I beg you, Gin, go about it discreetly, for if Mattie really is in trouble with wrong-doers of some kind, we do not want to make matters worse."

"Don't you worry, ma'am," said Gin, whose demeanour had marvellously improved the instant she realised that she would not have to set foot on any boat. "I'll be as careful as ever you could wish."

CHAPTER NINE

Follow you like Pilgrims through the World

Polly, the trailing hem of her riding habit gathered in one hand and her hat in the other, surveyed the Guldeford ferry with considerable misgivings. There was a sturdy, broad-beamed boat moored to the jetty, with room for several passengers and their baggage, and two ferrymen waiting, but where was the horse ferry? She was familiar with the one which took horses and carriages across the Thames from Westminster to Lambeth, and which was a large, well-constructed raft, but there was no such vessel to be seen. The tide was up, were the horses supposed to swim across? She glanced anxiously at Sam, and he gave her a reassuring smile. "If you are concerned about our nags, I suspect they go with us in the boat. It's large enough, after all."

Mr. Bird had assured them that their mounts would board the ferry without a qualm, and so it proved. Her bay and Sam's grey, led by one of the ferrymen, walked steadily along the plank and stepped into the boat as calmly as ladies entering church. The animals stood stock still while they took their seats, avoiding the obvious signs of previous equine or bovine occupancy. Then they were poled across to the other side and the horses were led back onto dry land, before she and Sam disembarked and paid over their coins, fourpence each and a shilling for the two horses. They were on the Marsh, and Lydd, and possibly Mattie, were perhaps only a few miles distant.

Sam helped Polly to mount, and they set off along the lane, pausing to allow a shepherd with half a dozen sheep to go past. Since the narrow road only led to the river, presumably they were planning to cross on the ferry. Polly wondered how the shepherd and the two ferrymen would manage, and was almost tempted to turn and watch the fun, but her need to find Mattie was more important, and she followed Sam towards Lydd.

The directions which Mr. Bird had given them had seemed simple enough, but it soon became obvious that the Marsh was a place where the normal rules of road and water did not apply. Lanes twisted and turned, divided and narrowed, followed the tops of banks or disappeared into stagnant pools, which Mercy had said were called fleets. There were no trees apart from a few stunted, windblown thorns, distorted and pollarded willows or patches of rough scrub and gorse, and only a few isolated houses or shepherd's huts, scattered randomly across the landscape like thrown dice. And everywhere was infested – there was no other word for it – with sheep. Sheep freshly shorn of their valuable wool, ambling down the lanes or resting in the shade of a bush, chewing the cud or busy nibbling the short sweet turf, lambs skipping up and down the turf walls and dykes which drained the Marsh or kept the sea floods at bay, and shepherds, crooks in hand and dogs at heel, looking curiously at the well-dressed gentleman and lady riding past. The bleating filled the air and provided a never-ending accompaniment which followed them through the Marsh, carried on the incessant breeze.

The Mermaid's landlord had drawn a quick sketch map for Sam, but it seemed to bear no relation to the lanes and tracks they encountered. They knew that Lydd lay seven or eight miles to the east of Rye, more or less as the crow might fly, and close to the sea, so there was little chance of becoming completely lost. After a while, though, Polly began to long for even the smallest hill to enliven this flat, desolate country which seemed unable to decide whether it was water, or land, or sometimes both.

They had been riding for nearly two hours by Sam's watch, and she had almost given up hope of ever reaching their destination, when they rounded a bend in the lane they were following, and saw a tall church tower in the distance, sailing above the marshes as Mercy had described, and a huddle of trees, red roofs and thatch about it. It was now nearly noon, and Polly felt suddenly hungry. Would this place boast some kind of inn where they could have something to eat and drink?

It did. The George was a handsome building, constructed of red brick and brown timbers, on the main street near the church. Their tired horses were led away for a rest and water, and Polly and Sam conducted to a private parlour where they partook of cold meats and bread and cheese, washed down with an excellent ale. This time, Sam asked the maidservant about the players, telling her that his 'daughter' had run away to join them.

"They be on the Rype," said the maid promptly. "They came yesterday, and how long they'll stay there, I don't know, but we be mortal glad to see 'em, little enough happens in this place when the Revenue men be about, stopping folk earning an honest living."

Polly had never thought of smuggling as an honest living before, but she let it pass. "The Rype?"

"If you head along south out of town, you'll come to the Rype, be a big open field where we hold the fairs and markets. There be a barn by the edge furthest from the town, belongs to Mr. Finn, and that be where they be playing tonight. They be putting on *The Country Wife*." The girl beamed at them. "And Mr. Blacklocks has said I can go!"

To give the horses more time to rest, they walked to the Rype. As strangers, they attracted considerable interest, and several urchins begging for pennies, though they were obviously much better clad and fed than any in London. Although it was a warm afternoon, Polly was shivering with apprehension. She was desperate to discover what, if anything, had happened to Mattie, though she did not relish the prospect of another encounter with Amos Crowley, otherwise Ambrose Rookwood. He was dangerous, in the same way that Dark was dangerous, a man who kept his power almost hidden, but allowing those who opposed him to see just enough to fear what he could do. He could not be a friend either to her or to her sister, who had seemed to be afraid of him.

They found the Rype easily enough. It was a broad green space on the edge of Lydd, at present grazed by a selection of scrawny cattle, as a change from the ubiquitous sheep. And yes, there was the barn, an ancient arrangement of tarred timbers and mouldering thatch, that looked as if it would fall down in the next stiff breeze. Several horses were tethered in its shade, dozing, and a couple of battered old carts stood nearby, but although there were more children playing in the dust outside, or looking hopefully at the doorway, none of the players were to be seen.

Polly had never been short of audacity. She gave Sam a bright smile, and marched up to the barn's entrance. The big double doors were wide open, and as she stepped inside, a familiar voice cackled. "Well, look what the cat's dragged in!"

It was Peg Ellis, sitting on a stool in a patch of sunlight, a pipe still between her teeth, wearing the same threadbare, filthy clothes that Polly remembered from their previous encounter. She added maliciously, "Want to join up? He'll give you a share of the profits, if there are any, and a place in his bed if you play your cards right."

"I'm looking for my sister," Polly said.

Peg cackled and jabbed the stalk of her pipe at Polly's chest. "You've wasted your time. She ain't here. She's gone."

"Gone?"

"Yes, gone, whistled off, scuddled, fled – whatever you want to call it, she's gone. So you can go. Go on, go, whistle off, scuddle."

Polly stood her ground. She said coldly, "You lied to me before. Why should I believe you now?"

A male voice intruded. "You came to us asking for your sister Martha. We only knew Matt."

Amos Crowley emerged from the shadows at the end of the barn, and came to stand before her. He was even more imposing, and intimidating, than her memory of him. He looked her up and down, his pale gaze lingering insolently on her breasts, even though her riding coat was buttoned up to the Steinkirk neckcloth at her throat, and it took every scrap of her self-control not to shudder. Then his eyes went past her to Sam, standing a few paces behind, and he smiled without using his eyes. "I did not know you had a new lover."

"Sam is a friend." To her fury, Polly knew she was blushing. "He has kindly agreed to help me with my search for my sister."

"Indeed. How very ... kind." Crowley's tone left no doubt as to what he thought of the nature of that kindness. "Well, as Peg has already told you, your sister is here no longer."

"And as I said to her, why should I believe a word of it, when you both lied to me before?"

"But you were looking for Martha," said Crowley, in a voice of sweet reasonableness. "And Martha was not with us then. Matt was. As you discovered. What did you offer *her*, to entice *him* away?"

"I offered her nothing except my love as a sister, and a home, if she so desired it. And she told me she did not."

"Well, I can only assume that she has changed her mind, and left us to find you. If you return to London, you will doubtless find her waiting on your doorstep. It is always a pleasure to see you, Mistress Paradice, but I regret that you and your ... *friend* have had a fruitless journey. I would be happy to spend more time talking with you, but we are getting ready for our play tonight, and if we are to give the good people of Lydd our best performance, we must have another rehearsal. So, my apologies, ma'am, sir, and good day to you both."

He turned away, but Polly said sharply, "Wait!" and had the satisfaction of seeing him wheel around to face her. Before he could speak, she added, "If I am to find her, I need to know – when did she leave? And where? Did she give any warning, or say where she was going?"

For a moment, she thought that he was not going to answer her. His eyes, that penetrating blue she remembered only too well, locked with hers, and she had the troubling sensation that he was playing some game in which he held all the cards, and she had no idea of the rules. Then he smiled suddenly. "Your concern for your sister does you credit, Mistress Paradice. She left us when we were in Rye, last week, and did not say why, or where she planned to go. It caused us great inconvenience, because she was due to play Silvia in *The Recruiting Officer* that night, and Hester had to take it instead, though she much dislikes the breeches parts."

"So, she told no-one of her plans? Does she have any friends in the company?"

"I regret to say that your sister is not the kind to make friends easily."

"All starchness and buckram, you mean," Peg put in, with a malevolent glare in Polly's direction. "Too high on a horse no-one else can see."

"So, she left the company without warning last week while the company was in Rye, she gave no indication of where she was going, she confided her intentions to no-one, and you have not seen her since. Is that the sum of it?"

"It is, ma'am. Now, if you will excuse me, I have much

to do." He turned and disappeared back into the gloom of the barn, where Polly could hear subdued voices and a sudden clatter as if something had been knocked over. She had the sudden, overwhelming urge to see for herself that Mattie was truly not there, and before Sam could stop her, she ran inside.

"Here, you can't do that!" Peg lumbered to her feet, but Polly avoided her clutching hand and followed Crowley to the end of the barn. The light was poor, but it showed her the same huddle of people she had seen in Amesbury months ago. A swift glance told her that Mattie, whether in her male or her female guise, was not amongst them. They stared at her, some with interest, others with hostility, and Bella Wright, attired in a faded blue gown adorned with frills that had been the height of fashion ten years ago, said loudly, "Come to join us, Poll? Well, there ain't no part for you tonight."

"I am looking for my sister Mattie. I know she is no longer with the company, but do any of you have any notion of where she might have gone? I fear she may be in trouble."

"If she is, it's of her own making," said Bella dismissively. "Good riddance."

One of the other women, whose name Polly could not remember, seemed more sympathetic. "She said nothing to me, Mistress Paradice, but I thought afterwards that she might have decided to join you in London. I am sorry I cannot be of more help."

The rest of the company were shaking their heads and looking apologetic. Polly knew she was wasting her time, but she thanked them, and added, "If anyone remembers anything that might be of help, my companions and I are staying at the Mermaid in Rye – "

"Oh, ain't we the dandy!" put in Bella, and Polly was pleased to see that the woman next her nudged her sharply in the ribs and whispered something that caused Miss Wright to frown and turn away.

"We will be there for some days yet, making enquiries," Polly continued.

"Alas, we are engaged to play next at New Romney," said Crowley, who had come up behind her. His voice was smooth and even, but she sensed his anger, barely concealed. "So I doubt that any of us will have the opportunity to visit Rye. However, I thank you for the information, Mistress Paradice."

"And I thank you for your assistance, sir," Polly said, giving him a very brief curtsey that was just the polite side of insolence. "Now I shall bid you all good day, and good fortune tonight."

As she left the barn, with a buzz of talk behind her, she heard Bella Wright's voice raised to carry above it. "And good riddance to you and all, Mrs High-and-mighty Paradice!"

The Marsh air smelt fresh and sweet after the frowsty atmosphere in the barn, and it was a relief to see Sam's familiar smile of concern. "I take it she was not there?"

Polly shook her head. "No. No-one will admit to knowing anything – nothing of where she went, or why. I am so afraid that something terrible has happened to her, and yet I have no means of helping her." She glanced back at the entrance to the barn, but none of the company had appeared. "Let us walk back to the George. There is nothing more to be gained by lingering here. And I want to return to the ferry before dark. I mislike this Marsh, something about it unsettles me. It feels unfriendly, somehow, as if it does not care for us to be here."

"It is not like you to be so fanciful," said Sam. "And of course it is quite untrue, as you well know, Polly."

She laughed, but could not shake off that feeling, even as they walked back across the Rype to comfortable, cosy Lydd, with the sun shining brightly down on them, and the gulls wheeling and crying above, reminder of the nearness of the sea. Sam said thoughtfully, "That man Crowley – I care as little for him as you care for the Marsh, and with better reason. I am not surprised your sister was afraid of him, Polly – I would be. He gives the impression of being a bad man to cross."

"Yes, I think he is." She paused, wondering how much to tell him. But he was her good friend, and there could be no harm in giving him the complete picture. "And that is not all. Dark told me that Crowley is not his real name, and that he is a Jacobite."

"Ah." Sam loaded the single syllable with a wealth of meaning. "I see."

"And I strongly suspect he is involved in smuggling. Do you remember our conversation on the *Susannah*? When I met him at Amesbury, he offered me some very good wine, and I do not think that any tariff had been paid on it. Perhaps he has brought the company here to meet some Jacobite agent, or pass letters on. It is a good disguise for such activity, under his direction the company can wander all along the south coast and no-one will guess the real reason why he chooses a particular route."

"You may well be right. Do you think it has something to do with Mattie's disappearance?"

"I do. And that is why I am so anxious about her. I can't help but feel that she has come to harm, and that Crowley has had a hand in it."

"What of the rest of the company?"

"I'm not sure. They were very firm in their denials, but of course they are all actors, they are trained to lie."

"I had not thought of it in those terms, but yes, that is very true."

They had reached the town, and began to walk towards the church. Polly said, "I am sorry for dragging you all the way out here, Sam, on yet another wild-goose-chase. But I needed to make sure that Mattie was not with the players. Now we know that she really has left them, we can concentrate our search in Rye."

"Do you think that Crowley might be right, and she has perhaps gone to London to find you?"

"If so, why did she send me that message? Something bad has happened to her, Sam, I know it has. And the worst of it is, I may never discover her fate."

"You will find her," Sam said, though she could tell from the tone of his voice that he was trying to convince himself as much as her. "And don't forget Gin's efforts. She may have acquired some vital information in Rye, by fair means or foul."

Polly smiled. "By foul, probably, knowing Gin. I hope she has not got herself into trouble in our absence."

*

Gin's day had begun quite well. Once Polly and Sam had set off for the ferry, she had gone down to the kitchens to find Mercy, who had seen the players perform in Rye last week. The inn's cook was fortunately nowhere to be seen, and the maid was busy washing plates. Gin's cheerful grin was sufficiently disarming to overcome any doubts that the other girl might have had about talking to her, and they chatted for a while, managing to make sense of each other's different accents, before Gin mentioned the players. "You said they played at – was it the Red Lion?"

"Yes, the Red Lion," said Mercy. "I went with my young man, and I haven't laughed so much in all my life, I tell you I haven't."

"What was it called, the play, can you remember?"

"*The Recruiting Officer*," said the maid. "There were two girls, each one sweet on a soldier, and one of them dressed as a lad to be near her true love."

This was a somewhat sentimental interpretation of the plot, which Gin had watched several times at Drury Lane after sneaking into the gallery without paying. She let it pass. "I know that play! Who was the actress what played that part?"

"I don't know her name, but it looked as if she weren't happy, and it were plain she weren't a lad, just a maid in breeches."

Gin thought about it. Mattie had been the actress who specialised in breeches parts, and she must have made as convincing a boy on the stage as she did in her daily life. "And what did she look like? Tall, short, fair, dark?"

Mercy screwed up her face in concentration. "Not tall, and fair. As fair as I am, nearly."

She had very pale skin and light blue eyes, and the hair tucked up neatly beneath her cap was the colour of flax. So the actress in breeches had definitely not been Mattie, unless she was wearing a wig. Gin came to a swift decision. "Thank you. I'll go ask at the Red Lion. Where can I find it?"

The streets of Rye were narrow, steep and cobbled, but they were considerably cleaner than those in London. Gin, puffing slightly, followed Mercy's directions – "To the top of Middle Street, past the church and turn left into Lion Street and you can't miss the sign," – and duly came to the Red Lion, a respectable inn rather smaller than the Mermaid, and a few doors down from the church. With her usual bravado – looking confident had given her entry to many places she should not have been – she walked under the arch and into the yard where Amos Crowley's company had performed.

It was not a particularly inspiring space, being cobbled,

unswept and edged by stable buildings. There was a large horse trough to one side, and two rather weary looking nags tethered to rings in the wall next to it. As Gin paused, not wishing to shout too loudly, a young man emerged from one of the empty stables, pushing a barrow laden with dirty straw with a pitchfork stuck in the top. He stopped when he saw her, and came over. "Can I help you, Miss?"

Gin had never been called 'Miss' before. She beamed at him. "Are you Reuben?" Everyone in Rye seemed to have names from the Old Testament: it was not long since the town had been a nest of Puritans and Dissenters, one reason why the players had only performed for one night.

"So I be." He gazed down at her enquiringly. Mercy's description had been vivid and accurate. "He be near twice as tall as anyone else, with a brown horsehair wig, and a mole on his chin shaped like a heart." And she had giggled, and blushed.

The mole was more of a blob than a heart, but she had obviously been looking with the eyes of love. Gin said, "Mercy said you'd be able to help. I'm searching for someone who was with the players what were here last week." And she described, as best she could, the young woman who could be either Mattie, or Matt.

Reuben scratched his head, pushing his wig slightly askew. "You say she plays breeches parts? It weren't her last week, I'll stake my life on it. And when the women were tiring themselves in the loosebox, I heard one of 'em talking about someone who'd left them, and she didn't sound too pleased about it."

"So you didn't see her at all? Or did you see a lad who could have been her?"

"Ah." There was more head-scratching. "Now you come to mention it, Miss, I did see a lad who was with them, but he left afore they'd finished setting up the trestles for the stage. I tell you, Miss, it was a miracle no disaster happened, that there stage was so rickety it was like to fall down at any moment!"

"Did it look as if he was going secretly?"

"Oh, no, Miss, the manager, Mr. Crowley is it? I saw him talking to the boy, if boy it was, and then the lad took a horse and rode off. And I didn't see him come back, though he could have done I suppose, but I didn't notice him again, but that's not to say he weren't there, if you get my drift."

Gin did. "Can you tell me what he looked like, that lad?"

"Slight, not tall, wore a brown coat and his own hair tied back." Reuben screwed up his face like a small boy with the effort of remembrance. "Now you say it, Miss, I bain't so sure it *were* a lad."

"What colour was his, or her, hair?"

"I suppose ... like that horse." He pointed to the nearest beast. Gin knew little about horses, but this one was a reddish brown that was certainly a very similar shade to Mattie's dark chestnut.

"And did you see which way he went?"

"No, I did not, Miss, but I heard Mr. Crowley say he'd meet him in Appledore." He obviously noted Gin's look of bewilderment, for he added, "It bain't far upriver, if you take the ferry across."

The very thought of that ferry made Gin shudder. She swallowed hard and said, "Did you hear anything else?"

"No, Miss, I did not, for then my Mercy came into the yard." He grinned with a mixture of pride and bashfulness. "And after that, I didn't pay them no more mind."

It was obvious that he knew nothing more, so Gin thanked him, gave him one of the sixpences that Polly had supplied for that purpose, bade him goodbye and walked out of the Red Lion's yard with her head high and a spring in her step. She would have some news for Madam, when she and Mr. Jessop returned from their jaunt to Lydd. Always assuming, of course, that they had not been drowned on the ferry.

Hoarding her golden nugget of information, she decided to take a turn around Rye. It was such a small place that there was no chance of becoming lost, and she might discover something else. Feeling hungry, she bought a pasty from a cookshop, and looked for a quiet space in which to eat it. A little walking brought her to an open area in front of an obviously ancient tower, square with four round turrets like a miniature castle, and a long wall running away from it. There was a gateway in the wall, and Gin peered through. She saw a rough grassy area with, surprisingly, what appeared to be a bowling green in the centre. A row of cannons lined the edge of a cliff, with the sea further away, set with numerous sails. There was no-one about, so she slipped under the arch and sat down in the sunshine, with her back against the wall, to eat her dinner.

From this distance, the silver sea did not seem terrifying at all, but Gin knew that was cruelly deceptive. A pretty picture, to be sure, but danger lurked in those harmless-looking ripples. She hoped that Madam and Mr. Jessop had negotiated the ferry safely, but she thought of what Reuben had told her, and suspected that it would turn out to be a wasted journey. Perhaps Mattie was in Appledore, as her words with Crowley had implied. *She's led us a merry dance and no mistake*, Gin thought with annoyance. *I hope Madam gives her a flea in her ear when they meet.*

"Hello?"

The voice made her start. Gin looked up and saw a girl, perhaps a little younger than herself, standing just inside the gateway. She had seen that russet cotton dress before: it was the child who had looked at them so curiously when they had walked up to the Mermaid yesterday evening.

Gin scrambled to her feet, brushing the crumbs off her skirts, and made a very brief curtsey, to be on the safe side in case she was gentry. The girl bobbed herself in acknowledgement. "I saw you all yesterday, going to the Mermaid. You are a stranger to Rye, I think? Where are you from?"

"From London."

"Were they your mother and father?"

Gin could not help laughing at this. "No! Madam is my mistress, and Mr. Jessop is her friend. They are looking for her sister."

"So you are their servant." It was said matter-of-factly, without disdain. "How old are you?"

"Fifteen." This was an approximation, for Gin had never known her real age: she only remembered her mother saying that she had held her up to see Queen Anne's coronation procession, and that had been in April, 1702: she could be fourteen, fifteen or even sixteen.

"I'm twelve." The girl put out her hand. "Philadelphia Tucker, but everyone calls me Phil."

Surprised but pleased, Gin said, "Jane Maggs, but I've mostly been called Gin."

They shook hands, and then Phil flopped down onto the grass. "So, your mistress is trying to find her sister? Is she in Rye?"

Gin sat next to her, looking out at the treacherous sea. There could be no harm in telling Phil about Mattie, and possibly a great deal of good. Briefly she explained, and was gratified to see the other girl's eyes widen with eager interest. "She was with the players! I would have loved to go see them, but Mama would not let me go, she said it would not be proper and in any case I was too young. But if my brother was here, I am sure we could have gone together."

"Your brother?"

"Yes, he is my half brother, for Mama was married before she married my father, so he is a deal older than me, he is nineteen and apprenticed to a lawyer in London, but he wants to come home." She sighed heavily. "It is very dull without him, he has the drollest notions! He is building a flying machine."

Gin's ears pricked up at once. This might be a way of traversing the Marsh without having to resort to a boat. "A flying machine? Does it really fly?"

"Well, not yet," Phil admitted. "But I am sure it will, for Tawny is so clever –"

"Tawny?"

"Oh, that is what I call him, for he wears glasses and looks just like an owl sometimes!" Phil glanced sideways at her and grinned, and Gin grinned back. She had never felt able to get close to the children she had associated with while in the guise of a link boy, in case one of them guessed her secret, and since then she had been almost entirely in the company of adults. This friendly, light hearted conversation was something new to her, and she revelled in it, even though Phil was obviously no servant, but the offspring of a well-to-do family.

"The flying machine," she ventured hopefully. "Is it near to being completed?"

"I think it may be, for that is one reason why Tawny wants to come home, to finish it. He has made the framework, but he can't decide whether to use sailcloth for the wing, or some other lighter material. He asked me to look over the cliffs all around the town, to see where there might be a good landing place below, because he must launch himself off a height in order for the machine to fly."

"It sounds very dangerous," said Gin, thinking that, searching the Marsh or no, she would never venture into such a contraption, not if she was paid a hundred pounds.

"That's what I said, but Tawny says it is no more dangerous than jumping off a chair, and he seems very sure that it will work."

"And you are not?"

"Indeed I am not, and although I have a sister, Bab, and three brothers, Tawny and Francis and my own brother Joe, who is the youngest of us and at present away at school, I do like Tawny the best, for he makes me laugh with all his wild schemes, and I would be very sorry to see him come to grief. But if God had meant us to fly," said Phil, with a touch of sanctimoniousness, "He would have given us wings on our backs."

"And if He had meant us to cross water," said Gin with feeling, "He would have given us fins."

They went carefully down the slope to look over the edge. It was not a sheer drop, and there were bushes and boulders on the way down to the river below. Phil shook her head emphatically. "No, he can't fly from here. He'd break his legs for sure."

"If not his neck," Gin said. "Don't take no offence, Miss Phil, but does your brother have windmills in his head?"

Phil did not take offence, but laughed uproariously. "No, though I'm sure some folk in the town think he has. Will you come with me along the Eastern cliff, and see whether that's more fit for his purpose?"

The two girls spent an energetic and interesting

afternoon scouting out possible launch sites for Tawny's flying machine. In the course of it, Gin learned a great deal about Phil Tucker and her brother, but sadly, she did not think that his invention would be of use in the hunt for Mattie, especially if Reuben was right and she was now in Appledore. However, her new friendship might well prove useful, and besides, it was a warm, sunny day, and she was enjoying herself.

They found a couple of places which Phil considered to be possible, and finished by the Land Gate, an impressive stone structure flanked by massive turrets. By this time the sun was beginning to sink, and it was some hours since Gin had eaten that pasty. Phil invited her back to her house in Middle Street for a cold drink and some refreshments, but although she would have loved to have taken up the other girl's offer, she had just seen two familiar figures riding towards the town. "Can't," she said tersely, noting with secret pleasure Phil's look of acute disappointment. "That's Madam and Mr. Jessop coming up to the gate. But thank you kindly for the offer."

"Another time, perhaps," said Phil. "And if you need any help in finding your mistress's sister, I'd be happy to oblige. I know most people in Rye and hereabouts."

This had been obvious from the number of times she had been greeted by name on their tour round the town. Gin thanked her, bid her goodbye, and watched Phil hurrying off up the main street which ran like a backbone through the centre of Rye. Then, with a feeling of pleasurable anticipation, she went to meet Polly and Sam as they rode in under the ancient arch of the Land Gate.

CHAPTER TEN

I late receiv'd a Letter

After supper, which they had ordered immediately on their return to the Mermaid, Polly called a council of war. Food, wine and candles had been brought up by two of the maids, including Mercy, who was obviously very curious about the progress of their search, but despite her eager interest, Polly had no intention of satisfying her until she had had the chance to talk over the events of the day in private with Sam and Gin.

Hunger assuaged, they cleared the dishes onto another table, and Sam poured out second glasses of wine, while outside, it was rapidly growing dark. Briefly, for Gin's benefit, Polly described their expedition to Lydd, and their encounter with Crowley and his company, with additions from Sam. Then Gin, gratified by their close attention, told them what she had learned from Reuben in the Red Lion.

"Well," Sam said when she had finished, "we have a conflict here. Crowley tells us straight that Mattie left his company in Rye without a word to anyone. The groom at the Red Lion tells Gin straight that Mattie rode away from his company in Rye after talking to Crowley and arranging to meet in Appledore. They cannot both be telling the truth."

"And I reckon I knows which one was lying," Gin said darkly.

"I agree." Sam folded his arms. "Reuben has absolutely no reason, as far as anyone can tell, to be lying. Whereas I would not trust Crowley if he said the sun rose in the east."

"The lad at the Red Lion might have been mistaken," Polly said. "It might not have been Mattie he saw."

"Well, what he told me certainly sounded like her." A

note of belligerence had crept into Gin's voice. "Brown coat, red-brown hair tied back, slight for a lad – that's your sister, ain't it?"

"I suppose it might be," Polly said. She felt a deep sense of unease. Something was wrong here, and she could not tell what it might be. No, she did not trust Crowley either, but if he was lying, what could be his reasons?

Thinking it through, she added, "But perhaps Mattie, if it was Mattie, came back later, and then vanished."

Sam's compassionate smile told her that he thought she was clutching at straws. Polly knew he was right. "Though that is not very likely," she added.

"No, it ain't," said Gin. "So what's her game, then? She sent you the locket what you'd told her would bring you back to her if she was in trouble. Maybe she just wants to see your kind face. Or maybe she left Crowley and then got into trouble. But she ain't in Rye, unless she's prisoned somewhere. So where is she? Appledore? A few miles up the river, so Reuben in the Red Lion said."

"Then I will go there tomorrow," Polly said firmly. "Sam, will you accompany me? I must make absolutely sure that Mattie isn't there." She looked at him pleadingly, and was relieved to see his smile.

"Of course I will. Mr. Bird can give us directions, and the horses we hired today will serve very well tomorrow. Gin?"

"There's a ferry, so Reuben said. And *I've* said I ain't going on no ferry. I'll stay here and ask around. I met a girl yesterday what lives here, and she said she'd help me look."

"Well, you did well today, Jane, so I think that is a good plan." Polly smiled at her independent maid. "So, who is this girl? Does she work at the Red Lion?"

"No, her name's Philadelphia, she likes to be called Phil,

and she lives just down from here." Gin looked rather smug. "She's *gentry*!"

After a startled pause, Polly said carefully, "Did you impart any of your history to her?"

"You mean me being a link boy and a bulker till last year, and my ma a common drab and not knowing who my father was?" Gin asked, with a glint in her eye. "No. But she knows I'm your maid." She grinned. "She thought you two was my ma and pa, till I set her right."

"Oh!" Polly had suddenly put two and two together. "Was she the child who came out of that house down the street and looked at us, yesterday evening when we were walking up from the Strand?"

"That's her. She's got three brothers, and one of them has built a flying machine. I thought it might be some help, but it's not finished yet, Phil said."

"I can't imagine that a flying machine would be any help, unless to a speedy grave," was Sam's opinion. "So, are we decided? I shall go down now and tell Mr. Bird of our plans, I can arrange for the horses and get directions. It will mean another early start, I suspect, so I will bid you good night now, and let us hope for some good news tomorrow." He finished his wine and got up. "Good night, Polly, good night, Gin, and sleep well."

"Before you go, Mr. Jessop – "

"Yes, Gin?"

"Do you want the rest of that pie, Mr. Jessop? Acos if you don't ..."

*

Appledore hardly deserved to be called a town, being a small huddle of buildings on rising ground above the Marsh. It gave off the same air of decay as did Rye, but not so gently. The church was obviously in need of repair, many of the cottages required new thatch, and some of them seemed likely to fall down if one of the occupants so much as slammed a door.

Polly reined in her horse and looked at Sam in some dismay. Why would Mattie come here? Surely it would not be to hide, for in so small a place a stranger would be noticed instantly. Indeed, a group of young children, raggedly clothed and barefoot, had silently appeared and were staring at them as if they had never seen a man and woman on horseback before. Fortunately, there was an inn just beside them: it did not look as decrepit as the rest of Appledore, being constructed fairly recently of warm red bricks, with a tiled roof and a sign outside bearing the arms of Her Late Majesty, Queen Anne. At least they would be able to quench their thirst, and have something to eat: it had been a long ride, and the day was warm and sultry.

Once more, Sam asked the questions, and received little information in reply. The potboy had some vague memory of some lad who might or might not be Mattie, but his description could have fitted almost any young man, and brown coats were common. Moreover, Gin had neglected to ask Reuben, the previous day, for details of the horse which Mattie had ridden. They finished their refreshing beer and the bread and cheese which had been offered, and by mutual consent went across the road to enquire at another Red Lion, hard by the church.

They had more luck there. Yes, a young man had stayed the night there the previous week, and had been visited by another, older man the following morning, who from his description was almost certainly Crowley. Then the two had ridden off together in the direction of New Romney, which was only three miles north of Lydd.

Sam thanked the landlord, and Polly gave him a shilling for his trouble. But this had, all too obviously, been yet another wild-goose-chase. She said as much, once they were out of the village and on the weary ride back to the ferry at Stone, the only route from Appledore to Rye.

"Pray do not apologise," Sam reassured her. "If we had not come, we would have run ourselves mad wondering if your sister was here. Now we know that she was, but has gone off with Crowley. The question is, why did he lie to us yesterday? There is something dubious afoot, Polly, and I do not like it."

"Neither do I." They drew their horses to the side of the road to allow a farmer's wagon, laden with sheaves, to go by: every field of grain hereabouts was being harvested before the weather could break. "But I have been thinking and thinking it all over, and I cannot for the life of me work out what Crowley is up to."

"Mischief, no doubt," said Sam drily. "However this ends, Polly, and no matter how much she protests, I think you will have to draw your sister away from him. That man is dangerous, and I do not trust him."

Their ride back to Rye was without incident, and they arrived at the Mermaid with a sense of relief. Polly was not used to spending so much time in the saddle – indeed, until this week she had not sat on a horse since last year's expedition to Bristol and Bath in search of Sam's errant daughter – and she ached all over, while she suspected that Sam, from his stiff gait as he crossed the Mermaid's yard, felt much the same. Gin, meanwhile, had spent the day, as she put it, nosing round the town, but she had not had the benefit of Phil's help, that young lady being kept at home to assist with the baking because the cook-maid was ill, and without her to act as guide, she had failed to discover any information of note. It was frustrating in the extreme, and Polly, though she did not admit it, was beginning to wonder if this was all an elaborate trick, with Mattie and Crowley laughing somewhere at the thought of their discomfiture. They could go to New Romney, but what would be the point? It was becoming plain that if Mattie did not want them to find her, they had small chance of tracking her down. Perhaps the best plan would be to stay in Rye and wait for her sister to emerge from her hiding place, and contact them.

She slept poorly that night, both because of the heat, which had turned oppressive, and her worries about Mattie, and looked so weary at breakfast that Sam suggested a day of rest. It was just as well that she agreed, for later in the day the sky grew very dark and there was a crashing thunderstorm, with heavy rain and frequent flashes of lightning. Polly, at heart still a farmer's daughter, thought of the men labouring to get the precious harvest in, and hoped that this would not ruin the yield. When the storm eventually passed and the sun came out, Sam suggested that they take a walk round the town, to which Polly readily agreed, and they set out.

Gin, who had had the advantage of seeing Rye in Phil's company, was eager to point out the various landmarks on their tour: the church, the tower looking out towards the sea, the town walls and the gateways through them. At the top of the hill, everywhere was clean and sparkling after the downpour, though there were deposits of rubbish at the bottom of every street, swept down by floods of excess rainwater. Last of all they came to the Strand, and saw that the *Susannah* was no longer moored there: presumably she had discharged her cargo and was sailing back to London, or continuing along the South coast towards Portsmouth. Her place at the quay had been taken by another, smaller vessel, and men were busy unloading sacks from her hold with the aid of a small crane on the dockside. Gin, however, was looking in the other direction, and said urgently, "Madam! There's Phil! I must speak with her!"

Polly turned, and saw a young woman and a girl walking across the Strand. Before Gin could shame them with a loud halloo, the girl spotted them. She said something to her companion, and both changed direction and came over. The younger was certainly the one who had watched them walk up to the Mermaid a few days previously: she wore the same russet gown, and an expression of lively curiosity. She glanced from Polly to Sam, and then addressed Gin. "Pray introduce us?"

Gin straightened her shoulders, puffed out her still scrawny chest, and said proudly, "Mr Samuel Jessop, Mrs. Mary Paradice. Miss Philadelphia Tucker and ..." She looked at Phil.

"Miss Barbara Jeake. My sister."

There was little resemblance between the two girls. Phil, although she was obviously the younger by quite a few years, was nearly as tall as Miss Jeake, her half-sister, and much sturdier, with an air of vigorous good health. The other was very plain, with a prominent nose and severe mouth, and clad in a grey wool gown which did her complexion no favours. Polly would have liked to have taken her in hand and shown her how to make the most of the limited assets which had been bestowed on her, but Miss Jeake did not look as if she would appreciate such an intervention.

"I understand you are seeking your sister, Mrs. Paradice," she said. "I have heard much about you from Philadelphia. I do hope she has not been troubling you, I regret to say that she is quite the hoyden."

"On the contrary, this is the first time we have met," Polly said, noting Phil's indignant flush. "But I believe that Jane here made her acquaintance a couple of days ago."

"And have you managed to discover your sister's whereabouts, Mrs. Paradice?"

"I regret to say that we have not – we seem always to be one or two paces behind. We have been to Lydd, and Appledore, but have no recent news of her, save that she may have gone to New Romney last week."

"And you have not yet been to New Romney?"

"No, Miss Jeake," said Sam, entering the conversation for the first time. "We are beginning to feel that we are on a wild-goose-chase, and that young Miss Paradice is making sport with us."

"Well, if she wants you to find her, she will let you know, I am sure," Phil said. "Mrs. Paradice, Mr Jessop, will you take tea with us tomorrow, if you have no other engagement? Mama knows everyone in Rye and for miles around, she will surely be able to help."

"Philadelphia, I don't think –" her sister began, and then stopped with a sigh. "Very well. But remember, your brother may be home soon, he is expected later today, or tomorrow."

"I haven't forgotten," said Phil, with a little skip of excitement. "I am so looking forward to seeing him again! I wish he'd never gone to London. Why couldn't he stay here?"

"You know why," said Miss Jeake wearily, as if this was a topic too often raised. "He is his late father's heir, he needs knowledge of the law, and where better to serve his apprenticeship than with a London lawyer? Far preferable to the pair of you getting up to mischief here in Rye. Now, it's been a pleasure to meet you all, but we must be on our way, for our supper will not prepare itself and our cook is indisposed. If you would wait upon us at three of the clock tomorrow afternoon, Mrs. Paradice, you and Mr Jessop would be very welcome to take tea with my mother and myself – and Philadelphia, of course. I am sure Mama will be able to offer suggestions for the next stage of your search."

"And of course you will be quizzed on the latest London fashions," said Phil, grinning. "Don't think you will escape scot-free. Mama is always very keen to know what the ladies are wearing in town, and my brothers have no interest in such matters."

"Of course, most willingly," Polly assured her with a smile. "And thank you, Miss Jeake, for your kind invitation."

They exchanged courtesies and farewells, and watched as the sisters hurried away towards the Strand Gate. Gin said triumphantly, "See? I said meeting Phil would come in handy, and so it proves!"

"That is if your friend's mother is able to help us," Sam pointed out. "And she may not. I am truly beginning to think that Mattie is playing some game with us – and so, I suspect, is Crowley. Why else summon us here and then prove as elusive as marsh fire?"

"Well, she didn't trust Madam, that was plain," said Gin. "So maybe she's happy to lead her a dance. But it still don't make sense, why send Madam that token if she didn't mean nothing by it?"

"Very little of it makes sense," Polly said. She was tired, and hungry, and the sun was beginning to set over the Marsh and the distant hills beyond. "Let's go back to the Mermaid. It seems a long time since we last ate, and I'm quite sharp-set."

They plodded wearily back up Middle Street. The house where Philadelphia and her mother and sister lived was quiet, though smoke climbed from a chimney at the rear. They were obviously a well-to-do and respectable family, with no notion that they had invited a notorious woman into their midst. *Though of course,* Polly thought wryly, *Sam is also very respectable, and comes from much the same world as they do. Gin and I, though ... that's quite a different matter.*

But all thought of the appointment tomorrow flew out of her head as they walked into the Mermaid, and were met by Mercy, flushed and eager. "Oh, Mistress, a note came for you while you were out! I do pray it's good news!"

Polly's heart lurched with sudden hope. She held out her hand, and Mercy fumbled in the pocket of her apron and produced a small square of worn and grubby paper, folded and sealed. Across the front, in uneven, ill-formed letters, she saw the words 'For Mrs. Paradice at the Mermaid'.

She did not know if this was Mattie's hand, but instinct told her that it was. Their mother had instructed them both in reading, but her sister had been too young to have learned much before being orphaned. Somewhere, at some time, she must have acquired the ability to read and to write – indeed, being able to read scripts was essential for an actress. Who had taught her? Had it been that woman Moll that she had mentioned? How old had she been then? Polly was beginning to realise that some elements of Mattie's life story, as related by herself, did not entirely add up.

It did not matter. Nothing now mattered save for the note. She thanked the maid, gave her a generous shilling, and bore it off upstairs with Gin following eagerly at her heels, while Sam, more practical, ordered a handsome supper to be taken in their rooms.

"Come on, Madam, open it!" Gin commanded, as soon as Polly had shut the door behind them. Despite her own desperation to see the message that Mattie had sent, she shook her head. "No, Jane, I must wait for Mr. Jessop, he should be here to learn what it says."

"And here he comes," said Gin, as loud footsteps sounded up the stairs outside Polly's chamber, and Sam, red-faced and out of breath, hurried in. "It's all right, Mr. Jessop, you ain't missed nothing, she ain't opened it yet."

Polly took a deep breath, feeling strangely reluctant. Was she about to read a hostile demand that she stop pursuing her sister? Or would this be a request for a meeting, at long last?

"You won't find out nothing till you opens it," Gin advised her, and Polly broke the seal and unfolded the paper.

"Sister I need yr help, meet me at the Blew Anker this evning at sunset I will be waiting and reddy, sorry for all the trubble I've put you to, but I'm sor feared of him, I need yr help, I will be in a privat room ask for Matthew."

There was no signature, but she had no doubts. The scrawled, mis-spelt words were almost illegible, and spoke of fearful haste. Polly felt a rush of sympathy and alarm. It must be Crowley of whom her sister was 'sor feared'. She remembered that sense of menace in the barn at Lydd, and shivered. Well, perhaps now Mattie would accept her offer of a home in London, however much it might curtail her freedom: for freedom was of little use if you were afraid for your life.

"What does it say?" Gin demanded, and Sam echoed her. "Could you read it to us, please, Polly?"

It took a lot of effort to keep her voice from trembling, but she managed it well. When she had finished, Sam said, "Where is the Blue Anchor? Presumably it's an inn, or a tippling house?"

"Ain't you got no eyes in your head, Mr. Jessop? We walked past it not half an hour ago, it's the tavern up against the Strand Gate."

"Thank you, Jane." Polly looked down at the note again, then turned the paper over. Apart from the direction, and the broken seal, there was nothing on the reverse. She folded it into four, and slipped it into her pocket. "Sam, when is sunset?"

"In an hour, I think." He took out his silver pocket watch and consulted it. "Yes, there will be time to have our supper, and then Gin and I will walk down to the Blue Anchor with you."

"I'm not sure if that is a good idea – I think it is best if I see Mattie alone, at first. Otherwise she may take fright."

"Then she'd be a bird-wit," Gin muttered.

"If she has bespoke a private room for your conversation, then of course you may see her alone, but I will escort you. Yes, Polly, I insist. No harbourside in any town, however genteel and respectable, is safe for a woman after dark."

It was sensible, of course it was, and Polly nodded reluctantly. "Very well. But be discreet. We have spent so much time and effort on tracking her down, I would be devastated beyond words if it all went wrong at the last minute."

"Don't you worry, Madam," said Gin, with chirpy reassurance. "She won't know Mr. Jessop and I are there."

Not surprisingly, when their supper arrived Polly found it very difficult to eat anything, even though the food – mutton chops, a roast fowl, fried mackerel fresh from the boat, a bowl of sallet and plenty of fruit and a bottled raspberry pie – was plentiful and delicious. She picked at the contents of her plate, and made no objection when Gin, who seemed able to consume unlimited quantities, offered to finish it for her. Outside, the light was growing dim, and the hour of her meeting had almost arrived. With fingers that did not seem to know what they were doing, she fastened her mantle, waited below while Sam procured a lantern and lit it, and then they all set off back down Middle Street to the Strand.

Even as darkness was falling, there were still several people about, walking home or setting off for an evening with friends, or in some tavern or the single coffee-house which Polly had noticed on their tour of the town that afternoon. Sam strode confidently down the hill, lantern in hand, and she and Gin followed close behind. Compared with London, though, those they passed were remarkably quiet and well-behaved, no raucous singing, drunken suggestions or threats of violence, and Polly began to think that Sam's insistence on escorting her was unnecessary. But the shadows beneath the town wall, on either side of the Strand Gate, were deep and murky, and she heard scuffles and whispers further along. They passed under the arch and there on the left, leaning against the gate and the wall, was a high building, weatherboarded and tiled, with a sign hanging outside depicting a device which was, plainly, an anchor.

"Told you," Gin said triumphantly. Sam blew out his lantern and pushed open the door. Full of apprehension, Polly saw candlelight, an atmosphere thick with choking tobacco smoke, and a babble of masculine voices which halted abruptly at the arrival of the strangers. A quick glance round told her two things: firstly, that this was no respectable inn, but a rough tavern catering for thirsty fishermen, sailors and quayside labourers: and secondly, that neither Crowley nor Mattie were amongst them, though there were a couple of slatternly women. Polly felt distinctly uncomfortable under their intense scrutiny, and then wondered at herself. It was not so long ago that places like this had been familiar haunts, and less than a year since she had told Hannah that she did not wish for respectability, since it would curtail the freedoms she craved. Respectable women had chaste and stainless pasts: they could not come and go as they pleased, they did not run coffee houses, and they certainly did not conduct passionate affairs with notorious artists.

One of the women was making her way over to them, a couple of dented pewter tankards clutched in one fist. Her knuckles were battered, as if she had recently hit someone. She addressed Sam. "Can I be of service, sir?"

Behind her, several of her customers were whispering to each other, and the rest stared at them with avid curiosity, mixed with some hostility. Sam said, "We were told to ask for Matthew."

"He bain't expecting a gentleman," said the woman, looking at him dubiously.

"No, he's expecting me." Polly stepped forward. "Will you conduct me to him, please?"

"And you be?"

"Mistress Paradice."

"Through there." The woman jerked her head at a further room. "Then the door at the far end. But just you, mind. Your friends will have to wait."

"Of course," Sam said at once. He smiled at Polly. "We shall be here if we are needed."

She smiled back at him and at Gin, who was looking round with a frown, though she was even more accustomed to such places than Polly had been. Then the woman led them off towards another door at the back, and she made her way carefully between the tables and benches, ignoring the comments, some appreciative, some contemptuous, which rose from all sides as she passed. The next room was very small, just a kind of antechamber, with trestles stacked against the rough plaster walls. She knocked on the door at the end, and gently pushed it open.

The parlour beyond was a little larger, and furnished only with a couple of chairs and a rough table, on which stood a bottle of wine and two glasses. In one of the chairs sat Mattie, in the brown coat and breeches she had worn at their first meeting, her hair pulled back and her face pale and strained. As Polly appeared in the doorway, she jumped to her feet. "You came!"

"Of course I came, dearest Mattie! Why would I not?" Polly walked forward, intending to embrace her sister, but before she could reach her, she heard the door slam shut. As she realised what the sound indicated, someone grabbed her from behind, pinioning her arms, and she just had time to see the expression on Mattie's face turn to triumph, before the hood came down over her head, plunging her into darkness.

CHAPTER ELEVEN

Seize me, they've sworn, imprison me's the next

Sam had intended to order beer for himself and Gin, while they waited for Polly and Mattie to finish their conversation, but the woman seemed to have assumed that as he was obviously a cut above her usual run of customer, he would require wine. They were conducted to a room which was plainly the tavern-keeper's inner sanctum, settled on cushioned chairs, and a bottle and two glasses were produced with a flourish.

"Good, ain't it," Gin observed after her first sip. "Run, I'll be bound."

Sam glanced round to check that no-one was listening, but the woman had gone out to the main room, and the talk there was so loud, not to mention the sound of a fiddle being tuned up, that no-one else could possibly hear them. "And what would you know about it?" he asked, not unkindly.

"Oh, I knows a lot about a lot," said Gin, taking another sip: despite her scruples, she was beginning to appreciate good wine. "And I'll wager you a guinea that this is the same as what Crowley gave me and Madam in Amesbury, *and* what we had at the Oglethorpes. Madam thought it too."

"I know, she said as much to me." Sam looked at the girl. With her sharp features and the general air of furtiveness which nearly a year in Polly's employment had done little to diminish, Gin was not, at first sight, an honest and reliable servant, but he knew her to be both, and also utterly loyal. He said, "You have met this girl who claims to be Mattie. Tell me truly, what was your opinion of her?"

Gin put the glass down and considered. "She's full of

grievance," she said at last. "I think she's got it into her head that Madam could have saved her and didn't, even though she was a kinchin-mort herself at the time. She ain't happy, Mr. Jessop, that's plain to see. She ain't happy being with them players, she ain't happy in that Crowley's company, and she'd rather be a man than a woman."

"So why didn't she leave them? Polly offered her a good home at the Paradise, you'd think if she misliked her lot so much, she would have jumped at the chance."

"I didn't say she was *sensible*," Gin pointed out. "Some folk are so contrary, they can't see what's best for them because they think the whole world's agin them."

"It goes some way to explain why she has led us such a dance," Sam said. "Perhaps she had some idea of punishing us, even though we have her best interests at heart. Well, hopefully she has now decided to put an end to dragging us all over half of Sussex and Kent, and will come back to London with us."

"But not on no boat, *please*, Mr Jessop!" Gin begged. "I'll gladly walk rather than get on that boat again, as heaven's my witness!"

"Don't worry. There is no coach direct from Rye to London, but we can ride to Tonbridge and catch one there. If Mattie does agree to come with us, we can be back at the Paradise the day after tomorrow."

"Can't wait!" Gin muttered, and buried her face in her wine glass.

In the outer room, the fiddle had now been tuned, and someone was singing a very lewd song with a catchy tune and a chorus that everyone in there, obviously, knew and loved. It made Sam blush, though Gin seemed entirely unmoved, merely commenting that they were not the right words and she knew plenty who could sing and play better. But of course she had seen far more, in her fourteen or fifteen years, than he had seen in his fifty.

They finished the wine, Gin taking a long time over it, but there was still no sign of Polly. Sam looked at his watch again. "We have been here nearly half an hour, and I have no wish to start another bottle. We should go and see what the situation is – discreetly, of course. Perhaps Miss Mattie is being difficult."

"Well, wouldn't that be a surprise?" said Gin waspishly.

They emerged from the comparative peace of the little parlour, and looked round for the woman who had helped them earlier. There was no sign of her, and the attention of the company was entirely taken up with singing. Gin said something, but Sam could not hear her for the noise. She made a gesture of exasperation, turned and made her way to the antechamber and the door beyond it. Sam hurried after, intending to urge her to caution, but before he could catch up with her, she had pushed it open.

There was no need for caution. The room was empty. A smashed wine glass lay on the floor, and a chair had been overturned. Gin stared round, as if she could conjure Polly and Mattie up out of thin air purely by wishing it, and then turned to Sam, her face anguished. "Something's happened to Madam, Mr. Jessop, it must have been a trap! Where are they? How did they get out?"

The woman appeared at Sam's elbow. He rounded on her angrily. "Do you know anything about this?"

The woman quailed. "N-no, sir, I don't. Looks like they had a disagreement, perhaps."

"Rather more than a disagreement, don't you think? Did you see them come out? Did anyone? Where did they go?"

"I didn't see no-one, sir, I be sure of that. But see that

door there, beside the hearth? There be a passage going out to the Strand. Maybe they left that way."

Now that he knew where to look, Sam saw that there was indeed a door, set flush and unobtrusive into the panelling. The woman went past him and pushed at it. It swung open, revealing a narrow sliver of passage, disappearing into darkness. Gin gave a cry and darted forward. She retrieved something that had been lying just inside, and showed it to Sam, safe in the palm of her hand. It was one of the silver buttons that fastened Polly's mantle.

"Someone's taken her!" Gin cried. "I'll kill them what's done it, if any harm comes to her!"

"The lantern," Sam said to the woman, so fiercely that she shrank back. "Fetch me the lantern from the room we've just left. And hurry!"

Without a word, she turned and fled. The singing had died away, raggedly, and the fiddle player, a scrawny young man with greasy hair and a patched coat, was looking at them with interest. Sam summoned all his fear and fury and said loudly, "Who was in that room? Someone must have seen something. Who took my friend?"

There was a hostile silence. "I only saw the lad," said the fiddle player. "Came in not long before you did. No-one else."

"Are you sure about that?"

"Yes. Sir."

"Aye, he be right," said a voice by the wall, and there was a chorus of assent. It was plain that no information could be gathered from these men. Sam would have liked to have shaken some truth out of the nearest, a shrunken ancient who looked as if a light breeze would blow him to Dieppe, but he knew obstinacy when he saw it.

"Here, sir," said the woman, returning with the lantern.

Gin handed him one of the candles that had illuminated the parlour, and he lit it and hurried back to the open door, the maid following close behind. With a terrible sense of dread, he made his way along the passage, the light held in a hand which he could not keep from shaking.

The way was very narrow, and the rough wall on his left was naked stone, while that on his right was brick. Something made Sam glance up, and he saw the dim evening sky, lit with stars. Then this must be a gap between the Blue Anchor and the face of the West Cliff, against which the tavern had been built – leaving a narrow space between the building and the rock behind, for what Sam suspected must be nefarious purposes.

The lantern light showed him another door, roughly constructed. Sam pushed hard, but it refused to move. Gin, hard behind him, said, "Try *pulling* it, Mr. Jessop."

Feeling more than a little foolish, Sam crooked his fingers into a hole where normally a latch would be, and obeyed. The door obligingly creaked open. Beyond it was the interior of a wooden shack, smelling strongly of tar and seaweed, with fishing nets festooned over trestles and lobster and crab pots stacked against the walls. Sam raised the lantern high, but the small space was empty of life, apart from a hasty animal scuffling in one corner.

"They ain't here," said Gin unnecessarily. "Come on, Mr. Jessop, don't just stand there gawping!"

The Strand was lit by a moon that was almost full. It illuminated the warehouses huddled along the quayside and glittered on the windows of the houses above on the cliff, while the cranes and the masts and rigging of the ships moored there cast black fantastical shadows across the rough ground. Sam looked round, but there was no sign of Polly or her sister. He ran across to the nearest boat, where a man was leaning on the gunwale, smoking a pipe. "Have you seen two women?"

"Can't say as I have." The sailor looked down at him and leered. "I'll go shares with you, though, if you find 'em."

Sam hardly ever swore, but he did so now. "Devil take you, I'm looking for – for my daughters! They've vanished, and I think they've been abducted!"

"I ain't seen nothing, *sir*," said the sailor. He took the pipe out of his mouth, spat on the deck, and replaced it. "Quiet as the grave since sunset."

Sam did not believe him, just as he had not believed those in the Blue Anchor who had claimed ignorance, but there was no point in arguing the issue. He turned away, to meet Gin, who had been looking all along the jumbled nets, pots, crates, tubs and other fishing and marine equipment stacked at the foot of the cliff between the warehouses. Together, increasingly frantic, with his lantern illuminating those areas where the moon did not reach, they searched the Strand from one end to the other.

There was no sign, no sign whatsoever, that Polly had ever been there.

*

She was on a boat. Why she was there, where it was bound, who had abducted her, were mysteries that she could not comprehend at this moment. Her world had shrunk down to physical sensations of discomfort, pain and nausea. Her captors had bound her hands behind her back with a swift and brutal efficiency that spoke of long practice in God knew what disreputable undertakings, and when she had tried to scream, a broad hand had been clamped across her face, almost suffocating her. Then a rag had been thrust into her mouth through the sacking hood, and tied so tight that she could hardly breathe, let alone cry out. After that, they had pushed and dragged her, still struggling, along a very narrow passage whose sides scraped painfully at her arms as she was knocked against them, pulled into the open air, smelling of mud and fish, propelled across a rough surface, and finally, shoved down into something that rocked queasily. She lay on hard boards, with water soaking her mantle, and heard oars being shipped into rowlocks, and the soft splashes as the blades bit. It had happened so quickly that she could hardly believe it, and all in complete silence.

Polly had never been so frightened, or furious, in her life, even as a child of twelve, when she had faced the implacable, callous magistrates and begged for compassion for her family. But then she had thought she might have the power to change their fate. Now, trussed like a fowl for roasting in the bottom of a boat, she was utterly helpless, and the thought was terrifying.

Terror must be fought. She tried to calm her breathing, which was fast and shallow, sucking at the coarse cloth which covered her head. As the boat moved out, presumably into the river, she heard the oars creak more swiftly, and the soft grunt of effort as her captors put their backs into their work, driving the vessel along. Was Mattie one of them? She did not think so. Intuition told her that these were two big, powerful men. Her sister had been the bait, to lure her into their clutches. Her role was now ended, and she had gone.

But why? As a measure of composure returned to her, Polly tried to think rationally and logically. Mattie had been doing Crowley's bidding, that seemed obvious. He must have some hold over her sister, and he must also have some reason for abducting Polly, though she could not think what it might be. Then suddenly a lurid, half-remembered tale came back to her. Had not the Oglethorpes, years ago, been supposed to have taken one of their maidservants to France, and imprisoned her in a nunnery while they tried to persuade her, by fair means or foul, to embrace the Catholic faith? The Oglethorpes and Crowley were Jacobites, they were connected by their beliefs and also, she suspected, by smuggling. It seemed very likely that her captors were smugglers, for they were obviously used to working with swift, brutal efficiency. But why France? It seemed a great deal of trouble and risk to go to, just to gain one more convert.

Her mind shrank from the possible fates that awaited her. *I will not let myself weep, or snivel, or beg,* Polly thought fiercely. *I have friends, they will find me.* But the thought of Sam and Gin, desperately searching for her in Rye, was almost enough to destroy her resolve. And what would Dark say, when he heard? Would he blame her for her foolish expedition, and think she had wantonly put herself in harm's way? He would be entirely justified in doing so. And would she ever see him again, feel his touch on her skin, and the delicious sensation of their bodies moving together, so close they seemed like one?

That thought nearly undid her. She squeezed her eyes tightly shut behind the hood, denying the tears and sobs that threatened to fall, and tried again to think it all through. She had been abducted, not killed. If they had gone to all this trouble to take her somewhere on a boat, they were probably not intending to murder her. They must have some other purpose. The idea that she was intended for a French nunnery seemed suddenly ludicrous. So what was their reason? Mattie had lured her – was she designed to be the bait to trap Dark?

He had known what Crowley was. It was perfectly possible that in return Crowley knew about Dark, knew that he was a government spy, and knew, also, that Dark had been responsible for Robbie Sinclair's death. Perhaps revenge was the motive, or simply the desire to eliminate a dangerous opponent. And if so, she might, unintentionally, be the means by which her lover would be drawn to his doom. How could she bear it?

This was a futile and disheartening exercise. Such

things were pure speculation, nothing more. She tried to fight down her fears, and instead concentrated on what she could hear. The steady splash and creak of the oars, and the hard breathing of the rowers: the more distant cries of seabirds, who did not seem to have noticed that darkness had fallen: and the wind, growing stronger, ruffling the water which lapped busily against the thin planks of wood that were all that separated her from the river. If she thought too much about that, she would panic, and she had determined not to show weakness.

They must be nearing the sea, because there was a swell now, she could feel the rise and fall of the boat, and nausea threatened, but she had to fight it because being sick into her gag was too horrible to contemplate. Even the idea of it was almost enough to make her retch. Desperately, she tried to concentrate on something completely different. In her mind, she made herself walk from the Paradise in King Street to her old house in Flying Horse Court, just off the Strand, trying to recall every shop front, every tavern and coffee house, every market stall that she might pass on the way.

But she had barely reached the end of the Piazza before one of the men above her said something, and the boat changed direction. Jolted out of her imaginary journey, Polly tensed, waiting. Were they approaching a ship, anchored out in the deeper waters of the bay?

No: the bottom of the boat touched stones, was pushed on by a wave, grounded again. It rocked wildly as one of the men rose to his feet and jumped off. The other soon followed, and Polly felt the vessel being drawn up onto dry land. There was a rumble of voices, and then hands grasped her and pulled her, not unkindly, off the boat. Her legs crumpled, and she fell awkwardly onto wet shingle.

Well, at least it did not appear that she was going to be shipped to a French nunnery or, worse, cast into the sea. Polly tried to struggle to a sitting position, failed, and found herself being helped. One man supported her, the other pulled off the hood, cut the bonds around her wrists, and untied the gag. The relief was so enormous that for a moment all she could do was suck in the pure, tangy air.

"Bain't no point skreeling for help out here," said one of the men. He came to stand in front of her, a hulking dark shape whose features she could not make out. His voice was thick and rough, and heavy with what she could already recognise as the local accent. "Bain't no folk for miles, and even if anyone was to hear you, they'd think it was a gull. No point trying to run either – there bain't nowhere to go, and in the dark you'd fall into a fleet and be drownded. So, miss, come along of us quietly, eh?"

She could see she had no choice, but she needed to know something first. "*Why?* Why have you done this? What have I done to earn such treatment?"

"You won't get no answers from us," said the other man, coming to stand beside his companion. "We don't know nothing about that, and even if we did, we wouldn't tell you. Owlers keep their dealings close, see? All we know is that we've been paid handsome, and told what to do, and warned to ask no questions about it. So save your breath, miss, for we've a rough walk ahead of us."

They helped her to her feet, and supported her as they all three struggled up the steep shingle mound. The massive hill of loose stones was exhausting to climb over, and when they got to the top Polly was gasping. She glanced back and saw the boat lying tilted a few feet above the water's edge, and the wide dark expanse of Rye Bay behind it, with the westering moon laying a glittering silver path across the gentle motion of the sea. So this must be the eastern bank. She tried to recall what little she knew of the land hereabouts. Were they quite close to Lydd? She had seen no map, and had no idea what to expect along this 'rough walk', what their destination might be, and how long it would take them to reach it.

Her captors, though, obviously knew this place as thoroughly as she knew the streets of Covent Garden, although she did not understand how they could find their way in the dim light when there were almost no landmarks visible. The Marsh stretched in front of them, flat, dark, and even more sinister at night than it had been during the day. But the men made their way unerringly past stunted trees and twisted gorse bushes, sloughs and fleets of mud and water, and heaps of shingle presumably left stranded by some long-ago inundation. And the silence was eerie, no sheep or sea birds here, nothing but the shiver of the wind and the sound of their breathing.

After a while, she realised that there were some taller trees ahead, ragged, darker shapes against the dimness of the Marsh, and an even darker rectangle within them. The men quickened their pace and arrived at a wooden shack, barely visible in the shadows. One let go of her arm, took out something which must be a key, and after some fumbling, found the lock. He pulled open the door with a creak which was sharply loud in the silence, and peered inside.

"Be it made ready, Ned?"

"When I've had a feel round, I'll tell you." The man Ned disappeared into the blackness. She heard him blundering about, and a curse as he bumped into something.

Polly felt it was time to assert herself. "Where is this place?"

"You don't need to know that, miss, you just need to know that no-one will pass this way for days and weeks. You've got a bed, and blankets, and water, and a bucket. Nothing else. Be thankful we weren't told to drop you over the side into the bay."

Polly opened her mouth to protest, but was shoved through the door so hard that she fell with a gasp of surprise. Behind her, she heard the slam, the turn of the key in the lock, and the rattle of a bolt.

The darkness around her was complete. Her knees were painfully bruised where she had landed, for the floor beneath her hand was bare earth, rammed hard as stone. Something soft and fluttery touched her fingers – a feather, perhaps. The air smelled musty, and tinged with some odour she could not place. Determined not to give way to tears and panic, she searched around, as far as she could reach. There was what appeared to be a heap of straw, and some folded coarse cloth – presumably that was the bed and the blankets. As her eyes adjusted to the absence of light, she thought she could discern a crack which might indicate the position of the door. Polly got onto her hands and knees and methodically began to explore her prison. It was a small space, about ten feet square, with the so-called bed in one corner, and beside it a stool on which stood a leather bottle containing the promised water. It tasted stale, but she took several sips, suddenly realising how thirsty she was. She replaced the bung, found the bucket in the opposite corner, and made use of it. Then she stood up carefully, and inched her way over to where she thought the door might be. But no matter how hard she pulled, or pushed, or rattled at it, it refused to budge.

Just as well I'm not afraid of the dark, Polly thought. She turned, found the bed after two brief steps, and sat down. There was just enough straw to shield her from the worst pains of lying on hard ground, but not sufficient to give any comfort. Nor would the blankets, rough, scratchy and probably full of lice, offer much protection from the chill. She shoved them as far away from her as she could, and then lay down, wrapping herself in her mantle, which was made of fine wool and, despite still being damp, provided warmth and a degree of solace. Morning, surely, would bring her some answers.

In the meantime, since there was nothing else she could do, she began to think about Sam and Gin, knew they must be searching desperately for her, but knew also that they could not possibly find her tonight. Then her thoughts turned inevitably to Mattie, and her betrayal. Why had she done it? Had Crowley forced her into it? But Polly remembered that look of triumph on her sister's face, and knew that Mattie had taken an active, willing part in her abduction. And the tears which she had not allowed herself to shed earlier were drying cold on her face, when sleep eventually claimed her.

*

It was very late when Sam and Gin finally accepted that any further search of the Strand was futile during the remaining hours of darkness. They had accosted every passer-by, to no avail, and had even returned to the insalubrious Blue Anchor, to find everyone still within the tavern claiming complete ignorance, many of them also with shameless expressions of bewilderment.

"They're lying," Gin said, as they made their way wearily at last up Middle Street. "Didn't you see their faces? They know what's happened and who's took her, sure as I'm standing here."

"I expect smugglers were involved," Sam said, keeping his voice low, though the street was empty and the houses on either side mostly shuttered and dark. "And it's dangerous even to talk of smuggling, leave alone inform on them. I'm not surprised no-one said anything."

Gin was silent for a while, and Sam suspected she was repressing sobs. Finally she burst out, "But who's done this, Mr. Jessop? And *why?* What has Madam done to anyone to make them take her? I don't understand, Mr. Jessop, truly I don't."

"Crowley has to be at the bottom of this. But as to why,

Gin, I'm as much in the dark as you are." They had reached the Mermaid, and Sam paused by the entrance to the courtyard, looking down at her. "But we will find her, I am sure of that, and I will move heaven and earth to do it."

"You can't be sure," said Gin, with a miserable snivel. "What if they've taken her to France? We'd never find her then."

"Why in the Lord's name would they want to do that?"

"I dunno. Perhaps someone wants to pay her back for Sinclair. But I knows this," Gin said fiercely, "if ever I catches up with him what's taken her, I'll put a knife through his heart meself."

CHAPTER TWELVE

He'll make exorbitant Demands

Polly was woken abruptly by the unpleasantly loud creak as the door to the hut was shoved open. Gasping in shock, her heart pounding, she sat up and saw, framed by the early morning light, the man who called himself Amos Crowley.

"Well, Mrs. Paradice, I see you've made yourself comfortable," he said, with a smile. "How was your night? I hope you had pleasant dreams."

"Very pleasant, considering." Polly surveyed him coldly. She was lying: the thin straw had made for an uncomfortable bed, and her worries about Sam and Gin, as well as her fears for Dark, for Mattie and for herself had kept her awake for many hours, only to reappear in a disturbing nightmare when at last she did fall asleep. She had begged her sister to tell her why she had betrayed her, and received the same answer over and over again. "You let them take me."

Was that really Mattie's reasoning? It was flawed and twisted, but to a six-year-old girl forced into brutal servitude, it might seem logical. She had come to that conclusion last night, and her thoughts had presumably influenced her dreams.

But she would not make this man privy to them, not in a thousand years. Feeling at a disadvantage, Polly scrambled to her feet, shedding straw. Deliberately, she brushed the remainder off her mantle, and only then looked at Crowley. She was shorter than he was, by a considerable margin, but she was determined not to let him cow her.

He was still wearing that expression of condescending

amusement. It infuriated her, but she kept calm, as she had decided during the wakeful hours before dawn. "So, Mr. Crowley, can I go now? My friends will be looking for me, and in great distress."

"I will let you go in due course, but you have something I want. Give it to me, and you can be free."

"Well, it cannot be my maidenhood, for I have not possessed that for some years now." She stared at him, challenging and defiant.

Crowley laughed. "No, Mrs Paradice, I want something more tangible, and very much more precious. I want the gold that you and your lover Sinclair stole from King James."

And suddenly everything became clear. Last year, Robbie had been entrusted with the task of planning rebellion in the southern parts of England, including Oxford and Bath, and to that end he had been given a very large sum in gold, to buy arms and cannon, bullets and gunpowder, and to equip horsemen and soldiers so that the English Jacobites could rise up, combine with the army in Scotland, and sweep Turnip George of Hanover from the throne.

But Robbie, greedy, unscrupulous and selfish, had diverted much of the gold to his own ends. He had taken a lease on a fine house, showered her, his mistress, with beautiful gifts, fine clothes and jewellery, bought a splendid horse and a silver-hilted sword. To be fair, he had also spent plenty of it on arming the English Jacobites, but at least a third of it still remained when he abandoned Polly and rode away to war, capture, prison, escape, and ultimately, death. And, left in charge of the remainder of the gold, she had paid Robbie for his betrayal of her by using much of it to buy Hannah, so that she could give her maid her freedom, and then to transform an almost derelict house in King Street into the Paradise, an undertaking which had not been cheap.

"There's no gold," Polly said. "It's gone."

Crowley laughed. "And you expect me to believe that? I reckon that when Sinclair rode off to war, there must have been five hundred guineas or more left in your possession. And not even you, my pretty, can spend so much in less than a year."

The purchase of Hannah's liberty had cost a hundred, but Polly would have paid twice that to help her friend. And the Paradise was the means to her own freedom, to have enough wealth to live as she wanted, beholden to no-one, controlled by no-one. The gold, what was left of it, was safe in her banker's keeping, and in the past six months she had augmented it considerably with the profits of the coffee house, and, of course, the fees for Molly Oglethorpe's singing lessons. So a goodly proportion of her wealth had been honestly come by, and Crowley had no conceivable right to it.

"And of course, you would immediately send that gold back to King James," Polly said.

"Of course." Crowley smiled. He had very good teeth.

"I am a loyal subject of King George. I would hardly hand over such a sum, *if* it existed, knowing that it would fund a rebellion against him."

"You? A loyal subject of the German? You were as ardent as Sinclair for King James."

"Opinions may change, and mine certainly have. Moreover, Sinclair was an unprincipled rogue who betrayed me and betrayed his cause. He deserved his fate. But he spent that gold, in Oxford and in Bath, to raise rebellion, and there is none left. You have wasted your time and effort, Mr. Crowley, and I would be very grateful if you would let me walk past you. Lydd can't be far away – to the north of here, at a guess?"

She took a step towards the door, and at once Crowley moved to fill the space. He was a big man, and blocked out most of the light. "You are going nowhere, Mrs. Paradice, until you tell me where I may come by that gold."

"And I told you that I don't have the gold," Polly said. "If you will not listen, that is your fault, not mine. Now let me pass!"

"No, you are staying here, madam, until you give me the information you require. This is a very lonely place, no-one will come here until late next month, when the wildfowl land on the decoy pond and the man comes to net them. This shack is where he hangs the dead birds, and over the winter he lives in a little house by the pond. It possesses more comforts than here, of course, there is a hearth and some sticks of furniture. But this has nothing, and I will give you nothing save enough water to keep you alive, until you give me the information I want."

"And my sister? What have you done with her?"

"Your sister? Or is she really your sister?" Crowley looked at her, his head on one side, pretending to ponder. "Well, she *told* you that she was, but how much reliance can we place on that? She could be anyone. There is little resemblance between you, after all, either in looks or in character, and you have not seen her since she was, what, six years old? I can see that you still have doubts, and probably even more now that she has betrayed you. After all, what true sister would do such a thing? I told her to, of course, but she was eager and willing to obey. She has been with my company for a couple of years now, and she is loyal to me and to the Cause. Besides," he added, with a cold smile, "I know things about her that would make your blood freeze."

Robbie had talked with apparent fervour about the Cause of the Jacobites, but had not scrupled to embezzle the money they had entrusted to him. Polly suspected that Crowley had similar intentions. She said, "Where is Mattie now?"

"Oh, she is back with the company, and much in their favour. They do not care for you, Poll Paradice, they think you have grown too far past your proper station, and too high in your own esteem. Not one of them would lift a finger to help you, and nor would Mattie. Your friends will never find you here, they are strangers to the Marsh and they will have no idea of where to look for you. They may even think that you have been spirited away on a ship bound for France – perhaps suspecting that those who espouse the Cause may want revenge on you, for stealing their gold and betraying Sinclair to his death. So you may not look for help from any quarter, madam, save from myself. And I will keep you here until you obey me. Without food, or any of the comforts you have become accustomed to, Mrs. Paradice, I do not think it will be long. I shall be back in the evening, to bring water, and to receive your answer. Good day to you."

Before she could say or do anything else, he had stepped back and shut the door. Light vanished, the key was turned, a bolt slid, and she was once more a prisoner.

*

"But what shall we *do*, Mr. Jessop?"

Sam surveyed Gin. Her face swollen with crying, her eyes red, she was a travesty of her usual chirpy, impertinent self. He said gently, "I don't know. The constables have been very little help."

"They said that she'd probably gone off of her own free will!" Gin wiped her runny nose on her sleeve. "Fat-headed drumbelos!"

Sam could not help but agree with her. They had spent all morning asking, and no-one they had spoken to in Rye seemed to give any credence to the idea that Polly might have been abducted: indeed, one of the constables had actually laughed aloud at the suggestion. And at the mention of smugglers, or owlers as they were known here, everyone seemed to become very deaf, or very obtuse, or very ignorant.

"We can hardly search the whole Marsh," he pointed out. "But you could ask your friend Philadelphia where the best places to look might be. You will have to explain what has happened, or she and her mother and sister will be wondering why Polly has not taken up their very kind invitation to tea." He paused, thinking how best to phrase it, and then added, "You should wash your face and change your linen first."

"Are you saying I'm dirty?" Gin demanded, suddenly looking very much more her usual self. "Well, thank you kindly for that compliment, Mr. Jessop, why didn't you say so before?" She bounced out of her chair and stamped over to the door. "I won't be long."

As good as her word, she was back before his pocket watch had recorded ten minutes of time. Her cheeks were rosy with scrubbing, and she wore her best striped cotton dress, with a fresh apron and her hair brushed and tied up under a cap. Her dark eyes were still rimmed with red, but only someone who knew her well would realise that she had been weeping for half the night and most of the morning. "Here I am, Mr. Jessop, will I do?"

"Admirably, Gin," Sam said, smiling at her.

"That ain't my name, though, is it, Mr. Jessop? Jane Maggs is what Madam calls me, and Jane Maggs I am, if I ever –" Here her voice wobbled, but she managed to control it with an obvious effort. "If ever I see her again, or if I don't."

"Of course we will see her again – and as soon as maybe, you can depend on it." Even as he spoke the words, their futile emptiness struck him. He had no idea what had become of Polly, or where on this earth she might be – or even if she were still alive. And he felt completely helpless.

"I shall go down to Mistress Tucker," Gin said. She gave

him a bright, brave smile, bobbed a curtsey and went out.

When she rapped on the door of the Tuckers' house, it was opened by their housemaid, a middle-aged woman with a kindly face. She looked enquiringly down at Gin. "Yes?"

"I'm Jane Maggs, and Phil – Miss Philadelphia spoke with my mistress yesterday on the Strand."

"Oh, but I thought you wasn't expected till later."

"I know," Gin said. She swallowed, and added, "Is Phil – Miss Philadelphia in? I wish to see her, it's very important."

"I know she's at her lessons." The maid looked very doubtful. "I'll go ask Madam if she can be spared."

"If you please – it could be a matter of life and death!" Gin said urgently.

As she had hoped, this statement had an immediate effect. "Come inside and I'll fetch her," said the woman, and ushered her into a small, panelled parlour with a window overlooking the street. Gin sat down on the cushioned seat in the bay, and wondered how long she might have to wait. The more she thought about it, the less likely it seemed that Phil would be permitted to leave her lessons to speak to a mere maidservant, however urgent the request.

"So you're Jane! I've heard all about you from Phil!"

It was a male voice, and Gin looked up, startled. A boy, perhaps eighteen or nineteen years old, stood in the doorway. He was tall and very lanky, his clothes seeming at once too big and too short for him, and his round spectacles gave his face an enquiring, owlish look. Gin jumped to her feet, bobbed a curtsey, and said, "Are you Tawny?"

The young man laughed. "Yes, for my sins. Phil has saddled me with that name for years. She's in the middle of some complicated sums and Bab says she has to finish them, and Mama is out and Papa's in Southampton on business, so

I'm afraid you'll have to put up with me for a while. You told Sarah that it was a matter of life and death, so can I help?"

Gin was an acute judge of character – it was one of the reasons she had survived for so long on the London streets – and she liked the look of Tawny, alias Samuel Jeake. She said, "I don't know as you can."

"Try me. Tell me what's happened." He sat down on the chair by the hearth and leaned eagerly forward. "I'm sure we can do something."

Despite herself, Gin was heartened by his enthusiasm. She explained about their search for Mattie, about the note that had lured Polly to the Blue Anchor, and about her subsequent disappearance. Tawny frowned. "The Blue Anchor has a very dubious reputation. Owlers – smugglers use it. Do you think your mistress might have been taken by them, for some reason?"

"I don't know," Gin said, trying not to sound too despondent. "I can't think why they would. Madam ain't – hasn't – had nothing to do with smuggling."

"It might have been a mistake," said Tawny, obviously thinking aloud. "They might have mixed her up with someone else."

"But her sister was there! And I'm feared that she might have been taken to France."

"Why?"

Reluctantly, Gin said, "Because the Jacks might want revenge on her."

"Jacks? You mean Jacobites? There aren't many of those hereabouts." Tawny regarded her curiously. "Except some of the smugglers, of course. Everyone knows they carry messages and spies to and from France. It's a long empty coast, easy to land a boat, easy to take people and goods out to waiting ships, all without being seen. And the smugglers don't care what they do, as long as they're well paid for it."

"Or it could be other Jacks what we met in London. I don't know," Gin said despairingly. "All I know is that Madam has gone and we ain't got no notion of where or how to find her, or even where to look."

"And my flying machine isn't finished." Tawny caught her eye and grinned. "Though it probably wouldn't be much use anyway. I've designed it to be launched from a cliff or a tower, and glide as far as the wind can take it. Did Phil tell you about it?"

"Did I tell you about what?" His sister burst into the room, hair flying. "Hello, Jane! What's happened? Sarah said it was very important, but Bab made me finish my lesson in accounts. I had to add up all last month's expenses and get it right, and I tried five times before I managed it."

Once more Gin explained what had happened at the Blue Anchor, and Phil's eyes grew round with astonishment. "And your mistress – she's disappeared?"

"It's as if she was never here," Gin said. "Them in the tavern, some of 'em must know for sure what's happened, but they ain't saying nothing. Your brother says it's because she might have been seized by smugglers, but I can't make out why they would have taken her."

"We should go down to the Strand and ask around," Phil said decisively. "Tawny and I have lived in Rye all our lives, so they might tell us something that they wouldn't tell you because you're a stranger here."

"Mr. Jessop should come along with us. I'll go and get him from the Mermaid."

A little while later, Gin and Sam met Phil and Tawny outside their house, and walked down to the Strand. In contrast to the previous evening, when it had been almost deserted, the place was now bustling: a ship had recently come into port, and men swarmed round her, beginning the arduous task of unloading her cargo of barrels and sacks. Tawny walked forward, threading his way through the labourers with practised agility, and approached a man who was standing by the gangplank, obviously directing proceedings. They engaged in animated talk for a few moments, and then he returned. "That's the *Cormorant*. She's fresh in from Dieppe, and her captain tells me that there have been no ships leaving Rye and bound for France for at least a week. So you may rest assured, Jane, that your mistress has not been taken overseas. She must still be nearby, and we will find her."

"Thank you, Master Jeake," Gin said, with profound relief. So her worst fears, it seemed, could not be true.

"That is good to hear," Sam added. "But even if she has not been taken far, the Marsh is a vast area that will take a very long time to search – not to mention Rye itself, and the towns and villages around."

"Which is why you need our help," said Phil. "Tawny knows the Marsh like the back of his hand, he and our brother Frank have been fowling there with Papa every winter since they were younger than me. He knows every looker's hut, every barn, every creek and fleet and wall. We'll track her down for you."

"But if she has been taken by smugglers, will that not be dangerous?" Sam objected.

"Well, I suppose so," Tawny said.

"Oh, if they threaten you, you will talk them out of any harm they might do," his sister said airily. "You could talk the wings off a dove and the back legs off an ass. That's why Father has apprenticed you to a lawyer."

"Evil necessity," said Master Jeake, with an expressive

grimace. "Now, I shall enquire at the Blue Anchor. It's owned by the Corporation, so if there's been mischief there, I can ask my stepfather to have a word in the right ear. Will you come with me, Mr. Jessop?"

The two girls watched as they approached the tavern door. Sam did not have to duck beneath it, but Tawny did. They disappeared into the gloom, and Phil looked at Gin. "I have never been in a tavern, and I would dearly like to see inside! The Mermaid, of course, is a respectable inn, but the Blue Anchor definitely is not. Have you ever visited a low tavern, Jane?"

This was a tricky question, for Gin had had an extremely close acquaintance for most of her life with any number of very low taverns and tippling houses in and around Covent Garden, the denizens of which would doubtless horrify Phil's respectable parents.

"I bin in one or two," she said cautiously.

"Oh, have you? Were they very rough and full of drunken men and – and –" Here, Phil's voice dropped to a thrilled whisper – "And ladies of the night?"

"You mean harlots? Yes, I dare say."

"And did they sing bawdy songs? I'm sure Tawny and Frank know some, but they won't teach me the words."

"Probably just as well," said Gin. In different circumstances, she might have been tempted to satisfy the other girl's curiosity out of mischief, but she liked and respected her new friend, and besides, they needed her help and her brother's if they were ever to find Polly – help which would not be forthcoming if Phil and Tawny were told not to consort with such a disreputable person.

"Oh, look!" Phil grabbed her arm. "There's Jem Fuller, see, walking across to his boat. He knows everything that happens down here at the harbour. Let's go talk to him."

Jem Fuller was a lean elderly man, with long wisps of white hair and a lined ruddy face. He turned as Phil approached, hailing him. "Miss Tucker! How d'ye do, maid? And who be your young friend?"

He was obviously a kindly man, and Gin felt hopeful. "This is Jane Maggs, who's visiting from London," Phil said. "Her mistress vanished last night, and we're trying to find her. Have you heard anything about a lady who may be in trouble?"

The twinkle disappeared abruptly from the fisherman's eye. "What sort of trouble?" Jem asked.

"We don't know for sure," said Phil. "But she was supposed to meet someone at the Blue Anchor last night, and she's disappeared, and we think she may have been abducted. Has there been any talk?"

"I ain't heard nothing," said Jem.

"Well, can you keep your ears and eyes open for me? Please?" Phil put her hand on his worn sleeve and opened her hazel eyes very wide.

"I will, miss, but you know what folk are like in these parts." He laid a finger to his nose. "They reckon 'hear no evil, see no evil' be safest."

"But Madam's life might be in danger!" Gin said despairingly. "And you're saying people will just turn a blind eye to it?"

Jem sighed. "Yes, because they be more feared of upsetting certain folk than they be feared of the law. Your mistress bain't the first to go missing round here, and I doubt she'll be the last. Sometimes they turn up, sometimes they don't. And sometimes they're washed ashore, or found in a fleet."

"That's murder!" Gin said, with a sob. "And no-one lifts a

finger – "

"The Marsh is different, see? The law don't run there like it do elsewhere. Some men set themselves up as kings, and make their own rules, and no-one dares go agin them."

"So you won't help us," said Phil flatly.

"I didn't say that, maid. What I'll say is that others might not. But there bain't no word of such, not this morning, not even from old Harry, and he be the biggest blabbermouth on the Strand. But if I do hear anything, I'll be sure to tell you, Miss Philadelphia."

"Thank you, Jem. Thank you." Phil paused, and then added, "Do you know if a boat has gone out, tonight or this morning?"

Jem rubbed at his thinning white hair. "Well, Miss, I didn't see one go *out*, but I saw one come *back*, a little after first light it was." He pointed to a large rowing boat, moored a few yards along the quay. "I was sorting my nets and didn't see who was in it, but it belongs to Tom Fowler, he was checking on his crab pots most likely."

He had just finished speaking when Sam and Tawny emerged from the Blue Anchor, and Gin gave Phil a discreet nudge. They thanked Jem and made their way across the quayside, dodging several men rolling barrels towards the Strand gate. As they came nearer, Gin saw the grim expressions on their faces and her heart lurched. What had they learned?

"Not here," said Sam, as soon as the girls were close enough. "Let's go over there, away from anyone." He jerked his head at an empty corner by the cliff, out of the way of the toiling labourers and busy sailors, and Gin followed him, feeling sick with dread.

"Well?" Phil demanded, once they were out of earshot of

any passer-by. "Did you discover anything?"

"She refused to say anything until I told her I'd report her to the Corporation for aiding criminals, and she'd lose her licence," said Tawny.

"And would you?" Phil asked.

"I doubt they'd listen to me, but she wasn't to know that. All she knows is that I'm a Jeake and my stepfather has considerable influence in this town. Anyway, then she just said, 'The angel took her.'"

Gin stared at him in horror. "But – but that means Madam must be dead! She's dead, and I'll never see her again!" And she let out a huge wail of anguish that bounced off the cliff and echoed round the Strand, before burying her face in her hands and sobbing as if her heart were broken.

CHAPTER THIRTEEN

Lost, beyond the possibility of hope

Polly had spent most of the afternoon in a fitful doze. She was hungry, uncomfortable and afraid, but she had also had very little sleep the previous night. After Crowley's departure, she had explored her prison minutely, making use of the limited but welcome light that filtered through slender gaps in the wooden walls, and through a rather larger hole in the roof, in the corner opposite the mass of straw which comprised her bed. The building was obviously old but quite sturdily built, of splintery planks on a solid brick foundation, with a tiled roof festooned with cobwebs. There were plenty of feathers lying about on the bare floor, but fortunately no other trace of the dead wildfowl which were presumably kept here when the decoy man was in residence, before being sent off to market or to some big house. The door had strong hinges, and was securely locked and bolted on the outside. The walls offered no loose plank or rotten corner which might be broken through. Even if she upturned the bucket and stood on it – something she had no desire to do now that she had used it – she would not be able to reach the gap in the roof tiles and make the hole big enough to squeeze through. And the stool beside the straw was even smaller.

After more than an hour, she guessed, of fruitless and increasingly hectic exploration, Polly had to admit defeat. She picked up the water bottle and sat down on the stool, trying not to give way to panic and despair. But try as she might, she could see no way out of this. She was not physically capable of breaking out of the shack, nor could she hope to best Crowley, who was so much larger and stronger than she was. Humiliatingly, she was entirely at his mercy.

But, she reminded herself, she had friends. Sam and

Gin must be searching for her. They could surely enlist the help of the worthy citizens of Rye. Gin had befriended the girl Phil – she must have family who could assist in the hunt. They would have guessed that Crowley was involved in her abduction. Perhaps they could track him down. It would be easy enough to trace his company. She would not, must not give up hope.

For she was quite certain of one thing: she would not give him what he wanted, for that store of wealth represented a secure future, and happiness. And without her information and assistance, he would never be able to lay his hands on it.

Outside, the sun climbed higher, and the little shack grew warm and stuffy. Polly drank most of the water and lay down on the straw, ignoring the rumbling of her empty belly. Without intending to, she drifted into an uneasy sleep, punctuated by strange dreams and intermittent periods of waking, until the sound of the door being opened wrenched her back into full consciousness.

"Get up." Crowley's voice, abrupt and commanding, sounded too loud and too close. Polly did not feel like obliging him. She yawned, stretched like a luxurious cat, and sat up. "Why, Mr. Crowley! How nice of you to call. My maid would bring you refreshments, but there seems to be a sad lack of victuals here at present."

Crowley strode forward, grabbed her by the arm, and hauled her to her feet. She blinked and tried to ignore the pain of his grip. "Well, Madam? What is your answer?"

"I have already told you. The money is mine, and you have no right to it."

"I have every right to it! That gold belongs to King James!"

"But it has gone. Every last guinea. There is nothing of that sum in my possession. All my wealth, such as it is, has been earned by hard work and careful saving. It is not yours, it is mine. And I will not give it to you if my life depended on it, for you are nothing but a thief."

"Your life may depend on it if you persist in this defiance."

"Well, if you take my life you will have gained nothing, for you still won't know how to get it," Polly pointed out.

Crowley glared at her. "I can make your life in this place so miserably uncomfortable that you will soon be begging me to take your gold. And I fully intend to. Let's see how stubborn you feel, madam, after another day with no food."

Polly smoothed her skirts over her hip with her free hand. "That is of little matter, I have grown a trifle too plump of late. But I will need water. After all, I may survive hunger, but I will not survive thirst, and you need me alive. I trust you have brought some? You did say that you would."

"I have." Crowley let go of her and turned away, and Polly, who had been waiting for just such a chance, dodged past him with a twist of her body, evaded his clutching hand, and ran out through the door and into the light.

She had a brief glimpse of scrubby bushes and trees, murky water, heaps of sand and shingle, tussocks of sea grass. There was a path in front of her and she ran along it, gasping, her skirts hitched high. Behind her, she heard Crowley's enraged shout, and knew he was coming for her. To her left, a long narrow slick of water waited to engulf her if she fell, and on her right there were bushes of gorse and stunted willow. Her legs ached and her throat hurt as she sucked air in, knowing that he must be gaining on her. There was one weapon left to her: somehow, she summoned up enough spare breath to scream, and scream again.

No good, he was almost on her, she could hear his footsteps and his breathing, harsh and urgent. Then her shoulder was grabbed with such force that she lost her balance, tried to save herself, and was only prevented from falling headlong into the water by the strength of Crowley's arm. "If you scream again, you stupid little bitch, I'll throttle you!"

In fact he gave her no opportunity to scream: he clamped one hand over her mouth and with the other, twisted her arm up behind her back so painfully that she could not struggle. Then he marched her back to the hut and flung her down in the approximate direction of the straw, so hard that her head banged against the wall. Dazed, gasping, Polly stared up at the man standing over her, a looming shape in the dimness, and rubbed the back of her head, trying not to wince. At least he could not see the tears of pain and fury which had sprung involuntarily to her eyes.

"Not so pert now, are you, you little whore?" Crowley said, his voice thick with menace. "Well, you've got all night to think about your answer, and I'll be back in the morning for it – and to make sure you don't try that again!" He picked up the water bottle, pulled out the bung, and slowly, deliberately, turned it upside down so that the contents streamed out to make a puddle on the floor at his feet. "In the meantime, you can go thirsty, it's no more than you deserve. Good night, Mistress Paradice, and sweet dreams!"

*

"Jane! Jane, she's not dead – that's not what I meant!" Tawny patted Gin's shaking shoulder awkwardly. "I'm sorry – please, stop crying and listen to me! I said, *listen!*"

At last, his words seemed to penetrate Gin's hopeless sobbing. She lifted her head, revealing a swollen face streaked with tears. "W-what do you mean?" she asked, with a hiccup.

"I mean that when the woman said that the angel took her, she did *not* mean that Mrs. Paradice was dead. She meant that she was taken by a man called Gabriel Tomkins – he's often called the Angel. After the Archangel Gabriel?" he added, seeing Gin's look of bewilderment.

Gin was unfamiliar with most aspects of the Christian religion. "Are you sure?"

"Utterly sure. Strike me dead if I lie." Tawny put his hand on his heart, looking particularly owlish behind his spectacles.

"If you say so," Gin muttered at last, scrubbing at her face with her hand and feeling suddenly foolish after her outburst of emotion.

"Gabriel Tomkins is a smuggler," Tawny went on. "He and his brother Ned are the leaders of the Mayfield Gang, they're much feared on the Marsh. But apparently if you pay them enough, they'll do almost anything criminal, no questions asked."

"*Almost* anything?" Sam glanced at Gin.

"I think they would stop short of cold-blooded murder," Tawny said. "There's a story that they were surprised landing a cargo on the beach near Jury's Gut, and rather than kill the Revenue men, they tied them up and left them to be found in the morning. Please, Jane, I think if we can only track your mistress down, she may well be in some trouble and discomfort, but she will be alive."

"That's easy for you to say." Gin looked up at Tawny, and he smiled at her reassuringly. "I do mean it, Jane. If they wanted to kill her, they'd have done it in the Blue Anchor, and made it look like an accident. And they haven't taken her to France, for there's been no ship. She is still here, either in Rye or on the Marsh, and we will find her."

His optimism was infectious, and buoyed them all up for some time, as they continued to ask around on the Strand, but received no answers, and no help. Eventually, by mutual agreement, they gave up the search, and plodded back up Middle Street, Phil and Tawny to their house for a late dinner, and Gin and Sam to the Mermaid. The landlord knew about Polly's disappearance, and had already offered his assistance, but beyond a list of names to ask, had no other information, and at the mention of Gabriel Tomkins, became noticeably more reticent. Gin slipped away to the kitchens, where she discreetly questioned the servants there, but no-one, not even Mercy, was forthcoming. The possibility of the smugglers' involvement was enough reason, it seemed, to keep silent, however heinous the crime they had committed.

By the time she had climbed wearily up to the chamber which, until yesterday, she had shared with Polly, Gin was beginning to feel the return of her earlier despair. Tawny's blithe cheerfulness had enthused them all, but he was not here now to lift her spirits. She looked round at the comfortable room, the canopied bed, neatly made up, with her truckle slid beneath it, the table at which they had eaten their supper only yesterday evening, and the old-fashioned clothes press below the window. If she opened that, she would see Madam's gowns and shifts, which she had folded just as Madam had taught her, and sprinkled with the dried lavender which Madam always carried in her bags. It was almost too much to bear, but Gin had broken down once already today, and it had been a humiliation which she was in no hurry to repeat, even now she was alone.

That state did not last long: a knock on the door announced Sam, looking as tired and sad as she felt. She curtseyed, and said, "I've bespoke our supper, Mr. Jessop. It should be up shortly."

"Have you, Gin? I confess I had not thought of it, even though now that I think about it, I do seem to be a little hungry. Thank you." He sat down heavily on one of the chairs and sighed. "It seems we have come to an impasse. A dead end. Apart from your young friends, everyone sighs and offers their sympathy and says how dreadful, but then they shrug and turn away, washing their hands of us. I had thought better of people here, I thought they would be anxious to help, but it seems not."

"It's because the smugglers have took her," Gin said. "They daresn't go agin them. There's no law in these parts where smugglers are concerned, because all of them here have got their trotters in the trough. The wine's smuggled, the brandy's smuggled, probably the tea they drink and the silks and lace the ladies wear are smuggled too. And I reckon Crowley's in it, up to his neck. He's a right wrong'un, Mr. Jessop."

"You're surely right, Gin. But it's no use tracking him down and confronting him. He'll play the innocent and deny everything, with a smile of sweet reason that I fear cloaks all manner of wickedness. And wherever Polly is now, she will not be in his company, I feel sure. What I do not understand, though, is why he has taken her. Revenge, perhaps, if he is the fanatic Jacobite that Dark suspects he is."

Gin slammed her hand down on the table, so hard that Sam jumped. "That's it, Mr. Jessop! That's it! Why did we not think of it before? There's one who will do all he can to find Madam, and never mind the cost. There's nothing else for it, we shall have to ask Dark to help us."

"That's if we can find *him*," Sam pointed out. "We have no idea of where he might be. He could be in France, or the north country, or anywhere."

"Or he could be kicking his heels at Half Moon Street, waiting for Madam to return," said Gin, with some exasperation. "But how do we know unless one of us goes back there?" She gave him a challenging stare. "If you sets off for London tomorrow, you can be in town the day after. And I'll lay you a shilling to a guinea that old hag Madame Rousselle knows a lot more about where Dark is than she bothered to tell you and Madam. If you lay it on thick, make it a matter of life and death, maybe she'll spill. But don't think of bullying her, she'll be as stubborn as an old mule if you do."

For a moment, she thought that Sam would refuse. But she could not go, not on her own, she was only a young girl and a servant, and she could not ride alone to Tonbridge. And someone had to stay in Rye, to carry on the search with the help of Tawny and Phil. Gin crossed her fingers behind her back, and waited for his answer.

"You are right, Gin, of course," he said heavily at last. "I do not like to leave you here alone, but there is no other way."

"I won't come to no harm in Rye," said Gin, with far more confidence than she actually felt. "And I'll have Phil and Tawny to help me carry on looking. They know all the land round here and where Madam might have been hid. You go and find Dark, Mr. Jessop, and once we have him back with us, it'll all come right, you'll see!"

*

Crowley returned, as promised, as the sun rose. Hunger and thirst had woken Polly some time before that, as the first light slunk into the sky and changed the absolute darkness within the shack to a vague grey. Her tongue filled her mouth, and felt gritty and harsh, as if she had swallowed sand. For a while after waking, she lay quite still, trying to think of something, anything, that would take her mind off the desperate longing for water and for food. And then she heard men's voices outside, low and urgent, and knew that her nemesis was back.

"Good morning, Mrs. Paradice!" Crowley seemed very pleased with himself today. "I have brought you a visitor."

For a wild moment, she thought that it might be Matty,

but then realised that the figure behind Crowley was far too large. Dark haired and thick-browed, with a pockmarked face, he stood menacingly in the doorway. Polly sat up, ignoring the sudden feeling of light-headedness, and said, "I see you have brought your minion with you. Is he content to see a lady imprisoned and abused?"

Her captor laughed. "Content? He should be, I pay him enough. Besides, he was one of the men who brought you here. Were you not, Gabriel?"

"Indeed I were, Mr. Crowley."

"You are as despicable as he is," Polly said to the dark-haired man. "Do you sleep well at night?"

"I should imagine he does," said Crowley. "He's the leader of a most notorious gang of smugglers, after all, so bringing you here is a very minor crime compared to everything else he gets up to. Now, Gabriel, will you do as I asked? I would not want Mrs Paradice to wander off again and come to some misfortune in the marshes. These parts can be dangerous. You never know who you might meet, or what accident might befall you."

"Aye, sir," said the man Gabriel, and came into the shack. He knelt beside Polly and before she had time to realise what he was doing, he had tied a thick loop of rope tightly round her left wrist. As she began to protest, he rose, reached up to the rafters, and fastened the other end to a large hook from which, presumably, dead ducks or geese would be hung. He tugged at it to check that it was secure, and nodded to Crowley. "She won't get away agin, sir."

Polly stared at them in furious astonishment. "You would tie me up? Like a common criminal in Newgate? What manner of men are you? You are a heartless barbarian, Crowley, and I wish you nothing but ill! And I won't give in to you, I can assure you of that!"

"So you keep saying." Crowley bent down and placed two water bottles on the stool beside her. He looked at Gabriel, and indicated the bucket. "Deal with that. Then we can go."

As the dark-haired man went out with it, Crowley turned again to her. "I will be back tomorrow evening. I will bring pen, and ink, and paper. I want the name and direction of your banker, and I want you to write him a letter authorising me, as your agent, to withdraw all your funds and take charge of them. Is that clear? You have two days and a night to think on it. And if you persist in your defiance, well, I can make your imprisonment even worse for you. Ah, Gabriel, thank you. Put it there, so that she can get to it. Of course it is very close to the bed, if you can dignify a verminous heap of old straw by such a name, but I am told you can become used to the stink if it is in your nostrils all the time. And now, Mistress Paradice, good day to you. Until tomorrow evening."

He bowed mockingly, and followed Gabriel out into the fresh bright air. The door slammed, cutting off the light, and she was once more alone.

At least she had water. She drank more than half of the first bottle immediately, ignoring the stale, slightly brackish taste, grateful for the relief to her mouth and throat. After that, she lay down, which was just possible if she chose the right position, and dozed for a long time, until woken by a fly, circling annoyingly round her. It was possible to tell that the sun must be high in the sky, from the short slivers of light across the floor, and from the heat, penetrating even this almost airless space. Polly drank some more of the water, too thirsty to consider where it had come from, even though it had probably been taken from some murky pond and would give her griping guts and other ills. And it assuaged, a little, the gnawing pit in her belly. She had been hungry often enough in her life, but not so savagely as this. When had she last eaten? It had been supper at the Mermaid, not yesterday, but the day before. Only a short while, but looking back, it seemed to belong in another life.

*

"Winchelsea," said Tawny. "That would be a good place to hide someone."

Gin looked at him. "Where's Winchelsea? Is it near here?"

"It's there." Phil pointed. "See that big hump of rock and trees? That's Winchelsea."

The three young people were standing in the Gun Garden, below the ancient and diminutive stone castle which Gin had now learned was called the Wipers Tower, or simply the Tower, and was used as the town gaol. They had conducted another fruitless search of the Strand and the boats, and encountered the same blank wall of supposed ignorance that Gin and Sam had met with, the day before. Now they had come to this unfrequented space, with bread and cheese and a leather jack of small beer, to rest and to satisfy their hunger before planning their next move.

Gin squinted at the distant hill, surrounded by more flat and dreary acres of marsh. "It don't look that far," she said.

"It's not. Three miles at the most. We could hire a horse and be there in less than half an hour." Tawny surveyed the girls with bright enthusiasm. "What do you say? Shall we?"

Gin looked hopefully at Phil, but she shook her head. "No, Tawny, we can't. Mama thinks I'm spending too much time in your company, and she's told me I have to do my lessons this afternoon. But tomorrow, we can bespeak horses from Mr. Bird and spend all day in Winchelsea, for Mama and Bab have arranged to have dinner with Mrs. Spencer in Playden."

"Tom Spencer is a very eligible young man," said Tawny,

with a wink at Gin. "Though Bab thinks he's far too much under his mother's thumb, so I fear Mama might be wasting her time. Very well, tomorrow it must be. I will arrange for the horse, and then I have an urgent appointment with a flying machine."

"You couldn't fly it from here without breaking your neck," said Gin. "Miss Phil and I looked the other day."

"I don't intend to fly it from here. Phil tells me that the cliff beside the Landgate would be a better place." He looked quizzically at Gin. "You think I'm mad, don't you?"

"Course I don't!"

"You do, Jane," Phil reminded her, "you asked me the day we met if my brother had windmills in his head."

To Gin's surprise, Tawny did not seem to mind in the least, but hooted with laughter. "Mama certainly thinks I do. She despairs of me. I never write to her, I spend far too much time neglecting my duties and my studies, and chasing foolish dreams. Frank is far more satisfactory – he writes home regularly, he works hard, and he doesn't frequent coffee houses and taverns and playhouses."

"He's not as – as *interesting* as you are," said Phil. "In fact, I can safely say that most of the time, he's very dull." She brushed the remaining breadcrumbs from the folds in her skirts, and turned to Gin. "I have to go, or Mama will be cross with me, and even more cross with Tawny. But I'll see you tomorrow. Goodbye!"

With a careless wave of her hand, she vanished through the arch that led back towards the town. Gin watched her go, and then turned to Tawny. "Why is Winklesea a good place to look?"

"Winchelsea. Because it's built on the rock, and many of the houses have cellars, to store barrels of wine, but they'd be ideal for hiding someone. And then there's Winchelsea Castle. See, there it is, to the left of Winchelsea but nearer to us. The people say it is haunted and that ghostly spirits wail and gibber in the ruins." He grinned. "But I think the 'ghosts' are far more likely to be smugglers who don't want people poking and prying. It would be a good place to store barrels of wine and brandy."

"Or to hide people," said Gin thoughtfully. "Could we go there tomorrow, as well as to Winchelsea?"

"Of course we can!" Tawny beamed at her, alight with an eagerness which was very appealing. "Don't worry, Jane, we will find her." He paused, and then said, rather shyly, "Would you like to see my flying machine? As long as you remember that it's not finished, nor anywhere near it."

Gin glowed with pleasure. This pleasant, friendly young man from a well-to-do family was not only taking notice of her, but treating her as his equal, in exactly the same way as he treated his own sister. "Indeed I would, sir," she said primly. "Where do you keep it?"

"In my late father's storehouse. You may have noticed it, it's a handsome brick building just over the way and down the street from our house. Since my father died, other merchants have used it, but it's never full, so Mama said I could have the use of a space on the ground floor. She thinks I'm planning to set myself up in business, starting in a small way just as my father did, but I would rather amuse myself with the flying machine." He grinned disarmingly. "It's a welcome distraction from lawyer's affairs. Will you accompany me, Miss Jane?"

He proffered his arm, and with a thrill of delight, Gin took it. They promenaded across the open space in front of the Tower, round the churchyard and so to the top of Middle Street. Passing the Mermaid, Gin was reminded briefly of why she was here, and wondered whether Sam, who had set off for London that morning, would manage to extract the information about Dark's whereabouts from the ancient and unsavoury Madame Rousselle. And then they were standing outside a very handsome brick building, that she had assumed to be a gentleman's residence.

"Look there, Jane," said her escort, letting go of her arm so that he could point at the wall not far above their heads. Gin tipped her head back and saw, set into the russet stone, a plaque with writing on it. Now she wished, how she wished, that she had paid more attention when Madam was attempting to teach her to read and write. But she had no intention of admitting, to this young man who was giving her his undivided attention as if he genuinely liked her, that she did not know more than the most simple words. She squinted up at it, as if her extremely sharp eyesight was actually not very good. "I can't quite see what it says, it's too far away."

"Of course you can't read it," Tawny said, and for the first time she detected a note of condescension in his voice. "It's in Latin, and girls don't learn Latin."

"Why not?" Gin demanded, her hackles rising instantly. "I could learn Latin if I wanted to."

"And do you?"

It was impossible to be annoyed by him for long. Gin looked at his smiling face, the warm brown eyes behind their round, heavy lenses – his eyesight was, obviously, genuinely weak – and felt a little jolt in the pit of her stomach. She grinned back. "Which I don't. So, Mr. Dry-boots, what does it say in Latin? And then say it in good honest English."

Obediently, Tawny recited the words, which he obviously knew by heart. *"Junii 13, 1689, culminante sole jactum fuit hujus repositorii fundamentum coelo se sic habante."*

"That ain't Latin, that's rantum-scantum."

"It is Latin, I can assure you. And this is the English. 'At mid-day on June 13th, 1689, the foundation of this warehouse was laid, the heavenly bodies being in these positions.'"

"Heavenly bodies? What's that mean? And what are all those marks below the writing?"

"My father was very interested in astrology." As Gin looked blankly at him, he elaborated. "He believed that the heavenly bodies, the stars and planets, influence what happens here on earth. So he worked out what he thought was a good time to build his storehouse, according to the positions of those heavenly bodies as it says, and that's what those signs and symbols indicate."

"It all sounds too much like Old Nick's doings," Gin said suspiciously. "Did he conjure demons or ride on birds?"

Tawny laughed. "I don't think so! He would be horrified at the thought. My father was a good upstanding Christian. That is what my mother says, but I have no memory of him, I was only two years old when he died, and Frank was not even born. My stepfather, Phil's father, Joseph Tucker, is the only father I've ever known."

Gin decided not to mention that she had no memory of her own father either: indeed, she did not even know his identity, although her mother, in her frequent drunkenly maudlin moments, had always claimed that he was a young lordling. She watched as Tawny fumbled in his coat pocket, producing a key, unlocked the door of the storehouse and pushed it open. Then she followed him inside.

To her surprise, the space within, lit by two large windows, was almost empty. There were some sacks and crates stacked up in one corner, but the rest was bare and dusty, with a few grains and some light drifts of what looked like dried flowers scattered across the floor. Gin bent and picked one up. A familiar aroma tickled her nose. "It smells just like beer!"

"That's because it's a hop," said Tawny. "There's a big trade in hops in Kent and Sussex. In a few weeks the new harvest will arrive and be stored here, before it's shipped on to the West Country and Ireland."

Gin looked at the papery little cone between her fingers, and rubbed it gently so that the pungent fragrance filled the air. Then she looked round. "Where's this here flying machine, then?"

"In here." Tawny led her to a further room, much smaller than the first. In the middle lay a confusion of sticks, tied together in a rough oval. Acutely disappointed, Gin said, "Is that it?"

"It's not finished." He sounded a little defensive. "That's just the frame. I have to decide what is best to cover it. It could be canvas, or a thinner calico weave. This is what it will look like." He went over to the windowsill and picked up something which Gin had assumed was a leaf. "I made this to see if it would work."

It sat flatly on his palm, a little larger than his hand. She could see that the frame was made of very light canes, covered with thin, almost transparent paper. There was a hole in the middle, occupied by a stick figure that was obviously intended to represent a man. Gin said, "I thought it would have wings like a bird."

"That's what I originally wanted, but birds are much lighter than we are, and even the strongest man would not have enough power in his arms to flap the wings and lift himself off the ground, because of a force that Sir Isaac calls gravity, which pulls everything down to the earth. So I studied the gulls and buzzards soaring high above the Marsh, and decided that it would be easier, and have more chance of success, to build a machine that would glide rather than fly.

And that's what this does. Watch."

He transferred the little model to his other hand, then picked it up and gently launched it into the air. To Gin's surprise, it did not plummet instantly to the floor, but floated gently forwards and down, to land in a patch of golden sunlight. She clapped her hands in delight. "It truly does fly!"

"It glides," Tawny corrected her. "So I thought that if the model works, it was worth the time and effort to make a much larger machine that would be capable of carrying me. Do you still think I've got windmills in my head?"

Gin looked at him sideways. "Maybe," she admitted. "But it's *your* head what'll be broke if it all goes wrong."

"I shall choose a good landing place, never fear. There's marshy ground below the town wall on the north side, I might try there." He grinned at her. "Though of course I might land on a sheep!"

In ordinary times, it would have been a splendid afternoon, Gin decided later, when she had returned to the silent, lonely chamber in the Mermaid. And even so, for an hour or more she had been so entranced by Tawny and his flying machine that she had almost – almost, but not quite – been able to ignore the lump of dread in her belly, the fear that Polly was lost for ever. Now, looking round at the desolate room, she felt despair return with a vengeance. She owed everything to Madam, the clothes she stood in and the food she ate, and above all the fact that she was still alive, rather than tipped into a pauper's grave after freezing to death last winter. Polly had held out her hand to haul Gin out of the gutter, and she knew that she had been fortunate beyond all deserving. If she could repay that kindness a thousand-fold, she would.

And Dark, too, had been kind to her, in his odd fashion, because once, long ago, she had saved his life. Gin sat down at the table, where soon her supper would be laid, and wondered where he was now, and whether Sam had managed to extract his direction from Madame Rousselle – assuming, of course, that she knew it. Surely, surely, Dark would be able to help. And they would find Polly. They *would*. She clung to that with all the fierceness in her nature, because the alternative was too dreadful to contemplate.

CHAPTER FOURTEEN

To mock at my Misfortunes

Polly dozed uneasily, prey to unpleasant dreams and eventually stabbed back into wakefulness by the harsh cries of seabirds, unseen in the air above the hut. The sun was sinking, and a fly, probably the same one that had annoyed her earlier, was buzzing too close to her face. She swatted it away, and it flew angrily up into the rafters. Then she sat up with an effort, and removed her mantle. It would be necessary tonight, but now she was uncomfortably warm. She leaned back against the wall of the shack, feeling the sweat start out on her forehead. At least she had loosened her stays yesterday, which was fortunate because she did not think she would have been able to do it with one hand tied. The rope round her wrist chafed a little, even when she was still, but it was bearable. The humiliation, however, was worse than any discomfort.

To raise her spirits, she began to hum the lullaby, 'Golden Slumbers', which her mother had used to sing. The gulls shrieking outside reminded her that she had been told there was no point in screaming, because there was no-one to hear, and even if there was, they would think it was the seabirds. Well, she must make a sound that could not possibly be mistaken for gulls. She stopped humming and then, feeling more than a little foolish, began to sing.

'Golden slumbers kiss your eyes,
Smiles await you when you rise.
Sleep, pretty baby, do not cry,
And I will sing a lullaby.
Cares you know not, therefore sleep,
While over you a watch I'll keep,
Sleep, pretty darling, do not cry,
And I will sing a lullaby.'

She was safe, for Crowley would not return until the following evening. Emboldened, she sang the next verses, feeling her voice grow stronger with every line. Then she embarked on other songs in her repertoire, feeling confidence and hope returning. This was a performance for a sleepy fly and a cluster of seabirds wheeling invisibly in the free air above her, but she sang as if she was at Lincoln's Inn Fields, on the night when she looked down into the pit, and first saw Dark, drawing her as she stood on the stage.

The thought of him almost made her falter, and tears pricked her eyes, but she finished the song, a tragic ballad, and began '*The Fair Maid of Islington*', with its amusing *double entendres*. She followed that with a selection of traditional songs, and then, feeling her throat growing scratchy, eased it with more water and rested for a while. She had no audience, but strangely she did not mind, for she was curled up safe in her own world, the world of music, where nothing could touch her.

So she tried songs she had always found difficult, and different phrasing of old favourites, and finally, when she was growing tired and her voice was beginning to fade, she began *Dido's Lament*. Isolated out here in the Marsh, imprisoned and tied, it seemed extraordinarily appropriate. And so lost was she in the words, the emotion and the tune, that she did not realise that she had been heard until the door swung open, throwing a spear of golden sunlight into the shack.

But it was not Crowley who stood there. It was Mattie.

Utterly astonished, Polly stared at the young woman who might, or might not, be her lost sister. She had last seen her, so briefly, in the room at the Blue Anchor, and that betrayal had struck hard and deep. Mattie was responsible for her present miserable situation, and the knowledge fuelled her anger. "I'm surprised you're here. I assume that you have come to gloat."

The other woman came into the shack. She was still in breeches and that brown coat, which at close quarters was distinctly shabby and worn at the elbows, with dark smears at neck and cuffs. She said curtly, "No, I have not."

"Really? I would have thought you must be delighted to see me in these unfortunate circumstances." Polly raised her left hand so that the rope around her wrist was obvious. "Your friend Crowley is no better than a brute."

Mattie flushed. "You tried to escape."

"And why should I not? I am not a common criminal held in Newgate. I have not been tried, or judged, or condemned, and I have committed no crime."

"You stole the king's gold."

"So he has infected you with his lies, has he?" All the terror that had been pent up during the past two days and nights fuelled Polly's fury now. "That gold was intended to fuel a rebellion against our lawful king, which is treason."

"And now you have it."

"I do not. My lover Sinclair spent most of it – on arms for the rebellion, yes, but also on himself – a fine horse, a comfortable house. rich clothing, a jewelled sword. Any wealth I possess has been earned by my own efforts, and is not Crowley's to take."

"Liar," Mattie said, her voice rich with contempt. "I know you're lying."

Polly stared at her. "What have I done to you, that you hate me so much? All my life I have loved you, and I did my best to keep the three of us together when our parents died, even though I was only twelve years old!"

"You let them take me. You stood and watched while that woman struck me, and you let them take me."

"Oh, Mattie, please understand, I couldn't have prevented it – Kitty held me back until they and you had gone. And if even I had tried, it would only have made things worse for you."

Her sister made a derisive sound. "Why should I believe you?"

"Because it's the truth! And I mourned you when I believed you were dead. Mattie, we are *sisters*. That should count for something, surely."

"You only have my word for it, that we are sisters."

"Yes – Cutty."

At her use of their father's pet name for her, Mattie flinched. Polly said, "You knew that word, and it proves you are either truly Mattie, or you have known her. Which is it?"

The other girl did not answer. Instead, she put her hand in her coat pocket and brought out a leather pouch. She threw it down by Polly's feet, and then turned and went out, slamming the door behind her. The key turned, the bolt rattled, and there was the sound of rapid footsteps diminishing, followed a little later, by hoofbeats.

Breathing hard, once more alone in the dim shack, Polly stared at the little bag, wondering what it might be. She could think of several things, most of them unwelcome. It was just beyond her reach, but by shifting her position, and stretching out her hand, she was able to pull it close enough to undo the drawstring at the top and peer inside.

The smell of fresh baking rose up. Polly stared in astonishment at the rough bread roll, the hunk of cheese, and the small rosy apple. Tears sprang to her eyes. She had been angry and unwelcoming, but Mattie had brought her food. She pulled out the roll and tore it into pieces, devouring each one hungrily, knowing she should not eat too fast but unable to resist. Only when the bread was gone, and the cheese nibbled and swallowed more slowly till perhaps half of it was left, did she pause to consider the implications.

Mattie had brought her food, even though Crowley had said that he had no intention of giving her any. That meant that her sister must have somehow stolen the key and come here without his knowledge. Therefore, to ensure her safety, Polly must be careful to hide all the evidence. It would be easy enough to do, she could secrete the pouch in the pocket of her dress, and she intended to eat absolutely everything, down to the last crumb, including the apple's core.

And if Mattie had gone behind Crowley's back to bring comfort to his prisoner, then her hostility was not as complete as Polly had assumed. She could not understand, though, why Mattie had conspired with Crowley to abduct her, and then deceived him. What was happening inside her sister's head? What motivated her? Polly broke small pieces off the cheese, which was fresh and ripe, and ate them slowly, still thinking. Crowley had said that he knew things about her sister that would freeze the blood, and there was something she sensed in Mattie, some wild, implacable darkness that made his words plausible. And for that reason, she could not imagine that her sister would have taken Crowley as a lover.

By the time she had finished the apple, including the pips, she was no nearer resolving the question. Perhaps Mattie had been coerced into doing as he asked. He must have a hold over her: it could be that she had indeed committed some dreadful crime, and he had threatened to denounce her to a magistrate. But it was all pure speculation, she reminded herself, hunting down a last piece of cheese which had crumbled and lay somewhere in the straw beside her. She found it, dusted off the dirt, put it in her mouth, still gritty, and chewed thoughtfully, savouring the taste because she knew there was a good chance that Mattie would not return. If only she had not been so angry, if she had welcomed her ...

But why should she have expected me to welcome her? Polly thought unhappily. *The last sight I had of her was her look of triumph as I was captured. She betrayed my belief and my trust, I could not help but be angry with her.*

She made sure that there was no morsel left evident of the food, and tucked the empty pouch into the pocket beneath her skirts. Her gown was very much the worse for wear, covered in dust and pieces of straw, and in sore need of a good brushing and hanging up to get rid of the dirt and creases, but that was the least of her worries. Crowley would be back tomorrow evening, and he had said he would bring pen and ink and paper. But he could not force her to tell him her banker's name, or write a letter to him authorising him to take her savings. And she was determined not to give in to his threats. She had been a whore, she had experienced many of the evil things that men could do to women they despised, what could he possibly inflict on her that would be vile enough to persuade her to abandon all her hopes for the future?

Besides, she realised as the warm day dwindled into a murky dusk, there was the very real possibility that once she had given him the information he desired, once she had written that letter, he would be free to kill her.

*

Gin eyed the ferry that would take them across the river westwards towards Winchelsea. She had sworn never to set foot in such a craft again, but Tawny and Phil were unaware of that, and she did not want to show herself up for a ninny and a chicken-heart in front of her new friends. So she swallowed hard, picked up her skirts, and clambered into the boat, hoping that she would not disgrace herself by being sick, even though the water, in the clear light of morning, was as smooth as a mirror. The two horses Tawny had procured stood calmly in the middle of the craft, looking as if they did this every day of the week, which was, Gin thought, probably very nearly true. She looked at the round and somehow threatening rump of the nearest animal, looming above her, and edged back a little, just in case.

But they were poled across the river without any incident, and safely disembarked on the other side, much to Gin's relief. Tawny paid the ferryman and mounted the taller of the two horses – though that was not saying much – while the two girls shared the other, a sturdy broadbacked pony with a sleepy eye and a white star on its forehead. It had been supplied with an ordinary saddle, and Phil rode it astride, arranging her skirts to show as little of her legs as possible. Gin, also astride, perched on the pillion pad behind her, clasped her friend round the waist and prayed that she would not fall off, for although the pony had seemed quite small when she was standing next to it, the ground now looked to be a very long way down. Then they rode in the direction of Winchelsea Castle.

This was the first time that Gin had set foot on any part of the Marsh surrounding Rye, and she was not impressed. Land that had appeared to be as flat as a pancake from the vantage point of the Gun Garden now revealed itself to be humped and ridged like a crumpled old length of cloth. The humps and ridges turned out to be made of shingle, inadequately covered with grass, and all too often the lower ground between them was boggy, or filled with standing water, evil-smelling and home to a host of small biting insects. And sheep were everywhere, their voices competing with the gulls. Gin hunched her shoulders, feeling dangerously exposed in this open landscape.

Tawny, who seemed to know a great deal about a great many things, told them that the ridges marked old shorelines. "Not so long ago, this was all under the sea. Winchelsea was a port, with a strand and harbour like Rye, and ships could berth right up by the walls. And the castle was built by old

King Henry, the one who had six wives, to protect Rye Bay from attack by the French, but the sea fled from it so fast that seventy years later any ships would be far out of range of its cannon, and it was useless. So it fell into ruin."

They were approaching it now. The only other castle that Gin had ever seen at close quarters was the Tower of London, and Winchelsea was nothing like it. Low round towers and curtain walls surrounded a squat central keep, also round. As they came near, sheep ambled away from their horses, and a flock of jackdaws flew up from one of the towers, squawking furiously at being disturbed.

"Well, at least that means there's no-one else here," Tawny said. He dismounted and tied his horse to a stunted hawthorn bush a few yards from the gatehouse. The girls followed suit. Gin looked up at the ancient walls, decorated with stray plants and crumbling stones, and suppressed a shiver. What if those tales that it was haunted proved to be true?

"I hope there aren't any ghosts," Phil said, sounding uncharacteristically anxious. Gin grinned at her, as much to bolster her own courage as her friend's. "There ain't no ghosts here, not in broad daylight with the sun shining down, they wouldn't dare!"

"No," said Phil. "Of course they wouldn't."

"Come on!" Tawny called from the entrance. "Don't tell me either of you are afraid of phantoms!"

That settled it of course, and the two girls followed him under the gateway. The keep at the centre was just a shell now, surrounded by an outer wall from which projected the gatehouse, and the four semi-circular towers. It was plain that the castle had not been habitable for a very long time, and also that despite its ruined condition, something, or someone, was using it, for there were paths through the undergrowth, and hoofprints that were definitely not those of sheep.

"Look," Phil said, pointing to a pile of dung. "That's from a horse."

Tawny went over to inspect it. "And quite fresh, too – yesterday, or the day before."

"Smugglers?" Gin enquired.

"Almost certainly. A looker – a shepherd – would be on foot, and who else would come in here with a horse?"

"We have," Phil pointed out.

Tawny grinned at her. "Yes, but we're not trying to hide ourselves. Our horses are in plain view outside the gatehouse. This animal was kept out of sight."

"You've been here before, haven't you?"

"Yes, this was a favourite place to come when Frank and I were boys. I tried to climb the keep once, and fell down and broke my arm, do you remember that? It was seven years ago, so you were quite small."

"I was five, and I do remember." Phil assumed a superior expression. "You made a lot of noise."

"Well, it was very painful when the bonesetter splinted it."

"Here," Gin said, "I thought we was supposed to be searching this place?"

For the next hour and more, they explored the castle. It was compact, but proved to have a veritable warren of passages, chambers and niches, all of which had to be investigated. There were certainly plenty of indications that people, and goods, had been here recently – trampled earth, a broken and discarded tobacco pipe, a button from someone's coat – but all the spaces which might have been used to store contraband were at present empty. Nor was there any place in which a prisoner might have been kept.

At length, hot, dusty, nettle-stung, bramble-pricked and

hand-scraped, they emerged from the gate house to find a lean, grey-haired man approaching. He wore a smock and carried a shepherd's crook, and a black dog trotted at his heels. The animal eyed them suspiciously, and lifted its upper lip in a silent warning.

"Good morning to you," Tawny said cheerfully.

The shepherd surveyed him, unsmiling. "What be ee doing in there? Bain't safe for maids." He indicated Phil and Gin, whose clothes were now considerably the worse for wear. "Be a deep well in there, you could have been drownded."

Tawny hesitated, and Gin, whose skill at talking her way out of trouble was the result of years of practice, stepped hastily in. "We was looking for our dog, he ran off after a rabbit and we can't find him anywhere!"

"Dog? What manner of dog?"

"Brown and white, with a feathery tail," Gin said, improvising with the description of just such an animal she had seen in Rye the previous day.

"Ain't seen one like that," said the shepherd. "And if I do see it, and it be chasing the sheep, I'll knock it on the head if I catch 'un." He brandished the crook menacingly.

"Oh, he's a good dog, he knows better than to chase sheep," Phil said in a conciliatory tone. "Anyway, we must continue our search. Thank you."

Under the man's hostile gaze, they mounted their horses, Tawny helping the girls onto the pony before swinging into his own saddle, and rode away from the castle in the direction of Winchelsea. Gin looked back after several minutes and saw the shepherd still standing by the gatehouse, his own dog at his side, watching them to make sure they were truly leaving.

"That was well done, Jane," Tawny said when they were beyond any possible earshot. "For the life of me, on the spur of the moment I couldn't think of a good reason for us to be in there. And you too, Phil, backing her up. I think he was convinced."

"Well, there was nothing inside the castle to find," Phil said. "So he needn't have been so hostile, unless he thought we were snooping for the Revenue men."

"And that ain't likely," Gin pointed out.

Winchelsea was plainly visible to the south-west of them, sitting on its outcrop of rock, rather as Rye did, the same distance to the north. However, the route to it seemed anything but direct, and involved skirting pools of water, clumps of twisted gorse, and riding up and down dykes and ridges, avoiding the ubiquitous sheep, many of which, on this warm sunny day, lay chewing the cud in the shade of contorted hawthorn bushes or banks of reeds. Gin suspected that this bare, bleak landscape would be very much worse in winter, with the wind scouring the Marsh and the rain stinging. London, despite its dangers, its heaps of refuse, the beggars and thieves, the constant noise and stink and the press of people, seemed cosy and welcoming by comparison. She longed above all else to be back in the Paradise, with Madam behind the bar, or singing, and the coffee house full of warmth and talk and tobacco smoke, Dan and Joe rushing to and fro with pots and pipes, and the heavy, familiar figure of Will Evans keeping the door. Even the thought of Hannah's gimlet eye upon her was surprisingly comforting.

And Dark. What would Dark do, if they were unable to find Madam, or, even worse, they found her corpse? Gin's imagination quailed from the prospect. That forbidding shell concealed a vulnerable core: she knew this because his previous lover had treated him vilely, and nearly driven him to take his own life, but she, Gin, had saved him. *Please let us find her*, she prayed silently, to God, or Fate, or some other unknown deity. *Please, we must find her, so much and so many depends on her.*

Eventually, after negotiating a great number of obstacles, including the fording of dykes, ditches or streamlets, and once making a considerable detour to avoid a very large bull with an impressive pair of horns, they arrived at the Strand Gate, at the foot of the cliff on which New Winchelsea was built. Tawny had earlier told them something of its founding hundreds of years ago, after Old Winchelsea had been drowned in a great storm, and the survivors had chosen this site for their new town because it was too high to be in danger from the waves. Then, the water had lapped the foot of this cliff, and ships had unloaded on the Strand by the gate, but in less than a hundred years the sea had cheated the inhabitants of Winchelsea again, and retreated so far that what had once been ocean was now swamp and shingle, and the town's trade went into a catastrophic decline.

Even so, Gin had expected to find a thriving settlement at the top of the long hill up from the gate, and was shocked to see that most of the few houses were in a state of decay, or even ruin, with broken glass, green and mouldy thatch and many overgrown plots where, obviously, the remains of a once-prosperous house was gradually sinking back into the earth. A cluster of children, as ragged as those in London, stood and stared at them with interest, and an ancient crone at the door of her even more ancient cottage glared at them as if they were personally responsible for Winchelsea's failure and poverty.

It was now well past mid-day, and it had been many hours since her early breakfast. Gin's belly growled in complaint. She was glad to see that, facing the huge but truncated church, there was an inn, quite a substantial building, which presumably could furnish them with some sustenance, even if it was only bread and cheese. They dismounted in the yard, and a stable boy led away the ponies for a drink, a net of hay and a rub down, while Tawny went in search of the landlord.

He was quite a while, and Gin and Phil waited for him in a parlour, talking over their search of Winchelsea Castle, and trying to ignore their rapidly increasing hunger until a maid brought bread and cheese, a pat of yellow butter and thick slices of ham. It was very simple fare, but delicious.

Tawny came in at last, his eyes going at once to the table. He grinned. "Thank you for leaving some for me – I was wondering if you would."

"Of course we have," said Phil, with mock indignation. She indicated the food still on the tray, and asked, "Did you learn anything from the landlord?"

"Well, it was interesting." Tawny cut himself a big hunk of bread, spread a layer of butter over it that was almost as thick, and topped it with a huge piece of pink, juicy ham. "I'm so hungry my innards are clapping together." He took a large bite and added through his mouthful, "I hadn't realised how many cellars there are in Winchelsea. Dozens! They were used to store wine, but once the sea retreated and there was no more trade, they're mostly empty or abandoned."

Dismayed, Gin said, "There are *dozens* of cellars here?"

Tawny was still chewing, so she had to wait until he had swallowed it all, and washed it down with a gulp of cool beer which Phil had poured for all of them from a big jug. He wiped his mouth with a napkin and continued. "There's one beneath this inn – the landlord insisted on showing me, that's why I was so long. Stone vaulted, very cool even in the hottest weather, but in winter it's warmer than outside. Perfect for keeping beer and wine, it's full of barrels." He looked at Gin. "Don't worry, Jane, it's not so bad as it sounds. Winchelsea is a small place now, and it should be easy to find the cellars that are still in use, because although the houses were built on top of them, they all open onto the street. Just let me finish here, and then we can go looking."

He made it sound very easy, but Gin was not so sure. She

tried and failed to be encouraged by his optimism. Madam had been missing for days now, and it seemed ever more likely that they would never find her. When would Sam return to Rye? And would he bring Dark with him?

CHAPTER FIFTEEN

Conscience you have none

When Sam Jessop arrived at the faded, peeling blue door of the house in Half Moon Street, he was in no mood to be polite. He had left Rye at dawn the previous day, and ridden the forty miles to Tonbridge along dreadful roads, only to find that there was no coach to London that week as the conveyance had been overturned a few days ago and was undergoing extensive repairs. There was nothing for it but to stay that night at the Rose and Crown, and continue the following day on horseback. As a result, he had arrived at his usual inn in Holborn weary, saddle sore and sick with fear for Polly and anxiety about Gin, left behind to carry on the search alone. A snatched meal and a change of clothing had done little to lessen his discomfort, and he had perforce to hire a hackney out of consideration for his aching legs. He bade the driver wait for him, and hammered the brass door knocker with no regard for the sensibilities of anyone within the house, or indeed within earshot.

It was eventually answered by the footman John, looking rather flustered. "Sir! There is no-one at home!"

"So Dark is not here?" Sam glared at him, and John visibly quailed. "No, sir, he has not returned since your visit last week, and we have had no word from him."

"And Madame Rousselle?"

"She has retired for the night, sir, and must not be disturbed."

"It's not seven o'clock yet," Sam reminded him, and with a boldness that he would later find astonishing, shouldered his way past the indignant footman, and into the hall. A young maid appeared from the back of the house, rather too obviously adjusting the neckline of her bodice, her face flushed and full of annoyance. "Sir! You cannot – "

"Oh, yes, I can," said Sam forcefully, and pushed open the door to Madame's chamber.

The ancient actress was indeed in her bed, but obviously awake: she sat bolt upright, propped by a bank of bolsters and pillows, a battered book on her lap and wearing an embroidered nightgown over a lace-trimmed shift. Her frilled cap did not disguise the unfortunate absence of her habitual red wig, or hide the straggling white hairs that made her look not only much older, but much more vulnerable. She leaned forward as Sam burst in, and pointed a claw at him. "You, you insolent malefactor! What is the meaning of this intrusion?"

Her words sounded like, and probably were, lines from some long-forgotten play. Sam, breathing hard, said, "I have to know where Dark is. If you know, or if you have guessed, or even if you have the vaguest notion, I beg of you, for the love of God, please tell me."

"*Dark?* You want to know where Dark is, Mr. Jessop? Well, I can give you a straight answer to that. He ain't here. Ain't been here for over a month. So you've wasted your time." Madame Rousselle shut her mouth like a trap, and fixed him with a malevolent and self-satisfied stare.

"I know he's not here! But I need to know where he's gone." Meeting her implacable gaze, he surrendered to desperation. "It could be a matter of life and death."

"Whose life? And whose death, pray?"

"His life," said Sam. "And Polly's death."

The hot airless room was suddenly very quiet. A scuffling in the hall outside reminded Sam that there were witnesses to this. Madame had obviously realised this as well, for she shouted suddenly, "John! Sukey! Get yourselves back to the kitchen, fornicate all you please, I don't care, but if you dare to eavesdrop, I'll dismiss you both and tell the justices you've made off with my silver! Now begone!"

She waited until the two sets of scurrying footsteps had diminished into the distance, followed by the shutting of a door. Then she turned back to Sam. "Explain yourself."

His earlier anger had vanished. Haltingly, under that basilisk stare, he related once again the events that had led up to Polly's disappearance, and their fruitless search for her. Madame Rousselle heard him out in silence, which was even more intimidating, until at last he faltered and stopped.

"You think she's in danger?" the old woman demanded. "What gives you that notion?"

"If Crowley has her, he may want revenge for Sinclair's death," said Sam, aware of how lame it sounded, because of course, in fact he did not know anything for certain: it was pure speculation.

"If that's the case, he'd want revenge on Dark as well," said Madame. "Perhaps she's a decoy, the bait to lure him into the trap. In which case, why should I tell you where he is, and put him into danger as well?"

Sam picked up on it at once. "So you do know!"

"I never said I didn't," she pointed out. "So what makes you think Dark will succeed where you've so pathetically failed?"

Sam flushed. "Because ... because he will move earth and heaven and cry down the moon, to find her," he said at last.

"A most poetic turn of phrase," was Madame's caustic comment. "Why not just say he loves her and have done with it? Oh, Mr. Jessop, pray do not look so dismayed. You know it's true, and so do I, even if neither of the fools will admit it, even to themselves."

"And if that is true," said Sam, "and if you have even the smallest regard for him, which I think you have, you must acknowledge that if Polly is lost, so is he."

There was a hostile silence. The fire, banked up for the night, glowered sullenly. Madame Rousselle made a small, vehement gesture. "Poof! You have a point, Mr. Jessop. Very well. But before I tell you, just check that neither of those miscreants is lurking behind the door."

Sam went quietly over, and opened it in a rush. To his relief, the hall was empty, though he heard a woman's laughter, rather muffled, coming from the back of the house. He shut the door and nodded. "There's no-one there, Madame."

"Because they know I'd turn them off without a character," said the ancient, with relish. She beckoned. "Come here, Mr. Jessop. Closer. Closer still, how can you hear me whisper from there? I won't eat you."

Reluctantly, Sam approached the bed. As soon as he came within reach, Madame Rousselle reached out and grasped the skirts of his coat with a clawed hand, pulling him towards her until he was touching the embroidered counterpane. He put his hand on it to steady himself, and bent down so that she could hiss into his ear, "He's gone to Godalming."

He had expected York, or Edinburgh, or even France or the Low countries. With what he thought was considerable presence of mind, Sam refrained from uttering the name too loud. "*Godalming*? Isn't that in Surrey? On the Portsmouth road?"

"Coach from the Elephant and Castle at Stone End, you'll be there tomorrow afternoon. Alight at the King's Arms and ask for Mr. Andrews. Say it's farming business. That's all I know." She released him, and he glanced down, seeing to his discomfort that his hand was resting on the plump breast of a naked, embroidered woman, languishing in a flower-strewn meadow. As he hastily withdrew it, Madame gave her cackle of a laugh. "Quite the prude, ain't you, Mr. Jessop?"

"Not at all," said Sam, stepping back with all the dignity he could muster. "Are you sure that information is correct?"

"Of course I'm sure," said Madame, offended. "He told me so himself, before he left."

Puzzled, Sam said, "But I was given to understand that he was visiting his sister."

"Indeed he was, but he came back here briefly before going on to Godalming. I'm the only one who knows." She winked grotesquely. "He certainly didn't tell your precious Polly. I trust you can be discreet? I wouldn't give that direction to any Tom Dick or Harry, Mr. Jessop, you should be flattered. Now be off with you, I'm tired. See yourself out."

There was much about this that Sam did not understand, or mistrusted, but the old woman had settled herself back on her pillows, and closed her eyes. She said, without opening them, "What, still there? Do I have to ring the bell and ask John to throw you out? *Go,* Mr. Jessop!"

Still bewildered, he said, "Yes. Thank you, Madame Rousselle. Goodbye." He bowed, although she could not see him do so, and thought he could discern a smile, before he left her in peace.

*

Crowley returned, as he had promised, about an hour before sunset that evening, accompanied by the man called Gabriel, who emptied the bucket and then stood guard just outside the door. Polly had prepared herself for his arrival, and Mattie's food had had a fortifying effect. She did not cower before him as he dragged the stool to within her reach, and dumped several pieces of paper, a badly cut pen and a corked pot of ink on it. "There, madam. Will you write that letter?"

Polly stared up at him. "You have had my answer. No, I will not."

"I will ask you again. Will you write that letter now?"

"I have already told you. I will not write it now or in the future. My savings are not yours to take, and your attempts to persuade me otherwise will be in vain. Now will you let me go?"

Crowley uttered a vicious exclamation and knelt down beside her. "I can tell you this, madam, I will keep you here until I have what I want."

"And I tell you this, that you will never have it from me. So we are at stalemate, are we not?" Polly gave him a challenging stare. "I propose a bargain. Let me go, and I will not peach on you, or any of your accomplices. Or on my sister. I will say that there has been a misunderstanding that has been resolved to our mutual satisfaction, and we can go our separate ways without any further contact."

"And you expect me to agree to that? I think not. But if hunger and imprisonment will not wear you down, Mrs Paradice, I have other means of persuasion that you may find more compelling."

Suddenly, there was a razor in his hand. Small, wicked, it shone sharply in the light from the door. Polly felt sick. She clasped her hands together to stop them shaking, and said, "And what do you plan to do?"

Crowley smiled. "Oh, all manner of things. I could mark that pretty face for ever with this – I have had it honed so fine, it will cut a single hair with one stroke. Shall I show you what it can do?"

To Polly's horror, he leaned forward and seized her free arm. She cried out and tried to twist away from him, but his grip was too strong. With a swift movement, he brushed the blade across, just above her wrist, and a thread of bright ruby beads sprang up in its wake. She flinched at the sting, and he laughed. "Not so defiant now, are you? That won't leave a scar, but just a fraction deeper, and you'll be wearing long sleeves and lace gloves for the rest of your life."

He was enjoying her fear and her humiliation. She was at his mercy, and they both knew it. Crowley withdrew the razor, and slipped it back into its leather scabbard. "That was but a foretaste of what I can do to you. Shall I remove one of your fingers next? This is sharp enough. Or maybe the tip of that pretty nose. Perhaps carve a few lines on your rosy cheeks, to make them rosier still. Well, Mistress Paradice? Shall I give you some time to think on it? Say ... three days? By that time, my dear, you should have realised that your defiance is pointless, and that all the gold in the world is not worth the ruination of your undeniable beauty." His hand went out to touch her face. The fingers felt rough and his touch was cold, despite the warmth of the day. She shivered, and he laughed. "There are all kinds of ways I can amuse myself with you. I am sure you will be able to think of many of them, once you are alone. I shall leave you to your thoughts. Good day to you, madam."

Sick with horror and loathing, Polly watched as he got to his feet and returned the razor to the pocket of his coat. The man called Gabriel stepped forward and slapped two bottles of water down on the earth beside the straw. She said quickly, "If you have any vestige of honour, any rags of decency, you cannot be a party to this cruelty! *Why* are you still helping him?"

He looked at her impassively. "He pays me well."

Polly sat helplessly as they went out, shutting the door behind them so that she was once more bereft of sunlight. She had three days. Three days to decide what to do. Three days to persuade Mattie, if she returned, to help her escape. And three days more for her friends to find her, before Crowley carried out his threats.

And she knew that if they did not find her, she would be killed. Crowley was in too deep now to set her free. Whether she wrote that letter or not, he must silence her forever, or risk the gallows.

The night was long, and very dark.

*

As instructed, Sam Jessop alighted from the Portsmouth coach when it arrived at the King's Arms in Godalming. It was still only the middle of the afternoon, but he was tired, hungry, thirsty, and very glad to leave his fellow travellers, four inebriated sailors and a woman who seemed to be more than happy to strike up an intimate acquaintance with each of them in turn. Fortunately, all of them were going on to Portsmouth. He asked for a private chamber and a good dinner, and then said softly to the landlord, "I am looking for a Mr. Andrews – a matter of farming business. Do you know where he might be found?"

The landlord was not true to type, being of a lean and forbidding aspect, though perhaps this was necessary to keep his nautical customers in order. He looked Sam up and down, and then said, "What name is it?"

"Samuel Jessop."

It seemed to mean something to the landlord, who nodded. "Very good, sir. I will see that he gets the message."

Up until that moment, Sam had not really believed that Madame Rousselle's directions would prove to be anything other than a wild-goose-chase. He thanked the landlord profusely and retired to his chamber, to change his shirt, which stank of the beer which had been spilt over him even before they left Southwark, to wash his face and hands, and eat.

An hour later, blessedly clean and refreshed, he was just finishing the last of an excellent lemon syllabub when there was a knock on the door. But despite his hope, it was not Dark: a boy stood there, with a folded and sealed paper in his hand. "I was told to give you this, sir."

Sam thanked him, and sent him away with sixpence for his trouble. Once alone, he unsealed the letter. It was indeed from Dark, the thick black scrawl unmistakeable, though there was no signature. He looked at the six words on the page, the last of them underlined. 'Churchyard, eight of the clock precisely.'

Ordinarily, it would seem unlikely that Dark would wish to skulk around in churchyards, but he was a government spy, presumably on government business, and skulking was what spies were supposed to do. His friend's clandestine employment had always left a sour taste in Sam's mouth: despite the fact that he himself was also a true and loyal subject of King George, he found eavesdropping and snooping morally repugnant, however noble the cause. And he knew that Polly and Gin had similar qualms.

Polly. He did not like to think of Dark's reaction when he told him what had happened. And when he walked out of the inn at five minutes to eight that evening, going by his watch, there was a knot of apprehension in his gut. He knew, none better, how obnoxious Dark could be if he was angered or distressed, and he was not looking forward to informing him that his Polly had vanished. Because Dark loved her, passionately and completely, even if he pretended otherwise: Sam was certain of that.

He had been for a stroll round the town earlier to get his bearings, so he did not have to ask for directions, but set off confidently down the High Street. It was now almost full dark, though there was still an afterglow of sunset in the west, and the moon, which was a little past full, had not yet risen.

Fortunately, many public-spirited inhabitants of Godalming had lit lanterns at their doors, and he was able to see his way without too much hazard. He turned right into Church Street, narrow and lined with ancient half-timbered houses, and soon saw a spire, sharp against the starlit sky. Hoping that Dark would be there, and would respond to his plea for help, he walked cautiously into the churchyard and looked around, seeing nothing in the blackness that could possibly be his friend.

"Sam?"

The quiet voice from the table tomb beside him almost made him fall over with shock. He swallowed a squawk of surprise and said, "Yes. Dark?"

"It is, extremely so. I have already fallen over one obstacle. No matter, this is not a time for levity. Sam, what the devil are you doing here? Something must be seriously amiss for Madame – I assume it was Madame – to give you details of my whereabouts."

"I told her that it was a matter of life and death," Sam said. "And I think it is."

A vague shadow rose from the tomb and took his arm. "Come over here," Dark said. "It's more private."

Sam thought that there could be few places more private than a deserted graveyard at night, wherever you might be standing in it, but he followed his friend across humps and around dim grey headstones to a deeper shadow under a yew tree. It was so black beneath it that Sam could not even make out Dark's shape, only hear his breathing.

"I hope the matter is serious," Dark said drily. "I would not be best pleased to find that you had tracked me down because the cat is ailing."

"It is serious." Sam swallowed. "It's Polly." And as briefly as he could, while still giving all the salient details, he told Dark what had happened in Rye.

There was an unpleasant silence when he finished, save for the other man's breathing, which had become ragged and irregular. Sam wished he could see Dark's face, and waited apprehensively for the explosion.

"Dear God, what were you thinking of? You let her go – no, worse than that, you *escorted* her, you numbskull! Into Crowley's trap!" A deep savage movement was visible even through the blackness. "So when was she taken?"

"Monday evening." Sam kept his voice level.

Another violent movement. "Oh, dear God," Dark said, and swore long and fluently. "She's been gone for *four days.* What in the devil's name have you been doing?"

"Looking for her. Then riding to London, questioning Madame Rousselle, and taking coach here. I have done my best, but you seem to think I must have wings," Sam said, with considerable annoyance.

There was a small pause, before the other man spoke. "I apologise. That was unfair."

Dark rarely apologised for anything. Sam said, "Apology accepted. Will you – *can* you – come to Rye and help us search for her?"

"You don't need to ask, Sam, of course I will – my business here has been a waste of time anyway. But when we find her, I shall leave her in no doubt about what I think about her going on yet another wild-goose-chase."

"You cannot blame her for trying to help her sister when she thought she was in trouble. She was not to know that it was a trap."

"And perhaps not a trap for her," Dark said grimly. "Mattie was the bait to catch Polly – is Polly the bait to catch me?"

"I confess that had also occurred to me," Sam said. "I have racked my brains to think of a reason why Crowley should have wanted to abduct her, and can come up with no other solution. Dark, I have asked for your help, but if you do not wish to put yourself at risk –"

"Risk to myself be damned to hell," the other man said vehemently. "What kind of coward would I be, if I went back to London and left her to her fate? How would I feel if she died and I could have saved her?"

"Then you think her life might be in danger?" Sam asked, moved by the uncharacteristic emotion raw in Dark's voice.

"If Crowley is responsible for this, then, yes, I do. He is ruthless and will stop at nothing."

"I can imagine that. As I said, we met him at Lydd." Sam remembered that smooth, intimidating man, his ready smiles failing to hide the menace, and the thought of Polly at his mercy made him shiver involuntarily. He was glad that Dark could not see him, and suspected that his friend felt likewise.

"So, we will go to Rye as soon as possible?" he asked, knowing the answer already.

"Does the sun rise in the east and set in the west? Of course we're going to Rye. At first light tomorrow. The King's Arms hires out horses, tell Patterson and he'll have his best nags ready and waiting. I'll see you then." He paused, and then added, in quite a different voice, "Thank you, Sam. You did the right thing by coming here. Never fear, we will find her."

"I know we will," said Sam, with a certainty he did not feel in the least.

CHAPTER SIXTEEN

The Tenderness of Pity

"It could be the marsh fever."

Gin looked up through hot, heavy eyes at Mercy, who was studying her sympathetically. "Whazz marsh fever?"

"What you have," said Mercy patiently. "An axey – an ague. Be bad airs and evil humours down on the Marsh, and you were down on the Marsh yesterday, weren't you?"

"What about Miss Tucker and Mr Jeake? Will they have got it too?"

"They be born to it, surelye? We all be, us folk who live on the Marsh, we be customed to it and we don't get it so bad. Incomers, now, that be different, they get the fever something terrible. Some of them even *die*," said Mercy, with considerable relish.

"Well, I ain't going to die," said Gin. "I got too much to do." She struggled to sit up, but her head swam to such a degree that she flopped back on the pillows and closed her eyes until the dizziness stopped. The room was warm, the sun shining in, but she felt as cold as winter, and shivered uncontrollably.

"You must stay in bed," Mercy said sternly. "I'll fetch the doctor to you."

Gin tried to protest, but the maid had already gone out, shutting the door behind her with a brisk and efficient click. A doctor! Who was going to pay? Doctors were expensive and as like to kill as cure you, from all she had heard. She had never been examined by one, for the parent of a child born into abject poverty, as she had been, could never afford the services of a physician. Those who fell ill either died, or recovered. Up until now, she had survived, but perhaps not for much longer.

She banged the mattress in angry frustration. Madam was lost, out on those deadly marshes somewhere most like, perhaps also suffering from this fever, but no-one to help her save only herself, Gin, and here she was, utterly useless, sick in bed and as weak as a new kitten. It was unbearable. Hot tears pricked her eyes and ran down her cheeks. Frightened, ashamed, alone, Gin rolled over, buried her face in the pillow, and sobbed.

She must have slept a little, for she dreamt that Madam was shackled in a stone cellar, like the ones they had inspected in Winchelsea the day before, the walls covered with green mould and a little light coming in from a tiny grilled window, high above. But it was not like the Winchelsea cellars, for they had been for the most part free of water, though stinking of damp and stale air. Here, the tide was rising inexorably, covering Madam as she struggled to free herself, while Gin, watching from somewhere above, like a ghost, could do nothing to save her.

She woke with a cry of despair, and found a man standing over her. For a moment, imagining the worst, she cowered away from him, and then he smiled and said, his voice calm and kind, "I apologise, did I startle you?"

He was quite a young man, though with a well-fed belly, and plainly but respectably dressed in a blue suit and a short full wig. Belatedly, Gin realised that this must be the doctor that Mercy had sent for, and indeed there was the maid, standing just behind him. She sat up with an effort, drawing her plain nightgown close around her, and said gruffly, "No matter."

"Now, Jane Maggs, is it? Mercy here tells me you are feverish and have chills and a headache, is that correct?"

"Yes, sir," said Gin, shivering despite herself.

"Well, it could well be the marsh fever, as Mercy has suggested. How long have you been staying here in Rye?"

Gin tried to persuade her foggy brain to work. Eventually she said, "It's Friday, ain't it? So a week."

"Ah. My observations have led me to conclude that in newcomers to Rye, marsh fever usually takes quite a while to make itself known – perhaps ten days or more, and sometimes even a month or two later, but I have noted some exceptions to this, and you may be one of them. Now, may I examine you?"

Gin sat, trying not to shiver or cough, with little effect, while the doctor took her pulse, inspected the contents of the chamber pot, and asked questions about her general state of health. Finally, he stepped back and smiled reassuringly. "Yes, I think it is the marsh fever. I will give you some powdered Peruvian Bark to take. A spoonful twice daily, dissolved in wine, should do the trick in a day or so. In the meantime, you should rest, and have plenty to eat and drink. I would also recommend the letting of several ounces of blood, to dispel the harmful humours. I shall ask Mr. Igglesden to attend you, he is a very competent surgeon."

"What?" Gin cried indignantly. "I ain't going to be bled, no matter what you say!"

"But Jane, it will hasten your recovery."

"Well, I ain't." She folded her arms and glared at him belligerently. "Not if the King himself was to ask me. So there."

The doctor sighed. "Very well, on your own head be it. Mercy, do you have the wine ready?"

Gin stared suspiciously at the small, greenish bottle he took out of his bag. He uncorked it, and measured out a spoonful of brown powder, which he tipped into the wine glass the maid was holding. A brisk stir soon dissolved it, and he held out the glass to her. "Drink this. It is bitter, but it will not poison you, so do not look so alarmed. Peruvian bark is a remarkably effective medicine," he added, seeing she needed reassurance. "It cured the late King Charles himself of his agues, and since then many, many gentlemen and ladies have been saved by its benefits. It will certainly help you, and quickly too. You will be right as rain in two days, if not before."

Two days! But, Gin reminded herself, with any luck Sam and Dark would arrive tomorrow, and then they could conduct a proper search. She trusted Dark. Dark would find Madam. He could do anything. If a miracle was needed, he would oblige.

She took the glass from the doctor, and with a shudder, but also with hope, drained it to the last dregs.

*

Polly had not thought that Mattie would return. She wished now that she had not been so angry and hostile. If she had known that her sister had brought her food, she would have spoken much more gently, and expressed her gratitude and thanks. But it was too late now to make amends, for she had surely driven the girl away for good.

So when the door to the shack opened, waking her from the light, uncomfortable doze in which she seemed to be spending most of her time, she thought at first in terror that it must be Crowley, come to threaten her again after less than a day, despite what he had said. Gasping with shock, she squinted up against the sudden light, and saw that the slight figure framed in the doorway could not be her tormenter. "Mattie?"

Her sister came forward into the hut. She bent, and dropped a bulging bag onto the floor beside the straw. "I've brought you some more food," she said, her voice neutral.

Polly sat up with an effort, and managed to prop herself against the plank wall at her back. She said quietly. "Thank you. And I'm sorry."

"For what?"

"For – for being so angry with you, when you last came. I didn't realise you had brought me food. I was rude and ungrateful."

There was a brief silence, filled by the never-ending cries of the seabirds. Mattie looked at her, the expression on her face hard to read. Then she prodded the bag with her foot. "You should eat. You can't have had any food for two days." She picked up the brimming bucket, and went out. A few moments later, Polly heard a distant splash, and then Mattie returned with it, now empty and dripping. She put it back on the floor beside the straw, then drew up the stool and sat, studying Polly. "You haven't looked inside. Go on, you must be starving."

Still suspicious, wondering if this was some elaborate prank, Polly pulled the bag onto her lap with her free hand, and fumbled with the ties. She drew out a small pie, its crust golden and gleaming, several apples, a piece of cheese and a chicken leg, and laid them down carefully on the cleanest part of her mantle. Then she looked up at her sister. "Thank you. From the bottom of my heart, I thank you. I take it that Crowley knows nothing of this?"

"No, he does not. For pity's sake, sister, eat!"

The pie was begging to be consumed. Polly surrendered to its urgings. She broke off a piece, finding spiced pork within, surrounded by rich jelly, and bit into it. The delicious flavour filled her mouth, and then nothing else mattered except for the need to assuage her desperate hunger. Quicker than seemed possible, the pie was reduced to a few stray crumbs, and she turned to the chicken. That too disappeared, and so did the cheese. Feeling suddenly very full, and slightly sick, she fumbled at the leather water bottle and took several gulps to wash it all down.

"Why were you singing?" Mattie asked abruptly. "I heard you, when I came before."

Startled, Polly almost upset the bottle as she put it back on the floor. "It filled the time. And I thought that someone might hear me, and come to my rescue."

Mattie looked down at the floor, and then directly at Polly. Her eyes were such a pale grey-blue, they were almost silver. Slowly, as if the compliment had been dragged from her by force, she said, "You sing beautifully."

"Thank you. Though I am sorely in need of practice."

"Do you sing in the playhouses, in London?"

"I have done, last year. But mainly I sing in my coffee house, for the customers. It draws many people in. And I am teaching a young lady." She smiled, thinking of Moll Oglethorpe, her naïve enthusiasm and her hidden unhappiness.

"I am no singer," said Mattie. "But I make a good boy."

"I know you do. You carry yourself like a man, and that counts for a lot." She remembered Madame Rousselle, boasting about her popularity in breeches parts, telling her that only a blind man could have mistaken her for a boy, and added curiously, "Do you wear skirts at all?"

Mattie made a dismissive gesture. "Only when I must. The last time I dressed in woman's clothes was when I went to see your old mistress in Bath. Lord, how those stays rubbed and itched! I was glad to throw them off that evening."

"So..." Polly picked up one of the apples and bit into it. It was tart, but juicy and refreshing. "Did you go to Kitty because Crowley ordered it?"

"Yes. We had been talking about you, for he knows of your connection with Sinclair, and I mentioned that you had spent time at the Bear, and that you might be found that way."

"And you came to meet us at the inn at Amesbury because Crowley told you to? When you lured me to the Blue

Anchor, was that also at his bidding?"

"He wants the gold," said Mattie. "You have it, and I was the means to reach you. That is all."

Without even noticing it, Polly found that she had reduced the apple to a core. She put it down and said bluntly, "Are you his lover?"

"What's it to you? *You* have had lovers aplenty, so I hear. But if it eases your mind, I will tell you plain that I am not. He wanted it, but I persuaded him that I would be more use to him as his accomplice, because I could bring you within his grasp."

"Yet in Amesbury, you seemed frightened of him."

"I am an actress. I act out a part." Mattie lifted her chin defiantly. "It suited our plan, that I should play the victim. And it worked, did it not? You came running when I called."

"Of course I did. I believed you were dead, I was overjoyed to find you were not. I thought you were in trouble when I received that token, and I wanted to help you. But in fact it was all a ruse to trap me. Why, Mattie? Why did you do it? And do not tell me that Crowley will return the gold to King James, because I will not believe you."

The fly, if it was the same one, was buzzing again in a patch of sunlight. For the first time, Mattie dropped her gaze. There was silence, and then she said, "When we have it, we will go to France, and begin our lives anew."

Polly stared at her. "France? Why?"

"He has friends there, he says. And I will be safe from – from things I have done, in the past." Her hands clenched in her lap. "I don't plan to stay with him, once I have my share of the gold."

"It doesn't seem to me that Crowley is the kind of man who would willingly share anything with anyone, least of all a fortune in gold. You would be lucky not to be pushed overboard on the voyage. He cares nothing for anyone, he is a brute, Mattie, a brute! This is what he did to me yesterday."

To illustrate her point, Polly lifted her free arm. The light cut that Crowley had inflicted the previous day was marked by an intermittent track, three inches long, of dull red scabs. "This is his way of persuasion. He wants me to write a letter to my banker, giving him permission to transfer the gold."

"Then why do you not do as he asks? It is only money, and you have plenty."

"You called me a thief, and yet you and Crowley are no better! That gold is not yours to take! In truth, there is very little of it left. Nine-tenths of the sum lodged with my banker is the profit from my coffee house, and he has absolutely no right to it. Which is why I have refused to give him what he wants, no matter what he threatens."

"What has he threatened?"

"He said that if I did not write the letter giving him the gold, he would – he would mark my face, scar me for life, cut off my fingers, one by one. And he seemed to relish the prospect of it."

There was another silence. Then Mattie said, "No amount of gold is worth that."

"It is worth my future. Do you not understand? The money that Crowley wants from me is not only money that is rightfully mine, it will provide the security and safety neither you nor I had, when we were children. Why should I give it to him? He has not worked for it, and he emphatically does not deserve it. Mattie, I can only offer you what I offered him. Free me, let me go back to my friends, and we will all return to London and say nothing of what has happened."

"And you expect me to believe that? What he has done could hang him, and he knows it."

"Which is why, when I have given him what he wants, he will surely have me taken out in a boat and dropped over the side, for he can't afford to let me go. Don't deny it, you must know in your heart that it's true. But what I'll wager he hasn't considered, is that if he kills me, Dark will pursue him to the ends of the earth for vengeance and justice."

"Dark. He is your lover. And a creature of King George."

"He is an artist. And, yes, occasionally an agent of the government. But unlike Crowley, he is at heart a good and honourable man." A brief vision of the likely expression on Dark's face, were he to hear himself thus described, almost made her smile.

Mattie snorted with contempt. "A spy is never good, nor honourable. I have heard enough."

She got to her feet, dusting down her breeches, picked up the bag, and surveyed her sister with a return of her early hostility. Polly said urgently, "Wait! I meant what I said when I said I would give you a home in London. I know Rich at the Lincoln's Inn Theatre well – he is always seeking men and women of presence and talent. You could take London by storm, have the town at your feet if you wanted. Is that not a future more preferable than anything Crowley can offer you?"

There was, surely, a tremble of doubt on Mattie's face. Polly continued. "Are you truly afraid of him? There can be no shame in that – anyone would be frightened of what he can do. He has shown himself to be cruel, greedy and utterly ruthless. And you are in danger from him, just as I am."

She had miscalculated. Mattie sent her a look of pure contempt. "You think so? You mentioned that he might push me overboard. But what if, my dear sister, I was planning to push *him*?"

Polly could only watch helplessly as she turned and went out. The door slammed behind her, the bolts rattled, and she was once more alone with the fly, the invisible gulls, and her unhappy, fearful thoughts.

*

"Gin! Gin, can you hear me? Wake up!"

Few people still called her that. Gin hauled herself up from the deep, dreamless and restorative sleep which she had been enjoying for most of the day, and opened her eyes, to find two of them standing by her bed, weary, filthy with dust from the road, but instantly recognisable. Hardly daring to believe it, she said, "You found him!"

"I found him," said Sam Jessop, smiling down at her. "Mr Bird tells me you have been ill with an ague. Are you feeling better?"

Gin took a brief mental inventory of her current state. No aches, no shivering, no swimming in the head: she felt tired, but otherwise very much better. She nodded. "I think so. The doctor's been," she added with sudden anxiety. "And I didn't have no coin to pay him!"

"Don't worry, Gin," said Dark, also smiling, though he looked exhausted and there were deep, dust-lined grooves around his mouth and nose. "I have taken care of that. But for now, if you are feeling better, would you like some food? The maid is waiting for us to order supper to be sent up."

With surprise, Gin realised that she was hungry. She agreed enthusiastically, and Mercy, who had been standing by the door ready for her instructions, went back downstairs. Once she had gone, the two men sat down at the table, and Sam said, "I am glad, and more than glad, to be here safe and sound. We have been riding all day with hardly a break and I am famished. And saddle-sore," he added ruefully.

"While we are alone," Dark said to Gin, "tell me exactly where you have looked and who you have asked. I have heard all the details of your searching earlier in the week from Sam, and I'd like to know what you have been up to after he left, and before you became ill."

"You makes it sound like I been misbehaving," Gin complained. "Well, we didn't find Madam, nor hear anything of her, so we knows where you needn't look tomorrow."

"We?"

"Me and Tawny and Phil. Master Jeake and Miss Tucker," Gin added, seeing Dark's look of enquiry. "They're my friends and they know this town and all the Marsh, and they've been helping me. We went to Winchelsea and the Castle on ..." She frowned, thinking about it. "What day is this?"

"It's the Saturday," Sam said.

"Thank Gawd for that, I've only been sick a day and a half! I must have slept for most of it, once the doctor had dosed me." She had only the vaguest memory of that time, save for her hideous dreams, many of which had concerned Madam, helpless, imprisoned, and menaced by something foul and terrifying. She pushed the thought of them from her mind and continued. "So we went to Winchelsea on Thursday, we looked round the castle down on the Marsh, but though it was plain as print that smugglers had been there, there weren't no place you could keep a prisoner. Then we went up to the town because Tawny – that's what his sister calls him, because he looks like an owl – said there were cellars there where she could have been hid. And we spent all afternoon looking in them. You ain't never seen such things, Mr Dark, Mr. Jessop! They're most of 'em reachable from the street, but lots ain't been used in years, you can tell, but they're proper rooms, all made of stone and vaulted like a church." Gin had never been in a vaulted church – most of those in London were new-built to Wren's designs and eschewed old-fashioned architectural styles – but Tawny had said so, and he must be right.

"But we didn't find any sign of Madam," she added. "And Tawny and Phil asked everywhere, and no-one knew nothing, and we could tell they really didn't. So you don't need to go to Winchelsea again. Tawny reckons the Marsh proper is more likely, there are shepherds' huts everywhere and she could've been hidden in one of those, and no-one would know save the shepherd, and he'd be easy enough to bribe."

There was a knock on the door. It opened at Dark's command and Mercy came back in, accompanied by another maid. Both were struggling with a loaded tray and accompanied by delicious aromas, both savoury and sweet. Gin's mouth watered at the sight and smell, and she could hardly wait until a laden plate – mutton chops, chicken, buttered cabbage and roots, all surrounded by rich gravy – was passed to her by Sam.

As she ate, sitting up in bed, she surreptitiously studied Dark, who was at the table in the window, opposite her. She knew him so well, had known him for years longer than had Polly or Sam, and despite his pleasant, apparently relaxed manner, there was a shadowing around his eyes, and he was talking too much and too fast. It was obvious to her that the news about Madam had greatly affected him. *And why shouldn't it?* Gin thought. *He loves her, no matter how he makes light of it.*

When they had at last done justice to the food, Gin put her cleaned plate back on the tray and hopped out of her truckle bed to return it to the table. Only when she had climbed back under the covers did she realise that despite the sudden exertion, she had not felt weak or dizzy at all. She drew her knees up, hugging them, and said to the two men, "What are we going to do tomorrow? I reckon you could ask some more questions at the Blue Anchor. Tawny got a few answers, and if you ask right, you might get some too, because everyone what was in there on that night knew a lot more than what they would tell us."

"Gin's right," Sam said to Dark. "And it might pay to

ask again at the harbour, too. Polly disappeared so quickly and completely, I am certain that she must have been taken away on a boat – not one of the bigger ships, but a skiff or a lugger. Someone must know something, and they can't all be in thrall to the smugglers."

"Then that is what we will do," Dark said. "Thank you, Gin, for all you have done. I think it best you stay here tomorrow, and continue to rest. Marsh fever can be very serious, and I do not want you endangering your health – and neither would Polly. So no gadling about on your own searches, understand?"

Gin was feeling so much better for the food that she was inclined to disagree, but was sensible enough not to voice any objection. "Yes, Mr. Dark," she said meekly.

Dark, who knew her as well as she did him, sent her a suspicious glance, but let it go. "So, we are decided. Tomorrow, Sam and I will look around the harbour and enquire at the Blue Anchor. Then the day after, we start a search of the Marsh."

"We shall need someone to help us there," Sam pointed out. "It's a curious place, almost featureless, and criss crossed by ditches and turf walls. And the roads seem to wander about with no clue as to where they're going. When Polly and I went to Lydd, it was no distance as the crow flew, but we must have gone twice as many miles because there are no signposts, and the land is so flat you can't see for any distance."

"Will your friends be able to guide us, do you think, Gin?" Dark asked.

"I 'spect so, and I can ask," Gin said. "If I feels well enough," she added hastily, seeing his look. "But Tawny said he'd have to go back to London soon, and Phil, her ma thinks she spends too much time in his company and she ought to be busy with her learning."

"How old is this Miss Phil Tucker?"

"Twelve, I think, and Tawny's six or seven years older."

"Well, Sam told me they live just down the street, so you will not have to go far. Gin, these are two young people from a wealthy and respectable family. Do they know *anything* of your past?"

"No, and they ain't going to. They're my friends, believe it or not, and ... and it's good to have friends," Gin said, and to her fury felt her eyes filling. "So don't say nothing to them, please, Mr. Dark, I don't want them to find out."

"Don't worry, I won't," Dark said, his voice unexpectedly gentle, and Sam echoed him. "They won't hear anything from me, Gin, I can promise you that."

"Thank you," said Gin gruffly, and turned away so that she could surreptitiously wipe her overflowing eyes. It was the illness that made her so easy to be upset, she told herself fiercely. The thought of what her former companions, the link-boys of Covent Garden, would say if they could see her now, leaking tears like a girl, spurred her to make a furious effort to compose herself, and when she turned back to face Sam and Dark, her voice was bright with hope. "With all this help, we'll find her, you see if we don't! And then we can go back to London and leave this horrible aguey Marsh behind for ever!"

CHAPTER SEVENTEEN

How happen'd this disorder?

The next morning, Dark rose in a mood of desperate hurry, broke his fast with extreme haste, and after looking in briefly on Gin, finding her still asleep, set off down Middle Street at a furious pace. The fine weather had come to an end in the night, with wind and rain, and although the sun was now making a hesitant appearance between swift grey clouds, there were puddles and slick, gleaming cobbles everywhere. Sam did not wish to suffer an undignified and probably painful fall, so he followed with considerably greater care, despite his anxiety about his friend. Dark had been outwardly composed on their ride from Godalming, though they had ridden faster and further than Sam would normally have done, however urgent their mission, but he knew that the calm concealed a simmering, desperate fear for Polly, and that it would not take much for his iron control to shatter, with possibly disastrous results.

By the time he reached the Strand Gate at the bottom of the hill, thankfully without serious incident bar a couple of minor slips, Dark was nowhere to be seen. In front of him, the harbour was much emptier than usual. It was Sunday, so the pious would later be visiting church or chapel, to be followed by spiritual contemplation at home, and those few who had not, were either uninterested in religion, or had work to do which would not wait until after the Sabbath. Sam was not sure if this would make their search easier, or more difficult. With fewer people about, there were of course fewer to ask, but also fewer to intimidate someone who might have information to impart.

As he looked round, he heard a violent hammering break out to his left, and saw Dark banging furiously on the door of the Blue Anchor. Of course, it was firmly shut, for the terms of its licence from the Council dictated that it must be closed today, but Sam suspected that Dark would batter it down if necessary. Fortunately, it opened almost immediately, and he recognised the slovenly woman who had served them on the night of Polly's abduction, wearing an old, stained gown and with a wet cloth in her hand. "What you making all that racket for? Be off with you, we're shut!"

For answer, Dark pushed his way past her and into the tavern. Sam, hurrying up to offer support, found the door slammed in his face. He stood for a moment, irresolute, staring at the flaking paint, and then decided not to intervene. Dark would not resort to physical violence, he was certain, though he could be extremely intimidating when angered. He remembered past confrontations and skirmishes, and did not envy the woman. But if she had information, perhaps threats would work where persuasion and bribery would not. And time, he was acutely aware, must be running out for Polly. She had been gone for nearly a week, and he had tried to imagine, and failed, the situation she might be in, especially if Crowley had her captive. He could not blame his friend for his intemperate action.

Ignoring the muffled sounds of dispute within, he walked over to the dockside. An old man was sitting there, on a battered stool, mending a net. His fingers seemed too gnarled and misshapen to do such intricate work, but they moved deftly amongst the tangled cords, weaving and splicing. Sam stopped a few yards away and waited, unwilling to interrupt until the fisherman had finished. After a while he looked up and gave him a nod. "You ain't found your friend, so I hear."

Sam wondered how he knew, but Rye was a small place, and everyone in it must have learned about Polly's disappearance by now. "No," he said sadly. "No, we have not, though we have looked almost everywhere."

"Young Master Jeake and Miss Tucker have been helping, but they bain't looked much on the Marsh yet." The fisherman put down the net, and studied Sam. "It's a mortal wicked thing what's been done. There be some as won't say what they know because they're feared, but I be an old man, I've had my three score years and ten as the Bible says, and I bain't planning on fetching up in Hell." His eyes were a faded blue, but very intent. Then their gaze slid past Sam's shoulder, and he said, "Young Joey's in a fearsome hurry, where's he going?"

Sam turned, and saw a boy running away from the Blue Anchor. He pelted through the Strand Gate, heading up into the town. With a feeling of apprehension, he said, "I think my friend may be causing some trouble in the tavern. He is desperate to find Mistress Paradice, and he is not a man to take no for an answer."

"Sweet on her, is he? Bain't surprising, saw her here the day you landed, pretty as a picture so she be." The fisherman fumbled in the pouch at his belt and brought out a battered clay pipe, half its stem broken off, and a crumbling pinch of brown leaves. With deliberation, he filled the bowl and struck a flint. Sam controlled his impatience and waited until the tobacco was lit, and the old man had taken a few long, satisfied intakes of breath. Then he said softly, "So do you know something?"

"I don't *know*, see? I only *heard* it." An evil smelling curl of smoke rose from the pipe, and the fisherman removed the stem from his mouth. "I were in the tavern last night, listening to them all nabbling away about it. I dunnamy chuckle-headed notions they had. Seems Gabriel Tomkins and his brother Ned were them as took her, but as to where, no-one knows for sure. But someone said 'decoy'." He looked up at Sam. "Mean summat to you?"

It fitted with Dark's suggestion that Polly was the bait to lure him into Crowley's power. He said cautiously, "It might.

Did you hear anything more of that conversation?"

"No, sir, I did not – my ears bain't so good in a small space, when others be talking thin. It could be why they took her, I don't know. And that be *all* I know, so the good Lord be my witness." For the first time, the old man smiled, revealing a sparse collection of stained and crooked teeth. "We bain't all wrong'uns on the Marsh."

"I'm sure you're not," Sam said. "Thank you –" He held out his hand, and the old fisherman half rose from his stool and shook it. "Jem Fuller, sir."

"Well, Jem Fuller, my heartfelt thanks. And if you hear any more about this, then my name is Sam Jessop, my friend is André Dark, and we are to be found at the Mermaid."

"Oh, I know that," said Jem, and winked. "Whole town knows that, sir. Bain't much that be secret in this place. But finding someone who be willing to tell you aught, that's a different matter." He pointed with the pipe. "Looks like your friend has got himself into a spot of bother. There go the constables."

Sam turned and saw two men, one tall and heavily built, the other shorter and thinner, running under the Strand Gate and through the open door into the dark maw of the Blue Anchor. They were followed more slowly by the boy Joey, who had obviously been sent to fetch them.

Alarmed, Sam said quickly, "Thank you, I must go," and hurried across the quayside to the tavern, his heart pounding with apprehension. What had Dark threatened, and, more to the point, what had he done?

After the bright sharp sunshine on the Quay, it seemed almost pitch black inside the Blue Anchor, and he halted on the threshold, blinking, while his eyes adjusted to the gloom. Then he heard the woman's voice, shrill with fury. "He just burst in here and laid hands on me and he was asking all manner of questions, I was feared for my life!" And then Dark, his voice as hard as steel. "A woman was forcibly taken from your tavern and you claim to know nothing about it? You're a bare-faced liar!"

"No, I bain't! I be telling you the truth!"

There seemed to be a danger of the scene turning into a farce. Sam followed the sounds of dispute, finding his way between the tables and benches more by luck than judgement, and once barking his shins on an unseen stool, which fell over with a clatter. At once, the woman said sharply, "Who be there? Tavern be closed!"

They were by the door to the private room, the one where he and Gin had waited, in vain, for Polly. The air stank of stale beer and tobacco, mingled with the more fragrant aroma of woodsmoke from the hearth. Dark and the slatternly woman had squared up to each other in the manner of fighting-cocks, while the two constables, each of whom were armed with short clubs, stood to one side, obviously ready to intervene. The woman turned as Sam entered. "I know you," she said. "You were there that night."

"Indeed I was." Sam made his voice level and authoritative, as he did with his apprentices and servants. "And I have to say that I find it very hard to believe that the men who abducted my friend from your parlour did so without your knowledge or consent."

The woman flushed with anger. "And I say you're wrong! You Sheere furriners don't know *nothing!* And as for him," she added, gesturing vehemently at Dark, "he be far too nosy for his own good, asking all them questions about boats and tides and France, wouldn't surprise me if he weren't a spy for the Jacks!"

"I am trying to discover the whereabouts of my friend," Dark said, breathing hard, his temper obviously in danger of exploding.

"Your *friend*?" the taller constable sneered. "Why waste your time on her? Get you back to London, you'll find plenty more whores and draggle tails there!"

Dark roared, and took a step towards him. It was all the provocation the constables needed. The taller man rushed at him and pulled him back. With a violent twist, Dark tore himself free and punched him full in the face. He staggered back, while the other constable raised his cudgel. Sam shouted a warning, and Dark tried to dodge, but could not move fast enough in time. The club caught him a glancing blow on the side of the head, and he fell.

It was suddenly very quiet in the room, except for heavy breathing from the man whom Dark had hit, and who was wincing as he felt the bruise on his cheek. The woman dusted her hands together and looked contemptuously down at the man lying at her feet. "That'll learn you, yer rough scandalising varmint!"

"My God, have you killed him?" Sam dropped to his knees beside his friend, fearing the worst: the constable, though a puny man and shorter even than himself, had wielded his club with considerable force. To his relief, Dark moved under his hands, and then uttered several choice oaths.

"Right, you," said the constable who had struck the blow. "Up, up on your feet, or I'll bannick you." He bent, reached roughly past Sam and grasped Dark by the shoulder. "Get up!"

"Let him alone!" Sam said sharply. "He's hurt, you brute!"

For answer, the other man stepped forward, one hand still to his injured face, and kicked Dark savagely in the ribs. The woman laughed. Dark grunted, rolled over and scrambled to his feet, gripping the nearest table for support. He looked as savage as a rabid dog, his eyes wild, his wig crooked, blood running down the side of his face. As the shorter constable made to grab him again, he raised his arm furiously, but it was seized by the other man and twisted behind his back. Panting, Dark glared at them. "Let go of me!"

"You're off to the Tower," said the shorter constable. "You'll be up before the magistrate in the morning."

"On a charge of assaulting an officer of the Council," the other man added thickly. "And on suspicion of spying for the Jacks."

Dark let out a bark of scornful laughter. "I'm no more a Jack than King George, you leather-headed hicks!"

"Dark," Sam said warningly, but his friend did not seem to hear. "I said, let go of me!"

The constables might be a pair of scrubs, but they knew their business. While the bigger man kept Dark's arms pinioned behind his back, the smaller one produced a length of rope from his coat pocket and tied his wrists tightly together.

"You can't do that!" Sam said desperately. "He's not a Jacobite spy, he's trying to find our friend, and this woman is protecting criminals and wrong-doers! For God's sake, don't do this!"

His feeble protests fell on deaf ears. The two constables pushed and hauled Dark, still resisting, through the door and out onto the quayside. Sam stared at the woman. "If Polly dies because of your intransigence, you will have that on your conscience."

"And you think I care?" she said, with an insolent sneer. "Away with you, and if you never dark this door agin, bain't a day too soon. You be lucky they didn't take you as well. Now cut your stick!" She picked up a broom that had been leaning against one of the tables and flourished it menacingly.

Accepting defeat, Sam turned and went out into the bright day. There was no sign of the constables and their prisoner, but a few small ragged children, of the kind that always appeared out of nowhere whenever there was something happening, were running through the Strand Gate. He supposed that Dark was being taken to the tower on the southern ramparts that he had seen during their searches of the town earlier in the week, and which was apparently Rye's gaol.

Now what? A confusion of emotions jostled in Sam's head. Anger with Dark, for allowing himself to be provoked out of his usual iron control: despair, for how were they ever to find Polly without him? And anxiety for his friend, who had not only just suffered a possibly debilitating blow to the head, but now faced the grim prospect of cooling his fury in prison, and the threat of a charge of spying for the Jacobites. A laughable irony, given that Dark was in fact a spy for King George, but down here in Rye, so close to France, such an accusation, however ridiculous it might seem to Dark and himself, would be entirely plausible to the magistrates. It would take a great deal of time to sort out, and time was a luxury that was fast disappearing.

He hurried to the Strand Gate and looked up Middle Street. The constables and their prisoner, attended by a growing and noisy crowd, were already almost halfway up the hill. Sam set his teeth and began the ascent, puffing in his haste. He hoped that there would be nothing unpleasant lying rotting in the gutter, that the mob could use as missiles, though most of the rubbish seemed to have been swept downhill by last night's rain.

As he passed the Jeakes' house, the door opened and young Miss Philadelphia looked out, her face bright with curiosity. When she saw Sam, she hailed him. "Mr. Jessop! Do you know what's happening? Who's that man, and what has he done?"

He paused, unwilling to discuss it in the street. Phil, who seemed to do almost entirely as she pleased, skipped quickly down the steps and ran to join him. "Is that man your friend?"

she demanded, fortunately in a much quieter voice.

Sam nodded. "Yes, that's Mr. Dark, and he's being taken to the Tower. The woman at the Blue Anchor accused him of being a spy for the Jacobites."

"Well, that ship won't sail," said Phil bluntly. "Everyone knows she's in the pay of Gabriel Tomkins and the Mayfield Gang – Tawny told me. She'll say anything to get them off the hook."

"That's as maybe, but he also punched one of the constables in the face."

Phil crowed with laughter, and clapped her hands. "Oh, did he? That's famous! Well, I expect he deserved it. If you follow them to the Tower, you can try and persuade them to let him go." She gave him a conspiratorial wink. "They're fond of a shilling or two."

"How do you know about such things?" Sam asked, diverted in spite of himself.

"Oh, I listen at doors," said Phil shamelessly. "Mama and Papa often talk about town business. And last year Tawny got into trouble with some of his friends, there was a fight and Tawny tried to stop it but he was taken up by the constables, they wouldn't listen, *so* unfair, and Papa had to pay them to keep him out of the Tower."

Sam could not imagine her mild, bespectacled half-brother being involved in a fight. He said, "Thank you, Miss Philadelphia, that's useful information."

"Oh, pray call me Phil, everyone does." Her face grew suddenly more serious. "How is Jane today?"

"She does much better, I think – she was still sleeping when we went out earlier. Miss Tucker – Phil – we are all very grateful to you and your brother for your assistance."

"We wanted to help," Phil said. "And it makes a change

from baking or sewing or arithmetic."

A voice called from the house, and she grimaced. "Or studying my Bible. I have to go, Mr. Jessop, but my brother might be able to assist you, if you can't persuade the gaoler to free your friend. And if I can get away before we go to the Meeting House, I'll go tell Jane what's happened, if she's awake. Goodbye!" And she whirled round and ran back to the house.

Sam felt oddly cheered by this brief conversation. Phil's optimism, like her brother's, was invigorating and gave him a sliver of hope. He turned and continued up the street, past the Mermaid, and just as he reached the top of Middle Street, he heard running feet behind him, and a voice said, "Mr Jessop!"

It was Tawny. He came flying up, his coat tails flapping, and halted beside Sam. "Phil's just told me," he gasped. "Would you mind if I come with you? I know the constables, and I might be able to sweet talk them into setting your friend free."

"Of course," Sam said, walking on as swiftly as he could manage. "But it may be a pointless exercise – after all," he added, "hitting a constable is a serious matter. Usually I do not approve of such violence, but Dark was provoked beyond endurance. He is beside himself with fear for Polly."

"The constable doubtless deserved it," said Tawny. Seeing Sam's sideways look, he added, "Perhaps I should not say such things, since I'm studying for the law, but they're a rough and ready crew. Besides, your friend obviously wasn't unscathed, Phil said there was blood on his face."

"The other constable hit him over the head with his club."

Tawny made an exclamation of disgust. "At least he doesn't seem to be badly hurt, but he could have been killed. Look, there they are!"

From the churchyard, they could see that the constables and Dark had reached the dark bulk of the Tower, surrounded by a jeering crowd. Sam paused, unwilling to intervene until they had dispersed. It would do no-one any good, least of all Polly, if he were injured or, even worse, imprisoned as well.

Tawny had no such qualms. "Come on!" he cried, and without looking back, set off towards the Tower, eagerness in every stride.

There was nothing for it. With a deep sense of apprehension, Sam followed him. No good would come of this, he was certain.

*

Gin woke in her truckle bed, feeling almost restored to health. For a moment she lay still, enjoying the sensation of the soft mattress beneath her, and the warmth of the covers above. A year ago, she had slept anywhere she could – in doorways, in outhouses, on the 'bulks', the stalls set up outside shops. An old coat to keep some of the cold at bay had been a luxury, any kind of mattress softer than a bare board, almost beyond imagining. And yet now here she was, as comfortable as any great lady.

She yawned, and stretched blissfully. Then she remembered. Madam was still missing, and Mr. Dark and Mr. Jessop were going back to the Blue Anchor this morning. Had they left already? The thick curtains were closed, but enough light was visible round the edges to tell her that the sun was well above the horizon. Gin leapt out of bed and ran to the window. She pulled back one of the curtains, and saw that it must be nearly mid-morning. They had almost certainly gone without her.

Cursing, she dressed hastily in a fresh shift, topped by stays, then her plain green gown and petticoat. After nearly a year, she was accustomed now to wearing female dress, but secretly she envied Madam's sister, who could enjoy the freedom of breeches. She looked in the mirror, seeing, to her satisfaction, a tidy young girl, her dark hair tucked under a cap, her clothes clean and her complexion for once mercifully free of the spots which periodically plagued her. There was little indication that she had been so ill, just two days before, and she felt completely restored. Admittedly, she was hungry and thirsty, but that could wait: helping in the search could not.

She went out into the passage that linked the two chambers with the stairs down to the courtyard, and knocked on the door of the room that Sam had shared with Dark for the past two days. There was no reply, so she lifted the latch and looked inside. It was empty.

"Devil take it!" Gin muttered. She turned and hurried along the passage and down the stairs. In the courtyard, to her surprise, she saw Phil, in earnest conversation with Mercy. They broke off when she appeared, and the maid came towards her with an expression of concern on her face. "Oh, Jane, should you be out of your bed so soon?"

"I am perfectly well, Mercy, thank you," said Gin firmly.

"I'm exceeding glad to see you up and about," the girl went on, with a beaming smile. "The axey's mortal wicked for anyone who han't had it before."

"I expect the doctor gave you Peruvian Bark," said Phil. "It's the best cure, everyone says so, even though it costs a mint."

And Dark had paid for it. Gin was pleased that he thought she had deserved such generosity. She was about to ask Phil if she wanted to come down to the Blue Anchor, when her friend added, "But I have come here to find you. I've just seen Mr Jessop following the constables up the street, and one of them had a bruised face, and they had your other friend captive with them! Mr. Jessop said that he'd hit one of them, and that's why they arrested him."

"But Dark don't usually make a habit of punching constables in the face."

"I should hope not," said Phil. "Anyway, do you feel strong enough to walk to the Tower? That's where they'll have taken him. I told Tawny and he went along too, he knows the constables and the town sergeant too, he's the man who oversees the gaol."

"I feel as if I could *run* to the Tower," Gin said.

"But, Jane –" Mercy began.

"Don't worry, I'm perfectly restored, I promise you. Shall we go, Phil?"

Leaving an anxious-looking Mercy in the yard, the two girls hurried out into Middle Street and up the hill. Despite her brave words, Gin found herself rather out of breath at the top, but she persevered, matching Phil's determined stride. A quick right and then a left turn brought them to the western end of the churchyard. They could hear shouting in the distance, and quickened their pace, dodging around the tombstones and through the gate. The Tower stood in front of them, a squat structure with a round tower at each corner, and with that same slightly shabby, seen-better-days air shared by so much of Rye. There was a crowd round the door, and as they approached, it was slammed shut, leaving a mob yelling insults at the oblivious wood. Gin stopped a little way away, and drew Phil close to her side. "They're angry," she said. "Best not let them realise we're his friends."

They waited by the churchyard wall until the crowd, who must surely have had better things to do on the Sabbath, had largely dispersed. Gin looked for Sam and Tawny, but could not see them. Presumably, they had followed Dark and the constables inside. She turned to Phil. "If we go and bang on their door, will they let us in?"

"I don't think they will. It is a prison, after all."

Gin surveyed the Tower. "Maybe, but it ain't Newgate. I bin in Newgate," she added casually, and was gratified to see her friend's look of horrified amazement. "*Really?*" Phil gasped. "Not – not as a *prisoner?*"

"No, just visiting," said Gin. She had no intention of going into details: the sheltered, innocent Miss Tucker should not learn about treason, spies, Jacobites and felons. "I expect this Tower's the same in little," she said. "You can have anything you want if you pay through the nose for it. And the gaolers all have blind eyes they're forever turning. Ain't that how it goes?"

"Well, they let Tawny out after Papa paid them," Phil said. "But he didn't hit anyone. Look, there's Mr. Jessop."

The door to the Tower had opened, and Sam walked out with her brother. He was red in the face and the boy's expression was set. Gin ran towards them, and Sam managed a smile as he saw her. "Hello, Jane! You look much better than you did yesterday!"

"Mr. Dark," Gin panted. "What's he done?"

There were still a few stragglers standing around, looking at them curiously. Sam said in an undertone, "Not here, too many watchers." Belatedly, he added in a normal voice, "Good morning, Miss Tucker."

"Good morning, Mr. Jessop," said Phil, with a quick curtsey, and followed Sam, Tawny and Gin into the churchyard. They stopped by a cluster of ancient, lichened headstones which were completely illegible, although a crudely carved skull was still visible on one of them, and the two girls looked at the men expectantly.

Briefly, Sam gave them an expurgated account of what had happened in the Blue Anchor. Gin said at once, "Mr. Dark don't usually lose his temper, so what did that constable do to deserve it?"

Sam looked uncomfortable. "I'm – I regret to say that the man referred to Mrs Paradice in very derogatory terms, to which Dark took considerable exception. As did I," he added.

"But you're still free, Mr. Jessop, so *you* obviously didn't hit anyone," Phil observed. "So what happens now? Will they bring him before the Council?"

"I don't think they will," Tawny said. "It's plain they don't take the accusation of spying seriously, but Bill Davy is making a great to-do over his bruises – which, from the sound of it, were thoroughly deserved – and they wouldn't accept any money to let him go."

"How much did you offer them?" Gin asked.

"A sixpence and a half crown," said Tawny, looking a little sheepish. "It was all we could muster between us. Perhaps if we give them time for their hot heads to cool, and offer more, they might listen."

Above their heads, the church bells began to toll the faithful to morning service. Phil gasped. "We have to be at the Meeting House! Mama will kill me if I'm late! Come on, Tawny, perhaps we can get back before she notices we've gone." She whirled round and ran off through the churchyard, hair flying. Her brother gave Gin and Sam a rueful smile. "I must go too. And certainly Phil will be occupied for the rest of the day, even if Mama hasn't realised that she's been out on the Sabbath. But I will try to visit you at the Mermaid later this afternoon. We can plan how best to go about releasing your friend, and also how we can best search the Marsh tomorrow. Your servant, Mr Jessop, Miss Maggs."

He bowed to them both and hurried away in his sister's wake. Sam looked at Gin. "I am so sorry. Dark was incensed, I have never seen him so angry. I think all his fear for Polly went into that punch, it is not surprising that the constable is refusing to let him go. And Master Jeake is right, I think it would be a good idea to leave them all be for a few hours to calm down, before returning. He has an excellent head on his shoulders, that young man."

"He and Phil have been so good to me," Gin said. "I don't know what I'd have done without them, while you was gone after Dark." She felt herself blushing, and cursed inwardly, but Sam did not seem to notice. He looked at the church, and said, "Perhaps I will attend the service. If someone has their conscience pricked in such surroundings, they might decide to help me with information, if I am ready to hand. Will you accompany me?"

Gin shook her head. "I think I'll go back to the Mermaid, Mr. Jessop, I'm dog-weary." She was indeed rather tired, but more concerned to avoid going into a church unless forced to do so. Such places were not, and never had been, for the likes of her, and she was so ignorant of the form that a service might take that she did not want to expose Sam, or herself, to public humiliation or scrutiny by kneeling at the wrong time, or saying the wrong thing.

Fortunately, Sam accepted her excuse without question. They walked back through the churchyard and parted company at the further side, Gin heading for Middle Street and Sam for the north door of the church, joining several other people heading in the same direction. Once back in the blessed privacy of her chamber, she flung herself down on the bed and allowed the tears to fall. Why, oh why, did Mr. Dark have to lose his temper? She could understand the reason for it, none better – she would have liked to have punched that constable herself for his insult to Madam – but to lose control at such a vital moment might be disastrous. She and Sam needed him, his help, his ideas, his competence, just as they also needed the local knowledge and enthusiasm of Tawny and Phil.

Despite her friends' buoyant optimism, though, it seemed very plain that their chances of finding Polly alive were now slender indeed.

CHAPTER EIGHTEEN

The man you justly hate

Since dawn, Polly had tried to prepare herself for Crowley's promised visit. He had given her three days to come to a decision, and left her with paper and ink and pen, to write the letter to her banker. And she had done neither of those things, although in those three days the thought of him had infested her mind with such dread and horror that he seemed to be more demonic than human. Rationally, she knew that he could not be as monstrous as she imagined, yet she knew that the reality must be worse. For a monster has no option but to be vile, but Crowley was a man possessed of free will, who had nevertheless chosen to follow the path of evil.

And Mattie, knowing this, had chosen to be his accomplice. Polly, who had experienced or witnessed most of the ways that a man could manipulate and coerce a woman, wondered how much choice she had had. She had mentioned that she had committed crimes in her past, but the contempt with which she had asserted that she was a danger to Crowley, rather than the other way about, had been chilling: there was a wildness and recklessness in her sister that made her statement entirely plausible.

Despite this, though, Mattie had twice brought her food, obviously without Crowley's knowledge or consent. That in itself must be at a considerable risk to herself, yet she had gone behind his back to give Polly sustenance. Yes, she had been hostile, defensive, contrary, full of bitterness and envy, but she was in an intolerable position. Sooner or later, she would have to choose between the gold, and her sister. And it was not a foregone conclusion.

So the sun moved slowly up towards its zenith, and then

slid down towards the west, and Polly thought about what she would say to Crowley when he appeared. She would defy him with calm and reason, at first. But what if he produced that hideous razor? Despite her brave words to him, she knew that she could not long hold out against the threat of pain and mutilation. There seemed to be no escape for her, for even if she avoided such horrors by surrendering to his demands, he would never let her go. And there was no sign of her friends. Where were Sam and Gin? Had they tracked down Dark? Were they even now frantically searching the Marsh for her? If so – and she knew they would not abandon her – then there was still hope.

The thought of Crowley's impending arrival had loomed so large and so menacingly in her mind for hours, that it came almost as a relief when she heard the sound of a horse. Polly sat up straight, her back against the wall of the hut, her skirts tidily arranged and her fingers laced calmly together in her lap to disguise their shaking, and awaited her fate.

Soon, the door was opened, and the sudden golden sunlight speared straight into her eyes. Squinting against it, she saw the dark bulk of her nemesis, framed in the doorway. And despite her wild imaginings, he was still only a man – taller than Sam, shorter but more broadly built than Dark. And he could not be invincible. She would defy him still, and buy herself the precious time in which she could be found.

"Good day to you, Mistress Paradice," he said cheerfully, and she realised that he expected her capitulation. It gave her more strength. She did not answer, though, but merely inspected him with disgust, as she might a rotten joint of meat on a butcher's stall. He turned, and beckoned. "Ned!"

One of the two men who had originally abducted her came past him and dumped a leather bottle beside her. He picked up the empty ones, and the stinking, brimming bucket, and went out. Crowley came further into the shack, and his smile vanished as he saw the crumpled sheets of paper discarded on the floor beside her. "You have not written the letter I asked you to write."

"No, I have not."

"Do you not understand what I can do to you?" In a single stride he was standing over her, his face abruptly suffused with rage. "I can carve your face so that your own mother would not recognise you, and children would run screaming from you in the street. You would end your days a noseless, fingerless, eyeless beggar. Is that what you want, eh, my pretty little harlot?" He knelt down beside her, his blue eyes hard as ice. "Though of course I can take my pleasure of you first, while you are still not too hideous."

It took an enormous effort of will not to shrink away from him as his hand came out to stroke her cheek. "Flawless," he said softly. "Entirely flawless. Such a shame that it must be marked." The fingers slid down past her jaw, lingered below her ear, where a pulse beat so hard she thought it must leap through her skin, and crept lower, like some vast and monstrous insect, to the swell of her breast beneath the light muslin kerchief above her neckline: lingered there, and then squeezed savagely. "Well? Do you really still think to defy me, you stupid trollop?"

"I do," Polly said, though the pain had brought involuntary tears to her eyes.

"Then perhaps I can change your mind. Do you know what symmetry is, my dear?"

"It is balance, when one half of something exactly matches the other." She had learned it, with so many other things, from the Colonel, who had loved her singing, and had educated her as if she was the daughter he had never had.

"You do know! And I thought you stupid and ignorant. My apologies, madam. Then you will understand that a lack of symmetry should be remedied."

As she was wondering what he meant, Crowley dipped his right hand into the pocket of his coat and brought out the razor. His other hand shot out and grabbed her bound arm, twisting it so that she gasped in sudden agony. "No, struggling will make me miss my stroke, and you don't want to make things any the worse for you, do you? Hold still!" And he pulled her wrist sharply towards him and before she could react, drew the blade of the razor across her skin. Blood and pain leapt in its track, and she could not suppress a whimper.

"There," Crowley said with satisfaction, inspecting his handiwork. "Almost perfectly like the other. Now, madam, what have you to say? Will you write that letter? I am generally acknowledged to be a patient man, but even my patience is beginning to run dry, and I have planned this for a long time. I do not utter idle threats, my dear Mrs Paradice, your defiance is merely prolonging the inevitable. I will have you begging for mercy sooner or later."

Her arm hurt, and there was more blood than before. *Not quite symmetry*, Polly thought. She clamped her mouth shut on a wild laugh and said nothing.

"Well?" Crowley demanded again, and when she did not respond, he hit her across the face, so hard that her head smacked into the wooden wall behind her, and her ears rang. "Answer me!"

The man called Ned had come back and was standing in the doorway. He said, "You had no call to do that to a woman, leave alone one that's tied."

Crowley turned and glared at him. "I didn't ask for your opinion. I pay you and your brother more than handsomely, to do as you're told and keep your mouth shut."

"Bain't right," the other man persisted. He held Crowley's gaze for a long moment, and then turned and went back out. Crowley swore under his breath and got to his feet. To Polly's overwhelming relief, the razor went back into its scabbard, and he dropped it into his pocket. "You're playing for time, aren't you?" he said, looking down at her, breathing hard. "Playing for time to give your friends a chance to find you? Well, you can forget that idea, madam, because your precious lover has been thrown into gaol in Rye, on suspicion of being a Jacobite spy. That's an absurdity, is it not? The spy for King George, accused of being a spy for King James! So there'll be no help from that quarter, they won't let him out until the Assizes come to town, or they might even send him back to London to explain himself. And by the time he gets free, my dear, you'll be a pauper with your beauty ruined."

In a single sentence, her hopes had been destroyed. She said, "You're lying."

"No, I am not. André Dark lies in the Tower in Rye, and all your hope is gone. So I'll give you tonight, do you hear me? A few more hours to think on what I've told you, and admit defeat. Then I'll come back tomorrow morning, and I'll be alone. No-one to hear us, no-one to see, no-one to interrupt or object. You'll write that letter, and if you still defy me, you'll wish you'd never been born." He gave her a brief, mocking bow. "Good day to you, Mistress Paradice. Sleep well – if you can."

*

It was the middle of the afternoon, and for want of anything better to do, Gin was sewing up the dangling hem of her striped gown. Mercy had brought her a simple dinner of bread, cheese and slices of ham, and a tart made with fresh, crisp apples baked in an egg custard, and she had eaten hungrily, still making up for meals not taken during her illness. There was no word from Tawny or Phil, and Gin suspected that their Mama, who obviously did her best to run a strict and godly household, despite the efforts of her wayward offspring, had insisted that they stay quietly at home, engaged in prayer and contemplation on the Sabbath. Nor had Sam returned, and she could only assume that he was still making enquiries about Polly and her captors. Of course, he could also have returned to the Tower to make another attempt to have Dark freed, but as the afternoon dragged on and he did not appear, that seemed unlikely.

So, bored and apprehensive, Gin had found Madam's little sewing kit, which she always took with her on her travels – a small rosewood box containing scissors, a thimble, a needle case and many lengths of thread in various colours – and sat down in the seat by the open window overlooking the courtyard, where the light was best and there was a cooling breeze, and where she could also keep an eye on the comings and goings in the Mermaid. She had laboriously sewn up nearly half a yard of hem, trying to keep the stitches small and neat as Madam and Hannah had taught her, when there was a bustle and commotion below. Praying that it might herald Sam's and Dark's triumphant return, she put down the sewing and peered out. A man in a workman's leather coat had entered the yard, pushing a barrow laden with baggage of all kinds. As she watched, he set it down and mopped his face with a large handkerchief. He was followed by a little group of women, two fashionably rigged and two who were obviously maidservants, with a footman also in attendance. Intrigued, Gin opened the window wider, the better to see and hear, as Mr Bird emerged from the inn and bowed very low. "Madame la Marquise! Miss Oglethorpe! It is a great honour to welcome you to my humble establishment."

Oglethorpe! Gin's ears pricked up, and she leaned a little further out. Miss Molly had mentioned that she had two sisters in France, and surely these must be they. One was decidedly plump, with dark hair elaborately arranged, and wearing a handsome gown in a delicious shade of blue-green silk, set off with lace ruffles at the sleeves and a mantle in a paler but toning colour. The other young woman was taller than her sister, with hair a warm shade of amber, and a dress of printed cotton that was far less grand, but more practical. Smiling, she said to Mr Bird, "Thank you, sir. Our apologies for arriving unannounced, but we had not intended to land here – after we left Calais last night, the wind altered to a very contrary direction, and the captain was forced to make for Rye rather than Dover."

"A happy accident," said the Marquise. She had a strong French accent, which Gin struggled to understand. "We are delighted to visit you, Mr Bird. I take it you are able to accommodate us? We require two chambers, one for my sister and one for myself. And our maids, of course, and the footman. Tomorrow at first light, we will be travelling on to London, to see our mother and brother and sisters. I understand there is still no coach service from Rye?"

"I regret not, madame. The roads..." Mr Bird spread his hands eloquently. "But a coach may be hired, although for the first part of the journey it's best drawn by oxen, rather than horses. I will arrange it for you. In the meantime, pray allow me to show you to your rooms. I trust they will be entirely to your satisfaction."

The little group moved into the inn. Gin sat back on the window seat, her sewing forgotten. The Oglethorpes! A happy accident indeed. Would they be able to help? After all, Polly had been engaged as a singing teacher to their sister, and their brother was a frequent visitor to the Paradise. Perhaps Madam's name had been mentioned in letters. It was a shot in the dark, but if it worked, it would be worth it.

Frowning, she began to think it through. It would not do to ruin her scheme for want of a little forethought, or to let any rashness make matters even worse. First, she considered the Oglethorpe family. They were Jacobites, who had plotted to install the Pretender, whom they called James III, in place of King George. Who was to say that they were not still plotting?

They had sought Madam out, and invited her into their house for what seemed, now, to be flimsy and spurious reasons. They had wanted something from her, and Gin racked her brains to think of what it might be. Was it Dark? If so, then they would jump at the chance to have him free and accessible. But that now seemed unlikely to Gin. What did they know of Dark, and what could they do to him?

Get rid of him by putting him on a ship to France. The thought popped into her head, but she rejected it. What if Dark had never been their quarry at all? Or Crowley's? What if Polly was their target? Or something she had, or something she knew? Perhaps her link to Sinclair? Some strange idea of revenge for her perceived betrayal of him?

But no-one had been responsible for Sinclair's death, save for Sinclair himself. *And good riddance*, Gin thought: she had met him only once, in Newgate, but recognised an out and out rogue when she saw one. She had little sympathy for the Pretender's cause, but he was infinitely better off without men such as Robbie Sinclair, full of pride, callous self-interest, recklessness and conceit. And he had intended, that icy January day on the frozen Thames, not only to assassinate the Prince of Wales, but, far worse, to murder Dark. No, she thought that very few people, if any, had mourned him.

It came to her that none of this was to the point. The point was, to free Dark so that he could search for Polly, because without him, she felt as if she and Sam were blundering around in blindfolds. And if the Oglethorpe sisters wanted something from Polly, they would surely listen to her desperate plea for help. Of course, they might be no more successful at getting Dark released than Sam and Tawny had been, but they were wealthy and perhaps would have more influence on the constables. It was a slim chance, but better by far than doing nothing.

Without Sam and his pocket watch, she only had the

church clock to tell her the time. Shortly after the Oglethorpe sisters' arrival, it struck three. Gin knew that it would be best to give them at least an hour to rest and refresh themselves, and in the meantime, Sam might turn up.

He did not. Perhaps, Gin thought, imagining the worst, he had been thrown into the Tower too. When she heard the four chimes through the open window, she put down her sewing, checked in the mirror that her appearance was tidy and respectable, and left the room. Her palms were damp, and her heart thudded beneath her stays. But she would not abandon this attempt, not now. *If you don't ask, you don't get,* she thought grimly. *And if they send me away with a tribe of fleas in my ear, at least I'll have tried.*

She had already deduced, from various sounds and her knowledge of the Mermaid's arrangements, that the sisters had been given the best chambers on the ground floor, immediately below theirs. So she went down the stairs, and encountered Mercy at the bottom, carrying a tray with two glasses and a bottle of wine. Inspiration struck. Greatly daring, Gin said, "Is that for the Oglethorpe ladies?"

Mercy stared at her in surprise. "Do you know them, then?"

"My mistress gave their sister singing lessons, in London." Gin swallowed. "I wish – I want to ask them something, if I may. Shall I take in the wine?"

The maid looked very doubtful. "I bain't sure – "

"I have often served ladies and gentlemen," said Gin, the accomplished and devious liar. "I won't disgrace you." She adopted what she hoped was a piteous expression. "Please? You can have a sixpence."

To an inn servant on small wages, any extra income was very welcome, and Gin knew from their talk during her illness that Mercy was saving for the future she hoped to share with

Reuben, the stable lad at the Red Lion. The other girl grinned suddenly. "Very well, you may do it. But please take care, the older one is a great lady in France and I heard her shouting at her maid earlier. If you offend her, and Mr Bird hears of it –" She made an eloquent gesture.

"Don't fret," Gin said cheerfully. She fumbled in her pocket, and proffered a worn coin that bore the head of King William. "I won't let you down, I swear it. Thank you so much, Mercy!"

The exchange accomplished, she bore the tray along to the nearer of the two chambers, which the maid had told her was occupied by the younger Oglethorpe sister, and knocked on the door. A voice within called, "*Qui est la?*"

Gin did not know a word of French, but that needed no translation. "I have brought the wine you ordered, Miss," she said.

There was a pause, and then the door was opened by a young woman who was obviously one of the two French maids. She stood aside to let Gin enter with her tray, and indicated a table placed, just as in her own chamber, close to the window. With demurely lowered gaze, she scuttled across to it, then looked round. Miss Oglethorpe, who seemed more approachable and less grand than Madame la Marquise, was standing by the bed, watching her. She said, in a pleasant, slightly accented voice, "Pray set the glasses on the table. Let me test the wine."

It was surely the same vintage that had been served by Amos Crowley, Jenny Garnet, and Lady Oglethorpe: Gin would have put a sizeable wager on it. Miss Oglethorpe came over to the table and poured a little of the wine into one of the glasses. It was a gorgeous colour, rich and ruby red. She swirled it gently round, then, to Gin's surprise, raised the glass not to her lips but to her nose, and inhaled deeply. Then she did taste it, but only a small sip, before nodding and smiling. "Yes, that is most excellent. Pray give my thanks to Mr Bird."

Now or never. Gin bobbed a curtsey and said urgently, "Yes, I will, Miss Oglethorpe. But please, begging your pardon, may I speak with you privately?" She glanced at the maid, who was unpacking clothes from a bag, shaking each garment out and laying it on the bed.

"You wish to speak with me?" Miss Oglethorpe was pretty, with an oval face and arched eyebrows above large blue eyes. She opened those eyes wide with surprise, and smiled. "Do not worry about Cecile, she does not understand English. So..."

"Jane, Miss. Jane Maggs. And I ain't a servant here. I'm in the employ of Mrs. Paradice."

There was a silence. Miss Oglethorpe put the glass down on the table with the slightest of clinks, and surveyed Gin with interest. Gin returned the scrutiny calmly, though inside her guts seemed to be tying themselves in knots. At last the other girl said, "The same Mrs. Paradice who has been giving my sister Molly singing lessons in London?"

"Yes, Miss."

"I see." Miss Oglethorpe addressed the maid in French, and she went out, returning almost immediately and holding the door open for Madame La Marquise. That lady had changed into an embroidered silk dressing gown, and her hair was loose around her shoulders, as if her maid had been halfway through brushing it. She looked curiously at Gin, and then at her sister. "Yes, Fanny? What do you want? This is hardly convenient."

Fanny Oglethorpe nodded to the maid, who was still holding the door open. "*Tu pou nous quitter, Cecile. Merci.*"

As the maid closed the door behind her, the Marquise came to stand by her sister at the table, and studied Gin with her eyebrows raised. "Fanny, who is this?"

"This is Jane, and she is Mrs. Paradice's maid."

The eyebrows – beautifully plucked and shaped – climbed even further. "The one whom Nan mentioned in her last letter? So, what does she want with us?"

"I don't know if you can help," Gin said, trying not to wilt under that intimidating stare, reminiscent of her fearsome mother's. "But my mistress has been abducted, we think by a man called Amos Crowley. We, her friends, are trying to find her, and one of us has been wrongfully imprisoned in the town gaol because there are people here who know the truth and are hiding it from us."

"And what is that to do with me, or my sister?"

Gin gulped. "My mistress was lured away here with a wicked lie, and taken. Crowley wants something from her, but we don't know what it might be. And he is an evil man, he may hurt or even kill her." Despite her resolve, tears sprang to her eyes. "Mr Dark was helping in the search, but he asked too many questions and they threw him in prison. Everyone claims to know nothing about it, because smugglers were the ones what took her, and no-one dares peach on 'em, but Mr. Dark's our best hope of finding her before Crowley ... before he ... of finding her still alive, she's been gone nearly a week now." To her shame, tears were spilling over, and she wiped them desperately away. "I'm sorry, Madame, I shouldn't have troubled you. I'll go now. Pray forgive me."

She was about to turn away, still sobbing, when Fanny said, "No. No, don't go. Here, have this."

Gin found an exquisite square of lawn, fine as a cobweb and embroidered with the initials FO, being pressed into her hand. She muttered her thanks and wiped her face with it, taking several deep breaths to calm herself, before looking up at the sisters. The Marquise was frowning, while Miss Fanny wore an expression of sympathy and kindness. She smiled at Gin, and indicated one of the chairs. "Why don't you sit down, Jane, and tell us your tale from the very beginning?"

A year ago, Gin would never have imagined that she would be on such terms with any ladies of quality, let alone a Marquise of France. She waited until the sisters were seated opposite her, and then launched into her story. Normally, she would have relished the chance to embroider and embellish, but it was vital that she spoke nothing but the simple truth, though she had no intention of mentioning the awkward fact, to these two Jacobites, that Dark had been accused of being a Jacobite spy.

As she finished, the sisters exchanged a significant look. Then Fanny said, "What a dreadful thing! Your poor mistress, what must she be suffering! My sister Anne has written to us mentioning her, and telling us that Molly has become quite the songbird under her tuition. Of course we shall do all in our power to help, though it may not be very much." She glanced at the Marquise. "Will we not, Nell?"

"But there is no time," said her sister flatly. "We are setting off for London at dawn tomorrow, to see Molly – she has run into some difficulty, and has requested our help."

That'll be to do with her debts, I'll wager, Gin thought, but did not comment.

"But that is tomorrow," Fanny said. "This is today, and there is still time to help free Mr. Dark. Tell me, Jane, are there palms eager to be greased?"

"I reckon so, Miss Oglethorpe."

"Good. That always makes matters easier. And you say that Mr Dark lost his temper when they called your mistress ... foul names?"

"Yes, Miss."

"Well, that is only what any gentleman of honour would do, when a lady of his acquaintance is vilified in such a way. I have every sympathy with him, and none for that wretched constable. He deserved to be struck. Indeed, he should count himself fortunate that he is not in France, or he might have been run through."

"In our country," said the Marquise through tight lips, "men such as that have a proper respect for their betters."

Fanny glanced at her, and grimaced slightly. Gin had already formed the impression that she was much more lively and less hide-bound by strict convention than her older sister. She said, "Indeed, Nell, that is true. However, if you recall, things are arranged a little differently here in England. Now, Jane, we will be happy to help you, and I think I know how it might be done."

"If what Jane says is correct, releasing this Mr. Dark will not necessarily mean that Mrs. Paradice can be found," said the Marquise, who seemed to have an objection to every strategy.

"I do know that, Madame," said Gin. "But if anyone can find her, he will, and he can't do it from a prison cell."

"Exactly," said Fanny. She leaned forward, her eyes sparkling, her face alight with mischief. "Listen, and I will tell you what I think will turn the key."

CHAPTER NINETEEN

Women love to see Men make wry Faces

A little later, those who were out and about in Rye on a pleasant Sunday afternoon witnessed a curious procession making its way up Middle Street. It was headed by a pair of very fine and elegant ladies, dressed all in the height of fashion, and talking to each other in a foreign language that most bystanders, in this port town, recognised as French. They were attended by a footman in livery and three maidservants, one of whom appeared to be their guide. Visitors were not so rare in Rye, but these seemed as exotic as popinjays.

Sam was one of those who stopped to look as they passed. He had been making his way back to the Mermaid, after several fruitless hours attempting to gather information about Polly's disappearance. As before, no-one had admitted to knowing anything, and he had met with obstinacy, professed ignorance, and even downright rudeness. Then he had returned to the Tower, where he had spoken with another constable, not one of those who had arrested Dark, and had received a flat refusal to even consider releasing him before the morning, when he would be interrogated by one of the town's magistrates. It had been frustrating and disheartening in the extreme, and he was not looking forward to telling Gin of his failure.

So it was with considerable surprise that he realised that the neatly dressed maid walking beside the fine ladies was, in fact, Gin herself. What on earth was she doing? Who were these French noblewomen? Did she know them? It seemed highly unlikely. As he hesitated, wondering whether to accost them, Gin glanced across to the side of the street and saw him. One eye closed in a deliberate wink, and she made a swift, small gesture that surely meant that he should not interfere. Sam nodded acquiescence, but he was not going to leave it at that. He waited until they had all climbed to the top of the hill, and then joined the ranks of the curious, and followed.

It soon became obvious where they were heading. They went round the outside of the churchyard and walked across to the Ypres Tower, perched on the edge of the cliff. Sam looked up at the turrets and wondered which of them held his friend, and whether he was watching. The footman turned and gestured at the little crowd to disperse, following it up with a threatening gesture. Most of them scattered, but Sam found an unobtrusive spot by a neighbouring house, close enough to see and hear clearly, and awaited events with interest.

The gaol keeper must have heard his visitors approach, but the door to the Tower remained firmly shut. The ladies halted a few paces away, and the footman walked forward and hammered forcefully on the old wood. After a pause, just long enough to be annoying, short enough not to appear insolent, it opened, and the keeper, the same man with whom Sam had argued not long before, stood looking at the group in front of him. If he was astonished by their appearance at the Tower, he managed not to show it. "Yes?"

The taller, slimmer lady stepped forward. In her flowered dress made in the new French style with a loose back, a straw hat elegantly perched on her immaculately coiffured head, she was splendidly intimidating. "I understand you have a man named Dark in custody here. Is that correct?"

"Y-yes, madam."

"Why is he here?"

"He struck one of the other constables. A completely unprovoked attack, and a serious offence."

"I have it from a reliable witness that, far from being it

being unprovoked, the man in fact uttered a foul slander on the lady Dark was seeking, rousing his quite understandable fury. I will also say that Dark has been in my mother's employ for many years and has always been a man of very upright and honourable character." Even from this distance, Sam could sense the power of her stare. "In short, this is an unjustified, trumped-up charge, and I demand that you set him free at once."

"I can't do that, madam."

"Can you not? Then your magistrate will receive a very forceful complaint from me regarding my servant's treatment at your hands. I am told he was injured, is that true?"

"He – he was resisting arrest," said the hapless gaol-keeper.

"I am not surprised he resisted, given the provocation. Any man of honour would do the same. Now, are you going to release him or not?"

"I can't," the man repeated.

"Are you quite sure about that? Do you know who we are? My sister is the Marquise de Mezière, and our father was Sir Theophilus Oglethorpe and the Member of Parliament for Haslemere in Surrey."

Oglethorpe, Sam thought, *where have I heard that name before?*

"We have good friends on the Council, and we can ensure that things are made very difficult for you. And if the injury that my servant has suffered turns out to be serious ..."

"I – I ..."

"Perhaps this will help." The tall lady turned to one of the maids. "Cecile?"

The woman stepped forward with a small bag in her hand, and passed it to her mistress.

"You can regard this as recompense for the very minor hurt which your fellow has suffered at my servant's hands. Believe me, it is far, far more than he, or you, deserve. Accept it, and we will say no more about this incident. Refuse, and I will ask the Council to strip you of your position, and the whole town will know of your disgrace. Is that clear?"

"Let him go!" one of the remaining onlookers shouted, and another called, "Davy had it coming to him!"

The gaol keeper hesitated, evidently torn between greed and duty. Finally, with a swift, furtive movement, he took the bag and shoved it into the pocket of his coat. "Wait here, madam," he said, and turned to go inside, but Miss Oglethorpe said sharply, "One moment! My maid will accompany you to see what conditions Mr. Dark has been held in. If they are noxious and unhealthy, it will be the worse for you. Jane?"

Intrigued and suddenly full of hope, Sam watched as Gin came up and bobbed a curtsey. The gaol keeper looked reluctant, but bowed under the combined pressure of two very threatening glares, and ushered Gin inside the Tower. The door slammed shut behind them, and Miss Oglethorpe turned and said something to her sister. The two women stood together, their maids and the footman a respectful distance away, looking round with disdainful interest at the open space before the Tower, and the curious idlers still standing there. Sam suddenly remembered where he had heard the name of Oglethorpe, and his puzzlement increased. These women were Jacobites, so why were they going to such lengths to have Dark freed? How had Gin come to be mixed up in this? And why had they sent her inside the Tower to see Dark's prison cell?

But of course, someone had to ensure that he went along with that cock and bull story about him being a servant of the Oglethorpes, and who better than Gin, whom he knew and trusted? Sam thought that he would give a considerable sum to be a fly on the wall when Dark realised who his rescuers were.

For her part, Gin did not relish the prospect of setting foot inside the Tower, but it had in fact been her idea, and she had to carry it through. The sound of the door shutting behind her brought back unpleasant memories of Newgate, and the visit that she and Madam had paid to Sinclair. But this place held none of the terrors of London's most notorious prison. She looked round the small space, some sixteen feet square, seeing a table laden with papers, a tankard and leather bottle, a couple of chairs, and a hearth containing a well-grown fire, with a trivet at the front of it, on which a kettle was beginning to steam. This pleasant room was obviously where the gaol keeper conducted his business. Somewhere below them, a muffled voice started to shout hoarsely, but it did not sound like Mr. Dark.

"He ain't down there," said the keeper, scowling at her. "*Gentlemen* get the best quarters."

"So I should hope," Gin said pertly, and was rewarded with an even more hostile glare. The man opened a door immediately to her left, and she saw a spiral staircase, obviously contained in one of the Tower's four turrets, leading both upwards and down. The shouting echoed up from the depths, and now carried a note of wild desperation.

"Drunkard," said the keeper, in response to Gin's querying look. "Your man's up here."

They climbed the stairs, Gin following with care and holding her skirts well up out of the way, for it was steep and the stones very worn and uneven. At the top was another square chamber, very similar to the one below, save that it had larger windows. There was a narrow bed near the empty hearth, and a door in each corner, so there must be much smaller cells in the turrets. The keeper crossed to the door diagonally opposite the stair, produced a large key, and inserted it in the lock. The door swung open to reveal a tiny circular room, lit by two narrow windows. Sitting in the embrasure, looking out over the river and across the Marsh to the distant sea, was Dark.

He turned abruptly as the door opened and his face changed from boredom to astonishment as he saw Gin lurking behind the keeper. "Jane! What are you doing here?"

"You're free," said the gaoler, with obvious regret. "So go, before I change my mind or before Bill Davy comes to hear of it. Go on, cut your stick." He held the door open and beckoned.

Dark got up, looking as if he could not quite believe it. "It's true, Mr. Dark," Gin said. "Your mistress has got you out." She saw his expression, and added swiftly, "Miss Oglethorpe and the Marquise are waiting for you, here below. They have explained everything, and the gaol keeper here has kindly agreed to set you free."

Not for nothing was Dark a spy. After that first look, he did not betray by a flicker that he had no idea what she was talking about. "Thank you, sir," he said to the man standing by the door. "I am most grateful to you."

"If it was up to me, you'd be here till Christmas," said the keeper. "Lucky for you you've got a kind mistress. Go on, out, look lively about it."

Dark stepped out of the cell. Gin saw the dried blood on the side of his face, and noted that he moved stiffly, as if bruised and in pain. Anger flared in her, but she swallowed it down and said, "This way, Mr. Dark."

The keeper followed them down the stairs and unlocked the main door. Dark gave him a bow which, to Gin who knew him so well, was just the right side of insolent. "Thank you for your hospitality, brief though it was."

"Out," the man said, and they obediently walked into the free air of Rye. The door slammed behind them with a blessed finality. Gin said, very softly, "We told him you're the

Oglethorpes' servant. Play the part until we're out of sight of the Tower, or he may change his mind and come after us."

"To be free of that place, I'd pretend to be a servant to the devil himself," Dark said grimly.

The Oglethorpe ladies had withdrawn to a shady spot beneath one of the trees lining the churchyard. Both sisters smiled as Gin and Dark approached them, though a derisive cheer came from a little group of onlookers who had stayed to see if the prisoner would be released. When they came close, Dark bowed very low, and Gin performed her best curtsey.

"Good afternoon, Mr. Dark," said the Marquise formally. "I am glad to see you at liberty."

"I am glad to be at liberty, Madame, Miss Oglethorpe, and I thank you both from the bottom of my heart for your kindness."

"I should thank Jane here," said Fanny Oglethorpe, with a lively grin. "She begged us for help, in such piteous and persuasive terms that we could hardly refuse her. Shall we move away from sight of that dreary prison? I would not want that unpleasant man to realise that I have been lying through my teeth."

The two women went through the gate into the churchyard, with the rest of their entourage following, and at once Gin spotted Sam, waiting for them beside a gravestone, and ran over to him. "Come and join us, Mr. Jessop!"

"However did you manage to free him?" Sam asked in bewilderment. "I have spent the best part of this afternoon trying to persuade that obdurate fool to let him go, with absolutely no result. And who are those ladies, and how did you make their acquaintance?"

"I'll tell you later, but for now, you must meet them, and please don't be surprised!" Gin took his arm and ushered him over to the women. A quick glance behind her revealed that the trees bordering the churchyard effectively hid them from any view from the Tower. Emboldened, she said breathlessly, "Madame Marquise, Miss Oglethorpe, this is Mr Jessop, who is a friend of Mrs Paradice and Mr Dark. He has been trying to find my mistress, but we have had no success so far, though we have asked far and wide all over Rye and beyond."

"But with Mr Dark free now," said Fanny Oglethorpe cheerfully, "surely you must have a much better chance of success." She ignored her sister's frown and smiled broadly at him. "I am very glad to make your acquaintance, sir, I have heard a great deal about you."

Ostensibly she would only have heard about him from Gin, an hour or so ago, but from the look in her eyes, it was obvious that she must have had other informants. Dark had evidently noticed too, for he bowed and said courteously, "As indeed I have heard much about you and your sisters. From Jane here," he added, after the slightest pause.

Gin looked at them with interest. It was plain to her that each of them knew very well what the other was about, and that despite this, they would not mention it. Perhaps Miss Oglethorpe, or her sister, had decided that having Dark indebted to them might come in useful at some time in the future. She resolved to quiz him about it later.

"Fanny?" said the Marquise, with a quelling glance. "I grow fatigued. Now that our errand of mercy has succeeded, I wish to return to our inn to rest."

"Of course," her sister said. "I collect, Mr. Dark, that you and Mr. Jessop and Jane here are also staying at the Mermaid? Then we can all walk back together. What a charming little town Rye is – so much quieter and less frantic than Dover."

She made prattling small talk all the way back to Middle Street, but Gin knew that it was a front. Miss Fanny might seem to be as frivolous and naïve as her younger sister Molly, but that girlish laugh and apparently innocent chatter disguised a lively intelligence and a quick wit, in addition to a well-honed sense of mischief. *I wish she and Madam could meet,* Gin thought sadly, as they entered the inn. *They would surely rub along very well together.*

In the hall of the Mermaid, Dark and Sam once more expressed their thanks, and Miss Fanny waved them away with a smile and a laugh. "Oh, that is of no consequence at all! It has been a most excessively diverting afternoon, has it not, Nell?"

"Indeed it has," said the Marquise, with considerably less enthusiasm.

"I am much in your debt, Madame, Miss Oglethorpe," Dark said, bowing. "When circumstances allow, which I trust will be very soon, I hope to repay you."

"Oh, pray do not trouble yourself about that, sir! It was but a trifling sum, though I think that gaol keeper thought it was riches. In any event, it was money well spent." She sent him a sparkling, significant look. "But it may fall out that you have the opportunity to return the favour in other, less *pecuniary* ways."

"It may," Dark said, with a smile. "And I am most grateful to you both, ladies."

They said their farewells, and the Oglethorpes and their servants returned to their rooms, while Gin, Sam and Dark climbed, in a rather tense silence, to the floor above. Gin had the uneasy feeling that a reckoning was due. They went into the chamber shared by Dark and Sam, and she said brightly, "Shall I go below and ask for something to eat?"

"In a moment," Dark said. He turned and gave her a long, hard look. "*Do* tell me how you have become acquainted with the Oglethorpe family?"

Gin swallowed. She wanted to lie, but under that stern gaze, evasion was impossible. She said, "Do you remember a customer at the Paradise, a greenhead what Madam called

Beaky Nose?"

"Yes, I do."

"His real name is James Oglethorpe, and he's those ladies' brother." Gin gulped. "And he invited Madam to sing for his mother and sisters at their house. Then they asked her to give Miss Molly singing lessons."

"And did she?"

"Yes." Seeing his expression, Gin added hastily, "They offered her a guinea a time, and she weren't going to turn that down, no matter what."

"And did she know what the Oglethorpes are? They're fanatical Jacobites, every last one. Their other brother Theo is in the pay of the Pretender, the eldest sister was Harley's mistress, and all the rest are enthusiastic plotters against King George."

"Well, she didn't know, not at first," Gin said. "But I went with her, and I heard the servants' gossiping, and I told her." She paused apprehensively, for whatever she said might anger either Dark, or Polly, or both.

"And?"

"She was torn," said Gin honestly. "She didn't want to, she knew you wouldn't like it, but that guinea was too good to pass up. And then at the third lesson, Miss Molly asked her about Sinclair, and that worried her, and she decided not to go again and give them some excuse. But before she could tell them, she had word from her sister, if it *is* her sister, and we came here."

"I see." The tone of Dark's voice was still hostile. "And why did Miss Molly's questions worry her?"

"Because she reckoned it meant they wanted something from her. And we couldn't think what that might be."

Before he could answer, there was a knock on the door.

Sam said loudly, “Enter!”

Mercy came in and stood aside. “A visitor for you, sirs.” She curtseyed, and Sam said quickly, “Can you bring us some food and wine? Thank you.”

The maid withdrew, and Tawny came rather hesitantly into the room. When he saw Dark, he smiled in relief, and bowed. “I see that you have been released, sir, and I’m heartily glad of it.”

“Not as glad as I am, Master Jeake.” Dark bowed in return, and then they shook hands. “Thank you for your efforts on my behalf, even if they did not bear fruit.”

“Then, if I may be so bold, how –”

“By a happy chance, some ladies whom Jane knows of are also guests here at the Mermaid, and they agreed to help Jane and Mr. Jessop.” He smiled suddenly. “They claimed that I was their servant, apparently, and then a sum of money changed hands.”

Tawny grinned in reply. “That does not surprise me, sir, for all the constables and gaol keepers are known to be fond of lucre. As indeed are many in Rye, for we are not a wealthy place, and what was once a huge and very profitable harbour, centuries ago, has now silted up almost completely. Anyway, I have come to offer my services as a guide for your search for Mrs Paradice, for I know the Marsh very well – my brother Frank and I have roamed it since we were young boys, and I don’t think there is a square yard of it that I have not crossed at one time or another.”

“Thank you very much, Master Jeake, we are much obliged to you.” Dark looked at Gin and Sam. “Shall we go over what has been done so far, and what conclusions we may draw from that? I do not want us to set out tomorrow with no plan and no clear idea of where to search next. And time may be running out.”

He spoke calmly, but Gin could sense the urgency behind his words. Tomorrow, it would be a week since Madam's disappearance. If she was still alive – and despite their hopes, that must be increasingly unlikely – then by now she must surely be in the depths of despair, thinking that rescue would never come. And Gin could not bear the thought that her lively, kind and generous mistress might feel that her friends and her lover had abandoned her.

Mercy and the other maid, Susan, appeared with trays of food and drink, and set everything out on the table. Tawny explained that he would be expected home for supper later, so would not eat, but at Dark's invitation he pulled up a chair, and joined Gin and Sam in giving him brief details of their searches.

"So, it seems fairly certain that she is not in Rye, or Winchelsea, or anywhere close at hand," Dark said thoughtfully. "If she is still in the vicinity, which is surely most likely, then the one area that has not been searched is the land between Rye and Lydd, and all around. And since Crowley and his troupe were in Lydd a week ago, it seems probable that he has hidden her somewhere close by."

"She could be in a looker's hut," said Tawny. At Dark's expression of enquiry, he explained. "A looker, sir, is our name for a shepherd. One man may tend several flocks, and there have been huts built all over the Marsh to accommodate them while they do their work. But at this time of year, with the sheep still out grazing and before this year's lambs are rounded up for slaughter, most of the huts will be occupied. Unless a looker has been bribed, of course," he added. "They are generally poor men, and any extra coin would be very welcome."

"So, that is one aim – to check all the huts we come across tomorrow," Dark said. "It would help if we knew why Polly – why Mrs. Paradice has been taken. What does she have that

Crowley wants? Or is it to keep her silent for some reason?"

"Or is she the bait in the trap to catch you?" Gin asked, forgetting that Tawny did not know that Dark was a spy and Crowley a Jacobite.

There was a brief silence, before Dark said cautiously, "That is also a possibility."

"But why –" Tawny was looking puzzled.

Dark sighed. "Dear Gin, you really should learn not to let your tongue run away with you."

"Sorry, Mr. Dark," she said, and meant it.

"Master Jeake, I trust that this will not go beyond the four of us, understand?"

Tawny nodded gravely. "Yes, sir. You have my word on it, as a gentleman."

"Amos Crowley is an agent of the Pretender, and an ardent Jacobite. I am an agent for King George and the government, and in the past I have done things which Crowley may want to avenge. I will say no more than that."

"Ah," Sam said. "While you were in the Blue Anchor this morning, Dark, I was talking to an old fisherman mending nets on the quayside. Jem Fuller, I think his name was."

"Oh, Jem," Tawny said. "I like him, he goes his own way and won't be told what to do or say or think. Phil asked him about Mrs. Paradice a few days ago, because she knew he'd help us if he could, but he didn't know anything."

"Well," Sam said, "he told me that he'd recently overheard some talk in the tavern which was plainly about Mrs. Paradice, but he could not catch all of it. He said that Ned and Gabriel Tomkins were the men who took her, which we already knew. But he also mentioned the word 'decoy'. So you could be right, Gin."

"I ain't never heard of a decoy, Mr. Jessop, I dunno what it is."

"It's another word for a lure, or a bait," said Tawny. "Or it's a trap to lure wildfowl into nets so that they may be caught and slaughtered." He paused, his eyes suddenly bright with eagerness behind his round spectacles. "And there's a decoy house on the Marsh."

Gin held her breath. Dark said carefully, "Whereabouts on the Marsh?"

"About a couple of miles south-west of Lydd, down in the Midripps – that's an area quite close to the sea, a place full of shingle banks and scrub and fleets – they're long strips and pools of water, left behind when the sea retreated. When the big flocks of wildfowl come back to the Marsh, in the autumn, the decoy man moves into the house until the spring, and traps the geese and ducks." Tawny's look of excitement was unmistakeable now. "But at present, late in August, the place will be empty. And there's no grazing fit for sheep, so very few people go there. I think smugglers use it sometimes to stow goods, or as a bolthole if the Revenue men are after them, but in the spring and summer it's usually deserted."

Gin saw Dark look at Sam, and knew what they must be thinking, for the same idea was filling her mind too. Suddenly, there was real hope. She said urgently, "So you think Madam may be kept prisoner there?"

"I think it's more than possible," Tawny said. "I think it's very likely. It's close to Lydd, the Tomkins brothers undoubtedly know of it, and it would be a better place to hide someone than a looker's hut."

"Then let's go now!"

Tawny shook his head. "It will have to wait until tomorrow. Look at the window, the sun is almost set. Trying to cross the Marsh in the dark is very dangerous – not only because smugglers may be about, but because you're likely to end up in a fleet or a bog or a sewer, unless you know the way. And the moon's on the wane, so there won't be enough light. Besides, the ferryman will have gone home – my father once missed the last one, so Mama told me, and had to spend the night on the riverbank wrapped in his cloak."

Gin could see the sense in what he said, but it was still agonisingly disappointing. Now that they had an idea, something to aim at, she was desperate to set out on the rescue at once, and knew that Dark and Sam must feel the same. However, it would do no-one any good, least of all Polly, if they came to grief in the dark.

"Then we must start at first light," Sam said. "I will go down directly and arrange for horses – we shall need three."

"I'm coming too," said Gin fiercely. "I ain't staying here twiddling my fingers all day in a terror, and that's that. Besides," she added, glaring at Sam and Dark, "if you try and leave me behind I'll just follow on after. You can't stop me."

Tawny winked at her, which was very encouraging. Sam said, "But you have just been quite ill, Jane, I don't think – "

"She can come," said Dark. "I know what she's like. You might as well try and stop the wind blowing, once she gets an idea in her head." He glanced at Gin, and gave her a sudden and unexpected smile. "You'll have to ride pillion behind one of us."

"I don't care if you drag me behind you on a rope, Mr. Dark, so long as I can go with you."

"Well, that's settled, then," Sam said, rising to his feet. "Three horses for first light tomorrow morning. I'll go down and arrange it now."

"Mr. Jessop?" Tawny said. "Mr. Bird is a good and honest man, but I pray you, do not let slip that we may know where Mrs Paradice is. I am sure *he* would not deliberately betray us, but someone less scrupulous might overhear you, and then we may come to the decoy house to find her gone."

"Good advice," Dark said, looking approvingly at Tawny. "Thank you, Master Jeake, thank you, Sam. And let us hope that tomorrow brings a successful end to our search."

CHAPTER TWENTY

Vengeance I will have

Amos Crowley had said he would return in the morning, but as the sun rose higher, Polly began to wonder if this was another of his games, intended to unsettle and confuse her. Had he said that, or had she misremembered? After so long in the hut, tethered and alone, she was beginning to lose track of time, to forget precisely when he had come, when he had cut her arms, when he had threatened her with mutilation or disfigurement if she did not tell him how he could gain access to the gold he thought she possessed. During the night, in a waking dream, or was it dreaming wakefulness, she tried to think of a way in which she might still keep him at bay. Time: she must play for time. Time for Dark and Sam and Gin to find her. Time for her to think of a way to escape this prison, even though she had already tried, already thought, endlessly, uselessly, about extracting herself from a place which had no exit but a locked door.

Or death.

She did not want to die, but she knew that was the most likely outcome of this. Whatever she did, Crowley intended to kill her, and not only because she could incriminate him, but to punish her for her defiance. She had seen it in his face as he sliced her skin with the razor, the longing to shed more of her blood. He had only restrained himself because he still thought that she would capitulate and give him the information he wanted. And she would never, ever give him the satisfaction of receiving her abject submission to his will.

It was far too much effort to sit up, so she lay in the stuffy warmth and dozed, letting her mind wander, as she had for days now. There had been no more singing, it seemed stupidly frivolous in the face of the horror Crowley had threatened, and in any case her throat was dry and parched from lack of water. How long was it since Mattie had last brought her food? Two days? Three? She could not even work out what day it was, or how long she had been kept here. But she was hungry, with a low, fierce, insistent hunger that lurked in her belly, reminding her that she was still alive, but slowly starving.

She dreamed that she was back in the Paradise, with the coffee steaming and fragrant on the hearth, and Dan and Joe hurrying between the customers, bringing them coffee and pipes and tobacco, passing newspapers along, or carrying, very carefully, the small cups containing Hannah's Arrack punch. She looked around, wondering why no-one was paying her any attention. There was Will Evans guarding the door, leaning against the jamb with a gently smoking pipe between his teeth, and she saw Hannah behind the counter, filling a fresh coffee pot from the kettle, and called to her, but her maid ignored her. Feeling indignant, Polly went up to the bar, thinking how rude today's customers were, to keep standing in her way. "How does it go, Hannah?"

But Hannah turned away to put the pot on the hearth without speaking, and then leaned over the counter to chat to a man who had come up to order a drink. As she poured coffee, he turned his head to look at Polly, the first person there to have noticed her presence, and she saw that it was Crowley. He smiled at her, and winked, and then turned back to Hannah, and she realised with horror that she had become invisible, she was dead, a ghost, and he was the only one who could see her.

Polly woke with a gasp, and lay bewildered and disorientated, her mind still partly in her dream. Gradually she came back to herself, and relief flooded her. At least she was still alive, and at this moment, the mere fact of living was enough reason to be grateful.

Then she became aware of a sound on the edge of her hearing, a different noise to the incessant shriek of the sea birds: the soft, rhythmic beat of a horse, being ridden in leisurely fashion. He was coming. Polly raised herself on her elbows and tried to struggle into a sitting position. Her wrist was chafed and sore, her belly ached for lack of food, she knew that her hair must be filthy and full of straw, her face drawn and pale, and she surely stank. *At least,* she thought grimly, *I'm hardly likely to tempt him to rape me.*

The horse's hooves halted, quite close. There was a pause, while its rider must be dismounting and securing it to one of the scrubby trees which surrounded the shack. Her heart began to hammer, and her palms were slick with sweat. This was it. This was the reckoning.

Footsteps approached the door, and stopped. Polly tried desperately to calm herself, to control the shaking and the frantic breaths, but could not. She heard the key turning, and the bolts being drawn back. Then light burst in, and with it came Amos Crowley.

*

The ferryman eyed their little party with interest. He knew Tawny, of course, but he was not the same man who had transported Sam and Polly over the river on their way to Lydd. It was only nine days previously, but seemed to Sam as if a lifetime had passed since then. Three horses, three men of widely varying ages, and a maidservant: it was an odd combination. But to Sam's relief, he asked no questions, merely led their docile mounts onto the boat, and then, when they were all aboard, he and his assistant began the laborious task of poling them across. The tide was filling, the mud flats silently disappearing beneath the softly rising water. They disembarked without incident, and Sam noticed that young Master Jeake was assiduous in helping Gin off the boat.

Dark paid the boatmen and they mounted, Gin riding

pillion behind Sam. Tawny had said that Phil was in disgrace after running away from her Bible study, the previous day, and their mother had forbidden her to leave the house for the rest of the week, unless in adult company. Sam suspected that, to his mother, Master Jeake did not count as an adult. Anyway, he was glad that the child was not accompanying them. All the signs indicated that their rescue mission might not turn out to be a pleasant jaunt in the country.

Tawny proved a reliable and competent guide. Sam was glad that he knew where to go, for as before, the Marsh presented a bare, bleak aspect, in which the horizon was delineated by the next dyke wall, the next tortured tree, the next huddle of sheep. He remembered what Gin had said about Tawny's flying machine, and he wished that a similar magic contraption could lift them up above the flat landscape, so that at the very least they might be able to see further than fifty yards away.

They passed one of the lookers' huts, a rickety, windowless wooden shack with, remarkably, a brick chimney attached to it. Tawny rode over to check, and reported that it was empty. The thought of Polly being imprisoned in such a place was appalling, and Sam tried, without much success, to push it away.

Behind him, Gin said quietly, "Do you really think we'll find her, Mr. Jessop?"

Sam gave her the optimistic answer, rather than the rational one. "I hope and pray so. And if she does prove to be the means to lure Dark into a trap, then at least he is prepared."

The gentleman in question was riding ahead of them, next to Tawny, on a shaggy-hoofed, ambling nag which was the tallest Mr. Bird had been able to provide at short notice. Sam had already noted that his friend had retreated into a controlled and intimidating silence, which must conceal a variety of intense emotions. Even the irrepressible Master

Jeake seemed daunted by his grim presence, and had entirely given up trying to make any small talk.

"Well, I got all me fingers crossed," Gin said.

The sun was gaining in warmth, but there was still a brisk and chilly wind, blowing off the invisible sea which lay both ahead of them and to their right. Their pace was steady rather than fast, for there were few roads or tracks in this part of the Marsh. Tawny had drawn a hasty sketch of their route, and Sam knew that they were heading roughly east-south-east, parallel to the coast, which lay probably a mile away to the south. But there were so many obstacles and necessary diversions that their actual route, if plotted on a map, would probably have most resembled a row of jagged, pointed teeth. Most notable were the long fleets, filled with murky water or mud. They could not be crossed, so a way had to be found around them. It was one of these, he said, that had been turned into a decoy pond, for trapping wildfowl in the winter. Sam wondered how he could find his way so unerringly in this bleak landscape, almost completely flat save for the turfed walls which had once been built to keep out the sea and were now made redundant by its retreat, and the few trees, mostly willow or hawthorn, whose unnatural, twisted shapes gave silent testimony to the power of the wind across the bare land.

After nearly two hours riding, they came to another broad bank, crossed by the track which they were following. At the top, there was a limited prospect of the way ahead. A few stray sheep scattered as they approached, but there was no other sign of life. They halted their mounts and looked around. The sun was still shining strongly, but the wind had grown sharp and mischievous, tugging at their clothes, blowing the horses' manes and tails out, threatening to snatch away their hats.

"See that clump of trees?" Tawny indicated a distant dark green hummock, perhaps half a mile distant. "That's where the decoy pond is. The house is close by."

"And that place there?" Dark spoke for the first time in about half an hour, by Sam's reckoning. "To the right of the trees?"

"That's the shack where the decoy man hangs the birds until they're taken away for market in Lydd or Rye."

Dark was silent for a moment, and then said, "I suggest we ride a little closer, find somewhere to tether the horses, preferably out of sight, and then proceed on foot." He prodded his horse down the bank, and the others followed suit. Now, they must negotiate long banks and drifts of shingle, interspersed with broad shallow furrows, looking to Sam's eyes remarkably like the waves of a frozen sea. It was not a scene to offer comfort or delight the eye, and he felt fear clutch at his belly. What would they find at the decoy house?

*

"Good morning, Mrs. Paradice." Crowley gave her that chilling smile, full of contemptuous amusement. "And how are we today? Not so good, to judge by your sorry appearance. Of course, you cannot see yourself, but I can assure you that you have quite lost your looks. What a pity."

She would still cling to her small crumbs of defiance, because that was all she had left, after he had taken away almost everything else: her liberty, her dignity, and her hope. "Ever free with the compliments," said Polly, matching his cold disdainful tones, determined not to let him guess the terror that filled her.

"Of course." He came further into the shack, and stood looking down at her. Casually, as if producing an innocuous handkerchief or twist of tobacco, he put his hand in the pocket of his coat and brought out the razor. Despite her efforts, Polly could not disguise a shudder at the sight of it, and Crowley laughed. "You are not so brave after all, are you, madam? So, will you give me what I ask? There is the paper and pen and ink, over there. You only have to write that letter, and all this will be over."

And very soon after that, I will be dead, Polly thought. She said thinly, "I have told you any number of times. That is my money, and you have no right to it whatsoever."

"Oh, I think I do. After all, what would a sixpenny whore – which is what you are, my dear, when all is said and done – want with so much gold? You would only fritter it away on gin and cheap finery and trumpery jewels. Whereas I can put it to good use. A chateau in France, perhaps, or a prudent investment in some productive vineyard."

He removed the razor from its scabbard and examined the blade, then pulled back his cuff and the sleeve of his shirt, and stroked it thoughtfully down his bare arm. A tiny flurry of dark hairs drifted to the floor in its wake. Smiling, he added, "Still very sharp, I see. More than sharp enough for what I plan to do to you, unless you comply. Ah, I see you are trembling. Have you reached your breaking point? Everyone has a breaking point," Crowley said, as matter-of-factly as if he was telling her that everyone had a shirt or a shift. "And I have found yours, and of course it is vanity. You are not so brave now, are you, madam, when faced with the prospect of losing what is most precious to you – your beauty. What shall I do first? Shall I carve your cheek? Or slit your nose? Your sneaking spying lover will not like you so well when you are hideous." He knelt down beside her and pushed her back onto the straw. "But first, I fancy a little amusement. You may not find it so amusing of course, but then you are not some shy virgin, are you? You have been a whore for years, what is one more man amongst so many?"

"No!" Polly tried to squirm away from him, but he put the razor down and hit her hard across the face. She felt her lip split, and tasted blood, and her head spun. Then he was kneeling astride her, fumbling with his breeches, before lowering himself down, his weight crushing the breath and the resistance out of her. Desperately she clawed at his face with her free hand, but the days of hunger had sapped her strength, and he gripped her wrist painfully and hit her again, harder. "Keep still, you little bitch!"

She would not, she would never obey him. Polly kicked and twisted and fought as he tried to pull her skirts up, still holding her free arm in a grip like a vice, and screamed for help as loud as she could, again and again, though there was no-one save the gulls to hear her. Crowley's flushed, avid face filled her vision, and his breath reeked of stale beer and tobacco. He bent his head and sank his teeth into the soft skin between her neck and her shoulder, and she screamed again in pain and desperation.

Behind him, a shadow moved, and fell. A judder went through him, he gave a roar of surprise and fury, let go of her, and began to turn and raise himself up. Polly, trying frantically to drag herself out from under him, saw with astonishment that Mattie was standing above them, wielding the stool. She lifted it again, and brought it crashing down on Crowley's head. With a grunt, he collapsed on top of her, and lay still.

"Quick!" Mattie said. She bent and, with some effort, heaved the unconscious man off her sister. "That won't keep him quiet for long, more's the pity. Come on, get up! He'll wake soon!"

Polly's head was swimming, her face and neck hurt, she felt utterly spent and breathless, but somehow she managed to sit up. Mattie picked up the razor, and with swift efficiency cut the rope around her wrist. "Come *on*!" she said again, with some urgency, and held out her hand. Polly took it and was pulled roughly to her feet. There was a groan beside her, and she saw that Crowley was already beginning to move. As he rolled over, muttering in pain and clutching at the back of his head, Mattie picked up the bucket and flung its stinking contents all over him. Then she grabbed Polly's hand again. "*Run*, before he comes after us!"

*

There was nowhere to tie the horses, so they rode on towards the clump of trees which surrounded the decoy pond. Gin, peering round Sam's shoulder, saw that the door of the wooden shack was open, and felt a dreadful pang of disappointment. This could not be Madam's prison.

Then two figures, a lad and a woman, suddenly burst out of the hut, running away to the right. Dark, at their head, pulled his horse to an abrupt halt, and the other two bunched up beside him. Gin recognised the boy's brown coat, and then, with a huge joyful leap of her heart, realised who the woman was. But a third person, a much bigger man, dripping wet, had emerged from the shack. Roaring incoherently with rage, he set off in stumbling, erratic pursuit.

"That's Crowley!" she yelled, and Dark clapped heels to his horse's sides and urged it into a trot, then a gallop. Sam and Tawny followed. Gin, bouncing up and down on the pillion, her arms clasped round Sam's ample waist, concentrated on not falling off. They rode past the shack, following Dark. Ahead, Gin could make out some stunted trees and bushes, growing around a patch of water which must be yet another stagnant fleet. Mattie and Polly had almost reached it, but it was obvious that Polly was failing, for her sister seemed to be almost dragging her along. Gin wondered where they were going, and then saw a horse, tethered to one of the trees.

Crowley was close to them now, but Dark, riding hard and silent on the soft, sandy path, had almost caught up with him. Then Polly tripped and fell, Gin gasped in horror, and the big man gave a cry of triumph. It turned to fury as Dark's horse drew level with him, and he launched himself from the saddle, knocking Crowley off balance. Both men fell to the ground.

"Dear God," Sam said, dragging his mount to a halt. He slithered down its side, leaving Gin to fend for herself, and ran towards Dark and Crowley. They were on their feet now, wrestling with each other. Tawny came up to Gin, holding out his arms. "Jump, I'll catch you!"

She obeyed, and was briskly set on the ground. "Madam," she gasped, "I've got to go to Madam!" and ran to where Polly was still sitting, gasping for breath. She stared at her maid as if she could not believe what she saw, and then, with a sob, tried to stand up. "Oh, Gin, is it really you?"

"It's me," Gin said, her rage swelling as she saw the blood and bruises on her mistress's gaunt face, and the raw red skin around her wrist. She bent and helped Polly to her feet, feeling the lightness of her with dismay, and then they embraced, clinging to each other tightly in an overwhelming flood of relief and gratitude, before she remembered Dark. She disengaged herself and turned. The two men were pummelling each other, gasping with fury and effort. As Crowley landed a particularly vicious punch, Polly cried in fear, "Oh, God, someone help him!"

Sam had drawn his sword, but stood irresolute, obviously unwilling to use it unless as a last resort, for the combatants were too close together, and dodging around so much that any thrust risked reaching the wrong target. Dark aimed his fist at Crowley's head, but the other man sidestepped and hit him in the face, before they closed, both of them wrestling feverishly for an overpowering hold. Crowley seemed to be trying to gouge at his opponent's eyes, but Dark seized his arm and twisted, and then suddenly they were both on the ground again, grappling together, rolling over on the sandy, barren soil, and coming closer and closer to the sharp edge of the fleet.

At last, with a mighty effort, Crowley managed to fight free, and staggered upright. Then Dark, with all the power of his pent-up rage and fear, hurled himself again at his adversary, who tried and failed to keep his balance. Together, they toppled down the slope and into the water with a huge splash.

Mattie ran back past Gin to the bank. She flung off her coat and stood poised on the brink, staring at the two men as they struggled to their feet, up to their waists in the fleet a couple of yards from her. Crowley swung a vicious punch at Dark's face, and he staggered backwards, floundering, into deeper water. The other man took a pace towards him, and with a cry, Mattie leapt onto his back.

Tawny had secured the horses, and ran up to Gin, his face full of astonishment and anxiety. "Is this your mistress, Jane? Thank God for that! Who's the man Dark's fighting?"

"I'll tell you later, no time now," Gin said. "Look after her, gotta help." And without waiting for his reply, ran back to the edge of the fleet. She saw that Mattie had her fingers spread across Crowley's face, seeking his eyes, and he was trying, without success, to throw her off. Then Dark was wading back towards them, blood running down the side of his face, his mouth set. He hooked an arm round Crowley's throat and wrenched at his neck. Forced off balance, he fell sideways, and all three disappeared beneath the thick brown water in an explosion of spray.

"No!" It was Polly, hurrying up with Tawny supporting her. "Dark – "

The water heaved and her sister's head broke the surface, quickly followed by Dark. Now Crowley came up, his mouth sucking air, his hands reaching out, and Dark pushed him back down. His arms flailed wildly, and then Mattie joined in, bearing down with all her strength. In horrified silence, those on the bank watched as the two held the thrashing Crowley beneath the water. Once a hand came up, frantically clutching at the air, and then disappeared again. Gradually, inexorably, the turbulent surface grew calmer, a few last bubbles rose, and still Dark and Mattie stood side by side, their arms sunk up to the shoulders, until long after all movement had ceased.

Dark released his grip first, and stood back. Mattie turned to him, and Gin saw a blade in her hand. "Shall I make it sure?"

"No! No, leave it, for certain he's dead." With a swift, unexpected movement, Dark snatched the razor, with which Crowley had threatened to mutilate his lover's face only a short while before, and threw it far into the further waters of the fleet. "Were you going to cut his throat?"

"He deserved it," Mattie said. There was a terrifying expression on her face, compounded of rage, and merciless vengeance. She brought her other hand up out of the water, and slowly backed away. Freed too late, a bulky shape rose up, and the shocked, silent watchers saw the body of Crowley, face down, break the surface and bob gently in an expanding circle of ripples. Gin stared anxiously, certain that it would suddenly come back to life, that he would rise roaring from the water and attack Dark and Mattie again.

But he did not. Instead, a gust of wind roughened the surface and pushed the corpse away from the bank towards the further side, where a clump of twisted trees overhung the water. Dark drew his own sword, and used it to prod Crowley towards the bushes. The shape, half sunk again now, was grasped in their wet, mossy fingers and pushed further beneath the water. For a long moment his killer stood, as if, like Gin, he feared he would come to life again. Then he returned to where Mattie was already clambering up onto dry land.

She rounded on him. "You should have let me!"

"No," Dark said emphatically. He pulled himself onto the bank and sat in a spreading puddle of water, looking up at her. "When someone finds him – which may not be for a while, days or even weeks – it will just look as if he accidentally drowned. Cut his throat, and it's plainly murder. That's why I didn't use my sword. And I for one do not want a hue and cry to be raised, or suspicion cast on us."

"Or for you to be hanged," Sam added. "He's right." He looked at the young woman in sodden shirt and breeches, her face as pale and implacable as an avenging angel, or demon. "I take it you are the supposed sister?"

"I am Mattie, yes."

Dark got to his feet, feeling his face where Crowley's final punch had landed, only a few moments before. "Thank you," he said to her curtly. "I think you have redeemed yourself." Then he turned away to where Polly stood, a few yards distant, staring at him. For a moment, his gaze took in her battered, bloodied face, her pallor and thinness, the hollows under her eyes and all the other signs that her imprisonment had inflicted. She gave a small sob, and a gasp, and at once he took her into his arms, holding her as tightly as if he never wanted to let her go, while she wept uncontrollably against his chest.

"Leave 'em be, for the moment," Gin said, feeling that someone ought to take charge, and that it might as well be her, since everyone else was standing round like lost sheep, staring at the water. "The hut – was that where he kept Madam prisoner?"

Mattie nodded. Gin decided that recriminations – and she had a tirade of them locked up inside her, ready to vent – could wait until later. "Then we need to clear it so no-one will guess that's where she was. Otherwise, when they find that sorry muckworm, or what's left of him, someone might put two and two together and then they'll come after us. Is that horse by the fleet yours?"

"Yes, and you'll find Crowley's in the trees near the

decoy hut. A big grey."

Gin turned. "Tawny? Mr. Jessop? Can you collect all the horses and bring them to the hut? But best to untie Crowley's and let it loose with a slap on the rump, then with luck it won't lead anyone back here. Don't just stand there, look lively, we've got a lot to do and someone might show up before we're done."

The inside of the hut stank, mainly from the bucket which Mattie had emptied over Crowley, but also of stale air, and misery, and despair. Working together and mostly in silence, the two young women cleared out the straw and scattered it, watching the wind whirl it away. The stool and blankets would be more difficult to dispose of, and eventually Mattie carried them off to a thicket of brambles and used a stick to stuff them out of sight. Gin rescued Polly's mantle, shook it out vigorously and laid it over a nearby bush in the sun, hoping it would air. Mattie returned with a willow branch and swept the hut as clean as she could, while Gin took the bucket back to the fleet, filled it and sluiced the floor.

"I nearly forgot!" Mattie indicated the severed end of the rope which had tied Polly to the hut. She stretched up, but even on tiptoe could not reach the hook to which it was tied. Gin, who was some inches shorter, did not even try, but went to the door and called to Tawny, the tallest of them apart from Dark. He obliged, with an expression of disgust, and hurled it under a nearby gorse bush. Now, to Gin's satisfaction, the shack looked as if no-one had been in it for months, apart from the dampness underfoot, which was already beginning to soak into the thirsty earthen floor.

"We're done," she said, dusting her hands, and then turned to Mattie, who was holding the bucket and the empty leather bottle which had held Polly's ration of water. "Thank you. What are you going to do now? I think Madam will want to put as much distance between herself and this place as fast as she can."

The supposed sister shrugged. "I don't know." For a moment, something like longing seemed to enter her face. "But I can't go back to the company. Not now he's dead. They'd suspect I had something to do with it, they know I hated him."

"So why did you stay?"

"He had – he knew things about me. Bad things. If he peached on me –"

That came as little surprise to Gin. "Anyway, that ain't the point now, the point is, will someone from your company come looking for him?"

Mattie shrugged. "I doubt it. They'll think he ran off with the gold. Or that he killed me. They know he had my sister captive, but not where he kept her. The only ones who know that are Ned and Gabriel Tomkins, and it was Ned who told me that Crowley planned to kill her, and ordered them to throw her in the sea afterwards. They drew the line at that." She gave Gin a brief, wry smile. "Seems there's some honour and pity still, even amongst smugglers."

"And you didn't like it either? Is that why you freed her?"

Mattie shrugged again. "Perhaps."

Gin said, more quietly, "Madam said she'd give you a home, and I reckon that offer still stands."

"It does." Polly stood in the doorway, looking round at the tiny space which had encompassed her world for seven terrible days. "Come to London with us."

Dark was just behind her, and from his expression, Gin guessed that he was not so enthusiastic, but he said nothing. Polly went on. "You saved my *life*, Mattie. I can't ever repay you for that, but the very least I can do for you is give you a home, as Jane says. And, if you want, I can also give you an introduction to Rich. But there will be no obligations and no expectations and no strings. You are my sister, and I love you, and whatever you want to do, I will help and support you."

Another of Madam's waifs and strays, Gin thought. She herself had always been grateful for her escape from the gutter. Mattie, however, did not look very keen. *Unthankful little jilt,* was Gin's opinion. *Be glad you have a sister what's happy to ignore all the wrong you've done her.*

Dark came further into the hut and looked around it. He said softly, "So you were held here all the time? For a week? And tethered like an animal, for God's sake?"

Polly nodded. Gin noticed, as Dark surely must, that she was trembling very slightly. "I tried to run away, and that was my reward."

"He didn't feed her," Mattie said. "Just water, and precious little of that. So I brought her something to eat, a couple of times. She's had nothing else."

"Dear God." Dark stared at her. "And you did not think to free her? Your own sister, held in such conditions?"

Mattie returned his stare, and shrugged. "I did what *he* wanted. The last woman who didn't, ended up in a ditch with her throat cut."

Polly said urgently, her voice trembling, "We can talk about this later. For now, *please,* Dark, take me back to Rye as quickly as possible. I don't want to be here a moment longer than we must." With a sob, she turned and went out, and he followed her. Gin and Mattie, left in the hut, eyed each other cautiously.

"You'll have to unveil sometime," Gin said at last. "Dark, he don't take no for an answer, and he's dangerous to them as what he don't like."

"That's plain enough," said Mattie. "But then, so am I."

There was no answer Gin could give to that: she had seen it with her own eyes, and the evidence was a sodden, lifeless corpse floating in the water fifty yards away. She gave a last look round the hut, making sure all was in order, and then said, "Let's go. They're waiting for us."

They went outside, and as calmly as if she were securing a house, Mattie slammed the bolts into their sockets, locked the door and hurled the key into a nearby bush. She gave Gin her tight smile. "Crowley thought he was so clever, but he was very easy to fool. He didn't believe a woman could have intelligence, or spirit."

And for that serious error of judgement, Ambrose Rookwood, alias Amos Crowley, had paid with his life.

CHAPTER TWENTY-ONE

Their Web is all unravell'd

Afterwards, Polly could remember very little of the long ride back to Rye. The lanky young man who seemed to be their guide, and who also seemed, she noted in passing, to be well acquainted with Gin, had offered her a battered mutton pasty from somewhere about his person, and she had devoured it, soggy crust and tough meat and bits of fluff and all, and washed it down with water from a bottle which Dark carried. And then her lover, handling her with extreme and tender care, had insisted on taking her up before him on his horse, while Gin resumed her pillion seat behind Sam, and Mattie and the young man, whom her maid addressed with startling familiarity as Tawny, each rode their own mounts.

Once they were on their way, everyone was very quiet. No-one seemed to want to talk about the horrific scene they had just witnessed, or about her own imprisonment, and Polly was glad of it. Later, back in Rye, she might be able to tell her story, but for now she just wanted to sink into the curve of Dark's arm, and rest her cheek against his damp coat, so that she could feel the solid, living warmth of him, and sense each breath he took. Even the stink of stagnant water, clinging to his clothes, seemed as fragrant as any exotic perfume, for it was proof that she was not dreaming, that she was no longer a prisoner, and alive and safe because Crowley was dead.

Dead, because Dark and Mattie, between them, had drowned him. She could not regret his death, he had imprisoned and tortured her, and he had intended to kill her, whether or not she had given in to his demands. But the law was not so forgiving of murder. She could only pray that Dark was right, and that when Crowley's body was found, perhaps days or even weeks hence, it would be assumed that he had died accidentally. And by then, they would be back in London.

She let the horse's soft, rhythmic stride lull her into a doze, and then to the welcome oblivion of utter fatigue both of mind and body, and only woke when they stopped. Dark said softly, "Poll? We have reached the ferry, and must dismount. You had an accident when riding with your young brother, do you remember? And he and I fell into the water, rescuing you. That is the story we have all agreed upon. Sam and I will do the talking if it is necessary."

Fogged by sleep and hunger, she did not really understand, but nodded. Then she was handed down into Sam's waiting arms, and helped to the boat. So many people around her, some dearly familiar, some less so. She still had no idea who the young man was, and it did not seem important. The boat rocked beneath her as she boarded, and she almost fell, but Gin was there, supporting her, and Mattie too, and the westering sun was warm on her face as they crossed over. They had to wait on the Rye side of the bank for the horses, because the ferry could not accommodate so many, but there was a step for her to sit on, and her maid beside her. Polly roused her mind sufficiently to ask about the young man.

"That's Phil's brother Tawny," Gin said. "Phil what lives in the house just down from the Mermaid, remember? You met her on the Strand. My *friend* Phil," she added, with palpable pride. "And he's her half-brother, and he's 'prenticed to a lawyer in London, and he's building a flying machine!"

There seemed little she could say to this surprising piece of information, but in any case Gin was chattering on, filling the silence, chasing away the memory of terror. "And Phil calls him Tawny because she thinks he looks like an owl with them spectacles what he wears. We was searching all over for you, we went to Winchelsea and the castle while Mr. Jessop went off to find Mr. Dark, and then I caught an ague ..."

Once the horses had crossed, she was helped up onto

Dark's mount once more, and they rode along the narrow causeway, between the marshes and the river, which led to the Land Gate. More aware now, Polly tried to ignore the curious looks of passers-by, and the jocular words addressed to Tawny, who of course was a native of Rye and well known to everyone. Once within the town, it seemed to take an age for their procession to negotiate the narrow streets, but at last they came to the familiar ancient façade of the Mermaid, and rode through the passageway and into the courtyard. She realised afterwards that she must have fainted, for at one moment she was being lowered from Dark's arms into Sam's, and the next she was lying on the bed in her chamber, and there was a smell of burning feathers under her nose, making her sneeze and cough, and Gin leaning over her, her face pinched with anxiety. "Oh, Madam, I almost thought you was dead for a moment! Mercy has brought up some wine and food for you, here, I'll help you sit up."

With pillows and a bolster piled up behind her, Polly took the glass which her maid handed to her and sipped the wine. The food was very plain, just bread and butter and cheese, but no ambrosia could have tasted better. She ate and drank slowly, savouring every mouthful, while Gin bustled about the chamber, selecting clean fresh garments from the chest, and pouring hot water into a bowl. When the plate and the glass were empty, Gin helped her from the bed and began to take off her dirty, stinking clothes, leaving them in a heap on the floor. Polly looked at it, and a surge of revulsion filled her. "Burn everything," she said.

"I'll tell Mercy, she'll see to it." Gin put the bowl of steaming water on the table, along with a cake of perfumed soap and a cloth, and laid a towel on the floor for her to stand on. "Shall I…?"

"I can manage, I think, but thank you," said Polly, and indeed she felt very much better for the food and the wine. While Gin began to gather up the ruined garments, she pulled off her shift, which was the most unsavoury of all, and washed every inch of herself, drying her clean wet skin with a second towel. She pulled the fresh linen over her head, and Gin helped her lace her spare stays over it. "You haven't half got thin," she said anxiously. "These are almost too big for you."

"I expect I'll grow plump again soon enough," Polly told her. And once her blue calico gown, now also rather large, had been fastened around her, she could almost convince herself that everything was back to normal, and that the past week had never happened.

But of course she could not forget, not now or for a long while into the future. She closed her eyes, hardly daring to believe that when she opened them again, she would not see the splintered rough planks of the decoy shack, or hear Crowley's soft, terrifying voice, describing the places on her body which he planned to carve with his razor. Her rational brain told her that she was standing in this pleasant room in the Mermaid, and that she was safe. But only a few hours ago, she had been Crowley's prisoner, in fear of her life, and she could not shake his malignant presence from her mind so easily.

A quiet knock brought her back to reality. She opened her eyes and discovered that she was still in her chamber, and Crowley was still dead. Gin went to answer it, and Dark entered, alone. He jerked his head significantly at the girl, and she dipped a brief curtsey and went out, shutting the door softly behind her. Then he came further into the room, and Polly saw, with a pang, that he was not sure of his welcome. *But neither am I,* she thought. *Is he going to berate me for walking blindly into danger?*

"Thank you," she said, giving him a rather hesitant smile. "Thank you for coming to my rescue."

Dark looked at her, and smiled in return. As she had so often noted, it made his normally rather grim face much lighter and more human. "You are looking a great deal better than when I saw you last. And more fragrant, too."

"You would not smell so pleasant if you had lain in the same clothes for a week," Polly pointed out.

"I do not doubt it."

"And are you not about to chastise me for entering into his trap?"

"You wanted to help your sister, how were you to know what she and Crowley intended? I would have done the same, if it was Bonne who had begged my help." He came closer, studying her. "Are you ready to tell me what happened yet? I would like to know, and I think it would help you."

"I – I'm not sure. Perhaps." She hated the wobble in her voice. Feeling suddenly weak, she reached for the chair behind her and sat down, taking long breaths to calm herself. After a pause, Dark pulled up another and sat beside her. Gently, he reached out and took her hand, his touch warm and dry against her skin. Then she heard his sharp intake of breath, and he moved his fingers up her arm to trace the line of rough skin and scab marking the place where Crawley had first used his razor. "Did he do this?"

Polly nodded. She indicated her other arm. "And this, a few days later. He said he wanted symmetry."

Dark bent his head and, with infinite tenderness, kissed both wounds, and then the slender wrist where the rope had rubbed her skin raw. Then he said, "He is dead, and deserved to die. For what he did to you, he would have gone to the gallows."

"He was going to kill me," Polly told him. "Even if I gave him what he wanted, he would have killed me, because he could not afford to leave me alive." A shudder ran right through her as she remembered. "And I think if Mattie had not come to the hut when she did, and if you had not found me, I would now be dead."

He said quietly, "What did he want from you? We had all assumed that you were the bait to catch me, but that was not right, was it?"

Polly looked up at him. There was nothing but concern on his face, and it gave her courage. "He wanted the gold – the Jacobite gold that Robbie stole from the Pretender." It had been a bone of contention between them before, but she did not want to have any more secrets.

Dark stared at her. "But there can be very little left of that, surely – if indeed there is any at all." He gave her a wry smile. "After all, Sinclair had spent much of it on himself and on you, as well as on funding the rebellion, and then you spent the rest on giving Hannah her freedom and setting up the Paradise."

"I tried to tell him that, but he wouldn't believe me. He said he wanted it to start afresh in France." She shivered. "And Mattie was to have her share, but I suspect he would have cheated her of it, as soon as he could."

"Mattie." He paused, and then added, "*Is* she your sister? Truly?"

"Yes, truly. She knows the pet name my father gave her, when we were children. Do not be too hasty to judge her, Dark. She has not had an easy life, and it has hardened her."

"But your life has not been a perfumed bed of roses either, has it? Well, she certainly possesses your gift for finding trouble. So she was in league with Crowley, but had a change of heart?"

"Yes, when it mattered most. I think she may have realised that blood is indeed thicker than water."

"Like it or not, I think we both owe her a considerable debt – indeed, our lives. She is a remarkable young woman. Does she ever wear female clothes?"

"She wore a dress when she went to see Kitty in Bath.

But she relishes the freedom that wearing breeches gives her. I have promised her an introduction to Rich. She makes a very convincing young man, and I think she would be a sensation on the stage."

"Well, neither Mr Bird nor Mercy seem to have realised that she is not a boy," Dark said ruefully. "But neither did I realise Gin's true identity. You see what you expect to see."

"Where is Mattie now? I cannot help but be anxious that she might run off again."

"Downstairs in the taproom, with Sam and young Master Jeake. I am not sure that he quite believes what took place today – he is still a little pale and quiet."

"I am not sure that I believe it either." Polly met his eyes. "You were right – it is good to talk quietly, like this. So how did Sam find you?"

"I think he bullied it out of Madame Rousselle."

Polly laughed in surprise. "I did not think that would be possible!"

"Well, it obviously was, or I would not be sitting here now. We have reason to be grateful to her too. I always give her some direction where I can be found, when I am away on 'business', but she knows only to divulge it to those whom I trust with my life – Sam being one of them. He told me she refused at first, but I fear she was having sport with him."

"She is a wicked old harridan, but I cannot help feeling some admiration for her – and even some fondness, now."

"Whatever she says, she will always cover my back, and yours." Dark paused, and then said quietly, "By a happy, or unhappy chance, I was in Godalming when Sam found me. I had been told to keep watch on a house there, home of a certain Lady Oglethorpe. And by a happier chance, two of the lady's daughters arrived in Rye yesterday, and Gin persuaded them to help free me."

"To *free* you? Dark, what happened? What on earth did you do?"

Briefly, he told her. Polly listened in astonishment. "You punched a constable? No wonder they locked you up."

"He insulted you, and as a gentleman, I was compelled to act."

"You mean, you lost your temper. Dark, you never cease to surprise me."

"Sometimes, I surprise myself," he told her dryly. "Anyway, to return to the Oglethorpes, Gin told me about your connection with that family."

No secrets. Polly said, "I should not have continued going there, once I realised they were Jacobites. They paid very generously, though, and I thought there would be no harm in it. But when young Miss Oglethorpe began asking me questions about Sinclair, I grew suspicious. I realised that they wanted something from me, but I couldn't guess what it was."

"I can," Dark said. "The gold. Except that I think they would have returned it to the Pretender, rather than stealing it for their own use."

Polly flushed, and opened her mouth to reply, but Dark put his finger to her lips. "I was making reference to Crowley, not to you and Sinclair. In any case, they could not know that your savings are now largely the profits from the Paradise."

She managed a smile. "And I told Crowley that, over and over, but he would not listen. He had nothing but contempt for me. If Mattie had not arrived when she did, he would have raped me. And then – and then I think he would have killed me, whether I had told him how to obtain the gold or not, for his patience was at an end."

Dark looked as if he were about to say something, but there was a tap on the door, and he went to answer it. Gin stood on the other side. "Beg pardon, Mr. Dark, but there's supper ready in the parlour. Is Madam ready to come down, or shall I ask Mercy to bring a share up here?"

"Thank you, Jane – I will come down," Polly said. "I am feeling so very much better."

"Are you certain?" Dark said, giving her a searching look. "They will understand if you do not."

"I am certain." Polly rose to her feet with a smile. "Apart from any other consideration, I would like to reassure them that I am not about to fade away entirely – and to thank them properly, for helping to save me. Though I would like your arm as we go down the stairs," she added, as an afterthought.

The table in the little private parlour at the back of the Mermaid was laid with a white cloth, and set with a fine china service, sparkling wine glasses, and a selection of cold meats, cheeses, savoury tarts, bread and fruit and cakes. When Polly and Dark arrived at the door, their friends – or accomplices – were already waiting. Sam was the first to come and take her hand and tell her how glad he was to see her safe. Young Master Jeake was also there, and bowed low. "Your servant, Mistress Paradice. I am so happy that you are safe at last, and glad to see you almost restored."

"I am very much better already, and will be more so for good food and plenty of rest," Polly told him. "And I wish to thank you, from the bottom of my heart, for all you have done to help find me. I have heard a little from Jane, and I owe you a great deal."

"It was the least I could do," Tawny said. "And if the truth be told, both Phil and I were more than happy to search for you. She will be delighted to learn that you have been rescued, and I'm sure she will want me to tell her everything that has happened."

Polly stared at him in some concern, but Gin leapt in first. "Don't do that," she urged him quickly. "You can say

Madam was rescued, obviously, but don't say anything about *him*. It ain't safe, she's bound to let it slip."

Tawny flushed, but nodded. "My apologies, Mistress Paradice, I was not thinking clearly. Phil often lets her tongue run away with her. Of course I will mention nothing of that, I'll just say we found her locked in a looker's hut. It's very close to the truth, after all."

"And that's *all*! Don't say nothing more to *no-one*!" said Gin, with considerable emphasis.

"Not to anyone," Tawny said, and smiled. "In any case, I must return to London very shortly, my mother is insistent on it. I have apparently been leading Phil into bad habits, and she has been neglecting her studies. And when my own studies permit, I will make sure to call upon your coffee house, Mrs Paradice – do I collect that it is in Covent Garden?"

"In King Street, just near the Essex Serpent," said the irrepressible Gin.

"And I shall much look forward to it. Now, I regret that I must go home, they will be wondering where I am. Your servant, Mrs. Paradice – Mr. Dark, Mr. Jessop. And Jane, of course, my companion in mischief." Tawny bowed again to the company, and went out.

"He seems a very pleasant young man," said Sam. "And we would not have found you in time, Polly, without his help – he guessed where you might be, and he was right. Now, let us do justice to this splendid feast."

For a while, as they ate, there was silence save for the chink of cutlery and the pleasant sound of wine being poured. Despite her earlier light meal, Polly found herself hungry again, and the savoury tarts, filled with eggs and ham, onions and cheese, were delicious. But she kept an eye on Mattie, who was seated at the furthest end of the table, still in the coat and breeches she had worn earlier, and picking at her food in a desultory way. Perhaps she now regretted throwing in her lot with her long-lost sister: or perhaps she was thinking about possible recriminations. Polly sent her a smile occasionally, but Mattie refused to meet her eye, and concentrated her gaze on her plate.

At length they were all finished, even Gin, although she could not resist nibbling at one of the small, sweet apples. Dark poured more wine, and Polly raised her glass. "I must drink a health to you all," she said. "I owe you my life, and my freedom, and I can never thank you enough." She felt her voice wobbling, and regained control with an effort. "So – to freedom, and a happy return to London!"

"To freedom," three voices echoed, with enthusiasm, but the fourth did not.

"Mattie?" Polly looked directly at her sister. "I meant what I said to you before. Will you come back to London with me?"

There was a long moment of silence. Gin broke it. "You're a fool if you don't," she said bluntly. "You bin given the chance of a home and a family. Maybe it ain't your idea of freedom, but I knows what that kind of freedom looks like and feels like, and if Madam hadn't done the same for me last year, most likely now I'd be dead. You won't be cold nor wet nor hungry, and you'll have half London at your feet, they love a girl what can do the breeches parts, and you're the best at it that I've seen." She fixed Mattie with an eagle's stare. "And you ain't had no better offers, have you?"

For a moment, the other girl said nothing. Polly could sense something of her internal struggle. London would give her some opportunities, and deny her others. Which would weigh heavier in the balance? Freedom, or security? She waited, tense, for her sister's answer.

When it came, it was almost inaudible. "Yes," Mattie said, and raised her eyes to meet Polly's. "I will come with you."

At last, she smiled, a proper smile of genuine warmth. “And thank you.”

*

Much later, tired, replete, Polly sat at the table in her chamber and looked at herself in her little hand mirror, turning it this way and that. The bruises and the damage to her lip would fade away eventually, and the cuts on her arms were already healing. Other scars, which could not be seen, would take much longer to disappear. She shivered as she remembered Crowley, his menace, his threats, and how slender the chance that she had escaped him. A week ago, she had thought herself safe from male brutality. He had reminded her, cruelly and maliciously, that she was not, that her freedom, her security and her power were limited, and dependent on a man’s good will and protection. Crowley was dead, but he was not unique, far from it. Would she ever feel safe again? Perhaps, once she was back in London, in her own home with her friends and servants around her, but she knew that it would take a long time.

A soft tap on the door signalled the arrival of Dark. He came up to her, and she rose and turned, moving gratefully into his embrace. They stood for a long while, just content to be close together, before he let go and said quietly, “Will you sit down? I wish to talk to you.”

Polly looked up at him with sudden anxiety, and obeyed. Her heart began to hammer a warning. Was he about to tell her that he wanted their affair to end? There was no clue in his face, except that the expression on it was very serious. He pulled up another chair and sat opposite her, taking her hands in his, and said, “This is difficult. I am not used to speaking so honestly.”

He was going to end it. She took refuge in the barbed banter of their earliest acquaintance. “Really, sir? I had thought you never did anything else.”

"But I have not said this. I have been very remiss, my dearest, darling Poll. I have never told you that I love you, and that a life without you is a life not worth the candle."

He was not going to end it. Something had happened to her breathing. She gulped for air, and managed a whisper. "Do you mean it? Is it true?"

"I would not say it if I did not mean it." His eyes, brown and flecked with green and amber, held hers. "I love you. Do you love me?"

A wild laugh escaped Polly. "You fool, Dark! Of course I love you! How could you doubt it?"

"If a man thinks he might not be worth loving, then he doubts it," Dark said. "And you have pointed out my faults to me often enough."

"As you have pointed out mine, even more frequently," Polly reminded him tartly. "But no matter. At least we have now established our mutual affection for each other." She eyed him suspiciously. "But there is more you wish to say, is there not? Sometimes, I can read you as well as any book."

"And other times?"

"You make sure the book is firmly shut. Come, Dark, pray do not keep me in suspense, spit it out."

For a moment longer he looked at her, and she saw the love she felt reflected back in his face. Then he said, so low she could hardly catch the words, "You love me, I love you, would you marry me?"

Astonished, Polly stared at him. "Did I hear you right?"

"I hope so. I said," Dark repeated, slightly louder this time, "would you marry me?"

Oh dear God. Part of her wanted to dance and sing and shout for joy, but the other, greater part shrank, trembling, from what he had proposed. For what was marriage, but the submission of a woman to a man, and the loss of her precious power and independence?

But as a wife, even as the wife of a man who lived as precariously as Dark did, she would have status and protection. This was, Polly realised suddenly, essentially the same dilemma that Mattie had faced: security, or freedom. And for her, it was too soon to choose.

Anyway, she could see that he already suspected what her answer would be. And because he deserved to know the truth, she weighed her words very carefully before she spoke.

"You do me great honour, Dark – "

"Honour be damned," he said, and grinned disarmingly. "You are going to say no, are you not? I thought so. But it was worth the attempt."

"We do very well as we are, I think," Polly said, feeling her heart lighten ridiculously. This was supposed to be a serious business, why did she want to giggle suddenly? "And now we have discovered the truth about what we feel for each other, I know that you will not go off with some flighty piece from the theatre."

"Or you with some overdressed nincompoop."

"Unless, of course, either of us are sorely provoked," said Polly, trying not to snort with laughter. "But I cannot imagine why you think I would provoke you."

"Sometimes, dear heart, you can provoke me with a single glance."

"Like this?" She batted her eyelashes outrageously, and fluttered an imaginary fan in front of her bodice.

"Exactly like that. Oh, Paradice, what am I to do with you?"

"Trust me," Polly said. "Respect me. Love me. Credit me with a little intelligence. Make me laugh. And in a few years I may have a different answer to give you, when I am tired of serving coffee and Arrack punch to bully-fops and lobcocks and hell-born babes, and yearn for a quiet life in the green glades of Chelsea or Richmond."

"*You?* A quiet life? That will never be. I shall make sure of it."

"I don't doubt that you will, Dark, and I shall relish every moment."

He got to his feet and stood looking down at her. "Do you mean it? About a different answer?"

"Yes," Polly said simply. She stood, and put her hands on his chest, looking up into his face. "I love you, but I also love the freedom I have. We neither of us own each other, do we? And that suits both of us splendidly at present. But when I have enough money put by, I plan to purchase a comfortable house in the country, and retire there one day to keep chickens and grow roses. I have already told Hannah that when that happens, she may have the Paradise. And then, Dark, *then* I will marry you. You have my word on it. If, of course, you have not changed your mind."

He spoke some lines of poetry, very quietly, his lips in her hair.

"'Let me not to the marriage of true minds
Admit impediments. Love is not love
Which alters when it alteration finds.'

I will not alter. Until the sun falls and the moon sails backwards, my mind is fixed."

"That's as maybe," said Gin, entering with only the most perfunctory knock. "But it's past ten o'clock Mr. Jessop says, and we got to rise early tomorrow because we're going back to London at the crack of dawn, and Miss Mattie's waiting, and some of us wants our beauty sleep." She looked at Dark and Polly, standing close, their arms around each other, and smiled broadly. “But it’s good when all’s come right with the world again, ain’t it?”

P.D.A.B. October 2024

HISTORICAL NOTE

Although most of the events described in *The Supposed Sister* are fictional, many of the characters I've portrayed were real people. The Oglethorpe ladies, incorrigible Jacobite plotters, were very much as I have described them, and travelled between France, Godalming and Little Ryder Street in London, carrying messages and promoting the cause of 'James III', the Pretender to the throne. Fanny Oglethorpe's entertaining, chatty letters are preserved in the Stuart Papers, discussing family affairs as well as plots and fellow plotters. Their brother James, dubbed 'Beaky Nose' by Polly (and it was an apt name), was not involved to the same extent as his sisters, and had a distinguished military career, culminating in his founding of the US state of Georgia many years later.

Mrs. Garnet (whom I have called Jenny) was a real person, though very little is known about her and her career. Rather more is known of Tony Aston, who wrote an entertaining 'Sketch' of his peripatetic life on the fringes of the theatrical world. Many hand-to-mouth companies of strolling players, like Crowley's, wandered through provincial England, and Mattie was not the only young actress to wear breeches in her daily life as well as on the stage: another autobiography, by the 'well-known troublemaker' Charlotte Charke, youngest daughter of the theatre manager Colley Cibber, proved very useful in this regard, although she acted a couple of decades later.

The Jeake/Tucker family is still remembered in Rye, where the second Samuel Jeake's impressive warehouse in Mermaid Street, known as Middle Street in the 18th century, is now a hotel. His son, also Samuel (I had his half-sister Phil nickname him 'Tawny' to avoid confusion with Sam Jessop), had a somewhat chequered career, but he really did construct a flying machine, which could still be seen in the town many years later. Unfortunately I could find no confirmation that it ever actually flew, and no description of what it looked like or how it worked, so I have borrowed the design of Emanuel Swedenborg, dating from 1714 and sketched in his notebooks. There is some confusion over Phil's birth date, and I may have portrayed her as a year or two older than she actually was.

Smuggling, of course, was famously rife on Romney Marsh and in the towns along the coasts of Kent and Sussex, and inland. The brothers Gabriel and Ned Tomkins were indeed notorious members of the Mayfield Gang, though they do seem to have been less violent than smugglers later in the century, for whom torture and murder were routine matters. And despite Rye's reputation as a hotbed of Whigs and Dissenters, smugglers were happy to ferry Jacobite agents to and from France, to carry messages, and to distribute pamphlets. The Rookwood family was distinguished, if that is the right word, by having two members called Ambrose executed for high treason in the space of ninety years (in 1606 and 1696, both for trying to assassinate the incumbent king) but there is no historical evidence that another Ambrose Rookwood, alias Amos Crowley, was active in the early 18th century.

I first became aware of Rye and the Marsh as a child when I read Monica Edwards' delightful books set in the area, and it was a pleasure to explore the town and the wonderful landscape around it for myself. Of course Romney Marsh has changed radically in the three hundred years since the events of *The Supposed Sister*, and I've spent long hours poring over old maps, many of which contradicted each other, such was the speed with which the sea, advancing or retreating, changed the shape and form of the land. The Decoy House really did exist, and there were apparently still traces of it until quite recently, when modern roads and tracks associated with the army ranges and Dungeness Power Station were constructed over the area.

The Supposed Sister was my 'lockdown book'. I planned to

return to the Marsh when it was all over, to finalise my research and fill in some gaps and details, but other events conspired against me. In consequence, there are bound to be errors and misinterpretations that I'm unaware of. Many apologies!
Finally, the adventures of Polly, Dark, Gin, Mattie and their friends will be continued in my next novel, *Foul Players*. Early 18th century London is a very rich source of inspiration, and there are many more stories to be told.

Pamela Belle
October, 2024

The quotations at the head of each chapter are taken from *The Duke Of Guise*, the play by Dryden and Lee which Polly, Sam and Gin go to see at the Theatre Royal, Drury Lane, in Chapter Seven.

The cover illustration is from a Victorian watercolour painting of Rye, which is in my possession.

ACKNOWLEDGEMENTS

As always, I owe a huge debt to the ongoing support of my family and friends, who have never failed to encourage me when times got tough, and have always believed in me. Particularly with *The Supposed Sister*, I'd like to mention, first of all, Jo Kirkham, fellow Dorothy Dunnett enthusiast and historian of Rye, who told me about the town's Jacobite links, at a time when this book was in the vague early stages of planning, and gave me a whole new direction for the plot. Thank you, Jo, and keep rocking those amazing embroidered jackets!

Huge thanks are also due to Sasha Garwood-Lloyd and E.M. Swift-Hook, who were kind enough to read The Supposed Sister and make numerous pertinent and helpful comments, even though they were both busy with their own commitments. Any remaining errors of spelling, grammar and plot are entirely my own! I'm also very grateful to the members of the Facebook group Historical Writers' Forum, who have been so helpful and informative. The staff of the London Library supplied me with many books on the history of Romney Marsh which would otherwise be very difficult to obtain, and my colleagues of the Wiltshire Library Service have been my enthusiastic supporters throughout. Thank you, everyone, it would be very much harder without you!

Pamela Belle, October 2024

ABOUT THE AUTHOR

Pamela Belle

I've been telling stories since before I could even read or write, and began my first book, The Moon in the Water, at the age of thirteen. Amongst many other jobs, I've been a primary school teacher, a charity shop manager, and a library assistant. I live in Wiltshire with Phoebe, my young Burmese cat, and I have two lovely adult sons I'm very proud of. Writing, though, is my passion, and I'm currently working on 'Foul Players', the next instalment in the 'Paradice and Dark' series begun with 'A Parcel of Rogues', and continued with 'The Supposed Sister'.

PARADICE AND DARK

In early Georgian London, the series follows the adventures and misadventures of Polly Paradice, singer and coffee house owner, her lover Andre Dark, Huguenot artist and spy, her servants Gin, once a street child, and Hannah, a freed slave, and their friend Sam Jessop.

A Parcel Of Rogues

London in 1715 is a vibrant and dangerous place, and into this ferment of rogues and harlots comes Sam Jessop, desperate to find his missing daughter. He is given unexpected assistance from Andre Dark, an enigmatic Huguenot artist, and the beautiful Polly Paradice, woman of the town, who bears a startling resemblance to his beloved Mary. In company with the homeless link boy Gin, who has a secret of his own, their quest will take them to Bristol and Bath as well as the teeming streets of Covent Garden, Newgate Prison and the frozen Thames, and lead them all into mortal danger as the search for Mary becomes a frantic struggle to foil a lethal Jacobite plot before it's too late.

BOOKS BY THIS AUTHOR

The Moon In The Water

My first novel - begun when I was about thirteen, and known in my family as The Epic.
The Heron Quartet, Book 1
In 1635, at the age of ten, Thomazine Heron is orphaned, and sent to live with her uncle, Sir Simon Heron, and his family. She is quickly accepted by her five cousins, especially Lucy, the only girl, and Francis, whose poetic, sensitive nature puts him at odds with his domineering father and his grimly conventional eldest brother, Simon. As the children grow up, Thomazine and Francis fall in love, despite the fact that she has been betrothed to another, more distant cousin as a child. Then civil war intervenes, and the Heron family must choose sides, while tragedy looms on the horizon ...

The Chains Of Fate

The Heron Quartet, Book 2
Believing that her beloved cousin Francis is dead, Thomazine, numb with grief, has married her cousin Dominic, a young man she dislikes and mistrusts. Then, astonishingly, she learns that she has been tricked, and that Francis is still alive, and in Scotland. She makes the heart-wrenching and momentous decision to leave her baby behind, and to set out in search of her lost love. But in the twists and turns of battle and siege, defeat and treachery, can she and Francis ever be reunited, and find happiness together despite the chains of fate?

Alathea

The Heron Quartet, Book 3
Alathea Heron, daughter of Thomazine and Francis, shows precocious talent as an artist. Her very first commission is to draw the boy she meets, by chance, on the hills above her home. Years later, a trained portrait painter at the beginning of her career, she encounters him again in London, and learns that the boy she knew as John Wilmot is actually the notorious Earl of Rochester. They are imediately attracted to each other, but can her desire to become a celebrated artist defeat her growing love for this wild, dangerous and supremely gifted young man, or will she give in to his advances, and risk destroying her talent for painting?

The Lodestar

The Heron Quartet, Book 4, but the first, chronologically.
Christie Heron, young, able and intensely ambitious, secures a good position in the household of Richard, Duke of Gloucester, younger brother of King Edward IV. The lodestar of his life is his beautiful sister Meg, about to enter into a prestigious marriage with Sir Robert Drakelon. Christie has serious doubts about the match, and promises Meg that if she is ever in trouble, he will come to her aid. Sure enough, Meg soon finds that her husband is a cruel and jealous man, but when she begs Christie for help, he ignores her plea because he feels the Duke's favour is more important. His betrayal devastates Meg, and she vows never to forgive him.
Years later, Christie has become the trusted friend and henchman of Gloucester, now Richard III, and is married to a wealthy heiress who loathes him. He is beginning to realise that his ruthless and selfish pursuit of his ambitions has come at a heavy price. Can he persuade his wife to love him?
And can he ever be reconciled with Meg, who plots her own

vengeance?
Then Henry Tudor invades, and everything Christie has worked for is in danger.

Wintercombe

The Wintercombe Quartet, Book 1
Silence has been married for years to Sir George St Barbe, owner of Wintercombe in Somerset, a very much older widower with three children. She has learned to keep her emotions hidden, and to be a good and dutiful wife and mother, taking pleasure in her garden and in her children and stepchildren.
Then civil war breaks out, Sir George and his eldest son leave to fight for Parliament, and Silence is left in charge of Wintercombe. But war cannot be kept at bay for ever, and a garrison of Cavaliers, led by the cruel and debauched Colonel Ridgeley, invades the house, bringing chaos, desecration and danger. Her only ally seems to be Captain Hellier, who protects her and her children and household from the worst excesses of the soldiers, but is it just friendship he offers her, or something more? And when Wintercombe becomes a battleground, will he take her side, or Ridgeley's?

Herald Of Joy

The Wintercombe Quartet, Book 2
At Wintercombe, Sir George St Barbe is dying, mourned only by his eldest daughter, Rachael, who is desperate to fulfil her father's last wish and marry his friend's son, a young man who, her stepmother Silence can see, will only make her miserable. But Sir George's death also means that his young wife is free to reunite with the man she loves, Nick Hellier, a member of the garrison that nearly wrecked Wintercombe six years ago. But she has no idea where Nick is, how to reach him,

or even if he is still alive.

Nick, however, is very much alive, and now a member of the army which the new young king, Charles II, has gathered in his attempt to take back his throne. But Cromwell and his army catch up with them at Worcester, and in the aftermath of defeat, Nick finds himself on the run, hampered by the aristocratic and idiotic Mervyn Touchet, who bears a dangerous resemblance to the king. The only place that might offer them refuge is Wintercombe, but their arrival will run the risk of putting Silence and all her family in deadly danger.

A Falling Star

The Wintercombe Quartet, Book 3

Silence's nephew, Sir Alexander St Barbe, returns from dissolute exile in Holland to take up his inheritance at Wintercombe. His arrival appalls his cousin Charles, who had hopes of inheriting Wintercombe by default, but delights and intrigues one of his other cousins, Louise, who has been brought up in France and is far more sophisticated than most of the St Barbe family. Before long, to her grandmother Silence's alarm, Louise finds herself increasingly attracted to the dangerous Alex, enraging Charles, who had hoped to make her his wife.

Rising tensions are exacerbated by the rebellion of the Duke of Monmouth, who lands in Somerset in a doomed bid to take the throne. As the St Barbes choose sides, can they avoid the tragedy and retribution that must come in the aftermath of crushing defeat?

Treason's Gift

The Wintercombe Quartet, Book 4

Louise and Alex's lively and tempestuous marriage is shattered by the death of their baby son. A catastrophic betrayal causes Alex to seek exile in Holland once more, and his cousin Charles

returns to Wintercombe, eager to take Alex's place and worm his way back into Louise's affections. But the king, James II, has alienated many powerful people: revolution is in the air, and Alex is at the heart of it. Will King James be overthrown? Can Charles be evicted from Wintercombe? Will Alex and Louise be reconciled, despite what he has done? And will his plain, bookish sister Phoebe accept the proposal of the courtier, Hugh Trevelyan, Alex's friend and the younger half-brother of Francis Heron?
The final volume of the Wintercombe quartet

The Silver City

My foray into fantasy, set in a world I first dreamed up at the back of the class as a teenager. Much more interesting than 'office practice'!
The first book in the Silver City trilogy
Young members of the Tanathi tribe are on a hunting expedition in the hills when they stumble upon a huge army of Ska'i, savage nomads fuelled by dangerous magic, and learn that they plan to attack Zithirian, known as the Silver City. Halthris is sent by her brother to warn the people there, and encounters a decadent royal family tainted by madness, magic and hidden ambitions. Her tale is believed only by Prince Ansaryon, widely assumed to be a sinister and evil sorcerer.
When the Ska'i attack, a terrible act of treachery leads to the fall of the city, and Ansaryon and Halthris are forced to flee. Together, they must seek help to free Zithirian and its remaining inhabitants of the murderous Ska'i and the evil witch D'thliss, who is aided by a mysterious small boy, Bron, who suffers under her spell and her command, and whose powers rival her own.

The Wolf Within

Book 2 in the Silver City trilogy.

Bron, son of the sorcerer king Ansaryon, grows up with the terrible knowledge of the extent of his own power, fuelled by the wolf-god who has taken up residence in his heart and mind. Fearing that his magic will endanger those he loves, he leaves Zithirian in search of some way of controlling the wolf within him. In the decadent city of Toktel'yi, centre of a cruel empire, he meets Mallaso, a former child slave who is a survivor of the empire's brutal invasion of her homeland, Penya. Together, they travel to the enchanted island of Jo'ami, seeking a way of banishing the wolf forever, but the sorcerers there know of a prophecy concerning Bron, and have their own agenda. And with the Silver City now in mortal danger from the Toktel'yan Emperor Ba'alekkt and his huge army, Bron must return to save Zithirian before invasion and brutal conquest destroy everything he once loved.

Blood Imperial

Book 3 of The Silver City Trilogy
Ba'alekkt is dead, and Zithirian is safe. But the Emperor left no direct heir, and his numerous relatives are free to employ any means, fair or foul, in pursuit of the wealth and power of the Onyx Throne. When the deadly dance is done, one sinister and devious man is left to become Emperor, and take Ba'alekkt's sister Djeneb as his bride. But his cruelty turns many against him, and there are other, hidden forces at work. Who is the Flamebearer, who enters dreams and spreads ideas of rebellion? And what part will Mallaso and her small daughter Kyu play, as the Toktel'yan empire stands on the brink of disintegration?

Printed in Great Britain
by Amazon

60120066R00217